THE WRONG BOY

With gratitude,

[signature]

CATHY ACE

FOUR TAILS PUBLISHING LTD.

PRAISE FOR CATHY ACE'S WORK

The Cait Morgan Mysteries

'Ace is, well, an ace when it comes to plot and description.'
The Globe and Mail

'In the finest tradition of Agatha Christie...Ace brings us the closed-room drama, with a dollop of romantic suspense and historical intrigue.' *Library Journal*

'...a sparkling, well-plotted and quite devious mystery in the cozy tradition, all pointing to Ace's growing finesse at telling an entertaining story.' *Hamilton Spectator*

'Cathy Ace is a fabulous writer. She has a great way with words. It is wonderful to read an intelligent woman's writing.' *MysteriesEtc*

The WISE Enquiries Agency Mysteries

'...a gratifying contemporary series in the traditional British manner with hilarious repercussions (dead bodies notwithstanding). Cozy fans will anticipate learning more about these WISE ladies.'
Library Journal, starred review

'In my review of Cathy's first book, 'The Corpse with the Silver Tongue' I compared her style of writing to Agatha Christie. While this book features four protagonists, the style is still the same. I also loved the setting...I strongly recommend this book and all of Cathy Ace's books.'
Lynn Farris, examiner.com

'A brilliant addition to Classic Crime Fiction. The ladies...of the WISE Enquiries Agency will have you pacing the floor awaiting their next entanglement...A fresh and wonderful concept well executed.'
Alan Bradley,
New York Times bestselling author of the Flavia de Luce mysteries

'Cozy fans will enjoy their chitchat as much as their sleuthing.'
Publishers' Weekly

'...a pleasant mélange with a garnish of death and danger.'
Kirkus Reviews

ABOUT THIS BOOK

'A disturbing storyline of family secrets, deftly told, and with a remarkable sense of place. Almost mythic in nature, it's narrated by a chorus of voices which stay with you all the way to the stunning ending and beyond.'
Craig Robertson, international bestselling author

'Family secrets stalk three generations of women in Cathy Ace's suspense-packed page turner, THE WRONG BOY. The ending is a stunner.'
Hallie Ephron, NY Times bestselling author of 'You'll Never Know Dear'

'...a truly gripping and strong narrative, coupled with a story line that is both intriguing and thoroughly entertaining.'
Yrsa Sigurdardóttir, award-winning, No. 1 bestselling Icelandic crime fiction author

'A clever plot with a web of intrigue and characters who stay with you.'
Jane Corry, author of the Sunday Times bestsellers 'My Husband's Wife', 'Blood Sisters' and 'The Dead Ex'

'Cathy Ace's skill at evoking place is a stand-out highlight of The Wrong Boy, a neatly wrought story which combines a mystery...with a study of tangled relationships within a close-knit community...'
Martin Edwards, author of 'Gallows Court' & winner of the CWA Dagger in the Library

ABOUT THIS BOOK

'A close-knit community in a quaint Welsh village in an area of outstanding beauty. Sounds cozy. But Cathy Ace's stunning new standalone, THE WRONG BOY, is about as cozy as a cornered snake. Told in a rising chorus of authentic voices, the story is deft and disturbing, creepingly claustrophobic, and with a grip that tightens to a choke-hold before its shattering conclusion.'
Catriona McPherson, multi-award-winning author of 'Go To My Grave'

'Drenched in Welsh atmosphere, forbidding weather, and mysterious folklore, THE WRONG BOY is a gem of a thriller that bewitches right up to the twisted ending you won't see coming. Masterful plotting and characters so real, you'll swear you know them. Ace is a master portraitist.'
James W Ziskin, multi-award-winning author of The Ellie Stone Mysteries

'Like a slow pot that boils, the author builds...this tightly-woven and intriguing mystery...grippingly riveting as the story came to a dramatic climax.'
Dru Ann Love, Dru's Book Musings, MWA Raven Award Recipient

DEDICATION

For my family and friends

5th November

John Watkins hooked open the bedroom curtains and wiped the frost-feathered window with his pajama sleeve. 'I thought that's what I could see. Somebody's lit a fire on the hill above the village.'

His wife tutted her annoyance at him letting in the cold. 'All the way up there? No.'

'Yes. Come and take a look.' Brass rings clattered as he pulled at the worn brocade. He breathed hard on a couple of panes to clear them.

Dilys gripped her steaming mug of tea with both hands as she shuffled across the room. The moon hung in the coal black sky, and glistened on the coal black sea. Her eyes shifted from the sparkling surf to the inky hillside above. 'That's up by the old RAF listening station, by the looks of it.'

'Guy Fawkes Night. Probably some kids,' mused John, rubbing his arthritic thumb. 'They had that do at the pub in Rhosddraig tonight, didn't they? Sparklers and hot dogs. Maybe someone had one too many and thought it would be a good idea to start their own bonfire up there.'

'That's dangerous, lighting fires all over the place.' Dilys shook her head with resignation as she turned toward the bed, eyeing its welcoming mounds with delight. Even her bones felt tired. 'It's nearly midnight. Who'd be out there in this temperature, doing that?'

Her husband's face creased into a smile. 'It's only one fire, not loads of them, Dilys. And I can think of a woman who — when she was a girl — would have been up for a bit of mischief like that.' He winked and smiled. 'Remember her?'

Dilys rolled her eyes. 'Even sixty-odd years ago I wouldn't have wanted to be out in this cold, not with you or anyone else, John Watkins.' She sat on the edge of the bed, placed her mug beside the alarm clock, and pushed off her slippers with her toes. 'Come on, let's get back in here to warm ourselves, and get some sleep. We're up early in the morning with a long day ahead of us. A diamond wedding anniversary, with a blessing in the church and a party afterwards, only happens once. You never know, there might be a surprise for you at the breakfast table.' She patted her husband's pillow.

'Who's that, now then?' said John, ignoring his wife's invitation. He was still at the window, bobbing his head to avoid the reflection of the bedside lamp. 'Well, well, I don't know how that family's got enough to pay out for the sort of get-ups they wear these days. That coat alone must have set them back a bit. And look at that – riding a bicycle on the footpath. I'll have a word with them about that, I will. And the fire, too.'

'John, come on, it's late, love.'

John clambered into bed, and kissed his wife's cheek. 'What were you doing sixty years ago tonight, I wonder?'

Dilys gave her husband a gentle shove. 'Crying myself to sleep because I was terrified about my wedding night, that's what. My mother – God rest her soul – had tried to tell me what to expect of being with a man for the first time; she didn't do a very good job of it. I had a bad stomach that night too. Butterflies they were back then, not this blinking wind I've got griping me now; I can't seem to shift it.'

John snuggled under the duvet. 'You were such a sweet girl. Carried away with you, I was. And I love you even more now. You know that, don't you?'

Dilys nodded and grunted.

John didn't like to see his wife in pain. He thought she looked more than usually peaky. 'Why don't you sit up for a bit; rub your tummy. Maybe that tea will shift it. You took some of your medicine, didn't you?'

'Yes, I did. Don't worry, love, it'll pass. It always does – one way or another.' Dilys chuckled. 'Now, come on, night, night. It'll be time to get up before you know it.'

'True enough.'

John turned off the lamp.

It was gone four in the morning when John rang for the ambulance. For once in his life he cursed the fact that the farm – high on the coastal moor between the villages of Rhosddraig and Lower Middleford – was so remote.

He held his wife's hand as the bedside clock ticked sluggishly, and put everything from his mind except Dilys's ragged breathing, and his prayers for the paramedics to arrive in time for her life to be saved.

6th November

Sadie

I hate double English. I hate double anything – it's too long to keep thinking about just one thing. I suppose it isn't so bad at the moment, because Aled's been picked to read Romeo in class. Though why Mrs Lee had to pick Rhian to read Juliet I'll never know. Priya Patel would have been better – at least she goes to elocution lessons and can read things aloud properly. Rhian stumbles over every line.

Aled reads Romeo like an angel, and I can tell he's thinking of me when he reads it, not Rhian.

She's just a big lump. Everyone says it, not just me. And it's true. She was always useless at PE. Can't run for toffee. And it shows. Wobbles about all over the place, she does. I mean, I know I'm not fast, but who could be with these boobs?

I hate my boobs. Mam says I can't have them made smaller until I'm an adult. Says I haven't stopped growing yet. Well, I'll be eighteen in six months and three weeks, so then I can do what I want.

But Aled likes them. Can't keep his eyes off them; sometimes he talks to them, not me. I might ask him about getting them made smaller. Maybe he wouldn't like it. I wouldn't want to do it if he didn't want me to. I'll ask him. When I'm eighteen.

Mam and I were talking about what I'll do to celebrate my next birthday, it being such an important one. Of course I have my own plans for the night, but she said she'd be happy to make me one last hare-shaped, white blancmange surrounded by green jelly grass, just like I've been having since I was little. I think that's a good idea, because after that night I'll be a totally different person, and that might not be suitable for me anymore.

Aled's birthday was weeks and weeks ago, lucky bugger. It must be great to be eighteen. No one treats you like you're a kid anymore. Nan's letting him serve behind the bar in our pub now, which is nice for him 'cos he gets more hours, so more money. But we don't see as much of each other as when he could only help down in the cellar, or in the kitchen, with me.

God, it was busy last night! I don't know why Nan wanted to do all that stuff with the hot dogs and burgers. Mam said it was a good night for the takings, but I was the one stuck listening to Hywel bloody Evans going on and on about the pivotal role the Welsh spy Hugh Owen had in bringing Guy Fawkes into the Gunpowder Plot.

Hasn't he got anything better to do than read all about boring old Welsh history, then try to tell everyone about it? Listen to him and you'd think everything ever done anywhere in the world had a Welshman at the heart of it. Always a man, of course, never a woman. We don't exist, apparently. Typical.

I was the one who had to clear away all those greasy plates and mugs coated with hot chocolate last night. My hands were raw after I'd done the washing up; Nan reminded me when I moaned about it that I was the one who said we shouldn't use paper plates and foam cups. I was right about that – they're a total blight on the environment, all those so-called disposable things. So I shut up; I didn't want a scene, I just wanted her and Mam to get off to bed, and go to sleep.

It was a big night for me, and Aled, of course. I wonder if I'll look different to other people today. I love him so much. More than anything. I know Mam and Nan wouldn't understand how Aled and I feel about each other, not for a minute. That's why we have to keep our love a secret from them.

Mam wouldn't have divorced Dad if she'd loved him as much as I love Aled. Couldn't have. And Nan never has a good word to say about Grampa, if she mentions him at all, so I don't think she could ever have loved him. Not really. Not even when he was alive. He was probably all that was left over after the war in any case.

Aled said he's missing his surfing. His Grannie Gwen won't let him go in the sea during the winter. She says the dragon might take him; it's true that when the dragon writhes in pain there are killer tides, but the dragon only takes bad people, not good ones, and Aled is good. He does everything for his grannie. Well, it being just the two of them, he has to. He said he's grateful she's brought him up as her own, since his mother died.

Poor Aled, he's had such a tragic life. But he never lets it get him down. He says life's for the living, and we've got to make the most of it while we're here.

Loves surfing, he does. It's not my thing, because I don't like the sea on my face, but it's fun to watch him in the summer, when his Grannie Gwen lets him do it. He looks fantastic in his wetsuit. He's got a gorgeous body. Perfect. His hair's lovely, too. Lush. All long and blonde with floppy curls. By the time we went back to school after the summer holidays it was so white I could see light coming out of it.

Oh Aled . . . when we get married I'll be Mrs Sadie Beynon. Mrs Sadie Beynon has a lovely ring to it. It sounds like I could be anything, with that name. Being married must be wonderful, if you're in love. And, of course, I could be Mrs Sadie Beynon who runs The Dragon's Head pub in Rhosddraig, if I want.

Not everyone's happy all the time, like me and Aled. I hear Mam crying at night sometimes, but that's to be expected, I suppose, because she's all alone. She said to me more than once when I was younger that this place felt like a prison.

Never known anywhere different, me. But Dad couldn't stick it. He told me that when I was little, too. Thinking about it now, I must have been very little when he said it, because he left when I was only four.

Funny that, the things we remember from when we were really young. I can't remember much about back then, but I do remember the way Mam and Dad would talk to me in the dark, when I was in their bed. But I can only remember being there with one of them at a time.

I wonder why Dad was with me there alone? Where was Mam, then?

She went away. But why did she go away? I don't remember that bit. Maybe I'll ask her. Or maybe I'll ask Dad when I see him next.

Mam let me sleep with her after Dad went away for good, I do remember that. She smelled of something sweet, and always cuddled my back, keeping me and Mrs Hare safe in her arms. Of course, I was just a kid then. Now I prefer my own room, my own bed; I can lie here and think of Aled touching me.

There's Mam calling again. I suppose I'd better get up; God knows Nan throws a fit when we don't all stick to our bathroom timetable. And I can't let Mam think I didn't get a proper night's sleep, or she'll start The Inquisition and it'll be awful. Besides, at least I can look forward to watching Aled while he reads Romeo's lines.

Love really is 'a fire sparkling in lovers' eyes'. Shakespeare must have known what real love was. A love like ours.

Sadie and Aled. Forever.

Helen

'Sadie Myfanwy Jones, it's time you were eating your breakfast, not still splashing around in the shower. You don't want to miss the bus to school.' Helen couldn't believe how her daughter always left everything until the very last minute.

'Lazy bag of bones, that girl,' sniped Helen's mother as she sucked on her first cigarette of the day at the breakfast table.

Helen did her best to hide her annoyance as ash fell onto the clean tablecloth; there'd be no point saying anything, because her mother would make a fuss about it being her tablecloth, her table, and her kitchen.

Instead of complaining, Helen defended her child. 'Come on, Mum, Sadie's still only seventeen, and she was up until all hours last night helping us clear around the pub. Just as well we closed early; she needs to be in bed by eleven on a school night. She works a lot more around this place than many other youngsters would for their families.'

'Got it cushy, she has,' replied Nan tartly. 'And I pay her.'

Helen felt her chest tighten as she watched her mother sitting at the rickety table in the center of the small kitchen, surrounded by the higgledy-piggledy collection of mismatched cupboards and chairs. 'You're the one who suggested that, Mum. Not her. Indeed, you insisted, as I recall.'

'Well . . .'

Helen watched as her mother stubbed out one cigarette and moved to light another. She knew she'd regret it as the words came out of her mouth, but she couldn't stop herself. 'I thought you said you were going to give that up, Mum. This year, you said. Well, it's November now, so there's not much of this year left. And no sign of you slowing down at all. Look at what happened to poor old Dilys Watkins last night. Well, in the early hours of this morning, anyway. Eleri from the next farm over sent me a text to say she went up to the Watkins's when she saw the lights; the paramedic in the ambulance told her it was Dilys's heart. They were there an hour with her before they took her away. Stabilizing her, they said. Couldn't say how she'd do. Poor old John was in a right state. Went in the ambulance with her.'

Nan Jones paused, her lips clamped tight, pushing smoke through her nostrils. 'I expect that means the service and the do at the church this afternoon will be off then. Diamond wedding or no diamond wedding, they won't be at a blessing at two o'clock. But as for me smoking, this is my home, and I will do as I please, Helen. My roof, my rules.'

Helen felt crushed. She'd been hearing exactly the same words her entire life, and they felt more weighty each time they were uttered. Never more so than now, when – at the age of forty-seven – she'd always expected she'd be independent.

'I haven't got time for breakfast, Mam. I'll be late,' called Sadie.

Helen turned at the sound of her daughter's voice; seeing her child's smile always cheered her. She'd come back to Rhosddraig to help her unexpectedly widowed mother, and had stayed to raise her unexpectedly conceived daughter in one of the most beautiful places on earth, believing she'd benefit from the stability of village life, and the richness of the natural surroundings. Sadie's smile was what all Helen's sacrifices had been about.

'I know you're late, but you're not missing breakfast, Sadie. I'll sort something out for you to eat on your way. And I've got your lunch ready. Where's your backpack?'

'By my bed. I'll get it.'

Helen watched Sadie's long, dark ponytail flick as she scurried out of the kitchen; her heart melted. She was so proud of her daughter; Sadie was well balanced, and her teachers said she had a good chance of doing well at her A levels. The only real issue was that her daughter couldn't decide what she wanted to do after she left school, so they were negotiating the idea of a gap year, while the January deadline for applying to universities was creeping ever closer. There was also the fact that, since the beginning of the school year, Sadie's bedroom had suddenly become off limits to her mother. Helen suspected it might be normal. She was giving Sadie the benefit of the doubt about her new desire for privacy, putting it down to her daughter becoming more mature. She tried to recall what she'd been like aged seventeen, but no memories surfaced.

'Morning, Nan,' said Sadie brightly as she passed her backpack to her mother. 'Lovely day for ducks.'

'Mmm,' replied Nan miserably through a wreath of smoke. 'Shame I'm not one.'

'Oh, come on, Nan, look on the bright side,' said Sadie, winking at her mother as she patted her grandmother's shoulder.

'Not your Nan's forte,' replied Helen quietly, kissing her daughter on the cheek. 'Lunch is tuna sandwiches. Don't scrunch your face up like that, you'll eat them and they'll keep you full. I put in an extra banana because they're on the turn; nice and soft, the way you like them. And there's some toast and Marmite too, for you to eat before you get off the bus. Be good. Stay as dry as you can, and – if you can't – there's a change of socks in your bag, rolled inside your school shoes.'

'Not wearing socks,' shouted Sadie as she clattered down the wooden stairs to the porch where the family's substantial range of outerwear was stored. 'I'm in thick tights today, 'cos it's cold. See, I'm so sensible, aren't I, Mam?'

Helen peered over the bannister. Sadie was already zipping her red, vinyl, hooded raincoat as she stubbed her feet into her blue wellingtons. 'Put a scarf on, you'll be glad later.' As the words came out of Helen's mouth they reminded her of her own mother, many years earlier.

'Already did, Mam. See you. Bye.'

The rain lashed through the open door onto the flagstones as her daughter ventured out into the early-morning darkness. Through the window at the top of the stairs Helen could see the distant headlights of the bus winding along the only road that served the headland, and the village perched upon it. The bus stop was only two minutes' walk away; Sadie would make it with time to spare.

Returning to the kitchen, Helen knew she should remind her mother she was taking a night off from working in the pub downstairs.

She braced herself. 'I'll make sure everything's in order before I go out tonight, Mum. You didn't forget to tell Aled Beynon he'd be starting early this evening, did you?'

Her mother looked up, hatchet-faced. 'No, I didn't forget. How could I? I'll have to pay him extra, even though we'll probably only have half a dozen of the old ones in, just to keep warm at our expense. What I take probably won't even cover what I give him. If only I were a few years younger I'd be able to manage on my own.'

Helen sighed. 'Mum, you know you can't, so that's that. It's not often I take a night off, is it? When was the last time?' Helen realized she couldn't remember. 'Besides, I picked tonight because it'll probably be quiet here. Last night was good; we made a pretty penny on the food, and the hot chocolates raked it in, especially the ones with a drop of Baileys in them. I worked hard to make it all a success. We've never had a turnout like that before on Guy Fawkes Night, have we? It could become a regular thing. You can't say people didn't enjoy it, despite the weather.'

'I don't know how it could go from being so clear and bitterly cold last night, to us having this rain now. It's a horrible time of year to have a thing like Guy Fawkes Night,' replied her mother sourly.

'Well, I dare say he wasn't thinking about the seasonality of outdoor celebrations more than four hundred years ago when he planned to blow up Parliament, Mum, so the 5th of November it is. We're stuck with it. Which is why we should be grateful so many people turned up.'

'The usual crowd would have come anyway. And as for the others? It's not as though there was anything else they could do around here, was it?'

'Oh Mum, don't be so negative. Why are you always like that?'

Helen's mother stood, tightening the belt of her quilted floral dressing gown around her theoretical waist. 'I'll have you know I am thought of as one of the jolliest landladies in the whole of the Gower,' replied Nan huffily. 'We might be stuck out here at the most south-westerly corner of this wonderful peninsular of ours, but I've often heard people say they've come from miles away especially to meet me. So there. Think you're too good for this place, you do, my girl. Always have and always will. It's why you took yourself off to university. Which was a complete waste of time, as I told you it would be. If you don't want to be here, I don't know why you stay.'

I stay because I've cut myself off from the world and any opportunities I might once have had within it – to help you, Helen screamed inside her head. 'Of course I want to be here, Mum,' was what she said aloud. She saw her mother nod twice as she left the kitchen, heading toward the bathroom. It was something Nan always did when she felt vindicated, usually at Helen's expense.

Helen began to clear the table of breakfast's detritus, focusing on mopping up crumbs to try to distract herself from thinking dark thoughts. It didn't work. The wind buffeted the small, ancient windows set into the foot-thick, stone walls. Helen hated November; there was only worse to come, with the short days and long, cold nights of winter stretching ahead, interminably. Hands on hips, she considered the damp-stained walls surrounding her; were they protecting her from the filthy weather beyond them, or holding her captive? One thing was certain, they were in need of sprucing up. As was her own life.

As she pushed the dirty dishes into soapy water, and swished them with a fuzzy green square, Helen wondered how different her life might have been if she'd stuck to her guns in telling her mother she should sell up when her father had keeled over with a stroke, from which he'd never recovered. If only she'd done that, by now she might have clambered her way up the ladder in the competitive world of archaeology. Somehow. Somewhere.

Or maybe not.

She admitted to herself she'd all but given up on that hope even before her mother had phoned her in a panic to say she'd found her father on the bathroom floor, unable to speak. So she'd come back, having achieved nothing but a degree she'd never used.

Of course, there was Sadie. Sadie was an achievement.

Helen rubbed moisturizer into her chapped hands as she contemplated the idea that, maybe, the only reason she'd been put on the face of the earth was to allow Sadie to exist. Was that why she'd been drawn to Bob? Just so they could create her daughter, then part, their reason for ever becoming a couple completed?

She'd only ever put up with his treatment of her for Sadie's sake. But she'd finally had to face the fact it would be better for Sadie to not have a father in her life at all, than to have one like him.

Maybe, if her mother hadn't fallen down the stairs and broken her leg so soon after her dad had died, Helen wouldn't have stayed to 'hold the fort' until Nan had recovered sufficiently to be able to get the pub up to snuff to attract the best possible sale price.

Maybe, if her mother hadn't taken that overdose, in her deep depression and grief so soon after she was back on her feet again, Helen would have taken Bob's advice and they'd have left when the pub was on the market.

But the pub hadn't sold, so she'd stayed, putting her head down and getting on with whatever menial task had been required at the time. Then Sadie had been born, and along with the joy of her arrival came the sourness of it all going horribly wrong.

After four long years of suffering, Bob had left. She and Sadie had stayed.

She felt the familiar feelings of helplessness as she reflected on how Bob had changed as the years had passed; each homecoming from his sales trips had become more dangerous than the last. He'd become ever more angry with her inability to break from her mother, the pub, and the village.

Maybe, if only her mother hadn't . . .

'Stop it, Helen Jones,' she said aloud in the empty kitchen. 'This isn't getting you anywhere. He's gone. That's all behind you. Pull yourself together, get your work done, and make sure everything's set up right for Mum and Aled tonight before you go. Then you can concentrate on having a nice time.'

Somehow the prospect of meeting a man for a drink at a pub in the Mumbles – a man with whom she'd so far only exchanged emails – didn't lead Helen to hold out much hope of having a 'nice time'; she found it difficult to settle in any pub without bringing her professional eye to bear upon the place. At least The Pilot had a reputation for good beer and no tellies or music. But the chatter was likely to get raucous as ten o'clock approached, because it always did in most lively pubs.

Stop it, Helen, she told herself, silently. *You're trying to talk yourself out of going. And you are going. Gryff seems very pleasant in his emails. You both enjoy classical music, you can talk about that.*

She turned from the sink, pleased to hear her mother's daily call of, 'The bathroom's empty,' signaling her chance to shower and get ready to face the day ahead.

Gryff might turn out to be nice. The entire evening might be nice. And sometimes 'nice' was all you could hope for.

Nan

Nan Jones dragged herself into her bedroom to get dressed. Even something so seemingly simple took forever nowadays, and involved a good deal of pain and other annoyances she could well do without. She sat on the edge of what had once been her grandparents' wood-framed bed to pull on her long woolen socks, but didn't seem to be able to get her toes up to where her hands could reach them. She wriggled about a bit, and made a supreme effort to stretch down, then felt dizzy, so had to sit up again.

'Bloody spots in front of my eyes,' she hissed quietly. 'I won't be stopped by spots.'

She squeezed her eyes shut, hoping the nausea would pass with the dizziness. It took a few moments, which she used to wrestle with her bra.

By the time she was fully clothed, Nan Jones was feeling anything but fresh. None of her body moved the way it used to; annoyed with herself, she had to admit that at seventy-eight she wasn't as young or lithe as she'd once been. She pulled a brush through her bobbed white hair, which had at least retained its thickness as she'd aged; she'd been proud of her hair when she was young, and Jack, her late husband, had enjoyed watching her brush it every night.

She finally put on her glasses and glanced at her reflection in the dressing-table mirror. Did her pain show on her face? Would Helen know? She didn't want her to; she wouldn't allow herself to appear to be weak.

She pulled her container of special painkillers from the secret drawer where she kept them hidden, and made some spit to get them down. If Mair Bevan, at ninety-two, could still kneel to take communion, she wouldn't moan about her aches and pains, she told herself.

She limped to the top of the stairs and shouted, 'Are you down there, Helen? Did you remember to wash the tea towels?'

'They're already in the drier, Mum,' shouted her daughter from the lounge bar, where Nan knew she'd be making a poor job of polishing the tables.

'So they should be, at this time of day,' replied Nan, pleased that Helen at least kept things moving along as she would have done herself, if only she were still able. 'I'll be down now, in a minute. I just want to find out how Dilys Watkins is doing. I'm going to phone Mair. She'll know.'

'Okay, Mum.'

Nan pulled the greasy length of string to turn on the standard lamp beside the telephone table and settled herself on the little sofa in the sitting room. It creaked as she sat; at least the board over the broken springs was holding well.

She wasn't surprised Dilys had suffered a heart attack, and said as much when Mair answered the phone. 'She's never been a healthy woman, hasn't Dilys,' she opened. 'So, has anyone told you if she made it?'

'Good morning to you too, Nan,' replied Mair, her voice cracked with age. 'She's alive. At least, she was an hour ago, I know that much. The son phoned me. She's in Morriston Hospital. Cardiac Unit. He's over from Australia for the diamond wedding thing. They'll cancel, of course. Poor Reverend Thomas, he put a lot of preparation into the service, I know.'

'He did, Mair. Went up to their farm and talked to them for hours about their life together. He told me last week, when I was polishing the pews. But there, if she goes, at least he'll have the eulogy ready.'

'And all the family would still be here for the funeral, if they can have it that quick,' replied Mair solemnly. 'Is she going into our graveyard, do you know? Or will she be a crematorium job, then the cemetery?'

Nan gave it some thought. 'The Watkinses haven't got any family in the graveyard as far as I know. I don't know where we'd put her, do you? There's only that little area over by the memorial for unknown sailors, and I don't think they can dig there because there might be some old graves from back in – what, was it the 1500s, or something? Not like you; you've got your place with your Dewi all ready and waiting. Like me and Jack; I'll go in with him, and my mam and dad. No, I don't think there can be any Watkinses there already. After all, these two only got here . . . when was it? In the seventies?'

'Later than that, I think. They already had the boy when they came here. Big Wig in banking in wherever he lives in Australia now, Dilys reckons.'

'So is he going to keep you in the picture then, Mair? The son.'

'He said he'd keep the vicar updated. The son only rang me to get the vicar's phone number. John knew mine off by heart; didn't know the vicar's. The son says John's not too good, neither. I'll phone Alis at the shop in a bit, to let her know. She'll be wondering what's happening. I'll let her get herself sorted out first.'

Nan pounced. 'Don't bother, I'll tell Helen to go over the road and fill Alis in when she opens up.' She checked her watch. 'Look at the time. It's so dark this morning I never thought for a minute it would be nine o'clock already. I'll tell Helen to go over now.'

'It's no bother for me to phone her, Nan,' pressed Mair.

'I insist,' replied Nan firmly, and hung up.

She heaved herself off the sofa and made her way slowly to the bannister to shout down to the pub. 'Helen? I need you to go over to the shop to tell Alis that Dilys Watkins is in Morriston. Alive. At least she was an hour ago. The son's going to keep the vicar informed.'

Helen poked her head around the bottom of the staircase. 'You want me to go over to the shop now? Can't I just phone Alis? Or maybe you could?'

Nan felt instantly annoyed. 'It's important information, Helen. It should be delivered personally. Alis and Dilys go back a long way. But, if you can't be bothered, I suppose I can put my mac on and do it myself.' Nan let out a little squeak of pain as she started down the stairs.

Helen pulled on her waxed cotton coat. 'No, Mum. You take your time up there. I'll go. I'll be quick.'

'Don't rush back. I'll be fine on my own. Well, you know that, otherwise you wouldn't be going out on the town tonight, would you?'

A gust of wind slammed the door shut behind her daughter. Nan made her way to the kitchen table, sat down on the chair that didn't wobble, and lit a cigarette. She reveled in the fact she was alone, at last. She was never alone anymore, it seemed. Helen, or Sadie, was always there. She missed being alone in the old place. It reminded her of the few years when Helen had been away, when it had been just her and Jack – and he used to make himself scarce quite a lot of the time. Then the entire place had been all hers, just like it was for these precious minutes. She smiled as she smoked, looking out of the small, square-paned windows at the grey light trying to pierce the rain. She loved the sound of rain. It made her feel safe.

It was times like this when she felt most content, and glad she'd allowed Helen to hang onto the fantasy that her late father had been a perfect man; she knew Helen was happier because of it. It had taken its toll, keeping the truth from her daughter, and the only way Nan could cope was to not talk about the man with whom she'd shared her life for four decades. At all. Ever. If it could be avoided.

She never liked to speak ill of the dead.

7th November

The rain had let up a bit, making it a slightly less-unpleasant walk than it would have been the previous couple of days. Hywel Evans let Nip off his lead knowing he'd head up the hill; during their last few walks he'd been kept close to heel. Nip made the most of his freedom by tracking down scents in the wet grass. Hywel followed his trusty companion, bedraggled and somewhat wind-weary, but glad that at least the wind was a little less biting than it had recently been.

Hywel loved the whole of the Dragon's Back area; he felt sorry for people who'd never experienced it for themselves, even on a day such as this, when the view was reduced to several feet in front of him. It didn't matter to Hywel that he could hardly see where he was going; born and raised in the village of Rhosddraig, he was one of the true 'People of the Dragon' – as the locals were referred to by outsiders – and knew his surroundings intimately.

The hillside path was crossed by narrow, winding sheep trails, but it rose ever upward despite these potential diversions. The still-heavy rain meant it was more like a trickling rivulet than a path, but he and his beloved dog pushed on, regardless – Nip with his nose down, Hywel with his collar up.

'Don't go too far,' called Hywel, unheeded by his keen Jack Russell. 'Oh buggeration,' he grumbled, conceding he'd have to go much further than he'd have liked. He whistled and called, but Nip didn't reappear, so Hywel battled on.

When he reached the old brick-built RAF listening station, now no more than a collection of crumbling walls and a once-flat concrete floor, he spotted Nip, dashing about, circling something at the center of what had once been the main room of the long-abandoned building.

'What's that, Nip?' enquired Hywel. The dog stopped, and turned his head toward his master.

Hywel was convinced Nip was saying 'No idea', because he certainly couldn't work out for himself what he was looking at. A mound of bricks and rocks was heaped on the floor, and the blackness of the concrete around them told him a fire had burned there at some point.

'Come away now, Nip,' he called, but the dog looked determined to stay; he sat down, his paws stretched out, sphinx-like. Hywel bent down to hook the lead onto his collar. Nip looked quite disgruntled.

'I said, come on, let's go home.' He shoved his hand into his pocket, then allowed Nip to sniff his fingers. 'Treats.'

Nothing.

Hywel decided to poke at the pile of rocks with his boot to prove to Nip there was nothing to keep him there. However, his boot dislodged a stone, which led to a mini-landslide. Inside the mound was a collection of what he immediately knew to be pieces of bone. A jumbled, blackened pile of bone shards that would have once formed part of . . . what? A sheep? A dog? No, too many bones for that. A wild moorland pony come all the way across the peninsular from Cefn Bryn? No. He let Nip's lead go slack as he pulled out his mobile phone and opened his jacket to provide cover so he could dial 999.

As he waited to be connected, he walked around the rock pile. He couldn't be certain, but he reckoned he could make out a bit of a crushed large joint. He shuddered, and it wasn't because of the icy rain.

Nip and Hywel were chilly and thoroughly soaked by the time the local community constable arrived.

Hywel wasn't surprised the officer hadn't rushed; after all, what he could see and describe sounded so . . . unusual.

But when the policeman replaced Hywel on guard, thanking him and telling him to go home but to speak to no one about his discovery, Hywel knew he'd done the right thing.

He carried Nip's shivering, wriggling body down the hillside under his arm, contemplating the brevity of life, and knowing in his heart that he'd been guarding something that had once been human.

Evan

As he sat down at his desk, DI Evan Glover caught his knee on the corner of a cardboard box he'd shoved into the space where his feet usually fitted. He swore quietly, then pulled out the offending item and pushed it along the floor into the corner of his small office, next to the potted plant he couldn't make a decision about.

'We've been asked to attend a weird one, in "Ross Thraick", sir,' said DS Liz Stanley as she popped her head around the door. 'If that's how you say it.'

'I expect you mean Rhosddraig, in the Gower,' replied Glover, not raising his head from logging onto his computer. 'It's a harder "th" in the middle, like in the word "the", with a hard "g" at the end. But a good first attempt by an Englishwoman.' He looked up. 'Good grief, where's all your hair gone?' He sounded as surprised as he was.

'New style, sir. Pixie cuts are all the rage, they say.'

Evan beckoned her in. 'Am I allowed to say that it suits you?' he half-whispered.

'I think so, sir. Thanks. It's an odd-sounding one this, sir. Will you drive and I'll bring you up to speed on the way?'

Evan stood and patted himself all over, checking for packets of strong mints and communication devices. 'Alright then, but give me a hint before we go.'

'Local community constable in Rhosddraig has what he believes might be human remains on his hands. Well, you know, not literally.'

'New ones, or old ones?'

'Pardon?'

'It's an ancient village, just a few miles from the Paviland Cave.'

'The Paviland Cave, sir?'

'Where they discovered the earliest human remains ever found in Britain. 34,000 years old they are. So, has someone come across something from a few hundred, or thousand, years back? You said "remains", not "a body".'

Glover followed Stanley as she walked sideways along the narrow corridor, talking over her shoulder. 'I don't know, sorry, sir. But I can get back on the phone when we're on our way, and the constable is sending some photos. Key point – it's outdoors, so we'll be getting wet, given the weather.'

Glover stopped in his tracks. 'Right. Got it. Wet. Lovely. You go on ahead, I'll get my wellies. And try to get us a decent car from the pool, alright? Not that dreadful thing we went to Cardiff Crown Court in last week.'

'Sir.'

Ten minutes later, Detective Inspector Evan Glover of the West Glamorgan Police Service was making adjustments to the driver's seat in the little courtyard parking area of police HQ in Swansea, as he scrolled through some pretty useless photos on DS Stanley's tablet. He saw what appeared to be a pile of rocks; the blurry images didn't give him any useful insight into what they were about to face.

There was only one thing he was sure of – the case was likely to be a pretty straightforward one, because his boss knew he was retiring in two days' time, so he'd hardly have assigned him to something complicated; he'd have given anything like that to someone who was going to be around to work on it.

The rain beat a tattoo on the windshield, and Glover cranked the wipers to full pelt as they set off. He saw the familiar streets of Swansea, then the hedged-in lanes of Gower, pass him by. Would he miss this – driving toward the unknown, wondering how he'd be able to help those caught up in, or caught out by, some criminal undertaking? On balance, he didn't think so. About six months earlier he'd been convinced he would never be able to give it up, but he and his wife Betty had talked about his retirement for so many hours since then, in so many ways and from so many angles, he knew his decision to leave was the right one.

Change had always been a feature of the world of criminal investigations, but now – more than ever before, it seemed to him – the shift away from the human interaction it involved was increasingly rapid, spiraling toward the use of more and more technology. Not something he cared for, or – if he was honest – completely understood. Stanley on the other hand? It was all normal for her. A graduate in her early thirties, she lapped it up. Yes, it was time to go.

Unfortunately, that wretched potted plant was preying on his mind; the victim of a particularly nasty mugging had given it to him as a thank-you gift, and he'd nursed the pathetic thing along for about six years. But, whenever he looked at it, all he could see was the poor pensioner's bloodied face, not the beauty of the plant itself. It belonged at HQ, not with him. There – he'd decided. It would stay where it was. Someone else could water it, and try to keep it alive in the pod he called an office.

'Much further, sir?' asked Stanley.

'Not far now. Believe it or not, the sea's just beyond the fields to our left. However, you'll have to take my word for it because we won't see it until we're in the village itself on a day like today, and maybe not even then. Do you know Rhosddraig, by the way, Stanley? Or the Dragon's Back and Head, at all? Having transferred in from Bristol, it might not be somewhere you've visited yet.'

'I've heard the area is picturesque, but, no, I've never been there under my own steam. Do you know it, sir?'

'I do, Stanley, and I love it; I've been visiting since I was a boy. My grandmother lived in a village hereabouts called Lower Middleford; we'll pass through it on the way. Rhosddraig's the sort of place we'd come for a day out in my dad's old Ford Anglia. There's a stunning arc of sandy beach; it's about three miles long – so loads of room for a good run about with a rugby ball, or even for a game of cricket, without bothering anyone. Like so many of the beaches on the Gower peninsular you can only get to it if you're extremely determined, or a sheep. It's an almost vertical path down the hillside, and I can recall how steep it felt when I would clamber back up at the end of a day playing in the sand and the surf, carrying buckets and spades, balls and towels, all of which felt as heavy as lead weights. Only my mother's promise of a sweet treat when we got back to the car would keep me going.'

Glover dragged his attention back to the winding road and lashing rain; it was an area where you could never guess when you'd encounter a farm vehicle or even a stray pony or sheep.

'And the name – what does it mean? I'm assuming it translates into something. Though these names don't always, do they?'

'You're right. And this one does. The village of Rhosddraig is on the headland – or the Dragon's Back, as it's known. *Rhos* means moor, and *ddraig* means dragon. Lovely place. Stone cottages lining the narrow road, some whitewashed, some left to weather naturally. There's a church that goes back to Norman times, which was substantially rebuilt in the fourteenth century – so the locals call it "the new church", of course. The original church, dating back to the seventh century, is now no more than a ruin in the dunes on the beach; its inevitable sandy demise was why they began the Norman replacement, and they took the chance at the time to change its name to St David's.'

'Why did they do that?'

'No idea. Though, of course, it's a popular name for churches in Wales. There's a memorial to Edgar Evans in this one – one of the blokes who went to the Antarctic with Scott, and never came back. Born there. As I say, the village isn't much more than a collection of cottages, with some 1930s cubes on the outskirts, between Lower Middleford and Rhosddraig. Farmhouses dotted about, too. There's an old pub with a beer garden I swear has the best view in the world, a tea room – ditto – and a newish shop. There's a pretty big car park; National Trust. The path that leads right along the back of the dragon is an offshoot of the Gower Coastal Path, so it's popular with hikers and strollers alike.'

'The back of the dragon, sir?'

'Ah yes, the dragon. It's a finger-like spit of land that'll be on your map. Google "Dragon's Head, Rhosddraig", and you'll see hundreds of photos of it. It's so ridiculously beautiful, everyone who goes there can't help but take a picture. Nowadays they also can't help but post their photos online. There's a significant rock formation that runs from the headland into the sea; it looks like the back of a dragon that's writhing up out of the waves, then there's another large, pointed bit that eerily resembles the head of the dragon.'

'Like the dragon on the Welsh flag?' asked Stanley, in what Evan suspected was a gently mocking tone.

He didn't bite. 'Sort of, I suppose. Anyway, you can walk out to the head along the back, but the head part becomes an island when the tide comes in. It's a dangerous and remote bit of coastline. There was an RAF listening post there during the last war, because it's a good place to be high up and checking for signals across the Bristol Channel, the Irish Sea, and even the Atlantic. It's the Atlantic swell that makes it a popular spot for surfers these days. Love it, they do; them, and those idiots who run off the top of the cliffs strapped into those hang-gliding contraptions. They seem to delight in the way the wind comes across the ocean and up the escarpments. Idiots.'

Stanley ran her hand over the back of her newly-shorn head. 'Oh, I don't know, sir, I should think you'd get quite a rush of adrenaline jumping off a clifftop. But, you're right . . . it looks lovely in these photos. It seems a lot of people like to take pictures of the sunsets there.'

'They refer to it as the dragon's fire. You'll notice a lot of that type of talk in the area – the fog is the dragon's breath, the wind is the dragon stirring, the storms tell you the dragon's writhing. You get the idea. The dragon's pretty much the reason for every natural phenomenon – and some that aren't so natural, too.'

'Hmm. We didn't have a lot of that sort of thing in Filton, sir. Very interesting. This says there are only about a hundred people living in the village, but it is Wikipedia, so I'll take that with more than a grain of salt. Does that sound about right to you?'

'Probably. Like I said, it's tiny, and there's no way it can ever grow; it's hemmed in by hilly moorland, and the Vile. That's agricultural land they've used in a strip formation since Norman times, so they can't build anything on that, of course. And it was Britain's first ever designated Area of Outstanding Beauty back in the fifties, so I can only imagine planning permission is a no-no in the area. I was there just a couple of months ago; Betty and I came down for a bit of a walk and lunch at what used to be a tea room, though it's called a *cwtch* nowadays.'

'A what?' asked Stanley, sounding truly puzzled.

Evan grinned. 'Ah yes, it's one of those words even we English-speaking Welsh use for several purposes . . . it means both a cuddle, and a safe, secure, welcoming place. My mum used to refer to the space under her stairs as her "*cwtch*"; she hid there during thunderstorms, which terrified her. She even used to cower there during the Swansea Blitz too, if she couldn't get to the air-raid shelter in the back garden before the bombs started to fall. Not that it would have been at all safe, if there'd been a direct hit, of course.'

'So the word is in use for restaurants as well?'

'Not widely, to my knowledge. But I suppose in their case they mean it's a welcoming spot to eat. It's certainly a wonderful place to do so; the view is still the same as when I was taken there as a lad. Thank God they still do fried egg and chips, that's all I can say, even if they do insist upon bringing you a photo of the blessed hens who laid the eggs when they serve you. A lot of this "farm to table" stuff, you know?'

'Just as long as they don't try to tell me the name of the cow in my burger, sir, I'll be alright,' Stanley chuckled.

'No beef on the menu the last time I was there; all lamb burgers. They say locally that once you've tasted lamb raised on the Dragon's Back you'll never be able to enjoy other lamb at all, it's that good. It's the sea salt in the grass there that makes the meat sweeter, I believe – or maybe it's because the sheep have the dragon's breath in them. Indeed, if you're searching out a lamb chop or two at Swansea Market you'll notice the signs telling you which cuts are from this area; some will pay extra for it, some won't touch the stuff.'

'And you said there's also a pub in the village, sir?'

Glover chuckled. 'A bit early for a drink, isn't it, Stanley?'

'Tea rooms, even those rebranded as *cwtchs,* sound small. Pubs are usually bigger. We might need a place to talk to the locals. You didn't mention a church hall, or community center.'

'You're right, I didn't, because there isn't one. But let's see what we're dealing with first. We might not need to herd the locals into one place to point shiny lights at them; it might just be some poor animal, and not human remains at all.'

'Yes, sir. I suppose we can but hope.' Stanley put away her tablet and phone.

Evan parked as close as possible to the deserted car park's entrance. To his dismay, the rain had soaked through his jacket before he could get his wet weather gear on, so he resigned himself to an uncomfortable day.

He reminded himself he'd only have two more to serve after this one, and mentally crossed his fingers for the sort of 'remains' he could either immediately determine were animal, or else hand off to the brainy folks who looked after ancient finds.

He even dared hope he'd be able to nip home for a change of clothes before going back to the office; he was supposed to be having a pint later on with a few old colleagues who weren't going to be able to make it to his leaving do on Friday night . . . he'd like to freshen up for that, at least.

Nan

St David's church was illuminated by scant daylight filtering through the stained glass of its small windows. The two members of the altar guild knew every inch of the place as well as they knew their own homes, so didn't need the extravagance of electric light to complete their duties.

'These can all stay for Sunday,' said Mair Bevan as she moved arthritically between the vases of lurid flowers set each side of the tiny altar. 'They shouldn't go to waste, however hideous they might be.'

Nan looked up at her co-villager and replied, 'Yes, they'll be fine. The Watkins boy got them for his parents' service. I don't know where they came from, but apparently Dilys likes orange and red, so that's what he ordered. Must have cost a fortune at this time of year. Luckily this place is like a fridge so they'll keep nice. If Dilys doesn't make it, they might even last until her funeral.'

Mair paused, hunched over. 'Not likely though, is it? I mean, they take forever these days to get you sorted when you've gone, don't they? Queues forever at the crem this time of year, too. All the old ones dropping like flies.'

It amused Nan that a woman in her nineties should always refer to 'old people' with disdain. 'I'd have thought they'd at least have a proper service here, even if they go to the crematorium afterwards. By the way, I'll do the numbers on the hymn board, Mair. Don't you go reaching up for it. If we get all this done today, I won't have much to do on Sunday.'

'But it's my turn to set up this week,' replied Mair. 'Isn't it?'

'No. You did it last week. Remember?'

Nan worried about Mair; she seemed to be forgetting things more and more these days. She'd have a word with the vicar about it. Maybe someone else could take on a few of her duties.

'Alright then,' accepted Mair, sitting in the front pew, straightening the navy leather kneelers.

'I hope it's not raining like this at the weekend,' said Nan. 'It's Remembrance Sunday and we're supposed to be having a procession out to the war memorial for eleven o'clock. Damn and blast.'

'Language, Nan,' chided Mair, vinegar faced. 'We're in the Lord's House.'

'Hmm,' grunted Nan, mentally swearing like a sailor about how much work a wet Remembrance Day service might cause her. Well, if there were extra cleaning duties to be undertaken at the church after the service, they'd have to wait until the Sunday lunchtime rush had passed at the pub. It was true that nowadays Helen coped with most of it – with Aled's help behind the bar, and Sadie's in the kitchen – but Nan pulled her weight as much as she was able, and she was still the one who made sure the roasts were doing well before she headed to church every week. It was a routine she'd followed for donkey's years, and with so many special services taking place on Sunday, she reckoned fewer people than usual would be out and about.

She stood as upright as she could at the thought. Special services? What if more people than normal decided they wouldn't cook their own Sunday lunch, and would therefore eat out this week? Had Helen thought of that? Should they be planning for an extra roast? More veg?

'I don't think we need to do anything else today, Mair,' she snapped. 'I know we agreed to clean in here, but with no anniversary blessing yesterday, there's not much else for us to do, really.'

Nan opened the ancient, heavy wooden door to the church's outer porch. 'I wonder who they are,' she said aloud, spotting the figures of what seemed to be a man and a woman crossing from the car park to the path that led up the hillside.

'Who *who* are?' asked Mair, joining Nan in the stone porch, safe from the worst of the weather. 'Oh they're probably more police.'

'What do you mean "more police"?' Nan was puzzled.

'Hywel Evans and Nip found something up at the old RAF place this morning. Didn't you hear?'

Nan was even more puzzled. If something – anything – happened in the village she was usually one of the first to know about it. 'Found what? When? Where exactly?' she needed all the facts, and fast; the people who came to her pub relied upon her newsgathering abilities.

Mair pulled on her ancient waterproof. 'I don't know the details. Alis phoned me. Hywel went into the shop for some of Nip's treats when he and the poor little thing came back from what turned out to be a very long time standing about in the rain this morning. He said he'd found something odd up at the old RAF place, and had phoned the police. That boy who comes round here in his funny little car turned up – you know, the one's who's like a policeman but isn't really. Well, he came, and he sent Hywel away, telling him to not say too much. Which Alis said he didn't. Very tightlipped she said he was. For Hywel.'

Nan decided to ask Alis some questions herself. 'Can you lock up, Mair? I have to get going. You'll be alright getting home, won't you? You'll be wet through by the time you get there, I'd have thought. Better put the kettle on and get into some dry clothes as soon as you can.'

Mair threw Nan a baleful look. 'I am *quite* capable of looking after myself, thank you very much, Myfanwy Jones.' Nan hated it when anyone used her full name. 'It's coming down alright, but my skin doesn't leak, so it can't go further than that. By the way, those flowers you put on your Jack's grave are looking a bit sorry for themselves in this weather, aren't they? Funny to think you'll be under that slab yourself one day. Is that why you keep it looking so nice? It can't be for love of Jack, can it? Not with the way you two were.'

Nan turned away from Mair, pretending to fiddle with the button of her collar. Mair was right, the silk flowers she'd put on her late husband's grave just a week earlier no longer looked jolly in the dim winter light; now they were a floppy, soggy mess atop some lurid bits of green plastic. And they were still too good for the likes of bloody Jack Jones.

'I'll be putting poppies there tomorrow,' replied Nan as sweetly as she could. 'I always put poppies for Remembrance Day.'

Mair pulled her hood over her head, and bent even lower than her normal stooping posture as she stepped into the rain. 'I don't know why you would. It's not as though he ever served. My Dewi, he was in the Welch Regiment and he had a terrible time in Sicily . . .'

'I know all about Dewi's war record, Mair,' snapped Nan, pushing past her friend and heading along the path, which wound through the graveyard, then toward the shop. 'It's not as though you haven't told me about it a hundred times. Now I've got to go. See you on Sunday.'

She didn't wait to hear if there was a response. Cursing Mair's late husband's wartime exploits, she made her way carefully over the uneven road surface, until she reached the easier going of the newly-laid path to the front door of the village shop. She sloshed through the garden area set with wooden tables, which were packed with visitors enjoying ice-cream cones and fizzy drinks in the summer months. At that precise moment, the rain was bouncing off them, and rivulets of rain were pouring from the scalloped edges of the blue-and-white striped shop-front awning that had been rolled away for the winter months. She noticed it was beginning to blacken with mold.

Pushing open the shop door, which stuck a bit in its frame, Nan didn't mess about. 'What's all this about the police being here, and something being found up on the hill by Hywel Evans this morning?'

Alis Roberts was perched on a tall stool behind her cluttered counter. She looked up from the magazine she was reading, closed it carefully and placed it on the display shelf beside the packets of crisps. Nan thought she sounded unnecessarily pleased with herself when she replied, 'Not like me to know more than you, is it, Nan?'

Nan shook her mac's hood forward, over her feet, creating a small puddle on the floor. Alis tutted.

Using her 'don't muck about with me' voice, Nan said, 'I know Hywel Evans found something he wouldn't tell you much about, phoned the police, and that two more police officers have just arrived. What else is there I don't know?'

Alis took a swig from the bottle of Lucozade beside her. 'Nothing, Nan. That's all I know. Keeping mum, was Hywel. I don't know why, but he wouldn't tell me anything. Which – as we all know – is not at all like Hywel. From the little he did let slip, I thought at first maybe someone had done something nasty to a sheep. We all know that's happened before. But at this time of year most of them are inside shelters, if they've got any sense – not that most sheep have, mind you. I don't know what else he could have found. Somebody's poor dog? But we'd have heard about a dog going missing, wouldn't we? And you're hardly going to find someone's dropped dead from walking up that hill, are you? I mean, who'd be up there in weather like this anyway?'

'Hywel was. Someone else could have been.' Nan cast her eyes along the shelves crammed with an assortment of everything a person might need in a pinch, and be prepared to pay through the nose for. She wondered how many of the products on offer were past their sell-by dates, or at least close to them; Alis had a reputation for keeping foodstuffs on display which should have been discarded, then claiming she hadn't had her glasses on to notice they were out of date when she sold them.

'Nip was out up there. Hywel just followed him,' replied Alis huffily.

'Well, there you are.' Nan nodded twice, having being proved right. 'So not a clue then?'

'Nothing. Did you want something, by the way, Nan? Or was it just a chat you came in for?'

'Those lamb and mint sauce flavored crisps will be out of date in three days. I'll take them at cost price if you want me to shift them over the road at the pub.'

Alis stood, sighed, counted the packets in the box, and pulled a calculator from beneath the counter. As she tapped away, Nan decided she'd get back to the pub as fast as she could to phone Hywel; there wasn't anything she couldn't winkle out of a person, when she put her mind to it.

Helen

'Mum, the Corries have started arriving.'

Helen had climbed to the top of the stairs to encourage her mother to come down to the pub, to join her group of fellow *Coronation Street* aficionados. She was surprised to find Nan wasn't in the kitchen, but sitting instead in the small living room, in the dark, with her feet up on a stool and a cigarette in her hand. Helen was instantly worried – her mother never put her feet up until after the pub had shut for the night.

'Are you alright, Mum?' She placed her hand on her mother's forehead. 'You feel a bit hot to me.'

'Stop fussing.' Nan batted her daughter's arm away. 'I'm fine. I'll be the right side of the grass for a good few years yet, my girl. And able to jump over your head, too. Is everything ready for them? Telly on? Seats arranged?'

Helen tried to sigh silently, but the expression on her mother's face told her she'd been heard. 'Yes Mum, everything's all set up for them. And you. I know you don't watch and discuss the program with them afterwards just to be hospitable; you really enjoy it. Will you come down? Or don't you feel like it? You could watch it here with your feet up, then come down afterwards, maybe. How about that? I'll put the telly on here, shall I?'

'I'll be there now, in a minute.'

Helen thought Nan sounded less certain of herself than she usually did. Which was another worry. She tried to not lend a helping hand as her mother rocked herself up off the sofa; it seemed to take her longer than usual.

Oh God, is this the beginning of the end? Helen hated that the idea had flitted, unbidden, through her mind, but she couldn't deny she felt less lighthearted when she descended the stairs than when she'd run up them. Someone on one of the online support forums she belonged to had mentioned the 'cliff' of ageing she'd seen her mother plummet over, transforming her from a nimble-minded, able-bodied woman at eighty, to someone who needed help with almost every aspect of her daily life just two years later.

Is that what's going to happen to Mum? To me? Helen wondered as she reentered the lounge bar. She looked at the faces dotted around; all of them over sixty, many over seventy. Was this her life already . . . surrounded by only older people? All of them gradually becoming more frail, then dying. With a feeling of dread she realized she herself wasn't far off fifty.

If they aren't legally old enough to be your parent, then they aren't really old, Helen told herself, smiling too brightly at the glowingly youthful Aled Beynon who was pulling a half pint.

She caught sight of Sadie's back disappearing into the kitchen. Had she been serving drinks? She shouldn't be, she was still under age. If anyone saw her there'd be trouble; several of the more vocal locals had made comments about Sadie needing proper adult supervision if she was going to serve alcoholic drinks. Sometimes people just didn't know when to mind their own business.

Helen lifted the flap in the ancient Welsh oak bar, carefully replaced it, and popped her head into the kitchen. Sadie was pouring beer from a glass into a pot on the stovetop.

'Just adding a last bit of flavor to the mix for the steak and ale pies, Mam,' she said cheerily. 'I got a drop of Guinness, alright? Aled pulled it for me. I didn't do it myself; I know you don't like me to do that.'

Helen nodded, relieved, and cast her eyes around the cooking area. Unlike their own kitchen upstairs – which looked cozy and homey with its cluttered countertops and eclectic décor – this was a symphony of stainless steel fittings, and gleaming, empty surfaces.

Health and safety down here, the realities of never having enough space, and always being too rushed to have a good old clear-out in our home upstairs. Fair enough. She thought.

'Thanks, love,' she said. 'You're just making enough for a dozen, right?' Sadie nodded, stirring. 'Good. When you've filled the basins leave them out to cool; I'll freeze six of them, make the lids tomorrow morning, and freeze those too. We've got a couple ready for tonight, haven't we?' Another nod from her daughter; more stirring. 'Good. I can't see us selling them, but you never know. We'll have them for tea tomorrow if they don't go tonight, alright?'

'Yes, Mam. But no lid for me. I've got to watch my weight.'

Helen's heart broke a little.

'Come on Sadie,' she said, reaching out to touch her daughter's shoulder, 'you've got a lovely figure. You don't need to lose anything. Unlike me,' she patted her hips. 'I need to get out and do a bit more walking. Like I used to.'

'And don't eat so many crisps. Nan brought almost a whole extra box over from the shop this afternoon. Why would she do that? We've got loads out the back already.'

'Did she?' Helen hadn't noticed. 'Where are they?' Sadie used her elbow to indicate the corner of the kitchen. Helen inspected the box. 'Lamb and mint sauce flavor? I didn't even know such a thing existed. Still, they might go down well. We could have a bit of a rush on Sunday, if people decide they don't want to cook for themselves after going to some of the special services taking place.'

'Nan said that,' said Sadie with a smile. 'Two peas, same pod.'

Helen chuckled wryly. 'Don't say that, love. Promise you'll tell me if I ever get like her?'

'I promise,' replied her daughter, with an air-kiss. 'Is Nan coming down to have a drink with the Corries?'

'She said she would,' said Helen. She heard her mother's voice calling out to one of her cronies. 'Yes, she's down. I'll go in and tend to them. You're sure you're alright here? Homework done?'

'I've got a bit left to do, but I thought I'd finish it after you'd got that lot settled, when you probably won't need me.'

'Good plan, love. You finish that, I'll do this. We make a good team, don't we, Sadie? You and me, together whatever.'

'You and me. Together forever, Mam,' said her daughter, shrugging off her mother's hug with a, 'Hey, I'm stirring.'

The Dragon's Head being a traditional pub, customers were expected to get their own drinks at the bar, but Helen made an exception for the Corrie lot. It was much easier for her to ferry drinks from the bar to their tables, rather than have a gaggle of elderly people hobbling about the place, bumping into stools, chairs and tables; it was like having a pub full of oversized toddlers when they arrived.

Finally all settled, with ten minutes to go before their program started, Helen was surprised the conversation didn't turn to the cliffhanger at the end of the last episode, as it usually did. Instead, the entire group peppered Nan with questions about the sudden – and surprising – arrival of so many police and official vehicles in the village. Helen couldn't believe she hadn't noticed the activity they were all buzzing about, so listened with genuine interest.

'It's all because Hywel and Nip found a dead body up at the old RAF ruin this morning,' announced Nan with authority. 'The police were here all day. It's all taped off up there now. No one can go anywhere near it. A crime scene, here in our village.'

Helen was completely taken aback by this news. Why on earth hadn't her mother mentioned this to her earlier? *Because she's loving being the center of attention here in the pub,* Helen answered herself.

Of course she wanted to hear all Nan's news, just like everyone else, and even took some delight in the relish with which her mother did what she was best at – showing off that she knew it all.

'I spoke to Hywel, who found it,' pronounced Nan brightly. 'He said it was definitely a human body, and he should know, having been a butcher. But he said it was burned . . .' She paused, to great effect. 'No flesh left on it whatsoever.'

Gasps and groans and a few '*Ych a fi's*' followed. Helen could tell her mother was loving every minute as she continued, 'Yes, it was just bones, all crushed under a load of rocks. Piled up on top of it they were, in the middle of the old control room up at the RAF listening station. Hywel phoned the police, and they sent that young bloke they've got over in Lower Middleford. He called in the big guns. Detective Inspector Evan Glover from Swansea HQ, and some woman with him. I've seen his name in the papers before now. Funnily enough, his grandmother used to live in Lower Middleford. Vi Pritchard, she was. Her daughter Shirley was his mother. You'll remember her, Eleri, I'm sure.'

Helen noticed that Eleri didn't look as though she did.

Nan pressed on, 'They wouldn't have sent someone like him if it wasn't a crime, would they? Then a whole lot of those special types turned up too, the ones who wear funny paper suits. They built a big tent, and they were taking photos for hours. And they started taking stuff away too. In that black van that's been back and forth all day. You must have seen it.' Silver heads nodded. 'They'll be back tomorrow they said, and they've even left someone on guard up there. Can you imagine it, being out there all night, in weather like this? Poor dab, whoever it is. I offered to send up refreshments, but they said not to because he already had a Thermos with him.'

Helen marveled at Nan's ability to have gathered such a wealth of information, thereby ensuring she was seen as the fount of all knowledge. The questions came thick and fast, and she enjoyed seeing her mother field them with an expert quip here, and a practiced glance there. She noticed her mum seed ideas about black magic, a serial killer, old tales about the wrath of the 'dragon' against those who wished ill of the villagers, and a nasty accident. All in five minutes.

During the lively conversation that ensued, it was generally agreed that any human remains couldn't possibly be of a person connected with the village, because no one was missing, that anybody knew of. As talk turned to people who hadn't been seen for a few days, Helen was impressed by her mother's ability to imply she knew more than she was telling, but had been sworn to secrecy.

You always like to have the upper hand, don't you, Mum? thought Helen to herself.

One of the group shouted, 'It's starting!'

All conversation stopped as the trumpet played the plaintive introduction, and the *Coronation Street* fans ceased to exist in the real world of The Dragon's Head pub in Rhosddraig – the possibility of a local dead body notwithstanding – moving in their minds to the cobbled streets of Weatherfield and the Rover's Return, hands reaching absently for drinks and packets of crisps, eyes fixed on the screen high above their heads on the wall.

Helen noted the look of complete satisfaction on her mother's face; like the Cheshire Cat licking cream off her paws.

No need to worry about her, she's in fine form, she thought to herself, moving behind the bar to give Aled a break.

'Off you go,' she said cheerily. 'Half an hour. You've earned it. Going home to make your Grannie Gwen her cocoa, and give her her tablets as usual?' Aled nodded. Helen watched as he headed for the back door, and the wind-whipped rain beyond it.

'Did you leave your bike outside?' asked Helen, annoyed she hadn't thought to ask earlier.

Aled told her he had, but assured her it wasn't a problem; he always left his bike outside his gran's cottage too, because there was no room for it inside. She was pleased to hear he'd kept it dry by covering it with his big old yellow rain slicker, which he reasoned would get wet during his ride in any case.

'Bye Aled,' called Sadie, popping her head out of the kitchen. 'See you later. Maybe we can talk about our history homework?'

Aled shrugged as he left.

'Is he good at history?' asked Helen. 'I know it's not your favorite subject at the moment.'

'He's better at it than me. Mr Hughes said he's got a real feel for the Tudor period. Leaves me cold, it does. I hate all the dates, all the acts. I wish we were doing proper history – you know, the sort we like.'

Helen nodded. She'd managed to instill a passion for ancient times in her daughter at an early age. 'Well, give it a go for yourself before he comes back, and see how you do, alright? I'll need him in the bar when that lot want their drinks for their post-episode natter,' said Helen, indicating the rapt customers.

She'd also hated all the dates, battles, and treaties in her history classes, much preferring the more lyrical Paleolithic, Mesolithic, and Neolithic periods, so knew she wouldn't be much help to her daughter.

As she tidied behind the bar, and gave a selection of glasses a good shine with a clean tea towel before replacing them on their storage shelves, Helen watched the Corries with interest. How could they find the imagined lives of a group of Mancunians more interesting than a dead body on their own doorstep?

For herself, she wondered what the lone policeman up on the hill was guarding. The remains, and the bizarre mention of a pile of rocks, intrigued her. For once, she might try to find out even more than her mother knew.

Evan

'I know it doesn't look too tasty, but I promise you it is. And it's low cholesterol. It's just veg and tomatoes,' said Betty.

Evan Glover looked up from the bowl of unpromising soup to his wife's hopeful face. 'I'm sure it'll be lovely, despite the lack of meat,' he replied, and suspected it would be.

But he wasn't in the mood for eating; he'd had a hell of a day, most of which he'd spent soaked to the skin and freezing cold. He'd even missed the get-together with old colleagues he'd been looking forward to for weeks. He was tired, miserable, and – truth be told – feeling a bit sorry for himself.

As if she'd telepathically picked up on his mood, his wife sat beside him at the kitchen table and cupped her face in her hands. 'You can tell me all about it while you eat, if you like,' she said quietly. 'Or not. It's up to you.'

Evan smiled as he allowed the warmed-through soup to begin to work its magic on him; the satisfying texture and myriad flavors bathed in a rich, tomatoey liquid soon soothed him. Betty waited quietly as he 'mmm'd' his way through a couple of mouthfuls, then he sat back and worked out how to express himself adequately.

'I thought this would be an easy week. Work-wise, not emotionally; I knew it would be a challenging one in that respect. After more than thirty years, it's my last week on the job, and I'd thought it would be all about clearing out my desk, and making sure I'd handed everything over properly . . . saying my goodbyes and thank yous, you know?' Betty nodded. 'I didn't expect today. But, there again, who could have expected today.'

'That's what you've always said you love about your career, *cariad*,' said Betty gently. 'Not knowing what each day will bring. What was it?'

Evan put down his spoon and raked his hand through his hair with a burrowing motion. 'Something I don't understand. Something I've never seen before.'

Betty's eyes grew round. 'That's saying . . . *something*.'

Evan smiled at his wife's loving attempt to cheer him. 'There's only one thing I *am* certain about – this isn't a case I'm ever going to be able to solve, because I leave on Friday and it's going to become someone else's problem.'

He took another mouthful of soup, and knew his wife was considering how to respond; she always tilted her head to the right when she was thinking. He loved that about her – that she was a thoughtful person. Having spent years as a practicing psychologist, and now also being an advisor at the local community center and Citizens' Advice Bureau, she used her professional training in all sorts of situations – even when it was just the two of them, alone together.

Betty finally spoke. 'I know you're truly ready to retire, *cariad*, but I can also tell you're not happy about handing this one off. Do you want to tell me why that is?'

Evan smiled. 'I read you, you read me, right?' The couple exchanged knowing looks. 'I love you, Betty,' he said simply.

'And I love you too,' replied his wife. 'Go on, that'll be getting cold. Have a think about your day, and tell me what you want, when you want.'

Evan watched as Betty stood, busying herself at the kitchen counter. 'I'll put the kettle on, so there's a pot ready after you've finished,' she said.

By the time Evan pushed the empty bowl away, he was ready to talk. He'd decided to tell his wife everything, not something he usually did, but – on this occasion – he knew so little, it couldn't matter if he shared it all.

The brewing pot between them, Evan began, 'A dog walker found some sort of remains out at Rhosddraig this morning. Locals called it in, Stanley and I were sent. I don't know why they gave it to me; probably thought it would turn out to be a dead sheep or something, I suppose. Anyway, I was immediately pretty sure it was human. But one of the weirdest things I've ever seen.'

Betty poured him a mug of tea, which Evan cradled as he spoke. 'You know they used to have an old RAF listening station out there on the hill above the beach during the Second World War?'

Betty nodded as she took full advantage of what Evan was convinced were lips made of asbestos to sip her scalding-hot tea.

'We've seen it in the distance on walks, haven't we?'

More nodding.

'Well, it's not much more than a ruin when you get up close – which I did for several hours today, hence me being soaked through.'

Betty reached out a hand to touch his arm, which Evan loved.

'So what we see when we get there is a mound of rocks – well, rocks, broken bricks, lumps of concrete even – all piled on top of what amounted to no more than a heap of shattered bones.'

Seeing Betty's eyebrows rise in surprise he added, 'See? That's what I mean. Weird. There's no indication how long this thing's been there, though it's obviously fairly recent, not an ancient burial site suddenly exposed by a run-off of heavy rain, or anything. Burn pattern all around the mound. The place has been awash for the past week or so, but the ruin itself is on level ground, so there was a fair amount of standing water about the place. Floor of broken concrete. We're not likely to be finding footprints or anything.'

Evan paused, and sipped his tea carefully. It was still too hot to enjoy, so he replaced the mug on the tabletop.

He continued, 'Not knowing when this might have happened exactly, nor what the cause of death might have been – despite the evidence of human intervention at least after death – I made all the necessary calls. Up came the lot from FIT – you know, the Forensic Investigation Team – with their tents and lamps and so forth, taking their own sweet time about it, I must say. Stanley and I were still hanging about in the rain at this point. Anyway, to cut a long story short, they shifted enough rubble for Rakel to come out and have a look at what was underneath it all, and she's as puzzled as the rest of us.'

'It takes some doing to puzzle West Glamorgan's very own Director of Pathology,' said Betty, sounding intrigued.

'It does. It was nice to see her professionally one last time before I bow out, though I know she'll be at Friday night's shindig. Her preliminary findings mean they'll hand this to someone else tomorrow morning, if they haven't already done so.'

Evan took an ill-advised swig from his mug. He pictured the scene again in his mind's eye. It was such a strange place for a life to end – if that was where the life in question had ended; there'd been no specific evidence of a killing.

He said, 'Rakel believes a human body was burned there; burned so thoroughly that all the flesh had been consumed. The resulting skeletal remains appear to have been shattered – literally smashed to about a thousand pieces, she reckoned – then burned again. *Then* covered in rocks, and bits of brick taken from the debris of the ruined walls.'

'How do you know – or how did she know – the remains had been burned twice?' asked Betty, sounding fascinated, rather than repelled.

'Rakel suggested it would have been impossible for the bones to be broken as they were – smashed to tiny pieces – without the flesh having first been burned off them. I agreed. The broken edges of bones were charred. So she reckons burned, smashed, burned again. It was slow-going trying to remove all the rocks while not disturbing what was underneath them.'

'So is it a man or woman? A missing local? Any idea?'

Evan loved the way his wife asked all the questions he'd asked himself. 'No idea of gender, or age. No reports of any local missing persons for the past few years, let alone during the past few weeks. Stanley checked. Door-to-door inquiries might reveal how long it could have been there. The ruined walls of the building come up to about shoulder-height, so you'd have to enter what's left of it to see the actual remains. The investigating team will have to establish the last time – before today – anyone was up there. The bloke who found it was following his dog, which had run off. Whoever gets to lead on this one will get the door-knocking started soon, I should think.'

'So – no timeline, no identity, no real forensic clues,' mused Betty. 'I think you're right; this isn't going to be your case at all, is it *cariad*? Does that bother you? That you won't get to follow through?'

Evan stretched his tired arms above his head. 'Ask me after I've had a hot shower and I'm in bed. At the moment it annoys the hell out of me, but maybe after I've given myself a bit of a talking to, it won't bother me so much. Rakel said it could take quite a while for the FIT folks to get everything from the site to her labs. But she said, even then, she's not sure what she'll be able to do with all the bits. And bits they are. Even though I didn't see it all, it was almost impossible to think of what I did see today as having once been a human being.'

'Not a pleasant sight, nonetheless,' said Betty.

Evan nodded, deep in thought. 'It's funny – I know we've both agreed it's time for me to leave this career of mine, but today made me ask myself some challenging questions. Have I actually reached the point where I can't connect a piece of bone to the idea of a person to whom it once belonged? Because if I can't do that anymore, maybe I should have left sooner. Maybe I've become immune to the horror of what I see, and don't even know it.'

After a moment or two of contemplation, during which he listed all the tasks he'd assign to people the next morning – if he were working the case – Evan added, 'You'd have to *really* hate someone to set them on fire twice, and smash their bones to smithereens, wouldn't you?'

'I dare say. Or maybe you'd have to fear them a great deal,' replied Betty quietly.

'Yes,' agreed Evan thoughtfully, 'hatred or fear. But which? Who knows? I certainly don't, and am unlikely to ever find out . . . for myself. So here I am, right at the end of my career, feeling really quite pleased with myself that there never was that one case that would haunt me in years to come, like so many of my ex-colleagues – and up pops this one. Wouldn't you bloody know it?'

'Well, first of all, maybe try to not think of it as *your* case at all, because it clearly won't be. And, if you can't manage that, you've always got me to talk to, *cariad*.'

They shared a wry smile. Evan hoisted himself from his seat to head for the joy of a reviving shower, hoping his neck muscles would stop their spasms before his head hit the pillow. 'I'm getting too old for all this,' he said, as he pulled himself up the stairs, the bannister creaking.

8th November

Sadie

I can't believe Aled has gone to sit at the back of the bus this morning with that idiot Stew Wingfield. I bet all they'll talk about is surfing this, and surfing that. Nothing sensible at all. But there, one of the reasons I love Aled so much is because he's so passionate about things he loves – like me, and surfing.

Nan was right about the police coming back to the village today, but they've brought a couple of cars this time, and they'd arrived before the bus came to take us to school. Mam reckons they'll be knocking on doors next; she and Nan were up until all hours talking about it last night.

Not that I mind – at least it keeps Mam from nagging me about university. Why can't she leave me alone? I'm not sure I want to go to bloody university. Just 'cos Mam went, she thinks everyone should go. I mean, what about me and Aled? Until he makes up his mind, I'm not saying, or doing, anything. Once I know where he wants to apply, if he does, then I'll do the same. But this one's up to him. He's got to make the first move. For both of us.

I know he was thinking about Exeter, because of some place called Bigbury, which I suppose must be something to do with surfing; then he said he'd rather stay here and go to Swansea. If we both went to Swansea University we could both still live at home, and save a fortune. And he'd be close to his precious Rhosddraig Bay and his surfer friends, too.

We could both earn some money while we study, to be able to afford our own place, later on. Mam and Nan would let us carry on working in the pub, I'm sure. That would be good. But all the traveling to and fro? It's bad enough having to get the bus from Rhosddraig to Killay every day to go to school, and the university's even further. But I suppose at least I could study on the buses.

They say a lot of students do that, especially now they've opened the new campus further along the beach from the original one. They've got a special bus that makes the trip between the two campuses, full of students all the time. Aled and I could catch it together. We could sit and talk to each other.

By then we won't have to keep us a secret, because we'll both be adults, and Mam won't be able to say a word about us. Nor Nan. I have no idea why she doesn't like Aled's family. She won't even mention his Grannie Gwen's name without swearing.

Old people are weird. No sense of priorities. No idea what's really happening in the world at all.

Always going on and on about who said what to who in church, is Nan. Not a clue about what was on the news last night, though. That's what really matters, the big stuff, not all her gossip.

What about all that plastic that washes up on the beaches? The birds dying from it getting stuck in their throats? All the rubbish in the sea – that's what she should be talking about, not who raised an eyebrow the wrong way in Mothers' Union.

She makes me sick, does Nan. Her *and* Mam. Always worrying about stupid things. St Melangell was a proper Christian, the patron saint of hares, small creatures, and the natural environment. There's even that horrible myxomatosis threatening the poor hares, now. That's what we've come to. Terrible. I suppose it's a bit ironic that the original church here was dedicated to St Melangell, and it's now buried in the sand dunes. But I still think her ideas about safeguarding all animals are something everyone should take to heart. That's the sort of thing that means something. People should be saving hares, not worrying about Victoria sponges for the cake sale next month.

But not even Mam gets that; there are important things going on in the world. She's awfully clingy these days. She'll have to get a life when Aled and I tell everyone about us. One of her own. I know she went on a date the other night, and when she came home she cried. I asked her why, and she said it didn't go very well; said she 'wasn't ready' yet.

I don't know what she means, 'cos Dad's been gone for ages. Thirteen years now. When's she ever going to be 'ready'? She said she'll find it hard to trust anyone ever again. What does she mean, 'trust anyone'?

Dad's alright; he's always fun when I see him. Not that I see him often, I know, but I get it – he's busy. Travels a lot for work. Sometimes he's in the area and just phones me out of the blue, and more often, these days. Like last Monday, when I had a coffee with him, then caught the late bus home from school. It wasn't the best day to meet him, 'cos Mam had wanted me home early so I could help her get ready for Guy Fawkes Night, but I made up for it when I finally got to the pub.

I forgot to ask Dad where he was staying overnight. Swansea, I think. Or maybe Mumbles. I don't know. Well, it doesn't matter, really.

It was nice to see him, even if it was only for a coffee. He looked thinner. He said I did too. Which is good.

Mam doesn't get it. Keeps saying I don't need to lose weight. God forbid I ever get as fat as her. Her hips are huge, and her neck's gone all blubbery. Nan's not so bad, but she's really old. I don't want to get like either of them. I take after Dad's side of the family, Mam always said that. Which is good. Not that I know them, because there aren't any of them left. But to end up like Mam or Nan? I'd shoot myself.

It makes me laugh when Mam says I've got to tell her if she gets like Nan, 'cos she's already exactly like her. Says loads of the same things. Just as useless.

And there I am again, back to the same thing. Useless old people.

Aled's stopped talking to Stew now. I'll text him to say he should come and sit with me, though we'll be there in five minutes. Then we'll be together again.

Double History first thing. I did alright with my homework, I think, even though Aled wasn't back at the pub in time to help me last night. If I can get an A he'll be dead impressed. He always gets an A, but I usually get a B something. Maybe this time I'll have done a better job.

It was quite interesting to think about how Elizabeth I treated Mary Queen of Scots when she had her in prison, trying to decide if she should have her executed or not. And if so, how. The things they all used to do to each other back then; such a lot of ways to torture and kill people. It's quite fascinating, really. So says Aled, anyway, and I agree with him – it's the only interesting thing about history.

Nan

Nan took her time looking the couple up and down, then invited them into the pub, ensuring both of them shook the rain off themselves in the porch and left their dripping coats there.

'We'll stay down here,' said Nan, making it clear that not inviting them upstairs was significant. Helen had called her down to the pub to tell her she'd seen two figures approaching the side door a few minutes earlier, and Nan had decided to ignore the thumping headache she had to be sure she didn't miss out on anything.

These two were most definitely The Police, even though they were in ordinary clothes, which she knew meant they were more important than the ones who wore uniforms. She also knew she had the chance to get every possible bit of inside information out of them before anyone else in the village knew what was going on; a legendary reputation for knowing everything didn't just appear out of thin air – it required a determined and sustained effort. She watched and listened with interest as the man formally introduced himself and his sidekick.

'Helen will make you both a cup of tea or coffee, won't you, Helen?'

Her daughter hovered and nodded. 'Of course I will, Mum. What can I get you? Detective Sergeant Stanley, Detective Chief Inspector Jenkins – what will it be?'

Nan watched as the woman deferred to her male superior, as was right and proper, even if the man looked like a pathetic wimp. The woman seemed to have a bit more about her.

'Thanks very much,' said Jenkins. High voice, reedy. 'Coffee, black, no sugar. Tidy. Ta.'

'Me too, please. Same thing. Thanks ever so much,' said Stanley. Nan thought it an unfortunate surname for a woman.

Deciding to make sure they knew she was no fool, Nan said to the woman, 'I can tell he's from the Valleys, but you're not Welsh.'

The young woman blushed. 'No, I work here now, but I'm from Bristol. Not far, really.'

'If it's over the bridge it's far enough,' replied Nan, keen the sergeant should know that being English in a Welsh village mattered a great deal.

'Yes, DS Stanley has joined us from across the Severn,' said Jenkins, 'but, you're right, I'm from the Valleys, myself. The Rhondda.' To Nan's mind, he smiled too brightly as he held out his hand to shake hers. 'Pleased to make your acquaintance.'

'Being from the Rhondda doesn't have anything to do with anything,' replied Nan tartly. 'Most people can't wait to get away from there, I hear. And with good reason too, I should think.'

Helen's curt 'Mum' was totally uncalled for, and she made sure her expression told her daughter so. If the police wanted to ask her questions in her own pub, they'd have to know who was in charge before they started.

Jenkins continued, 'I've heard a great deal about you, Mrs Jones. I understand this pub is the heart of the village.'

'As for this pub being the heart of Rhosddraig, well, we all know that, so telling me something I already know won't work if you meant it as flattery. Say what's on your mind.' Nan paused, glowering at her still-hovering daughter. 'I'll have tea, of course, Helen,' she said pointedly. 'Now then, tell me – what's occurring? Your lot's been disgruntling the entire population. I think it's time you told us why.'

Jenkins exchanged a look with his English subordinate that Nan couldn't quite fathom; she wondered if the two of them were at it, then thought maybe not, because the woman seemed to think she had to look as much like a man as possible – with her short hair, trouser suit, striped cotton shirt and thick-soled black lace-ups – while the man . . . what was it about him that Nan didn't like? She couldn't put her finger on it. Then she did.

'Remind me a bit of my late husband, Jack, you do,' she said quietly.

'Ah . . .' was all the policeman said; nodding his head gently, his emotions were masked by a blank expression. To be fair to him, Nan didn't know what else he could have said without understanding the nature of the relationship she'd had with Jack. If he'd known anything about that he'd have said something more telling.

To business, Nan told herself. 'So, what's up?' she asked.

'Knowing everyone from hereabouts, as you undoubtedly do,' began the sergeant, 'we wondered if you could tell us if anyone's gone missing, or not been seen around for a few days. You know the sort of thing.'

Nan did. 'No one,' she replied confidently.

'You seem very sure of that,' noted Jenkins.

'I am. A group of us had a lengthy conversation about that very matter last night, here. Bound to when you hear a body's been found in the area. No one's unaccounted for. Well, those who haven't been seen out and about in a while have since been contacted, and are just hiding from the weather, or aren't here for a good reason. Like Dilys and John Watkins, for example; she's in the Morriston cardiac unit and her husband's with her. Not long for this world, if you want my opinion. Her, not him, of course. Though apparently he's not too good, either. What is it, anyway? The body you've found, is it a man or a woman?' Nan didn't see any point mincing words.

'We're not at liberty to divulge that at the moment, Mrs Jones,' said the Englishwoman. Nan quite enjoyed the way the Bristolian spoke; a rare treat to hear the accent.

Nan made no attempt to help Helen when she brought the tray of tea and coffee to the table. It was best to let her get on with it her own way, and if she messed it up then they'd know how useless she was. But Nan had to admit Helen managed alright.

Helen sat. 'Mum and the Corries did a good job of working their way through everyone in the village. Lower Middleford too. All present and accounted for, as of this morning,' she said brightly.

'The Corries?' asked Stanley.

'A group of Mum's friends who come here to watch *Coronation Street* then chat about it afterwards. They're a very active part of the pub community,' replied Helen. She offered a plate of chocolate digestives, which Nan thought was a bit much; custard creams would have done just as well.

'Well, that's a big job taken care of for us right there,' said Stanley. 'Thanks. We knew we'd come to the right place, didn't we, sir?'

'We did indeed, Stanley,' replied Jenkins.

Nan reckoned these two didn't know each other very well, after all. In fact, they both seemed to be on pins with each other, and she couldn't work out why. Didn't the police work in pairs, always together? Like Morse and Lewis, or Barnaby and Jones . . . or whoever it was in each series of *Midsomer*; they chopped and changed a bit, but Jones had been her favorite. They even got themselves a new Barnaby at one point, which Nan didn't understand at all. Why couldn't he just have a different name? He was a completely different person, after all. She thought they'd been stretching it a bit with that one.

She straightened her back in the chair and asked, 'So, if you're asking if anyone's missing, and if you can't say if it's a man or a woman, that means it's definitely a person you've found up there, then.'

Stanley and Jenkins exchanged a glance. Nan was delighted; she'd caught them out on that point.

Jenkins took the lead. Nan had expected he would; the woman had messed up. 'I was hoping we could keep that confidential for a while longer but, you're right, we have discovered human remains up at the old RAF listening station.'

'How long have they been there?' asked Helen, which was just what Nan was about to ask. She glared at her daughter, who sipped her coffee.

Jenkins sighed. 'It's hard for us to be exact at this stage. The conditions up there, the weather the past week or so, you know.'

Nan pounced, 'I watch my fair share of police series on the telly, chief inspector, so I suppose you're trying to make the window of opportunity as small as possible. I suggest you ask who was up there last, when you carry out your door-to-door enquiries. I believe Hywel only went because he was trying to get hold of Nip. No one might have been up there for weeks. Could the remains have been there that long?'

'It's hard to say, because of their condition,' said the sergeant.

Got you again, thought Nan. 'Hywel mentioned only bones were visible. I don't think a body would have had the time to go to just bones in the past few weeks, do you?'

'We believe a fire was involved,' said Jenkins. 'Have you, any of your friends, or maybe even anyone else who's been in the pub and talking about this, seen a fire up there recently?'

'Fire, you say? Well, now, that's something, isn't it? A fire?' Nan was delighted to have a fact confirmed. 'We can't see the place in question from the pub. We'd have to be out and about. Have you seen anything, Helen? I haven't.' Nan poured herself a cup of tea.

Helen shook her head. 'Sorry, no. Like Mum says, we don't have a view up the hill, only out to sea on one side, and along the back of the dragon on the other. The people most likely to see something up there would be the ones who live on the road to Lower Middleford. Or people who were out and about, you know.'

'We'll be asking everyone in the village. Thank you, Mrs . . . um?' said Stanley, her pen hovering over her pad.

'She's Jones again,' said Nan quickly. 'Ms Helen Jones. Got rid of her married name when she got rid of her husband. Better to be a Jones around here than a Thistlewaite. I mean, *Thistlewaite*. Sadie's a Jones, too. Thank God. Don't know what they were thinking calling her Sadie Thistlewaite. It's like a tongue-twister.'

Helen piped up with, 'You know very well that Sadie was named after her father's grandmother.'

Nan glared at Helen, who started to nibble on a chocolate biscuit, something Nan believed she could well do without, given the size she was getting to be.

Nan snapped, 'Sadie's my granddaughter. In school at this time of day, of course. She'd have mentioned a fire if she'd seen one.' Then she decided to give it one more try. 'Any idea when this fire might have been?'

This time, Jenkins's sigh was heavier. 'It's early days yet, Mrs Jones.'

'Ah,' Nan nodded sagely. 'Still establishing a timeline, I see. Well, there's no one local missing, but I dare say you'll be expanding your enquiries. It must be difficult for you, not knowing when it happened. Doesn't help you know where to start really, does it?'

'Not as such,' replied Jenkins.

He's a cagey one, thought Nan. 'Do you have an idea of age?'

'Again, not something we can talk about at this time,' said Jenkins. Nan reckoned he was beginning to sound a bit snappy.

She decided to be helpful. 'We get a lot of youngsters down here for the surfing, you know, and those people who do hang-gliding. Plus there are the birdwatchers, and the people who just like to go for a walk. The dead person could have come from anywhere really. A visitor.'

'Have there been any unclaimed vehicles in the car park, or in other areas around the village that you, or your customers and friends, might have noticed or mentioned?' asked the sergeant.

'Good question,' said Nan, acknowledging that maybe the woman had a brain after all. 'We can see the main car park from here, as you can tell.'

She turned and waved toward the window behind them. 'There's a few other places you can park legally – in the church car park, for example. But I'm intimately connected with the church and I can tell you for certain there haven't been any abandoned cars, motorbikes or bicycles left in either car park since the summer. September, anyway. About six weeks ago a couple of young friends of the son of the family who own the café a couple of doors along left their bicycles chained up in the church car park for about two weeks, then one of the fathers came and took them away on the back of his camper thingy.'

'You mean the Rhosddraig Cwtch?' asked Stanley, making notes.

Nan couldn't help herself but tut. '*Cwtch*, my eye. It's been a café and a tea room, but nowadays – because there's an English couple running it, I daresay – it's a *cwtch*. Full of driftwood and fancy coffee machines, and they charge an arm and a leg for food that's no better than we serve here, it's just all lah-di-dahed on the menu. Nice enough woman, I suppose. Husband's one of them lot who do all that gliding stuff. But that son of hers? A bit on the wild side, I'd say.'

'Oh come on now, Mum,' said Helen. 'They've done up the old place a treat – it looks lovely now; light, bright, and welcoming, not like it used to be. And they sell some interesting bits and bobs there, too. Though I will admit it's stiffer competition for us; still, we can cope.'

She turned her attention to the officers. 'Stew's alright. Him and Aled are good friends, and he's very enterprising – got his own little surf shack in the garden around the back of the place there. He makes some lovely little birdhouses in the winter, when he's not doing so much business with the board rentals. Nice boy, chief inspector. In school with my Sadie, and with Aled, who works here some evenings and lives in the village with his grandmother. Both good boys. Both servers for communion at St David's. Reliable types.'

'Could I get some full names, do you think, please?' asked Stanley.

Helen replied before Nan could. 'Aled Beynon, lives at Green Cottage – though it's white nowadays – with his grandmother, Gwen – though it's really Gwendolyn – Beynon. And at the Rhosddraig Cwtch it's Maggie and Stephen Wingfield, and their son Stewart, known as Stew. Stephen's away a lot; he's a consultant in something or other. Travels about all over Europe.'

'English like you, they are,' Nan managed to insert, nodding at Stanley. 'Moved here not long ago from up north somewhere.'

'They moved here from Colchester, five years ago,' said Helen, with what Nan thought was a totally unnecessary sigh, 'not that that's got anything to do with anything.'

'And I take it your ex-husband is no longer in the area, Ms Jones?' asked Stanley.

'He can't be far enough away,' snapped Nan.

'He lives in Slough. I believe he still travels a fair bit for work, but only around the south-west of England and Wales. He hasn't lived in this area for many years, and certainly doesn't come anywhere near Rhosddraig anymore, nor even to the general area.'

'Thank the Lord,' said Nan, with feeling. 'I don't know what that waste of space has got to do with this. You don't think he's come here and murdered someone, do you?'

'We don't know that anyone's *been* murdered, Mrs Jones,' said Jenkins sharply. 'All we can say is that we have found human remains.'

'Well, whoever it was you found, they didn't drop down dead of natural causes, then cover themselves up with a load of old stones, now did they? So there's got to be something underhand going on, hasn't there? Just 'cos we live out here in Rhosddraig it doesn't mean we're all *twp*.'

'No one's saying you're *twp*, Mrs Jones,' replied Jenkins. 'That's a local word suggesting a slowness of comprehension, Stanley,' he added quietly, looking at his puzzled sergeant, 'and I would tell you more if I could. Really, I would. But, given you're a woman who certainly knows her onions when it comes to police work, Mrs Jones, I'm sure you understand we have to be very circumspect about what we say, because we could let something slip we don't want people to know.'

'Ah yes, the thing only the killer would know,' said Nan, glowing.

'There might not have been a killer,' snapped Jenkins.

Nan wasn't having that. 'Oh rubbish. You're not telling me that someone spontaneously combusted on our hill, then someone else came along and covered them nicely with stones for no good reason, are you? No. A deliberate attempt to foul-up a crime scene, that's what it is. Anyone who watches telly knows that much. It might be a serial killer's work. They're popular at the moment, on telly, aren't they? Someone might think it's a good idea – you know, to become famous. I might work every hour God sends in this place, but I record all my favorites on TV. Sometimes Sadie and I watch them one after the other to catch up. Highly educational.'

Jenkins stood, rather abruptly thought Nan, so she must have touched a nerve. 'Sergeant Stanley and I had better be getting along, Mrs Jones, Ms Jones. We have some uniformed officers coming to talk to local residents, and you'll continue to see some activity on the hill.'

'When will we be able to get back up there?' asked Helen.

'It'll be too early for him to say, Helen,' replied Nan, keen to retain the upper hand. 'All that lot in those bunny suits are still up there, so it'll be a while. Luckily for us it's hardly peak tourist season, so I don't think you'll be turning a lot of people away, chief inspector.'

'That's good, isn't it, sir? I'm sure it's lovely here when the weather's a bit better,' said Stanley, also rising. 'One of our officers, Detective Inspector Glover, has been coming here since he was a boy. He was telling me all about the beach, and the church. I look forward to being able to see out to the Dragon's Head, one of these days.'

'Glover? Yes, he was the policeman they sent in the first place,' said Nan. 'I recognized him. I used to know his grandmother Vi, and his mother, before she married. Lived in Lower Middleford, they did. Nice girl Shirley Pritchard, even if she was a bit of a lump.'

The pair left, as Nan waved at their backs.

'Going sideways is that rain,' said Nan as the figures disappeared and the door slammed shut. 'Horrible weather.' She picked up her cup. 'You can take this lot away as quick as you like, Helen. We don't want people seeing you serving me at a table like this. They'll think we're turning into a restaurant instead of being a pub. Can't have that.'

'Yes, Mum,' said Helen as she loaded the tray. 'I'll leave the pot so you can have another cup. Did you get everything you wanted out of them?' Nan wondered if her daughter was making fun of her.

'I'll manage with what I've heard, ta,' replied Nan, thinking about how best she could present her findings when the Corries arrived that evening.

Sadie

That stupid cow Rhian can't do anything right! I've been looking forward to hearing Aled read Romeo's part in the balcony scene for ages. I know it off by heart, I've gone through it so many times, imagining him saying those words to me in front of everyone in class.

And she messed it all up. That bit where she's supposed to say, 'My bounty is as boundless as the sea, My love as deep; the more I give to thee, The more I have, for both are infinite.' Well she said it nice and loud alright, but she sounded like she was talking to a log. No passion. No feeling. If Mrs Lee had let *me* read Juliet instead of her, they'd all have seen how it should be done.

Aled and me as Romeo and Juliet? There'd be no stopping us. Not in class, and not in life.

But maybe it's just as well Rhian is doing it, after all, because everyone would guess about us if we were reading it together. And we can't have that. Our grandmothers wouldn't hear of it, though I don't know why. Nan just goes on and on about me having to be careful to choose the right boy. Maybe Grampa wasn't nice to her, I don't know. He was dead before I was even born, so all I know is the little Nan has said – which isn't very nice at all – and the few bits Mam has told me, which isn't a lot, though she seems to think he walked on water. Maybe I should ask her – though I might not, because then who knows where that conversation would go.

I don't like lying to them both, really. I'm not sure I'm even very good at it, so I'd rather not say anything to set either of them off asking questions about me and Aled. They haven't guessed so far. Not at all. It's amazing, really. They're both so wrapped up in their own stupid worlds, I suppose.

If she's not down in the pub, Mam's on her computer, in one of her chat rooms. She thinks I don't know, but sometimes she's not quick enough to clear the screen when I go into her room, so I know alright. I wonder who she's chatting to. About what? She doesn't do anything to chat about.

Chat rooms are weird. The only ones I've visited were full of idiots who want you to tell them everything about yourself. Though there was one interesting conversation about how young people can get themselves set up with a place to live if they fill in some forms the right way; the bloke writing said he could fill them in for me if only I paid him. I left then. Just trying to get money out of people, that's what that was.

I never did tell Aled about that. I didn't want him to think I'd gone behind his back to try to plan for when we're on our own.

If that's what happens.

I heard him and Stew talking today about how they're going to be out in the surf in Rhosddraig Bay in the spring, which is when his Grannie Gwen will let him go back in, and Stew said how good the surf would be again next autumn, because that's when everything's in its favor around here. So it looks like Swansea Uni is in the lead for now. I'll shut Mam up by making sure she sees I'm doing some research into courses at Swansea tonight, after I've done my homework.

If I can do well at my A levels, she'll be chuffed. And I know I have to knuckle down and work, like she says. Aled has to, too. He was saying just the other day how much longer he's spending studying these days. All our teachers have turned serious lately, going on about how this is the most important year of our lives.

As though we don't know that.

This is the year when everything changes. It's started to change for me and Aled already, after the other night. Even though things didn't go quite the way I'd expected them to.

But they never do, do they? There's always something that comes up at the last minute, and you have to cope with it. To be fair to Mam, she's always recognized how good I am at that. I noticed it when I first joined the Girl Guides. It's a shame they closed them down at St David's; Aled misses his Scouts, too. There was that few years when about half a dozen families moved away, and then there just weren't enough of us, at the right age, to keep it all going. And Mam couldn't get me to the meetings in Killay back then, so I didn't make a fuss about it. Aled went there for Scouts for a few years, but then he dropped out. About the time he got that job making bicycle deliveries of take-away food. Then, eventually, he came to work here at the pub.

They said it might stop raining this weekend. That would be nice, because I like my walks up on the hill, even if it's freezing – but not so much in the rain. If I don't get up there regularly, I miss my walks a lot.

It's the only time when I feel connected to anything. Anything real, that is. I like the way the wind feels in my hair – it's usually all tied up, but I let it down in the wind. Best feeling in the world.

Well, second best – the best would be being in Aled's arms, of course. His wonderful, muscular arms. That surfing means he's so strong. You have to be if you're not going to drown.

If it stops raining, maybe Aled and I could somehow manage to find ourselves together with a chance to go for a stroll.

If I can, I'll make it happen – all innocent like – so no one would notice anything was up. But I'd have to make a plan, and stick to it. Sometimes, improvisation isn't the answer.

Evan

'It'll be your last morning to get up and go off to be a policeman, tomorrow, *cariad*. How do you feel about that?'

Evan gave his response some thought. 'Not too bad. Not too bad at all. Though I don't think it'll hit home that I've actually retired for quite some time. Not until we come back from our cruise, and I don't have to go back to work afterwards. Until then, it'll just feel like I'm on holiday. A once-in-a-lifetime, *very* special holiday – thanks to your great Auntie Barbara. By the way, did you manage to find that suntan lotion I asked about?'

'Yes, but I got factor 30, not factor 20, like you put on the list. The Caribbean sun is more dangerous than you think, and we're both blue rather than white at the moment, so I thought it best to get the stronger one for you, and for me too. I also got a bottle of factor 50 for the very tender bits.'

Evan chuckled. 'I'm not planning on letting the sun get at any of my tender bits, thank you very much. As for you? Well, I'd be careful if I were you.'

Betty hugged him from behind, her arms around his neck as he put down his tea on the table beside his armchair. 'I've got to put some laundry away,' she said. 'When I come back, you'd better have decided what we're watching for an hour. I've had a long day, and you have too. For all that you say you're not tired, what you mean is you can't relax because your mind is racing, trying to think if you've forgotten anything you're supposed to do before five o'clock tomorrow. An hour of vegetating and viewing is what we both need to slow us down. How about *Death in Paradise*? You know, to get us in the mood for the Caribbean.' Betty shouted louder as she finished her point while walking into the kitchen.

'No, not tonight,' Evan replied, 'I can't face it. It drives me mad the way they solve the whole case in just under an hour. Though, you're right, the locations – and the actors – aren't too difficult to watch. It's hard to believe we'll be somewhere just like those beaches in a week or so. It doesn't seem real.' Evan realized Betty had gone upstairs, so lowered his voice to talk to himself. 'It didn't seem real when we were planning this cruise, and it doesn't seem more real now.'

'All done,' said his wife, plopping herself down onto the settee, which sagged beneath her; he had to admit the furniture in the sitting room was a bit tatty.

'Do you think I'm past my best?' he asked aloud.

He noticed his wife's expression soften as she put down the magazine that listed everything on TV. 'Evan, you twit, you're in your prime. Look, with Auntie Barbara's money in the bank, you can afford to retire now, while you've got good years ahead of you. While *we've* got good years ahead of *us*. Thank heavens she was a real miser, owned that massive house, and didn't last long in that horrifically expensive old folks' home.'

Evan decided to play. 'Really? Glad she dropped off her perch, were you? You didn't help her along, by any chance, did you? Should I be investigating my wife for murder?'

Betty held her hands toward him in mock-surrender. 'It's a fair cop, guv. I'll come quiet, I will. No bovver, me.' She aped a cockney accent, and he loved the way her face took on a mournful expression.

Evan's phone began to trill and buzz in his pocket. 'Damn, I thought I'd plugged this thing in out in the kitchen,' he said, annoyed that he felt compelled to answer. 'I'll be quick. It can't be anything urgent, not this evening.'

As he rose to leave the room – that being the normal practice in the Glover household – Betty waved at him. 'Stay there, comfy, *cariad*. Tonight's a treat – last time.'

Recognizing the number on the screen, Evan answered, 'Hello Rakel. What can I do for you this fine – well, alright wet, but still quite special – evening?'

Rakel Souza was not only the head of pathology at West Glam General hospital, but also the region's Home Office approved pathologist; she and Glover had worked side by side on many cases, and had become firm friends over the years. The fourth daughter of immigrant Goan parents, she'd been raised in what was locally known to be the pretty dodgy area of Hafod, but was now at the top of her field. Evan wondered what she wanted. Never one to beat about the bush, Rakel launched into her topic with few niceties.

'I know it's your last evening on the job, Evan, and it's not your case, but I thought you'd like to know those remains we saw in Rhosddraig have revealed some of their secrets. Well, one in any case. It was a male. We know that much.'

Evan was impressed. 'Well done, Rakel. Good job. That was a lot faster than we thought. Anything else?'

'Wasn't me who worked it out. As soon as I saw the remains on-site, I knew it wasn't for me. Everything – skeletal remains, rocks, stones, any detritus and therefore anything of potential forensic value gathered at the scene – was sent up to London, to the Metropolitan

Police Laboratory. They're the only ones with the equipment and expertise to work on something like this. I'm not much use if there aren't any juicy bits left, and they've got access to all sorts of specialists there. So they're the ones who determined gender. From the bones. They managed to locate the sciatic notch. Which just goes to show I made the right call in sending it to them; I'd have been hard-pressed to find it, given the absolute mess it was all in, and the number of cases I'm working on with this flu thing going around. They've been able to take a look at it straight away.'

Evan was immediately engaged. 'They must be treating it as a possible murder; Superintendent Lewis has given it to Ted Jenkins. He'll be the right DCI for it, I should think.'

'Yes, I heard about Ted being given the job of heading up this one. London concurred, generally, with what I suggested to you at the site. They also say they know the type of accelerant used, and have confirmed what I first suspected – all the teeth have gone. Someone did a pretty thorough job.'

'Hang on a minute, Rakel – what do you mean, all the teeth have gone? Do you mean someone actually took the time and trouble to find all the teeth and pick them out of that pile?'

'No, Evan, don't be *twp*, they'd have pulled the teeth from the skull before smashing it about, I'd have thought. At least, that's what I'd have done. If there were any to start with, that is.'

Betty hovered beside her husband, trying to get his attention. 'Hang on a minute, Rakel, Betty wants me.'

'Alright, Evan, say hello to her from me, and tell her Gareth and I are looking forward to seeing you two at your leaving do tomorrow night. I hope neither of you is planning to drive. Do you need a lift? I'll do it, you know. Happily.'

Not wanting to get sidetracked, Evan, said, 'Thanks, we're fine,' to Rakel, and 'What is it?' to his wife.

'I'm going to change for bed while you talk about missing teeth. But don't be too long, alright? Remember what we agreed – this one's not your case. Never was, never will be.'

Evan nodded at his wife's back and said into the phone, 'So does that mean the killer knew a good deal about forensic manipulation of a crime scene?'

'Hang on a minute there, Evan. It might be being treated as such by Lewis – who always likes to cover his backside, as we all know – but I, personally, cannot be certain it's murder. They haven't yet determined the age of the remains; the skeleton might have been dug up from somewhere, then smashed and burned. As a scientist, I can't yet assume it's a current-day case at all – except for the smashing and burning bit, which is why I believe Lewis is treating it the way he is; imagine the blow-back he'd face if he didn't take such a discovery "seriously" enough. All we know for certain is that it was a male.'

'Fair enough,' replied Evan, 'but if you and I assume for a moment that it was a recent killing, or death, there might well have been forensic countermeasures taken. Or it might have been some judgement, with a bit of luck thrown in.'

Rakel sighed. 'I suppose a person could have a general idea that they'll burn a body to hide evidence, then observe the wicking that's likely to happen – the process of the body's fat becoming its own burning medium – and realize it's all going to take longer than they imagined. That said, you could have a total loss of all but bone inside two hours. Then they could get the teeth out, maybe with a hammer or something, then they smashed the whole thing to bits, then burned it again.'

'So you're certain about that too? The second burning.'

'Yes. Confirmed by London. It was pretty obvious that the broken ends of the bones were charred, and that's the only way that could happen. But we don't know yet when the bones were originally burned and smashed, you see. They have a great deal of testing ahead of them.'

'What about DNA?' Evan had to know.

Rakel snorted. 'That's where they might start, but I'll be largely out of the loop on this one, and I'm not them. They might have been told to make establishing the provenance of the bones as a priority.'

'How do you mean?'

'They have budgets and resources I cannot even imagine. They might be instructed to work out if they have the remains of a recently deceased person, or something from some time ago.'

'Would that take long?'

Rakel hesitated. 'Given all the machinery they've got in their swanky labs up there, maybe not. I'll be honest, if it were me, I'd go for DNA first, because they'll have to do that in any case if they discover it's a recently deceased person. They might get something they can work with, but I'd put money on any DNA being quite badly degraded. Heat's a bit of a bugger when it comes to DNA, you see. It's true they can run tests on tiny amounts these days – microscopic, if you've got the right kit. But who knows what the burning will have done to the shards, however old they are. The teeth would have offered the best chance to get hold of a less compromised sample, and it looks as though the person trying to hide the identity of the remains knew that much at least. Or – and this is a possibility – if it's an old, or even ancient, skeleton, there might have been no teeth to begin with.'

Evan gazed at the silent TV screen in front of him. It showed a majestic whale swimming through a sea littered with plastics. Even without sound, and bearing in mind the fact he'd probably already seen the clip a dozen times before, it was heartbreaking. For a fleeting moment he wondered why he felt so bad for the whale, whereas he felt nothing but curiosity about the human being whose remains he'd glimpsed in the rain just a couple of days earlier. Shouldn't he feel more compassion for the person, than the whale? He closed his eyes. Tight.

'So what's the next step?' he couldn't help but ask.

'As far as I'm aware, you pack away your things at HQ tomorrow, then drink a bucket of beer, and relax on a wonderful cruise,' said Rakel. He could tell by her voice she was smiling as she spoke. 'Jenkins is running the case. You're not on the team,' she added. Quite unnecessarily, thought Evan.

'I know,' he said quietly. Betty sidled into the room in her thick, snuggly dressing gown, and he knew it was time to wrap up his conversation. 'Thanks for this, Rakel. I know you won't be able to keep me in the picture after tomorrow, me having no official standing after that, but this means a lot. Ta. See you both tomorrow evening. Best bib and tucker, mind you. Betty's even bought me a new tie for the occasion.'

'Last one I'll ever choose for him. Cost a fortune. He'll probably be buried in it,' shouted Betty at the phone. 'Bye.'

Evan returned the phone to his pocket, telling himself he shouldn't forget to charge it overnight.

Betty said, 'If the teeth were missing, it might be an older person, you know. Someone who wore dentures, and the person who did all that horrible stuff just took them away. Or would they melt? I don't know.'

Evan smiled. 'God, I love you, woman! You'd have made a wonderful detective. But, you're right, I shouldn't get caught up in it all, and it could have been someone who had no teeth anyway. I'll mention that to Rakel, you know, just in passing.' He winked.

'So,' said Betty, 'a novel way to kill someone on a Caribbean beach, or the latest head-to-head in cake-baking? What's it to be? It's up to you.' Betty pulled the remote control from its little pouch hanging on the arm of the settee.

'Better make it cakes,' said Evan. 'I don't think I'm up to hyper-fast clue collection, and a denouement that takes place in a bar with a view of a beach behind it. Not tonight.'

'Cakes it is then, *cariad*. I could do with a bit of rose-tinted dreaming of perfect bakes, followed by stress and disaster, triumph and tears. If you drop off, I'll wake you up to send you to bed, as usual, alright?'

Evan's heart literally missed a beat; how had he been so lucky to find Betty? And how had she put up with him and his job all these years? This was it, the beginning of the end for him, and the start of something new for the two of them. As the perfect white marquee, with its picturesque setting within a stately, yet bucolic, idyll filled the screen, Evan allowed himself to wonder if he'd been right to miss the retirement preparation seminars they'd offered him.

Ah well, it's too late now, he told himself, and he did his best to give himself over to enjoying the variations between the artist's impressions of the bakers' descriptions of their creations and the eventual output.

Poor buggers, he thought, *I bet it all seemed a lot easier when they were in their own kitchens, and just having to treat their families.* Though he knew from experience that, sometimes, family members were the hardest to please.

Helen

Helen scrolled through the replies to a fellow support group member's question about how she might get a better night's sleep when her dreams were wild, and full of menace. As she read she recognized many of the tricks she'd tried for herself: hot milk, white noise on a bedside radio, lavender smelly things, the sound of the ocean. None of it had worked for her, and it seemed none of it had been working for this poor soul. Her fingers hesitated above the keyboard. Would it be silly to suggest the woman might try what had worked for her?

She typed, retyped, read, then deleted her comment. It was best to not post something like that on the Internet. Even though the group was supposedly surrounded by layers of security, you had to believe nothing on the Internet was ever truly private. That was why she always used a false name. She supposed many others did too. After all, she couldn't believe anyone really wanted the world to know what had happened to them, and what they'd had to do to survive it.

Bob had been gone for thirteen years, and the thought of him lying next to her in the bed she was perched upon still made her sweat; her heart still thumped at the thought of his touch, at what might make his mood, and demeanor change.

Deep breaths, Helen, deep breaths. He's gone. You're safe. Sadie's safe. He can't touch you now.

She counted to twenty, breathing slowly, deeply; she closed her eyes, and visualized herself walking along the golden sand of Rhosddraig Bay, the waves bubbling over her bare feet, the sun warming her upturned face. She felt her heart rate normalize, her hands stop trembling.

If only she'd had the physical strength back then that she had now; years of moving barrels, taking long runs in the early morning, shifting furniture, and carrying heavy loads of all types of supplies into the pub had allowed her to develop a satisfying level of physical superiority she'd not possessed when Bob had still been around.

Alright, she'd put on a few pounds recently, but she was still strong. Too late she'd grown into the sort of woman who might have had a chance of overpowering him. If she'd dared. Or maybe she wouldn't have; she'd worked hard at being quiet, not allowing her mother or daughter to hear her from their bedrooms. Trapped in her nightly prison.

She realized she was no longer in the mood to be supportive, or seek the solace of discussion. The bed creaked as she rose to plug her laptop into the socket on the wall to recharge. The bed had always creaked. So loudly. She'd hoped to get rid of the noises that still echoed through her dreams by pulling the bedstead to pieces. She'd greased and tightened every bolt and screw when she'd put it back together, but the creaking remained.

Helen had to acknowledge to herself, silently, that her mother had been right to warn her she was choosing to spend her life with the wrong man, but Helen had never admitted it aloud, and certainly not to her mother. She didn't need to; the day Bob left had told Nan all she needed to know – she'd been right all along.

Helen recalled when her then-prospective husband had first met her parents; it had been a beautiful day, and the four of them shared a meal after the Sunday rush. It started not too badly, but it hadn't gone well overall, largely because her mother had – as usual – spoken her mind. It had broken Helen's heart at the time.

She shook her head as she thought about how that disastrous dinner had brought her and Bob closer together – to battle her mother's disapproval as a couple. They'd developed a united front; became a force to be reckoned with. Of course it had been easier to do at that time because they'd been living in London. But the hurt ate away at Helen between the phone calls to her parents, which became less frequent as time passed.

Hindsight – and the reading of many books about the techniques used by abusers – had granted Helen the ability to realize Bob had been extremely clever at exploiting her emotional weaknesses; raising her mother's dislike of him in the middle of conversations Helen initiated about visiting her home, and pointing out how any woman who voiced a strong opinion he disagreed with reminded him of her mother.

Looking back, she knew the years she hadn't visited Rhosddraig at all were her least memorable, and she'd lost so many opportunities to spend valuable time with her father.

I miss you, Dad, she mouthed at a photo, taken by a fellow climber, of the pair of them out on the Dragon's Head, windblown, ruddy-cheeked, and triumphant they'd made it to the top.

Dad must have been about the age I am now, in that photo, she thought, wondering what it must have been like for him to see his daughter diminished, years later, by the man she'd chosen to love, and marry.

Did he know? she wondered. *He can't have done. Before he died we were never here long enough, or often enough, for anything to really happen.*

Helen switched off her bedside lamp, and snuggled under the duvet.

Eventually she gave in to her final resort when she needed to get to sleep; she visualized Bob being consumed by eternal hellfire, his screams unheard by anyone but her.

It usually worked.

9th November

Betty

Betty Glover was nervous. More nervous than she'd been about anything since her wedding day. She wanted her husband to enjoy his send-off, but was terrified something might go wrong.

'Almost everyone's here, where is he?' she asked Rakel Souza, who was hovering at her friend's elbow.

'Ted Jenkins is bringing him,' replied Rakel. 'He was supposed to come up with some sort of delaying tactic so we could all be here to greet Evan.'

Betty glared at her watch. 'They were due to be here twenty minutes ago. What's going on?

Rakel looked around. 'There's no sign of Liz Stanley either.'

Betty didn't want to say the words, but they blurted out of her anyway, 'You don't think anything can have happened to them, do you? I hate looking forward to things, because I'm always afraid they won't go as planned. Maybe Evan got dragged back in to look into this Rhosddraig thing.'

'You do remember you're a trained psychologist, don't you?' asked Rakel, her eyebrows arched. 'Good grief, woman, give yourself a good talking to. Hey, Gareth, come over here and have a word with Betty about her giving herself permission to expect good things to work out, will you? I'll get her a drink from the bar. It looks like she needs one. Give me a couple of those ticket things. Don't panic, I'll get you a pint too, husband dear. You're not driving home, after all.'

'I love being married to a woman who doesn't drink,' said Gareth, as he enveloped Betty in his long, strong arms. 'Don't worry, Evan will be here before you know it. Probably with his work-wife in tow, as per. Funny that, isn't it? Both his work-wife and his life-wife are named Elizabeth.'

Betty's eyebrows almost met her hairline. 'Work-wife and life-wife?'

Gareth had the good grace to look embarrassed. 'Oh, just ignore me, we're like a load of kids ourselves in the teachers' common room at school. Forget what I said, let's just enjoy the chance to take in the magnificent surroundings they've splashed out on for Evan, and what we can see out there. A million-pound view if ever there was one.'

He steered Betty to sit on a window seat, between faux-curtain swags of scarlet and gold. 'Look at that moon on the sea. Swansea Bay is one heck of a place, isn't it? All the lights down in Mumbles, twinkling away. I can't help but remember doing the old Mumbles Mile donkey's years ago when I see that. I don't suppose anyone bothers with it any longer . . . there just aren't the pubs along the front that there used to be, and Wind Street's a lot more convenient these days, I suppose. Youngsters today, eh? Can't even be bothered to put a bit of effort into getting drunk. Let's hope they all start earning enough to pay taxes to support us in our old age, otherwise we're up *cach* creek, without a paddle. What's this?' he said, looking with dismay at the glass his wife handed him.

'It's called Old Speckled Hen,' replied Rakel. 'It's bitter. It's that or Stella on tap, and I know you always call that stuff "a hangover waiting to happen". They've got something called Brewdog Vagabond in a bottle, but I think that's pale ale. I thought this would be the best choice.'

Gareth mugged a look of horror. 'Dear God. Belgian or English beer, or Scottish pale ale? Don't they bloody know this is Wales? We do make our own beer here. Bloody hotel chains, they think we'll drink anything.'

'You will, love,' replied his wife, smiling. 'Four tickets each for free drinks, so you'll drink your four, and probably use all mine, and by then you'll have got used to it, so you'll drink a few more, I shouldn't wonder. All those years of swilling down a gallon of dark mild after a game on the rugby field will come into play, I've no doubt. So stop grumbling, and be grateful the West Glam Police are paying for you to drink tonight – for a while, anyway. Oh, look, Betty, I think they're coming. There's a bit of a fuss over at the door. Let me hold that for you.'

Betty took a swig from the gin and tonic Rakel had just given her, then passed the glass back to her friend, wiping her hands together to try to dry them. She was about to hold her husband for the first time as a non-policeman; he'd already been on the job when they'd first met, so she'd had some inkling of what she was letting herself in for, and she'd been supportive of him every step of the way through his career, even when she herself had been working full time.

Nowadays, with a good amount of money in the bank thanks to Auntie Barbara, he could retire; she only put in a few days of volunteering at local places, and still did a little consulting work – mainly in Cardiff, because she didn't like to practice too close to home where she might bump into clients in the aisles at the supermarket. And there were the online support groups she belonged to, of course, which were essentially anonymous. But, still, they'd have more time together after his retirement.

She'd been thinking about what she might cut back on now that Evan wouldn't be going out to work anymore, but hadn't made any decisions. They'd agreed that too much change for both of them at the same time would probably not be for the best, so they'd have a proper talk about it during their dream cruise, as they pootled around the Caribbean.

A cheer rose as it dawned on the crowd that the Man of the Moment had arrived. Betty rushed forward and threw her arms around her husband, whose expression told her he was a bit overwhelmed by the set-up.

'I love you, Evan' was all she had a chance to say before she let him go; he had to shake hands with everyone who pressed toward him, including Superintendent Lewis. 'I'll get you a drink,' she shouted, as corks popped.

Ted Jenkins called for order, 'Bubbles all round, followed by the speeches. Then we can get on with the serious business of the evening.' He made drinking motions with his hand while rolling his eyes, and elicited a roar of approval from the crowd. 'We're all off duty here, and among friends. The man we thought would be one of us forever is leaving our ranks, so let's celebrate his career.' Another cheer.

Rakel handed Betty a tapered glass of fizzing Prosecco. 'Here, you take this, I'll nurse your G & T. If you like that one, you can have mine too, and Gareth's. There's no way he'll be touching it.'

'Thanks, Rakel. I might not see much of Evan tonight, by the looks of it. There's such a lot of people here. Do you know many of them? I don't.'

Rakel stood on tiptoes. 'Yes, I recognize most of them, but there are a few who might never have crossed my threshold. The office mice.'

'Office mice?' asked Betty.

'Not involved with the nasties I get to deal with, just the paperwork, filing, online stuff, that sort of thing. Some of them are civilians, too, of course. They'll be the ones who leave early, I should think. But you'd better prepare yourself, Evan's going to have quite a night of it. Good idea to have the speeches early – otherwise it'll drag on, and everyone will be maudlin before they get to say anything. Are you speaking, by the way?'

Betty shook her head. 'I wasn't planning on it.'

'Sometimes the wives do,' said Rakel with a smile. 'I should say "significant others" because they aren't all wives, of course – some are husbands, or partners. I've already told Gareth he's not to say a word when I eventually retire, but that'll be a whole different kettle of fish – it'll be a hospital do, not this sort of thing. Dried-up sandwiches and a variety of juices usually . . . my word, we know how to party at West Glam General. No swanky hotel conference rooms like this for us, oh no; just the canteen, and a collection of people who are either on-call, or have been for so long they need coffee, not alcohol.'

The evening progressed through a few blessedly short speeches, with Evan choosing his words wisely after being presented with a silver-plated tray and a travel voucher, and Betty taking the chance to simply thank everyone as she carefully cradled the large bouquet she'd been handed.

After the official bits were over, Betty noted how those who were about Evan's age patted him on the back with something she read as a mixture of envy and understanding. She was also aware of the pinched faces and the bags under the eyes of the senior officers, the fire of enthusiasm and even a little triumph in the expressions of the younger ones. As she was smiling and nodding, aware of the increasingly wide and heavily populated gulf between herself and her husband, Betty was pleased to see Liz Stanley making her way toward her.

The women hugged, and Liz said, 'Come on, let's grab a seat while we can.'

'Good idea,' agreed Betty. As they wandered away from the melee she added, 'Nice new hairdo, Liz. It suits you. But he's not leaving you, you know. He's leaving the job.'

Depositing her drink on a tiny glass table Liz replied, 'How do you mean, he's not leaving me? I know that.' She sounded puzzled, and a little uncomfortable.

Betty sat down, and patted Liz's hand. 'The haircut. It's a thing some women do as a sign of taking control, when real control in a relationship is beyond them, or the whole thing's over. Is that how you feel?' Betty always thought it was best to be as direct as possible when speaking to friends.

Liz's brow furrowed. Eventually she smiled. 'I always forget your professional background, Betty. There's really not much that gets past you, is there? But I hadn't thought about it that way at all; I'd just got annoyed with having to use a hairdryer every morning, and force my natural curls to do what I wanted them to. This way, all the curls have gone and I can run from the shower to the car with my coffee in my hand, and be none the worse for it by lunchtime.' She grinned, sat, then sipped her Diet Coke again.

Betty couldn't help but notice that Liz hadn't responded directly to her question.

She decided to press the point; she wanted Liz to know how highly Evan thought of her. Laying her hand on Liz's she said, 'Good. So long as you understand his leaving is nothing to do with you, personally. Indeed, but for you, he might have left some time ago. He's enjoyed working with you more than most. Says you're the face of the new service – a woman with a brain, a life outside work, and a healthy attitude toward upholding the law. He's also said on more than one occasion that you're intelligent enough to be able to investigate crimes, discover the culprits, and bring them to justice with enough evidence to allow the courts to do their work. Unlike many of the older ones here who joined a force, not a service, he thinks you get it. He's often said you're a good detective sergeant, and I know he believes you'll make a good DI one day.'

Liz stared into space. 'Thanks.' She smiled shyly. 'DI Glover really is one of the good ones. A bit of a legend, even. Known as fair. But there's still a lot that goes on that makes me feel . . .' Betty wondered what Liz was really thinking as she paused to choose her words. 'That we could be doing better,' she concluded.

Liz's gaze refocused on the events surrounding her, and Betty sensed the woman had surrendered a chance to speak her mind.

Betty ventured, 'I hear you're working with Ted Jenkins on that case out in Rhosddraig. How's it going?'

Liz sipped. 'It's a weird one. Has Evan told you about it?'

Betty nodded. 'A bit.'

Liz winked. 'I understand. He'd have loved it, you know. He said when we found the remains it would have been the most interesting case of his career.'

Betty wondered how best to reply. 'Maybe that's because he knew it wouldn't be a case he'd get to work on.'

Liz nodded thoughtfully. 'Possibly. Not too many grisly cases for him, I believe, over the years. And no job-related injuries, either. He's been fortunate.'

Betty agreed. 'He has been. Though you know only too well what it's like to leave home not having a clue about what you'll face that day; never being sure if you're going to be able to help a victim of crime, or become one yourself.' She sighed. 'I won't miss that feeling. Of not knowing whether he's safe. That'll be a huge weight off my shoulders.'

Liz put down her drink. 'It must be difficult, feeling helpless like that. We're alright, you know; we're trained to deal with pretty much anything we might come up against, and we have the authority to act. But you make an important point; it's the ones we leave at home when we go to work who do the worrying about us. *For* us, really, because we haven't usually got time for it.'

A young male server dressed in black topped up Betty's glass with Prosecco, then weighed the bottle in his hand, and left it on the table beside her. 'Not much in there,' he said. 'You have that and I'll get a fresh one.'

'Ta,' called Betty as he darted off. Rolling her eyes at Liz, she said, 'I'd better watch it; I don't usually drink much, and certainly not this fast. I'll be the one who'll be pie-eyed by nine o'clock, not Evan.'

'Cheers,' said Liz, raising her glass. 'I hope you two will be very happy together.' She paused, and Betty judged she was choosing her next words with care. 'Does it feel like you're getting married all over again? Someone – I can't remember who – said that to me once. That when he retired he and his wife needed to rethink their marriage altogether, for the new life they were about to live that differed from the one they'd known for decades.'

'If you mean do I think we'll be able to share our home without one of us bashing the other over the head with a frying pan or something, I think we'll be fine.' Betty smiled. 'But, if you're wondering what on earth Evan will do with himself all day, well, I'll be honest, and say I'm not sure. We've got this cruise coming up, and I know that'll give him a psychologically important chance to wind down and have a think about the future, without the present getting in the way. But after that? I don't know.'

Liz asked, 'No hobbies?'

Betty shook her head. 'One of the spare rooms is half full of books. He's never had time to get to them the way he'd like. I know he's looking forward to catching up with reading.'

Liz arched an eyebrow. 'Crime fiction?'

Betty grinned. 'No. History. Specifically Welsh history. It's his thing. Loves it. Not something I know a great deal about – other than the usual bits and bobs I remember from school – but him? From thousands of years ago to contemporary times, he loves it, he does. And connected stuff.' She leaned in. 'I've picked up a nice book for him to read on our cruise – all about Captain Morgan, the Welsh pirate who became governor of Jamaica. He'll enjoy that – loves to read about the impact the Welsh have had upon the world.'

'I'm not surprised he hasn't got much lined up other than reading – though reading with an interest is good. Joining group activities is pretty much out of the question for us, because if you join they expect you to turn up on a pretty regular basis. I've met a few here in Swansea who try to belong to choirs, for example, but they often get given the heave-ho for concerts because they haven't been able to attend all the rehearsals.'

'Evan's never been a big joiner,' said Betty.

'That's pretty common, too,' replied Liz.

'But I thought you were involved with scouting. Aren't you?' asked Betty.

A wry smile crossed Liz's face. 'Much more so when I was in Bristol than I am here, now. More responsibilities because of my promotion. Less predictable hours. I'm only a part-time assistant leader here; I help when I can. The job has to come first.'

'You're right,' replied Betty, half-smiling. 'It has to, or what's the point? But he hasn't usually brought it home with him, I'll say that much. Until recently we've hardly talked about it, in detail. That all changed during that business with GGR Davies, of course. You must have seen how that case affected him.'

Liz shrugged. 'They say it's best to not meet your heroes, and I'm sure that's doubly the case when you find them dead at the bottom of a cliff, then discover they weren't quite the person you'd always imagined them to be. A rugby hero that man might have been but, as for the way he lived the rest of his life?'

Betty nodded her understanding. 'That case was what brought up the idea of this early retirement. That, and my Auntie Barbara dying.'

Liz smiled sadly. 'I was sorry to hear about your aunt; sir said it was quick, and that you two weren't close, which I suppose is the best you can hope for.'

'I think you can call him Evan, now,' said Betty.

Liz chuckled. 'It might be okay for me to do it, but I'm not sure I'll be able to. He'll always be "Sir" to me, or "DI Glover".'

Betty countered, 'And he's always been Evan to me, even when he became DI Glover. I wonder if we both know the same man?'

'Back to being a psychologist?' asked Liz.

'Can't help myself, I suppose. Like you lot. Always on the job, aren't you?'

'You're right, and sir . . . Evan . . . is retiring, not having a personality transplant, so I'm sure you're in for some interesting times as he comes to terms with his new life,' said Liz with a grin. 'There you go, there's the first lot leaving. It'll go in waves from now on, I should think. It might be Saturday tomorrow, but some people here are on duty rotation; I know DCI Jenkins and I will be going down to Rhosddraig first thing to coordinate the team doing the door to door there.'

'I hear it's a man. The remains,' said Betty.

Liz looked surprised. 'Really? How did you "hear" that then? I thought we'd kept that bit of information pretty quiet.'

Betty blushed. 'Sorry. I shouldn't have said anything.'

'Let me guess – Doc Souza told Evan, and he told you?'

'Sort of. I overheard part of a conversation, then Evan filled me in on all the gory details. Quite literally. I wasn't too keen on the information he gave me about body fat melting. I wouldn't have made a good detective. Too squeamish. How do you cope?'

'I didn't, not to start with. However, you tell yourself you have to, so I got over being disgusted by human remains early on. Nowadays it's the actions of living beings which worry me more; the level of violent crime in the area is alarmingly high.'

'Drugs?' asked Betty, knowing the answer.

Liz nodded. 'Sadly. Same all over the UK nowadays. They use a system we call "county lines", which is just another way of talking about child slavery. Forced to sell drugs, given instructions by dedicated mobile phones, kids as young as eight or nine are involved.'

Betty could tell Liz was on a bit of a roll, so didn't like to tell her that Evan had she had shared this conversation several times in the past.

Liz looked anxious as she added, 'These kids are vulnerable, being exploited – but they have the advantage that they can get everywhere, usually unnoticed. It's like gangrene, eating its way into every part of life. There isn't anywhere you can name that drugs aren't available these days – it's not just a club thing, or something that affects a certain sort of person with a particular background; it's permeated every level and every part of society. Even rural areas aren't exempt; they use this process called cuckooing, where young kids are sent to live under the seeming oversight of an adult – often vulnerable themselves, for some reason. And they offer a direct line of access for all sorts of drugs into any type of community.'

'Do you think this burned body in Rhosddraig is drug related?' Betty asked. 'It's so beautiful and peaceful there. I mean, there's hardly a "there" at all, really. It's just a tiny village. Surely there's no drug problem in Rhosddraig?'

'The area gets a lot of visitors each year – and they all might seem to be healthy, outdoors types, but – like I say – drug users, and dealers, come in all shapes and sizes, and from all walks of life. It's not all begrimed, wild-eyed, rough sleepers with mental health issues; many people who use, and therefore sustain the supply chain, manage to function in what most would see as a "normal" way.'

Liz paused and shrugged. 'But I'm sure you, being a psychologist, would understand all that, wouldn't you?'

Betty looked across the now less-crowded room to where her husband was being hugged with great affection by a short, stout man wearing an ill-fitting sports jacket. She recognized him as someone whose own retirement party she and Evan had attended just a couple of years earlier. His beer belly, ruddy nose, and veined cheeks suggested he'd taken up heavy drinking as his hobby since then.

'Indeed I do understand, Liz. Sadly quite a lot of the people I've come into contact with over the years have struggled with addiction, of some sort or another. But there, that's all I can say about that. Like you, I have to be careful about what I say, and to whom.'

'No tales out of school? I understand.' Liz smiled and stood. 'I'd better do a bit of mingling before I leave, and that ought to be soon-ish. Up and at 'em in the morning for me. I'm meeting DCI Jenkins out at Rhosddraig at eight. And then it begins in earnest; the people who live there will have their lives changed forever because of this – we'll have to poke and pry, and they won't like that. Very soon they'll see the police as the cause of the infection of unrest and suspicion, when all we're doing is trying to unearth truths.'

Betty also stood, catching her husband's eye. 'I expect you're right about that; a crime in a community impacts everyone's life in some way or other. And you're certainly right about the mingling. Time for me to do a bit too, now the crowd's thinned out. You be careful, Liz.'

Liz hugged Betty. 'Don't you go starting to worry about me, now that you're able to stop worrying about him.' She nodded in Glover's direction. 'Give yourselves some time to get used to your new way of life, and enjoy it.'

The women parted, Liz walking toward a group of younger men, and Betty heading for her husband, who reached out his arm and placed it around her waist. She mirrored his actions, knowing they would be just fine working out how their new lives would be lived.

11th November

Nan

Damn and blast, I should have put the heating on in this blessed church yesterday morning, not last night.

Nan felt cross with herself as she pushed the communion wafers into the silver ciborium from which Reverend Thomas would take them during the service, counting them out appropriately for the number of congregants.

She filled the cut-glass cruet with wine, right up to the top, and even filled a second, which the vicar wouldn't bless if not enough people attended to warrant it; then she set up the credence table, off to one side of the altar, so it looked perfect. The water was fresh, and the lavabo was ready. The gold one, for a special occasion.

She'd polished the chalice at her kitchen table the previous night, and she made sure to wear a clean pair of her white cotton gloves when she placed it on the altar in the exact center of the nine freshly pressed squares in the starched corporal, which she'd aligned perfectly with the edge of the fair linen on the altar top. She carefully placed the purificator over the chalice; she loved the way it smelled comfortingly of Pears Coal Tar soap – by far the best thing for getting wine stains out of linen, she'd found – then set the paten at dead center, and added the priest's wafer. She'd also laundered the linen cover of the pall during the past week, and was pleased it looked fresh as she popped it on top of the wafer.

Nan spent quite a few minutes fiddling about with the veil, making sure its points looked crisp from the front and back. Finally she popped the burse on the top, and stepped back to admire her handiwork. She was pleased with it. Mair was a bit slapdash when it came to positioning the veil, she always thought. Hers was perfectly draped.

She looked around. Yes, everything was as it should be. Nan had always enjoyed the process of setting up for communion because the special items connected with the sacrament entranced her. Also, she was able to enjoy the service more when she knew everything was just as it should be, because she'd made it so.

The only problem was that the church was freezing, and even more cold air would rush in when people opened the door. There might be a magnificent old porch on the church, but there was only a little distance between the ancient wooden door and the new, inner glass one – installed to try to prevent the wind from gusting inside.

If a lot of people all arrive at once, both doors'll be open at the same time. They might as well not be there at all, thought Nan. *Still, there's nothing I can do about that.*

She headed for the vestry where she pulled the old poppy wreath out of its box and dusted it off. It took a while, but she finally managed to make it look quite presentable. She propped it at an angle between the floor and the center of the altar, so it showed up nicely against the green hanging.

The red and green together look almost Christmassy, she thought. *Not long now and it'll be Advent.*

'Oh no, where's my poppy?' gasped Nan aloud. She patted her bosom, then looked around the floor of the church. She was sure she'd pinned it to herself before she'd left the pub. She checked the vestry and behind the altar, but it was nowhere to be found. Where would she get another? She couldn't be seen without one; that would be scandalous. She eyed the wreath, wondering if she could pull just one of the flower heads off it, and somehow attach it to the lapel of her coat. But she'd need scissors. At least she knew where to find them.

Nan bustled into the vestry again and pulled open the little cupboard that held all manner of supplies, looking for the box containing stationery items. Finding it on the lowest shelf, she noticed they'd almost run out of the oil used to fill the reservoirs in the everlasting candles they'd invested in a few years ago. She'd have to have a word with the vicar about that; he'd have to order more to be sure they had enough for all the special advent and Christmas services.

Finding the scissors, Nan lost no time in selecting a decent looking poppy from the wreath, snipping it off, and rearranging the remaining flowers. She rushed back to the vestry to try to find a safety pin, which she managed to hide inside her coat while securing the poppy head to her chest. By the time Hywel arrived to ring the bell at nine thirty, calling communicants to the ten o'clock service, Nan was feeling quite hot around her collar, and was glad to sit out in the porch for a couple of minutes.

'Lovely day for it. Cold though,' said Mair when she arrived. 'Nice to come out without a mac on for a change, isn't it?'

'If you say so, Mair,' agreed Nan, gazing up at the pale blue sky and puffy clouds. 'No rain up there, though the wind's still got a nasty nip to it.'

'It has. But at least we won't all get wet when we go outside to the war memorial for eleven o'clock.'

'If it stays like this,' said Nan.

'Everything ready inside?' asked Mair as she pushed open the heavy door. 'Anything I can help with?'

'No. I've done everything.'

'I'll go in then. Hywel will be playing the piano, won't he?'

'As soon as he's finished with the bell, yes. Something appropriate for the occasion, he said. The servers should be along any minute now, to dress for the service. Both Aled and Stew are on today, I see from the list.'

'I saw Aled on his bike. Went right past me he did, fast as you like. I'd have thought he'd have been here ages ago,' replied Mair. 'Where could he have been going at speed, if not here?'

'No idea. Not the pub. He doesn't start there until noon today. He should be here already, by rights. So should Stew Wingfield.' Nan was annoyed. Boys would be boys, but Aled should have known better; he shouldn't be cycling around the village like a madman on a Sunday morning.

'You staying out here, are you?'

'I'll be in now, in a minute,' replied Nan, shutting the door to the church behind her friend, and finally feeling the sweat around her neck cooling off.

A gruff voice behind her made her jump. 'Morning Myfanwy.'

It was Gwen Beynon.

'Morning Gwendolyn,' replied Nan, instantly angry.

How she hated that woman.

Gwen had always given herself airs, and the red, white, and black Welsh tapestry cape she was wearing was one of her prized possessions. Nan would have chucked a tin of paint over it if she could have done; the thing stank of mothballs – she must have had it for forty years or more.

'Style never goes out of fashion,' Nan had once overheard Gwen say to someone or other.

And nor does showing off, Nan had thought at the time.

Still did.

The two women exchanged as few words as they could, whenever it was impossible for them to avoid being in each other's company.

Nan had been glad when Gwen had stopped attending Mothers' Union; quite right too, the way that daughter of hers had died.

Nan had said at the time, 'That sort of an end can only come after bad parenting.'

She still believed it.

She supposed Gwen had done a slightly better job with her grandson, Aled, but there was still time for him to go off the rails; his mother had seemed like a nice girl, and even a nice woman, until she obviously wasn't.

And then she died.

Best out of it, with a life like that. Just a few years younger than Helen, she'd been. And Aled only ten when she'd been found dead.

Awful.

Even 'accidental' drug overdoses were just like suicide, to Nan's way of thinking.

She took her revenge on Gwen for her past evils every way she could; employing Aled at the pub was her most recent strategy.

She rather enjoyed the fact that Gwen's grandson had to do whatever she told him to, because she was his boss.

Loved that he had to ask just the right way to get extra hours to work.

Was delighted that he was, to all intents and purposes, her servant.

Deeply satisfying.

Sadie

Aled looks so angelic in his cassock and crisp surplice. Even though his hair's not quite as blond as it was in the summer, he still looks so beautiful with that little ruffle around his neck. He's got the bluest eyes. So pale. Beautiful. And his voice? He'd do well as the lead singer in a band. But then other girls would get to look at him all the time, and I wouldn't like that. Not at all. There's not much room up there by the altar for both him and Stew; they keep bumping into each other. But I suppose the vicar does need the extra help today.

I can sit here and mouth the words of the service easily – I know them off by heart. It means I can just think of Aled and me, together. Think of his hands on me. I wonder what that would feel like if he was wearing what he's got on now. A bit odd, maybe?

Why is that? They're just clothes, after all.

All this church stuff doesn't mean anything to me. Nan goes mental about it. Washing things, then ironing them like her life depends on it.

Sometimes she has that long white tablecloth-type thing hanging around in our kitchen for hours and hours, until there's just the right amount of dampness left in it for her to press it. Then Mam has to help her carry it up to the church, flat. It's stupid. Why can't it have any creases in it?

If her God's all Nan says he is, he would understand a few creases. I had to help her once, and she went on and on about it all being perfect.

Oh my God, Mam's kneeler just let out a noise like a fart. That's hilarious, but I shouldn't giggle, I suppose.

There are people here I usually only see at Christmas and Easter, and there are even some faces I've never seen before. Nan said it was nice we had some visitors to contribute to the collection today.

Typical!

At least it was fun to belt out 'For the healing of the nations' to the tune of 'Bread of heaven'. Hywel and some of the other men sang the harmonies, and Aled did an especially good job.

I mustn't stare at him, but it's really hard not to. He's looked at me a couple of times, but he has to keep an eye on the words in the hymn book, like me.

Aled looks so regal, carrying the cross at the head of our procession out to the war memorial. At least the sun's shining properly now.

Everyone's so quiet; unnaturally so. It makes me want to laugh out loud, but I mustn't.

The linnets are singing their hearts out this morning; I love the way they hop about, nibbling at the grass here on the Dragon's Back. And that song of theirs? Perfection, it is.

Everyone's looking over at the lane that leads up the hill. Can't help themselves, I suppose. Dad and I had a chat about what they'd found up there. Mam doesn't know we talk, or meet. I don't really like keeping those secrets from Mam, but it's in everyone's best interests that I do; that's what Dad said, and he's right.

All those names carved on the memorial we're all singing at? I don't know why anyone ever thinks of any war as 'great'. All wars are bad. And they called it the war to end all wars too – but it didn't. None of them ever do. Because no one wants to talk about them when they're over – not the people who fought in them, anyway.

I wonder how many people here today are really thinking about the effects of war, and how many are just thinking about the body up on the hill.

That's all anyone's been talking about. In the pub, anyway.

Aled said the police had been to his Grannie Gwen's house asking about people who might have gone missing, and I heard enough at the pub last night to know they've been to every house asking the same thing.

But everyone agrees it can't be anything to do with the village because no one from here is missing. Which is comforting.

This two minutes of silence seems like a long time. Aled looks ethereal, with his eyes downcast, his lips moist and pink, and his surplice billowing.

That police tape fluttering in the wind sounds like an injured bird's wings when it panics because it finds it can't fly.

I suppose I'd better concentrate on the words again now. I hate 'Abide with me'; it's too sad. But that's the general idea, I know, to be thoughtful about the lives lost in war. Just between 1914 and 1918 there were eighteen million dead, and twenty-three million wounded, the vicar said. Forty thousand of them Welshmen. That was a lot.

I wonder how many of them burned, like the body up on the hill.

Helen

Glad to finally be sitting on the edge of her bed, Helen was pleased she'd managed to get through the day without crying in public. She had no idea why she'd always been so upset by thoughts of the First World War; it was specifically that one that got her – the idea of the second one didn't seem to touch her at all. No, it was being able to visualize the trenches, the mud, and the squalor that did it for her.

When she'd been little, she'd been regaled with stories about both her grandfathers' war experiences. By her dad, not by her grandfathers themselves. Her father's father had been gassed at the front in Ypres, and had never been the same man afterwards, she'd been told. It was usually at that point her dad would whisper, 'But he was a bit lazy too, you know? I think he used his weak lungs as an excuse to get out of any hard labor on the farm,' and they'd giggle together.

Her mother's father had been shot in the leg during the infamous battle of Mametz Wood in the Somme. She'd found out in school about how the 38th Welsh Battalion had lost a thousand men, and three thousand more had been wounded, all in just five days of bloody and brutal hand-to-hand combat. Their history teacher had talked to them about the historical perspective portrayed by the Welsh memorial sculpture at Mametz Wood, which was being erected at the time. All her dad had told her was how her mother's father had enjoyed showing off his scar in the pub when he'd had a few pints.

Both her grandmothers had been nurses, she'd been told: one at the front where she'd driven an ambulance, which Helen had always thought sounded fun – like a grand adventure, because in those days women hadn't generally done such things. The other had been stationed in a manor house somewhere in the north of England, where they looked after men with shell shock. PTSD they called it now. Or had they changed that again? Helen couldn't remember.

Someone had been talking about PTSD not being an appropriate term for the condition in one of her online groups recently, but Helen couldn't see the point of quibbling about the name. Did it really matter if it was called a disorder or a syndrome, or just called PTS? She couldn't imagine it did. But years ago the then-new PTSD website had been useful; even if she couldn't afford to keep going to any of the psychotherapists it listed as being available relatively close by, at least it had eventually allowed her to find her online chat rooms. Places where she knew psychotherapists visited, and commented. Well, usually they asked questions, encouraging you to answer them for yourself, rather than offering any advice as such. But why would she reply online? Put her soul out there into the world like that?

As she rubbed her tired feet, Helen wondered what she'd have ended up doing if she'd been called upon to serve in a war. She couldn't have been a nurse like her grandmothers; she didn't have the stomach for it. She stared at the tall brass cylinder full of dusty dried flowers sitting in the middle of her bedroom windowsill. It had been made from a shell from World War One. Trench art, they called it. She wondered how people could have had them in their homes, on display like that, so soon after the war. To torture themselves with the knowledge they were that close to a once-lethal object. It was weird.

Then she wondered why she still had it there, now.

It's always been there, she told herself. Like so many items in the living quarters above the pub.

A bit like her; the possibility of any original function removed. Essentially without purpose.

The rest of the stuff from World War One had been consigned to the attic, she recalled. Her grandfathers' improbably small uniforms, caps, medals, and some other stuff piled in a rusty heap at the bottom of an old trunk. Sadie had dressed up as an old-fashioned nurse for something at school, and she'd had a great time rooting about up there until she'd found what she wanted, Helen recalled.

She flipped the switch on her little speaker to play ocean sounds, and snuggled down to try to sleep.

But her ex-husband found her in her dreams, and that never went well.

30th January

Evan

With his Caribbean tan all but gone, and his waist a little slimmer as a result of the diet Betty had put him on after their over-indulgence on the cruise and during the Festive Season, Evan Glover studied himself in the wardrobe-door mirror; he reckoned his retirement wasn't something that had overly affected his appearance. Maybe he'd lost a couple of layers of bags under his eyes, which were possibly a slightly more vivid blue than they had once been. That was about it.

'They'll be here in half an hour. Are you ready?' called Betty up the stairs.

'Down in a minute,' he replied, then let his stomach distend, and made his way down to the pot of chili he'd spent half the day preparing.

'It smells fantastic, *cariad*,' said Betty, patting him on the bum. 'Thanks for this. I knew you could do it. I'd have been home an hour ago, except the traffic on the M4 near Port Talbot was horrific. I caught it at just the wrong time.'

'Not sure there's ever a right time on that stretch,' replied Evan, blowing steam from the tiny sample of food he'd put on a wooden spoon to taste.

'Here, try this,' said his wife, putting a metal spoon and a small glass bowl on the counter. 'Put a bit of chili in that bowl,' she said, 'then roll it around with the spoon, and it'll cool a lot faster. Touch the underneath of the spoon with the tip of your tongue before you put it all in your mouth. You don't want to go burning yourself, do you?'

Evan took her advice. 'That's a lot better. Ta. Your years of experience of tasting hot food paying off?'

'Absolutely. I know Rakel and Gareth might be disappointed we won't be offering them my famous lamb stew, but this smells wonderful. I'm sure they'll be pleased to try something you cooked. It's perfect for a cold and damp night like tonight. Can I have a taste?'

Evan poked the spoon into his wife's mouth. 'Oh, lovely,' she said. 'Maybe a final drop of red wine, to punch it up a bit? And stir in a knob of butter, at the last minute.'

Evan chuckled. 'That's your secret, is it? Slosh in the wine and dollop in the butter? What's happening to our diet tonight?'

'It never hurts to have a bit of a treat now and again, *cariad*,' said Betty grinning. 'And I haven't ever heard you complain about how my cooking's tasted all these years so, yes, take good advice when you're given it, but don't go passing it on. We all have to keep some secrets.'

Evan poured out half a glass from the box of cooking Cabernet that always sat on the counter; now he knew why it was there.

He quipped, 'I bet that's not what you've been saying in Cardiff all day, is it? Your entire career's based upon getting people to reveal their secrets, and deal with them.'

Betty headed toward the stairs as she replied, 'Secrets? Bury them and they can bury you, that's what I say. Well, that's what my tutor for my counselling qualifications used to say, and she wasn't wrong. Now I'm going to change into something more comfy, then I'll come back down and lay the table.'

'Ha! The old "changing into something more comfortable" routine, is it?' called Evan. 'And laying the table? *Just* the table? What's wrong with this picture, Betty Glover?'

'Be good, or it's no afters for you,' shouted his wife, sounding happy. 'I brought home some of that lemon ice cream you like so much, so you'd better be on your best behavior, or it'll stay in the freezer.'

As the front door bell rang, Evan looked at the table he and Betty had prepared together. He felt a strange sense of pride; he'd never played so active a role in having friends over for dinner before, and it felt . . . it felt wonderful. It might just be a quick midweek visit by some people he'd not seen for months, but this was a special night for him; Betty had been doing her counselling thing all day in Cardiff, and he'd done this. He'd even cleared and sort-of cleaned the house. The living room smelled of the Brasso he'd used to buff up his late-mother's horse brasses – an aroma that took him back to the security of his childhood, even if there was no smell of coal smoke to accompany it, which there always had been when he was growing up.

'Evan, lovely to see you after so long,' said Rakel Souza as she entered, throwing her wiry little arms around him. As they hugged, Evan thought he caught a whiff of the dissection suite, despite the fact he knew she meticulously shoved every strand of her thick black hair into protective headgear before she went anywhere near a cadaver.

'Looking good there, Evan,' said Gareth, extending his large hand. 'Lost a bit of weight, by the looks of it, *mun*. Got you off the beer, has she?' He winked as he patted Evan on the back. 'Here's a few now.' He handed Evan eight cans of Felinfoel Nut Brown Ale. 'They're a present for you, so she can't stop you from drinking them all.'

'Who's "she"? The cat's mother?' quipped Betty as she hugged Rakel, then Gareth.

Evan cradled the beers; the cans were the same temperature as his hands. Perfect. 'Thanks, Gareth,' he said. 'They'll go lovely with the chili I made for dinner.'

Gareth feigned mock shock. 'No lamb stew tonight? Oh my God, I knew it would happen. Got you cooking now, too, has she? Been wearing a pinnie all day, slaving over a hot stove, have you?'

'It's only fair,' replied Evan, slapping Gareth on the back. 'Betty's been with clients all day today, so I did what I could here. My humble efforts might not be as good as her stew, but I'll be checking to make sure you lick your bowl clean, right?'

Dinner was an enjoyable experience for Evan, during which the foursome managed to solve most of the problems being faced by the Welsh parliament, the church in Wales, the NHS, and the education system. And all before second helpings had been offered. Evan was happy to be able to express opinions he could only share with true friends, and reveled in the camaraderie of a good discussion.

However, he had to admit to himself he was anxious about how his food was being received; he couldn't believe he kept asking if everyone was enjoying it. He told himself he should comment more often about how good Betty's cooking was.

He'd always tried to tell those who'd provided him with information and insights at work how much he'd valued their contributions; but at home it had never occurred to him that the same sort of behavior might be appropriate. Now it did. Just planning, preparing, cooking, and serving one single meal to a couple of people who weren't his wife had taught him that. And no one had ever accused him of not being a fast learner.

He pondered how weird he felt about the evening as Betty chatted about a couple of women wearing old-fashioned headscarves she'd encountered in Cardiff a week earlier who'd been arguing in the street in Welsh; she'd been horrified when a young professional-looking couple had told the women to 'Go back where you came from'.

The women's retort – in English – of 'What, you mean Blaenavon?' followed by howls of laughter and a torrent of Welsh-language insults hurled at the posh English pair made the threesome at the table giggle; Evan was the only non-Welsh speaker among them.

'What did I miss?' he asked, puzzled.

'It wouldn't work in translation, *mun*,' replied Gareth. 'I haven't heard a few of those words since my days on the rugby field. I'm sure you'd remember some of them; you'd have heard them being screamed at you often enough as you scarpered down the sidelines.'

'Water off a duck's back, old chap, for we Anglophones, don't you know,' mugged Evan.

'Now, now, don't go making fun of the cook, Gareth,' said Betty, a playful smile on her face. 'He's good at many things, but picking up Welsh just isn't one of them. Not like Rakel here. Is it five languages you speak now?'

Rakel replied, 'Six. Well, nearly seven. There were three spoken at home, because my parents were keen that we children retained what they always called "our native languages", so we spoke Konkani and Portuguese, plus English. I'm sure that training meant the part of my brain used for understanding language grew in an elastic way. I didn't find Welsh especially difficult to learn, nor French. German was a bit of a slog, but the compound words are quite a joy, in their own way. I'm almost there with Swedish now, but I'm still working on it.'

'Good for you for wanting to keep on bettering yourself; for continuing to learn new things,' said Betty. 'Standing still can feel like going backwards, sometimes, don't you think?'

Was Betty trying to make a point, Evan wondered? Had he been 'standing still' since he'd retired? Did she think he should be trying to improve himself somehow? Had she noticed?

'So how's retirement treating you, then, Evan? Managing to keep yourself out of trouble?' Rakel asked the questions with a warm smile.

'To be honest, I'm managing to keep myself out of trouble alright, but I'm not thriving, Rakel,' replied Evan.

He noticed his wife's eyelids flicker.

There suddenly seemed to be less air in the room.

'Right, well that's out in the open at last,' he added. 'Betty knows it, but we haven't talked about it. Properly. I'm missing it. The job. No question.'

'All of it?' pressed Gareth.

Evan admitted, 'No. Not the hours, nor the stress, nor the constant annoyance of oversight by someone I feel doesn't understand a case as well I do. And certainly not the ever-revolving conversations about possible reorganization. I miss investigating. Following leads. Finding things out. Making sense of bits of information. Catching culprits.'

'Evan doesn't miss the politics or management shenanigans, but he does miss the puzzle solving,' said Betty.

For the first time that evening, Evan noticed her eyes were glistening in the flickering flames of the tea-light candles on the table.

Betty's voice was full of something Evan believed to be sorrow when she added, 'Though this is the first time he's admitted it.'

The awkward silence lasted for about three long seconds.

Rakel said, 'Remember the case that was almost yours down in Rhosddraig?' Evan and Betty nodded. 'They think they've found out whose remains they were. Came in from London today. I dare say it'll be all over the news before too long.'

'Who was it?' Evan was desperate to know. Hoping the knowledge would . . . he wasn't sure what.

Rakel's back straightened a little as she replied, 'A twenty-three-year-old drug dealer from Townhill. Dean Hughes. Partial DNA match. They had him on file because of previous charges. It seems this bloke's been missing from his usual dealing patch since the beginning of November last year, so the timeframe's right. No one reported him gone. No one put two and two together. Why would they? The woefully run-down estates of Townhill and the magnificent isolation of the village of Rhosddraig seem worlds apart, and they are in many ways, even if only about twenty miles separates them by road.'

Three heads nodded in understanding.

'But this is just for us, around this table, alright?' added Rakel. 'You're no longer within the golden circle, Evan, and you two know nothing at all. Not until it's out in the open. Understand?'

'Who am I going to tell, anyway?' asked Gareth. 'I'm just a maths teacher. We're all too busy whining about the kids in class to have anything approaching a sensible conversation during our lunch break in the staff room.'

'You know I understand confidentiality extremely well,' said Betty.

'I'd never drop you in it, Rakel,' said Evan. He thought it an unnecessary statement, but felt it was right to say the words anyway. 'Cause of death?'

Rakel shook her head. 'They put finding an ID at the top of their list. I can't imagine it would be easy to discern cause, or method, from the pile of burned bone shards they got. They might get lucky with a microscopic examination of the remains, I suppose, but only if something was used that resulted in recognizable markings on the fragments.'

'Is Liz still on the case?' Evan couldn't help but ask.

Rakel shrugged. 'I expect so, but there's not been anything anyone could do until now, really. There was no ID, no one missing from the vicinity of the scene, and no one they'd questioned giving off an aroma of guilt, it seems. Now at least they've got something to work with; I dare say it'll float back to the top of the pile pretty quickly. Isn't that the way it goes, Evan? You should know.'

Evan sat back in his chair, his mind whirring. 'It depends on what she and Jenkins are working on now, or if they're even still working together at all. I don't know. I've made a particular effort to not get in touch with people since I left; to not pick up the phone and suggest a friendly pint.' He glanced at Betty to try to gauge her reaction. 'It hasn't been easy, but I knew I needed to make a complete break with it all.'

He leaned forward and clenched his hands on the tabletop. 'Did they get a time of death? Or maybe a nice tight window for the crime itself?'

Rakel glanced nervously at Betty. 'I think they got it down to no earlier than Halloween in terms of the site we saw, but I don't know the details.'

Evan nodded to himself. 'Halloween? And I was there on the 7th November. First on the scene.' The fug of the evening's beers was lifting.

'You told me Liz got up the hill faster than you did,' said Betty, forcing a smile, 'so you'd have been there second.' She winked at him.

'At least third,' added Gareth, surprising everyone. 'Well, some poor pleb must have found it before you lot showed up, right?'

'See what a clever husband I have?' said Rakel with a chuckle. 'You're right, my dear, there was a community constable there to begin with, and the chap who discovered the remains in the first place, of course. So you were fourth on the scene, Evan. Fifth, if you count the dog.'

Evan decided Rakel was attempting an impish grin, and his wife wasn't making eye contact with him at all.

He picked up his near-empty beer. 'Alright, I give up. I wasn't ever involved with the case in any way that counts. It was never *my* case. And I'm retired now. I've got it. Alright?'

'Damn!' said Betty, slapping her forehead.

Evan's tummy flipped. 'What's wrong?'

Betty shook her head and stood. 'Just a minute.' She left the room, and its three puzzled occupants, returning a couple of minutes later with a container of ice cream in her hand. She knocked it against the back of her chair. 'I forgot to take this out of the freezer to thaw. It's like a brick. There'll be a bit of a wait if you want afters.'

The spell the evening had cast upon the group had been broken; farewells, and promises to do it again very soon, were made all round.

Rakel made sure Gareth had his seatbelt properly fastened before they left, 'He'll be asleep before we get to the end of your road,' she said as their car pulled away from the kerb.

Betty put the ice cream back into the freezer, and Evan managed to convince her the world wouldn't end if they just shut the door on the front room, and left the clearing up until the next day.

'At least let me soak the pot, Evan? The bits of chili in it will be like cement by the morning.' He gave in to that request, believing it was best to know which battles weren't worth fighting.

Evan wasn't surprised he couldn't sleep; within an hour he'd worked through what he felt should be the entire investigative plan for the Rhosddraig case, and had mentally sent subordinates scurrying to gather information from a dozen sources.

Then he lay awake, frustrated that he'd never get to see that information, to know those facts, or dig out any leads. The emotions were alien to him, and he didn't care for them one little bit.

'You're not managing to get off to sleep, are you?' said Betty in the darkness. She sounded concerned.

Evan grunted. He didn't dare do more.

Cold air wafted under the duvet as Betty shifted onto one elbow. 'I know you know all this, but – because I love you – I'm going to say it anyway. We have to get this out into the open, and talked about. It wasn't your case then, Evan. And it isn't your case now. You're no longer a police officer. You're no longer a detective.'

'I know I'm not,' he said, the words feeling like a lie in his mouth.

'I know you know that as a fact, but I'm not convinced you're coming to terms with what it really means. Look, if you get in touch with Liz and ask her about it, you'll be putting her in a difficult position, because she's not allowed to discuss an ongoing investigation with you.'

'I know that too.'

Betty gently touched his cheek. 'Oh *cariad*, I understand that you're going to want to know what's happening, but you'll have to be content with being like the rest of us outsiders who follow along with whatever is made public. Please don't let this become an obsession. An interest can become so much more, very quickly. Please, *cariad*, let it go. For your own good.'

Evan turned to face the dark lump beside him. 'I've given a great deal of thought to the whole thing. Let's be honest, I've thought about

little else. I don't mean this case. I mean the challenge of not knowing –
of not being on the inside. And I admit it's harder than I'd imagined it
would be. I will come to terms with it, eventually. But it's going to take
time. And maybe longer than I thought.'

He reached out until his hand connected with Betty's face.

'That was my eye,' she said, chuckling.

'Sorry. I was trying to be gentle.'

'I know. Night, night. Try and get some sleep.'

'Night, love.'

Evan squeezed his eyes shut, hoping peace would come, but fearing
it wouldn't.

8th February

Sadie

It's been horrible at school all day today; every class had a visit from the police, and we were all told we had to report any drug dealers or drug users we know. Told us it was our 'civic duty'. God knows why they bothered. Having some sort of a clampdown, or something, I expect.

What a complete and utter waste of their time. And ours. What do they think – that we're all going to stroll into the Head's office and give up the names of the users and dealers we all know? They're nuts. Try living a normal life after doing that.

The instant they showed up I recognized one of the blokes in plain clothes from when they found that thing up on our hill. Jenkins. He was the one who came over to the sixth form center and talked to us all there too. For a whole period. Lovely.

At least I won't be held captive in school for too much longer; the 22nd July is my absolutely official last day as a schoolgirl. Then I'll be free. But I won't have anything to do after the middle of June, so I might not go in at all for that last bit. Why would I? Why would anyone? What would they do if you didn't turn up after all your exams? Chuck you out?

Tidy.

A few of the girls have said they're going to meet up on the 23rd July to burn their school ties. Sounds a bit pathetic to me. I might be working by then, anyway. If I can get a job with more pay than I can get at the pub.

Aled's dead set on getting into Swansea Uni, and I've applied there too. They've made us both offers; we both have to get the UCAS Tariff points equivalent to two As and a B in our A levels. I think I can manage an A in English Literature, and maybe one in Film Studies too. I hope I can manage a B in History. Aled will. In fact, he might even get three As. He's cleverer than me. Well, not always, but most times. Sometimes he does really stupid things, but not usually when it comes to his schoolwork.

I've got to tell Mam she's to expect an email from the school tonight, and that she has to reply to it. For anyone without an email contact within their family, they handed out printed letters. There weren't a lot of those flying about, but Aled got one, 'cause his Grannie Gwen doesn't do email. He read it aloud in the coffee room before we left school. It was all about drugs, so no surprise there. It gave a lot of online resources for parents to use when they talk to their kids about drugs. Fat lot of good that'll do the ones who don't even have email.

Aled said he'd give the letter to his grannie, because she has to sign something and send it back with him to prove he gave it to her, but he said he'd talk to her about it too, because he doesn't want her to worry. I dare say it's times like this he really misses his mother.

I've got to talk to Mam tonight, about my uni costs. They've got this new package thingy which means the government will give me enough to pay my tuition fees for the year, either as just a loan, or as a mixture of a loan and a grant. And I might get a grant for my living costs too. But it will all depend on how much the household income is. I don't know how Mam and Nan will feel about that. Very private about money, is Nan, and she's the one who owns and runs the pub, not Mam. Mam's just an employee there, like me. So maybe what the pub makes doesn't matter. Maybe it'll only matter what Mam earns. I don't know. It's all so complicated. I don't know why they make it like that. Anyway, Mam and I can go online to read about it tonight. Maybe earlier, rather than later.

I can't believe Aled sat at the back of the bus again today. I thought he'd realize that I want to talk to him about all this drug stuff that's come up today. The bus is full of it, of course. Everyone's whispering, and giggling. Like I can't hear everything they're saying. I know all the dealers they do, it seems. Some people share the mobile numbers that keep changing all the time; in class, sometimes. It's laughable that they think no one notices what they're up to. Well, maybe the teachers don't. But I do.

Nan

Nan was boiling with anger, and well within her rights to be so, she believed. She stared across the bar at the chief inspector and the sergeant, and couldn't believe they'd said what they had.

'You're telling me you think people are dealing drugs here? In my pub? The pub I have run for over forty years. The pub where I myself was born and raised. My home. Do you think I'm completely *twp*? I'd lose my license, my income, and I'd end up having to sell my home.

You're barking up completely the wrong tree. Now get out. You're both barred. For life.'

Liz Stanley and Ted Jenkins exchanged a look; Nan instinctively knew what they were thinking. She lifted the flap in the bar, allowing it to slam down behind her as she moved toward the couple. 'And don't you dare imagine I'm an old woman you can intimidate. I know my rights, and I know my business. And my clientele, too. I can bar anyone I please if they give me reason, and I'd say coming in here and as good as accusing me of running a drug ring is a very good reason indeed. I won't stand for any of that stuff on my premises. If I so much as catch a whiff of that whacky baccy when people are smoking at my tables outside, I chuck them out and throw their drinks after them. And I bar them for life too. Don't I, Helen? You tell them. My roof, my rules.'

Nan was delighted when her daughter backed her up with a sound, 'Mum's rules are well known; she stands for no messing about or horseplay, and absolutely no drugs.'

Nan reckoned DCI Jenkins knew he wasn't going to win with her, and was delighted when he spoke to her in deferential tones.

'I'm terribly sorry, Mrs Jones. My sergeant here used her words clumsily. What she meant to say was that we are making inquiries to gather as much information as possible from people here in Rhosddraig about local drug availability. We certainly didn't mean to imply such business was ever conducted on your premises.'

Nan nodded twice and sat at a table. She invited the DCI and his sidekick to join her.

'Just so long as you understand that,' she said. 'I'm sure you haven't got time for a coffee, so my daughter can stay here with us, to be a witness to anything you might say. Sit, Helen.'

With her daughter at her side, and the policeman and his sergeant sitting in front of her, Nan knew she was in control. 'So why the big interest in drugs around here all of a sudden? Our Sadie just got home from school and tells us your lot's been there all day today, and that the Head's sending a letter to all parents. Got some secret information and you're hoping for a big bust, are you?'

Nan looked at Liz Stanley and added, 'I don't mean *you're* looking for a big bust, love. It's perfectly obvious you'd have one by now if you were ever going to get one. But you might be alright; I hear some men actually like flat-chested women. I meant a drug bust, of course. Is that what this is? Some sort of sting thing?'

'I don't think you quite understand what a sting operation is, Mum,' said Helen. Nan shot her a glance to shut her up.

The Jenkins bloke spoke slowly. Nan wondered why. 'This isn't an operation, Mrs Jones, just a fact-finding mission. We're always working our hardest to prevent the supply and spread of illegal narcotics, of course, and we're just having a bit of a push in this area, at this time. Knowing your important role in this community, I thought myself and my DS should come to speak with you personally; your neighbors will be visited by our colleagues.'

Nan was pleased the man understood her rank in the local hierarchy. 'Ask away then. What do you want to know?'

'Simply put, do you know of anyone in the area who uses, supplies, transports or sells illegal drugs?' said Stanley, almost politely.

Nan noticed her daughter shaking her head. 'They're asking me, Helen, not you, so I'll thank you to let me answer for myself. And my answer is that I do not. As I said, I won't have the stuff under my roof.'

'Mum's even averse to taking any unnecessary medications herself, aren't you, Mum?' said Helen. Nan thought it wise to agree, having kept her special tablets a secret from her daughter so far.

Stanley pressed the point. 'No passing customers – not regulars, of course – who seemed out of place, maybe meeting here, then departing at different times? Random-looking encounters, where it would be easy to exchange a package for cash – that sort of thing?'

Nan said, 'We have some "irregulars" – as I like to call them – I don't care for very much. Friends of that Wingfield boy. They're all turning eighteen now, so I have no reason to not serve them, but that doesn't mean I have to like them. Look like they live on the side of the road, most of them do. Straggly hair, and jumpers that are all stretched. And the tattoos? You wouldn't believe some of them.'

Helen added, 'Mum, they're young, a surfing crowd. That's how they dress these days.'

'Like the people begging for money, or selling the *Big Issue* up in Swansea? I don't see what's appealing about looking like they're sleeping rough.' Nan wasn't convinced the way they chose to dress was normal.

'Would they also be friends of Aled Beynon?' asked Stanley.

'They are,' replied Helen, 'though they're not in school with Stew and Aled. I think they're from somewhere in the West Country; they tend to come for the weekend, and stay at the Wingfields' house. The one they rent out for holiday lets, not the one they live in.'

'Thank you, Ms Jones,' said Stanley.

'I knew that too,' snapped Nan. 'And I also know they have late parties up at that place. I can see the lights from my bedroom. A whole wall of glass they have there, looking out along the Dragon's Back – rebuilt it from a small barn they did. It should never have been given planning permission. Ugly as sin, it is.'

'Is Aled due to be working this evening?' asked Jenkins.

'Starts at seven, though – as you can tell – we're not exactly rushed off our feet. It's been hard work to keep this place afloat since the smoking ban, you know,' said Nan, deciding to play the sympathy card. 'I've worked my fingers to the bone to keep it going, because every village needs a pub. But, other than the summer months, it's a worry, I don't mind telling you.'

'The village doesn't have an off license, does it?' asked the sergeant. 'I expect that helps a bit. If people fancy a drink, they'll have to come here for it.'

Nan suspected the sergeant was trying to make some sort if ill-advised point.

She wasn't having that.

'If people can be bothered to plan ahead they can get whatever they want to drink at home from the supermarket, easy enough. But you're right; Alis doesn't sell alcohol in her shop, and I don't sell ice creams.' Nan felt the reasoning was obvious.

'And nothing, or no one, comes to mind, when it comes to drugs?' pressed Jenkins.

Nan admired his persistence.

'Absolutely not.' She reckoned that would do it, and it seemed to work. The pair stood.

'Might I have a word with Sadie?' asked Stanley. 'As her mother, you are more than welcome to be present when I speak to her, Ms Jones.'

Helen stood. 'Of course. I'm sure she won't mind. She's upstairs doing her homework in the kitchen. I'll come up with you. Will you join us, chief inspector?'

'Thanks, I will,' he replied.

'I was just about to go upstairs myself, Helen, but I'll stay here and hold the fort while you all go up and do that then, shall I?' Nan used her pathetic voice.

'Thanks, Mum,' was all her daughter had to say as she led the detectives to the stairs.

Well, I never, thought Nan, then she moved to the end of the bar to answer the phone that had started to ring.

'Who is it?' she snapped.

'It's Mair.'

Annoyed that she was unable to find an excuse to be in on the action upstairs, Nan was even more irked that now she was expected to take a personal phone call in the bar. 'What is it, Mair? I'm trying to run a pub here, you know.'

'The vicar just phoned me to say John Watkins has only gone and had a heart attack, in Australia.'

'No.'

'He has. The son phoned the vicar just now. The vicar said it was only a minor one, like the one John had in the hospital here when they told him Dilys was dead. But I think it's sad he's gone all that way, and now he might not have time to enjoy being there.'

'They haven't even had a sniff about selling the house, I hear,' replied Nan.

'I expect someone from outside will buy it. Do it up to rent to holidaymakers, probably. Dreadful, isn't it? Another good house will go by the by.'

'It is. So will they bury John there, or send him back here? Did they say anything to the vicar about that?'

Mair sounded shocked. 'I don't think they expect him to die, Nan. And they took Dilys's ashes with them, remember? So at least the son will have them both near where he lives, in some form or another.'

Nan pounced. 'That's about the only thing the son did that suggests any compassion for his parents at all. I still can't get over the fact they didn't even have a service for Dilys's funeral here in the village. And we haven't seen hide nor hair of John since the night they took her away in the ambulance and he got in to be with her.'

Mair's voice softened, to the extent it ever could. 'Well, to be fair, he was by her bedside for the whole week she lingered, then he had that heart attack himself. The son told the vicar his father wasn't up to clearing out the house, so he got that company to do it for them while John was in the hospital, then on the mend with them in that house they rented up near Mynydd Bach Common. And then off they all went back to Australia, once the doctors gave John the all-clear to fly. So what can you expect?'

'I expected John Watkins to come and at least say goodbye to us all. Known him for years, we have. And he must have understood how difficult it would be for some of us to get to Morriston crematorium for the service for Dilys there. Thoughtless, I call it.'

'Well, now he's had another attack. At least the son thought to get word to the vicar about that.' Mair sounded miffed.

'Why?'

'Why what?'

'Why did the son bother to tell the vicar about it?'

'I don't know. Maybe he thought people would like to know his dad wasn't well?'

'What are we going to do? Send a card?'

Nan heard Mair sigh heavily. 'Well, I'll say bye for now then, Nan. At least I've told you. That's all I wanted to do.'

'Bye.' Nan hung up.

Helen

What's that song from The Sound of Music *called? Something about doing something good in her youth or childhood?*

Helen couldn't recall the details, but was congratulating herself on her daughter's interview with the police earlier in the evening. Sadie was a star, there was no question about it; mature beyond her years in many ways – but still her little girl in so many others – she'd answered the questions she'd been asked politely and fully, and the police had clearly been impressed by her composure. They'd looked a bit disappointed that she hadn't been able to give them any information at all about drugs, but Helen hadn't expected her to be able to do so.

Nestling into her pillow, Helen thanked everything that was holy for her Sadie; given all the temptations surrounding youngsters, and the horrible things going on in the world, she couldn't have hoped for a better daughter. She'd been so lucky. She knew from the conversations she read in her chat rooms that not everyone was so blessed; children, and especially teenagers, seemed to be the cause of great stress for so many who turned to the Internet for advice, guidance, and the solace gained from knowing you weren't completely alone.

Helen had read the email Sadie's school had sent, had dutifully acknowledged its receipt, and had even taken time to follow some of the links it contained. She understood why they'd sent it, and thought it was a good idea to offer some sources of information for parents who – unlike her – might be worried that their children were experimenting with drugs.

She'd taken the chance to talk to Sadie about the whole matter after the police had left, and was in no doubt her daughter was telling the truth when she'd confided in her mother that she knew some kids at her school did manage to get hold of drugs, but that mostly they only smoked a bit of cannabis. Helen hadn't mentioned the fact she'd smoked it herself at one time, agreeing instead with her daughter that only 'idiots' did so.

She was also pleased that Sadie seemed excited by the idea of attending university – at last – and had been doubly thrilled to see her daughter's enthusiasm for the offer she'd received from Swansea. She'd have her baby at home for a few years yet, safe and sound. It was a relief, and not just a financial one.

Sadie had always been good at handing in all her homework on time, but now she seemed to have finally focused on getting some proper revising done for her A levels. Helen knew it wasn't going to be easy for her to get the points she needed, but she was bright, and Helen hoped her hard work would pay off.

If it didn't, Helen couldn't imagine what would happen. She wanted her child to reach her full potential, to have all the chances she'd had, but then to follow through and actually take them.

And then there she was, thinking about bloody Bob again, just as she was trying to get off to sleep.

Maybe she'd try the whale-song tape.

14th February

Nan

I can't believe it, thought Nan when she stuck her head into Sadie's room. *She's got it in here. She's no right to hoard towels like that.*

She'd been looking for the big, old, blue towel she liked – because it had become so thin and absorbent after years of use – and there it was hanging on the end of Sadie's unmade bed. She knew the girl had almost missed the bus to school that morning, but she hadn't expected to find this sort of state in her room. She'd have a word with Helen about it, that's what she'd do.

Grabbing the towel off the foot of the bed, she noticed something pink poking out from beneath Sadie's pillow.

What's that? Never been a girl for pink things, Sadie.

The envelope was in her hand before she knew it, then she could do nothing but take out the card it contained. On the front of it was a cartoon puppy carrying a giant heart. Inside was printed: 'My heart belongs to you, my Valentine' and it was simply signed with dozens of Xs and the initials AB.

Nan's heart pounded. She sat on the end of the bed, feeling a bit dizzy.

That bloody Aled bloody Beynon was after her Sadie.

Nan threw back her head and shouted, 'No, no, no, no, no.'

She heard Helen running up the stairs. 'Mum? Mum, are you okay?' Where are you, Mum?'

Nan barked, 'I'm in Sadie's room. Come in here and look at this. Quick.'

As her daughter rushed through the door her face showed concern, then surprise when she saw what was in her mother's hand.

'Why are you in here, Mum? You know what Sadie's like about her room being her private place. We've talked about this before. And what's that you're holding? Where did you get that?'

'Don't start,' said Nan, once she'd caught her breath. 'That daughter of yours lives under my roof, eating the food my hard work provides for her. All I did was come in to get a towel, and I found this.' She threw the card at her daughter. 'That Aled Beynon's sent it to her. Aled bloody Beynon. I won't have it. This has to be nipped in the bud. I'll fire him. Bar him from the pub altogether. I don't want him anywhere near her.'

Nan felt her hands shaking with rage, the way they always had when her dead husband used to get the way he did. She didn't want Aled near Sadie anymore. However much she'd enjoyed bossing Gwen's grandson around, it wasn't worth it if this sort of thing was going to happen. She tried to calm herself by counting backwards, but it wasn't working.

She watched as her daughter bent down to pick up the card, and read what it said.

'See?' said Nan, feeling vindicated. 'AB. Aled Beynon. It's got to be him.'

Helen still looked puzzled. 'Oh come on, Mum, it's just a card. Aled's a nice boy. He and Sadie have known each other all their lives. They're young. It could be a lot worse, you know. She could have got a card from Stew, who was born in England.'

Nan finally felt she had the strength to stand. 'If you're making a joke of this, you're playing a dangerous game, my girl. Aled Beynon isn't just the wrong boy for her, he's the worst possible boy for her. If there's something going on between them – more than just this card – there'll be trouble. I've warned her about him. There's things I know about his family you couldn't possibly imagine.'

Nan was horrified that her daughter had the cheek to say, 'I think you're overreacting, Mum.'

That was it! 'Overreacting, am I? Well, just you wait.' Nan had a plan, and she knew exactly how she'd put it into action when Aled arrived for his shift that evening.

Until then, she was quite happy to stew on it.

Helen

Completely dumbfounded by her mother's outburst, Helen took herself downstairs into the pub kitchen to empty the dishwasher. She heard the post clatter through the letterbox, and automatically picked it up from the doormat. She noticed the card among the bills immediately, and was surprised to see it was addressed to her.

The envelope was thick, heavily embossed. She opened it curiously. It was a Valentine's card. She checked the envelope again. Yes, it was definitely addressed to her, not Sadie. She opened it, and her heart began to thump as music played. It was the chorus of 'I'll be watching you' by The Police. It was signed 'Bob x'.

Helen couldn't feel her feet, nor her hands. Everything she'd been holding fell to the floor. She reached out for the wall to steady herself, then pressed her body flat against it. As soon as she could move, she went to the window, and peered out.

Not again. Dear God, please, not again.

Sadie

Today has been the worst day of my life. I don't know how I can face tomorrow. Maybe I won't. Maybe I'll just end it, tonight. I can't see a way forward. Not at all.

It started well enough. I had Aled's card under my pillow all night, then I opened it first thing this morning. It was the best possible way to start Valentine's Day. I must have got a bit carried away, because I took too long in the bathroom and almost missed the bus. Aled wasn't on it this morning; the past couple of weeks he's been getting a lift in with Stew. Stew's parents bought him a car for his eighteenth birthday, and he drives Aled to school now. They can go faster than the bus, so they leave later. I miss seeing Aled on the bus every day, but sometimes he gets it just so we can be together. I love him so much. I'll be his Valentine forever, and ever.

School was the normal rubbish, then I came home and did my homework, like I usually do, but there was something going on between Nan and Mam, I could tell. They kept looking at each other, like dogs circling before a fight breaks out. I didn't know what it was then, but I found out as soon as Aled got here for his shift. I could hear it all start from upstairs.

Nan shouted at Aled. No – she screamed at him – that he was fired. Just like that. Fired. Told him he had to keep his distance from me, and then threw a handful of money at him. I'd crept downstairs by then, so I saw that bit.

Aled was as confused as I was, but he gave me a look, and didn't say anything. He even started to put his coat on. Just like that. Mam actually had to hold Nan back, or I think she would have hit him. Nan. Hitting out at Aled. I couldn't believe it.

Then, before he'd even had time to open the door, there was a police car with all its lights flashing right outside the pub, and in came that Jenkins and Stanley duo, and they told Aled he had to go with them to answer some questions.

That shut Nan and Mam up; but I was just standing there, at the bottom of the stairs, staring. I didn't know what to do.

Jenkins said something about how he wanted to question him about the death of Dean Hughes. Then he went on about some other stuff. I couldn't take it in.

'Who's Dean Hughes?' asked Nan, which was exactly what I was thinking.

'I'm not at liberty to say,' was all that idiot Jenkins said back.

'Was it him dead up on the hill last year?' asked Nan.

That was a good call, I reckon, because the Stanley woman says, 'I'm sure you'll find out soon enough.'

One of the policemen in uniform said to the other one, 'I wonder how many dead bodies they have down here?' then Jenkins told him to shut up. Spoke volumes, that did.

They marched my darling Aled out of the front door. Thank God they didn't put him in handcuffs, or anything like that.

I ran out after them, of course, with Mam trying to grab onto me. All I could do was shout, 'Don't say anything, Aled. Not one word. I'll phone your grannie,' then he was gone. Just like that.

Mam hugged me. I cried, of course, and I could see people poking their heads out of their doors to see what was going on.

I don't get it. Aled gone?

Nan was horrible to me, like she can be. 'I've always told you he's the wrong boy for you,' she said. God that woman's a bitch. I hate her so much.

What can I do? I can't go on without Aled. He's my life. If I take all Nan's tablets – the ones she thinks I don't know about – I could end it all right now.

I could leave a note, saying the actions of the police meant I had to do it. That would show them. I can't go on without Aled; he'd understand that.

All I want to do is to be *cwtched* up, here on my bed, holding Mrs Hare close to my heart. She's my solace when I can't get out onto the hillside. I've had her since I was very small, so she's mainly bald, but I like to hold her close anyway.

I wish there was a lock on my bedroom door, but Nan's never let me have one. If there was, I could lock myself in now, then they'd know how upset I am. As it is, I don't think they've got any idea. Gone bonkers down in the pub tonight, it has; so many people coming in to find out what happened. Nan's in her bloody element, of course, telling everyone Aled's killed someone – this Dean Hughes, the person they found on the hill. And she's going on and on about how Gwen Beynon shouldn't have been allowed to raise him after his mother died, then reminding everyone how that happened – drugs.

To listen to Nan you'd think Aled's been wandering around the village stoned out of his brain all the time killing people right, left, and center, that his mother was a total junkie, and his grannie is an evil woman who raised him specifically to murder people. God Nan's a bitch. How can she do this to Aled? *My Aled.*

I bet Mam needs me in the kitchen down there; with just her and Nan in the bar there's no one to do food at all. If I clean myself up a bit and go down, pretending to be all nice and helpful, maybe I'll have the chance to speak up for Aled.

Mam phoned Aled's grannie to tell her what had happened, then she phoned the vicar, so he could go over to Green Cottage to offer his support. Nan said Gwen doesn't deserve any support. Maybe I could go over there later on, to see how she's doing. Find out what's happening with Aled. She'd know, if anyone does.

That's what I'll do – be helpful downstairs, be involved. There's no point killing myself if I can actually help Aled. Maybe the police will realize they've made a mistake by tomorrow and let him out. I wonder how long he has to stay there? I hope he doesn't say anything until they give him someone to advise him; they twist everything you say, the police do. He could end up making everything very bad if he says the wrong thing.

15th February

Helen

Helen could only categorize her day as totally weird. It had all started when Sadie refused to go to school, and now here she was, alone in the pub, because her mother had gone to talk to the vicar.

Helen had ended up having to drive Sadie to Killay herself because their argument about her needing to attend classes had dragged on long past the time when the bus had left. Then, having taken the chance to nip into Swansea Market straight afterwards – to pick up some supplies she needed for the pub at the weekend – Helen had bumped into her old counsellor from years ago; the one she'd liked, but who'd caught her at the wrong time to be of any real use, because she hadn't been ready to face the truth about Bob back then.

Chatting over the cauliflowers, they'd decided to stop for a coffee, something Helen never did, because she usually didn't have the time. But she'd been looking for an excuse to stay out of her mother's hair for a while longer – her still being in such a tizzy about Aled Beynon and his grandmother – so she'd taken the chance encounter as an opportunity to act like a normal human being for a change.

She hadn't meant to stay for so long, but it seemed that once she started chatting, she just couldn't stop. *Oh dear.*

Thinking back to that hour, as she dusted the bottles displayed on the bar's glass shelves, Helen couldn't remember exactly what she *had* talked about, but she knew she felt a great deal better for having done so.

To her shame, she realized she'd let it slip that she'd received a Valentine's card from Bob, and had even told Betty – the counsellor had told her to call her that when they'd first met – how that made her feel.

It had been nice to talk. It dawned on her, in hindsight, that Betty hadn't said much herself, though Helen could tell she and her husband were having a bit of a time of it coming to terms with his recent retirement, even though she said it was working out well. Helen wondered what it was he'd retired from; Betty was probably only in her mid-fifties, so maybe her husband was a good deal older than her, or had retired early.

Helen took a moment to enjoy the fruits of her labor, noting how the glasses glistened with points of light reflected off the dozens of small lamps dotted about the whitewashed stone walls of the pub. No doubt her mother would soon be instructing her it was time for all the shades to have a good cleaning.

Sighing aloud, Helen wondered if she should do as Betty had suggested, and think about going to her for some real sessions. It seemed Betty now used an office near the *Senedd* building in Cardiff Bay to see her clients. Helen hadn't actually said she wouldn't go, but she knew there was no way she was going to drive all that distance to talk to someone about problems she didn't have any longer.

If nothing else, she couldn't possibly be away from the pub for so long without having to tell her mother what she was doing, and the last time she'd admitted to seeing a counsellor, her mother had blown her top, citing it as a damning sign of weakness on Helen's part.

But Betty had also mentioned she put in a few hours at the Citizens' Advice Bureau in Swansea and Clydach now and again, and had given Helen the website address for the Suzy Lamplugh people, the ones who helped with information about what to do about stalkers. Helen hadn't mentioned she already knew about them. Upon reflection, Helen reckoned she must have said more than she thought she had, or had meant to, about Bob.

Stephen Wingfield wandered into the pub and stood absently at the bar; he was looking a bit lost and carrying a newspaper. Helen was surprised, because he didn't usually drink in the pub in the evening, let alone in the middle of the afternoon.

She served him with a pint, and watched as he seemed almost unable to choose which of the empty seats he wanted to take, then he sat staring at his paper, not reading it.

She decided to engage him in conversation.

Ten minutes later it was clear he'd left his wife at home to read the riot act to their son, Stew, afraid of what he might say or do if he'd stayed. It seemed that Aled Beynon being hauled away by the police was sending shock waves through the community, and people were beginning to question what sort of a boy he really was.

It also appeared that Stew's close friendship with him was now giving the Wingfields cause for concern; she noticed Stephen mentioned the recent police enquiries regarding local drug distribution three times in quick succession.

Helen returned to the safety of her station behind the bar and looked at the clock. Stew Wingfield should have been at school, where Sadie was.

Had she been wrong to force her daughter to go in that day? Should she have kept her at home and tried to find out more about the true nature of the relationship between her and Aled? She'd been sure Sadie had been telling the truth last night when they'd talked; Aled was Sadie's friend, and he'd given her the Valentine's card as a joke as much as anything, because she'd never had one before, from anyone.

Sadie was just a kid, after all; Helen knew her daughter had never had a real boyfriend, and didn't think that was odd because she knew what it was like to grow up in Rhosddraig – there weren't that many boys in the first place, and it was hard to see a childhood friend as a romantic option.

Of course, there were the boys at school with Sadie, who Helen supposed might offer the chance of a liaison, but she remembered what she'd thought of boys her own age when she was seventeen – all useless. Girls grew up so much faster than boys, it was natural they'd prefer someone they weren't in school with. Maybe someone a little more mature. And she knew for a fact Sadie didn't go out to meet anyone like that – she was almost always at home.

No, Helen was sure there wasn't anything she should be worried about with regard to her own daughter. But as for what a group of eighteen-year-old boys might get up to in their own time – especially now that Stew Wingfield had a car – well, that was anyone's guess. Not for the first time, Helen was glad she'd had a daughter, not a son. She also had a suspicion that Stew wouldn't be revving his engine late at night any time soon, because his father quite clearly saw taking his son's car keys away from him as something he could do to control him, without resorting to more stringent measures. It looked as though things were going to be interesting around the village, for the foreseeable future.

Evan

'Only me,' called Betty as she came in through the front door. Evan loved that – he was finally starting to get used to being the sort of husband to whom his wife would return at the end of the day, instead of it being the other way around.

'I'm in the kitchen,' he shouted.

'So my nose tells me,' replied Betty, joining her husband in the steamy room. She dumped her bags of shopping onto the table beside him. 'And what wonders do we have for dinner tonight, *cariad*?'

'It's my version of Jamie Oliver's turkey risotto. I got it off the Internet, and this is the last of the turkey we froze after Christmas. We didn't have any thyme, nor Prosecco, so I used dried basil and red wine from the box instead. I reckon it'll be fine.' Evan felt rather pleased with himself. 'It should be ready in about ten minutes, but I can't stop stirring it. Thanks for phoning when you left the Post Office; it's helped with my timing.'

'You're welcome,' said Betty, patting Evan on the bum. He liked it when she did that.

He concentrated on not letting the rice stick in the corners of the saucepan as Betty bustled about, putting things into cupboards around him, then warned her that food would be on the table in two minutes, so she'd better change her clothes in double-quick time, unless she wanted to eat as she was.

The risotto hadn't turned out too badly at all, though its reddish hue was a bit unsettling; they were at least both satisfyingly full when they'd finished. It was while he was trying to get the gloopy mess out of the pan that Betty said, 'They've picked up someone for questioning in connection with that business down in Rhosddraig, I hear.'

Evan didn't turn around, and tried to keep his voice from betraying his excitement. 'Really? Who's that then?' he asked, as innocently as possible.

'Some local youth. From what I gather they seem to think he's connected, somehow. Liz and Ted took him in last evening, apparently.'

Evan gave in, and turned. 'Interesting, I suppose. Especially picking him up in the evening. That'll cause problems for them – who knows how long they'll have to wait for a solicitor, then they'll have to let him sleep for eight hours. Yes, interesting.'

Betty shook her head. 'Oh Evan, how on earth did you interview people and hide what you were thinking from them? You're useless at keeping a straight face. I didn't mention it until now because I knew you'd be excited by the news. But I don't know much – just that an Aled Beynon was picked up last night, and the village gossip is that it's all to do with drugs somehow. Seems the kid's mother overdosed some years ago and his grandmother's raised him since then. He works as a part-time barman at the pub, apparently. Good cover for a dealer, if he is one, I'd have thought.'

'Nothing else?' Evan sat down, disappointed, then realized this was an interesting situation – Betty knew something about an ongoing investigation that he didn't. 'How do you even know that much? Was it on the radio when you were driving home?'

'No; I ran into an old client of mine when I was at that nice veg stall in Swansea Market. She's the daughter of the woman who owns the pub in Rhosddraig, and was there when they hauled the kid off last night. That's all she knew.'

Evan's thoughts raced. 'I'll phone Liz. She'll know what's going on.'

'Evan, *cariad*, you can't do that,' said his wife calmly. 'You *know* you can't. Besides, you can imagine only too well what it'll be like for her at the moment – that clock you were always going on about will be ticking, and they'll have to decide if they're going to release him, or charge him. She'll be up to her ears in it. Now's not the time.'

Evan knew Betty was right, but hated it, nonetheless. 'Maybe in a few days I'll just check in with her,' he said. He knew he sounded as deflated as he felt.

'Good idea,' replied his wife. 'Anything for afters, by any chance?'

'Tinned pears and Ideal milk?'

'Lovely. I'll get the tin opener.'

'So who was it you saw in town, exactly?' asked Evan, doing his best to sound nonchalant.

'Helen Jones.'

'And she used to be one of your clients?'

'Years ago.'

'Problems, then?'

Betty put down her spoon. 'Because she was a client back then, I shouldn't really talk about her situation – back then. But, since she and I had an informal chat over coffee today, I suppose I can at least tell you what she's facing at the moment. I'll tell you one thing first, though – I liked her back then, and I like her now. She's a woman who's been through a lot, but she's got a good head on her shoulders, and she's more about tomorrow than yesterday. But today? She wasn't good today.'

Evan grunted.

'Her ex-husband sent her a Valentine's card, and it's thrown her into an immediate tailspin.'

Evan admitted he was puzzled. 'I don't see why a card should do that.'

Betty sighed, and scratched her hand through her hair the way Evan knew he did when he was thinking hard; totally focused on something knotty.

Finally his wife replied, 'If a person's been the victim of unwanted attention, like stalking for example, the slightest communication from – or sight of – the person who victimized them can return them to a high state of alarm and agitation almost immediately. It's a characteristic of the form of post-traumatic stress those who've been stalked can often experience. That's where she is today. Infer what you will from it. I encouraged her to come back to me as a client. I don't believe she will, though; she said she'd think about it, but her eyes told me she wouldn't do it. It's so sad; I think I could help her now. You see, when I was first involved with her she was still in denial about her ex; she appears to have got past that, but now there's this.'

Evan decided he'd wade into his wife's world for once. 'Do you find it difficult to let go of past clients' problems? I'll admit I'm having a hard time forgetting about this Rhosddraig case, and that worries me. I know it worries you, too. But you are the one who brought it up this time, aren't you?' He tried a winning smile, and was heartened when he saw his wife's worried expression melt into one of warmth and understanding.

Betty sat back in her chair. 'Yes, I did. And I told you because I understand something of how you feel about the case. You ask if it's hard for me to let go? Yes, sometimes, though these days I'm better at being able to grasp the fact I can't help everyone I work with; some don't really want to take the advice I give them, or aren't willing to believe they need it, while others aren't even able to get to the root of their problems in the first place.'

'Isn't that why they come to a professional, like you?'

'True, but sometimes – like it was with this Helen Jones – it's just a question of me not being involved at the right time in that person's life. I was pleased to at least discover she'd managed to extricate herself from her marriage and move on with her life with what I gather has, until now, been something of a sense of security and comfort. She dotes on her daughter; I recall her attachment to the child.'

'Good for her.'

'Well yes, and maybe no. Helen stuck it out with the father as long as she did because she thought the girl needed a dad about the place; she'd rather idolized on her own late father, you see. But then Helen's child became a repository for all her mother's love, and need to be loved. Which can sometimes turn out to be quite unhealthy for both the parent and the child. Apparently the daughter's off to university soon. She was just a toddler when I knew her mum; time certainly flies. And I've said far too much.'

'And is the kid connected to this bloke they've brought in for murder?'

Betty smiled. '"The kid" – Sadie – helps out in the family pub; Aled also works there, and they're in school together.'

Evan wondered what to make of it. He knew Helen was right – he couldn't beg for information from Liz, and he certainly hadn't got along well enough with Ted Jenkins to play the 'old mate' card with him; they'd been colleagues, never mates, and Evan had always been keenly aware of their difference in rank in any case.

Oh to be working on this one, he thought. Could this Aled be the culprit? He was desperate to get inside the head of someone who could burn a body twice and smash it to pieces. Why would anyone do that to another human being? And what about the dealer Dean Hughes? What could he possibly have done to Aled Beynon to receive such treatment?

'How old is he, this Beynon bloke?'

'Why?'

'Is he over eighteen? They'll be dealing with him as an adult if he is.'

'I don't know. Though if he was working behind a bar in a pub, surely he'd have to be over eighteen? But, there, I'm not the one in this house who was a detective for umpteen years, so what would I know?'

Evan chuckled. 'Touché. Good point. I must be slipping.'

'Has that ever seemed right to you?'

'What?'

'That the minute you turn eighteen you're an adult in the eyes of the law. You know, aged seventeen and eleven twelfths: you're a boy; aged eighteen: you're a man. It's not as though everyone develops psychologically, or even physiologically, at the same rate. This eighteen-year-old might have the moral compass of a child, and the development of his prefrontal cortex might be slightly less advanced than others of his age. If the part of your brain that deals with decision making and judgement is still undergoing changes until you're in your mid-twenties, why on earth do we insist upon treating eighteen-year-olds as though they are the same as someone in their forties when it comes to committing a crime?'

Evan had finished his dessert, and sat back in his chair. 'I know you're looking at it from your professional point of view, love, but we have to draw a line somewhere. Do you think we should treat everyone as though they're a child until they're thirty? If we did, then should we also stop them having the right to vote, drink, join the armed forces, or have sex until then? All those things need good judgement applied to them. You can't have it one way for some things, and another way for others.'

Betty stood and cleared the table. 'But we already do, Evan. There are different ages at which society deems it acceptable for young people to be able to make a decision about different aspects of their lives. Couldn't it be the same for crimes?'

Evan sighed. 'They'll make an assessment of the individual in question; but if this youth killed someone, and then did what we know had been done to the body, then – frankly – he should be treated as an adult. If you'd seen it, you'd agree with me, I'm sure; it was a scene that told me whoever did it was trying to get as close as possible to completely erasing a human being from the face of this earth. It would have taken a certain sort of person to do it. That's all I'm saying.'

Betty grunted, her back turned toward her husband as she stood at the kitchen sink.

Evan added, 'And may I just say how pleased I am that we're able to discuss this sort of thing like the two loving adults we are?'

Betty spun around, and grinned. 'It's good, isn't it, *cariad*?'

16th February

Sadie

Nan says I have to go to church in the morning. I really hate her. She has to be the least Christian person I know. Wasn't Jesus all about forgiving people? 'Do unto others . . .' and all that stuff. Even I remember all that guff from Sunday school, but she doesn't act that way at all.

I even remember the same stuff in *The Water Babies*, which is a lot about forgiveness and saving people you don't like, even though it's one of the most horrible books ever written.

I remember I liked Mrs Doasyouwouldbedoneby in it; Nan used to read it to me in bed when I was little. Mam didn't like that, but Nan did it anyway.

Nowadays, Nan's like Mrs Bedonebyasyoudid. Horrible. Cruel. It's funny, I haven't thought about that book for years.

I liked Tom in it, the poor little chimney sweep who drowned; Aled's like Tom, and I'm like Ellie – we belong together.

What if they don't let him out? People around here are saying the police can only keep Aled in for questioning for such a long time because they think he's killed someone. That Dean Hughes person. But no one really knows for sure. No one's telling us anything.

So I Googled it, and that's what it says online too.

That's serious, that is. Really bad. I don't understand; why would they think he'd do that? What if he never comes back to me? But that can't happen. They wouldn't lock him away forever. I wish I could help him, somehow. Maybe Mam could help me to help him, somehow?

No, Mam wouldn't be any use at all – especially the way she's been the past day or so; I've no idea what's got into her, she's all jumpy, and she keeps snapping at me.

She's been like it since they took Aled. Maybe she feels the injustice of it too?

Maybe if she knew how much Aled and I mean to each other, she'd help me. Should I tell her about us? I don't know . . . she's not right in the head at the moment. Not like her at all. Nearly had a fit when the phone rang in the kitchen last night.

And Nan's being so hateful about Aled's poor Grannie Gwen. The way she's talking to everyone who'll listen – and some who obviously don't want to – it sounds like she's always thought prison is where Aled belongs, and his gran with him. I've no idea why; she didn't seem to mind having him working here in the pub. What's changed? I don't get it. How can she do this to me? To Aled and me.

I wonder if Aled's Grannie Gwen will be at church tomorrow? She never misses. She'll probably go to pray for Aled. If I go, I could ask her what she knows when I see her there. That would be good. Mam and Nan have been watching me every minute since Aled got dragged away, so I haven't been able to get over to his house at all. Yes, maybe I can talk to his gran in church.

Alright, I'll get up really early to go for a walk up on the hill, then I'll do what Nan told me and go to church, but I'll use the opportunity for my own ends.

Shove that in your pipe and smoke it, Nan.

17th February

Helen

Sitting on the edge of her bed massaging her feet, Helen wondered, *I was worried about Mum getting old, but what about me?* She cursed herself for not having put the special arch supports she'd invested in into her pub clogs that afternoon. As she rubbed and twirled her swollen ankles, she noticed how the condensation in the room was starting to get a bit out of hand; it often did as the colder months wore on.

The pub might have been built to withstand everything the elements could throw at it, but that meant the moisture created inside didn't have a chance to escape. She'd have to give the walls a good wipe down in the morning, and leave the tiny window open as often as possible to air the place out.

Best to catch it before the mold sets in, she told herself. *But that's for tomorrow. Tonight, I think I'll sleep well; I'm tired enough.*

It had been a strange, and challenging day. She tried to sort through it for her own peace of mind.

When she and Sadie had left for church that morning the dragon's breath had been really thick. Helen reckoned people who didn't live in Rhosddraig couldn't even begin to imagine what it was like when the mist rolled down from the moors, and the entire area was bathed in the eerie light that filtered through the thick, swirling eddies of milky air.

It was magical, but not in a good way.

She'd grown up hearing older villagers spouting dire warnings about the effects of the dragon's breath, and – over the years – it was true there'd been some nasty smashes on the road, and people had fallen and hurt themselves quite badly when it was at its worst. In the daytime, the entire landscape would disappear, terrifying her when she was a child; there'd be no Dragon's Back, no Vile, no village, and no moors or cliffs. But Helen knew the sayings went back a long way, and had real menace in them, telling of times when people would disappear into the fog, never to be seen again – because the dragon had breathed on them, then the devil had taken them.

Helen didn't ever like leaving the pub completely unattended, but on Sunday mornings it had to be done. She'd especially hated leaving her safe cocoon that morning – the pub had smelled lovely when she locked up; she'd already roasted half a dozen chickens, and the beef was in the oven ready for the lunchtime crowd.

Outside, it was as though the seaweed down on the beach had somehow found its way up to the village; there was a pungent, unpleasant smell in the air. Every sound was deadened by the fog. Sadie hadn't been in a particularly talkative mood, which was good, because Helen suspected she couldn't have coped with the chatty version of her daughter. And hanging over her was the dreadful fear that maybe Bob was somewhere close by, waiting to pounce on her, and her child.

It didn't help matters that the nervous tension in the church was palpable, especially when Gwen Beynon arrived. Helen's mother stared daggers at her, and the poor woman was ignored by almost everyone. Helen's heart had lifted when Sadie went to help Gwen get her hymn book, and sort out a kneeler. *She's a good girl*, thought Helen.

Sadie even had a little chat with Gwen, who looked as though she'd aged a decade over the previous couple of days. Helen hadn't been surprised; she couldn't imagine what Gwen must be going through.

As she contemplated the situation, Helen had to admit to herself she'd never thought badly of Aled; but then told herself the police wouldn't have taken him away if they didn't have a good reason. She was glad he'd only given that Valentine's card to Sadie as a laugh, out of friendship; it would be dreadful if he'd been her boyfriend. She was grateful Sadie hadn't formed an attachment to a boy who might turn out to be a killer.

Helen plumped the pillow beneath her head. She hoped Sadie would make better choices of men in her life than she had. She'd never forgive herself for having been so stupid about Bob. But how could she have known? He'd been so charming, so wonderful when they'd met, and even for about a year after the wedding. What had made him change so much? She'd never known then, had spent countless hours thinking about it, so wasn't likely to have a breakthrough now, she told herself.

In her chat rooms, people talked about patterns of behavior being passed from one generation to another, but Helen supposed she must be the outlier in her family, because her mother couldn't have picked a better man as a husband than her dad. *I miss you, Dad.* He'd always told Helen to keep her head and her temper, and her marriage would all be alright. *Well, Dad, it wasn't, but I know what you meant.* If her mother had been able to pick a good man, how on earth had she managed to get it so totally and utterly wrong? And would Sadie pick the wrong boy too?

As her thoughts returned to her daughter, Helen recalled the moment that morning when they were halfway through singing the first hymn and the door to the church had banged open. The dragon's breath had twisted its way into the nave, and there, in the midst of it, stood Aled, looking like an abandoned child, with tears running down his face. Of course every head had turned to find out who was coming in late, and there'd been an audible gasp when people saw him.

His grandmother had let out a little yelp, dropped her hymnal, and then the two of them had stood in the aisle, holding each other tight, rocking gently, both crying.

Everyone had stopped singing, and eventually Hywel had stopped playing the piano. The Reverend Thomas had joined the pair where they stood, blessing them both and praying with his hands on their heads. It was an incredibly moving moment. It had even brought Sadie to tears.

That in itself takes some doing, thought Helen – though she knew her daughter could turn them on like a tap when she wanted something.

Seeing Aled like that – desperate to have his gran's arms around him, sobbing his little heart out – Helen had realized how much she'd allowed her mother sway her opinion of him; he'd always been a good boy, so how could Helen have gone along with her mother's reconstruction of his personality the way she had?

And if the police could come and haul away a decent boy like him without giving any good reason for doing it, then maybe it could happen to anyone. Like Sadie. Or someone else, for that matter.

Did the police really know what they were doing?

They'd never been able to help her, not even when she'd been desperate for their intervention.

Maybe they really were as useless as her mother was always saying they were.

20th February

Sadie

It's so weird being in school without Aled. Him and his Grannie Gwen came in to see the Head on Monday; Mr Wingfield from the village gave them a lift – I saw them getting out of his car when we were walking to English. Aled didn't see me; he was cuddling his gran.

The Head's told us he's allowing Aled to take this week off, so he can catch up and concentrate on his studying, and that we're all to understand he's been released from questioning, without being charged. At least somebody's telling us something. The whole village is pulsating with gossip. And Nan's to blame for most of it. The really nasty stuff, anyway.

I hope it helps Aled to be back at home.

I suppose it's helping me to concentrate with him not being around, though it's terrible to not see him, to not be able to talk to him. I miss his voice, his glances, so much it hurts. We're not even texting much. It's like I'm hungry all the time and I can't eat. I feel so useless, so hopeless. I don't know what to do.

But, at least he's at home, safe, now. So that's good. Maybe it's all over. I hope so. That's all I've wanted all along. For it to be over, so we can be together, like we want.

I reckon the best thing I can do for us both is to work as hard as I can to get the points I need from my A levels. I expect that's how he sees it too. We think very much alike, I know that much. The trouble is, none of us know why the police even took him in. It makes no sense. I have no idea who this Dean Hughes is, or how they might think Aled is connected to him. I've seen his photo online, and I've never seen him before. It's a real mystery to me.

I wish I could stop people saying horrible things about Aled, his mum, and his gran. But no one listens to me. They all think of me as a little kid. And even if they don't think I'm a kid, because they're the same age as me, no one seems to take much notice of me, anyway.

So I had an idea, and I *did* something. Something for us. I hope it works. I went into the Internet area of the library in Killay today and got myself a new email address and a new account on Twitter. No one uses Facebook these days – well, no one who really matters, anyway –

and Instagram is good for photos, but I don't want to get photos out into the world, I want to get ideas and words out there.

I worked out that if people don't know I'm me, they might take notice of what I have to say, because they don't think it's me saying it. I've seen such a lot on Nan's favorite TV series about how they track people down using their IP address that I think it's best to take precautions from the outset. I don't want people to know I'm me. At all. Ever.

The good thing about being anonymous is that it lets me say what I want about the police – about how they dragged my Aled away from people who love him when they didn't need to, and have maybe messed up his chances of doing as well as he might at his A levels. That could be our whole future gone, in a flash.

It's not fair.

I said all that in Tweets. Well, not the bit about our future, because I don't want people to know it's his girlfriend who's saying all this; then they'd take no notice. I did a few little things that would make clever people think I was a boy, not a girl; people take more notice of boys, even if they're not supposed to.

I Retweeted the Tweets as myself – because that's something I would do – and quite a few people in school picked up on them too; I tagged the school, and we all have to follow the school's Twitter account because they use it to talk to us, or if there's an emergency. So I'm starting to get the word out.

I set up the account @wrongboy10, which I think is a good handle because it's the main thing I want to say – that the police focused on the wrong boy, and I used the hashtag #wrongboy10, too.

Well, it's clear now that even the police know they had the wrong boy because they let him go; but I don't want people to think they had even one tiny real reason to pick him up in the first place.

It's funny, I wanted to use @wrongboy, but there must be at least ten other people who wanted that name, so @wrongboy10 it will have to be.

It's not much – but that, and doing my best at my exams – is about all I can do. And I'll be there for Aled when he comes back to school next week. Maybe by then my Tweets will be beginning to change what people have been saying about him.

Thinking about it, it's possible that going to Exeter University would be better for us than staying in Swansea; that way Aled could have a fresh start, without this all hanging over his head. As long as I'm with him, and I can take Mrs Hare with me, of course, I'll be happy.

1st March

Betty

Betty was enjoying a delightful evening. Much against her better judgement she'd gone along with Evan's idea to invite a group of people to drop in for *cawl* to celebrate St David's Day. She wasn't usually one for big displays of what she thought of as over-simplified nationalistic pride brought on by the celebration of Wales's patron saint, but had agreed it would be a good way for a bit of a get-together.

Evan had plopped daffodils in vases around the house, but she'd made a poster to go above the door to the front room that read NO RUGBY TALK – in an attempt to staunch the tide of conversation that was bound to flow after the match played between England and Wales the previous Saturday.

She'd spent the best part of that memorable day in the kitchen making about a hundred Welsh cakes in preparation for the soiree, while Evan had screamed at the television as though every player and official on the pitch could hear him if only he shouted loudly enough. She preferred to listen to the rugby on the radio – her years of avidly watching Evan on the field, and her father before him, allowing her to see in her mind's eye every move described by the commentators.

They'd agreed on a sort of open house arrangement, to run from five until ten o'clock; the shifts and hours their guests worked made it impossible for there to be a definite start time. Evan was serving a couple of his long-time colleagues with bowls of the hearty mutton and vegetable stew-like soup in the kitchen, while Betty was happy to sit in the front room where Gareth regaled her with stories about Evan's early days on the rugby team where they'd played together – this topic having been accepted by her as not counting as the sort of 'rugby talk' she'd intended to discourage.

Evan entered the room just as Gareth was wrapping up a story that involved an inflatable sheep, a pair of rugby shorts, some electrical tape, and a large pot of vanilla ice cream. Evan stopped Gareth from bringing the story to its conclusion, leaving Betty in a state of suspended horror at the thought of her husband being caught up in such shenanigans.

People came and went, with Rakel Souza arriving just in time to pour her husband into the car to drive him home; Betty insisted Rakel took a plastic container full of *cawl* and a few Welsh cakes to eat when she finally got him there. It was gone ten when everyone had left, and Betty and Evan were left to survey the shambles in their front room.

'That was fun,' said Betty as she kicked off her shoes, and shoved her feet into her slippers. 'How about we have a bit of a sit down, then give it a fifteen-minute clear around to get rid of the worst, so we don't have to face it in the morning?'

Evan agreed, so they sat in silence, Betty internally recalling some comments made during the evening. She wondered if Evan had heard them too.

'Sounds like they're about to bring that lad back in for the Rhosddraig thing,' he said.

Betty smiled. She'd had an instinct he wouldn't have missed it. 'Apparently so,' she used her most innocent-sounding voice.

'I couldn't get much out of anyone. Seems Jenkins is running a pretty tight team on the case.'

'Was that the doorbell?' Betty stood. 'I'll go.'

Betty was surprised to see Liz Stanley on the front step. 'I'm sorry,' said Liz looking a little ashamed. 'I know I'm late, but I just wanted to drop these off, and say hello to you both.' She held up six cans of Felinfoel Nut Brown Ale.

Betty stood back for Liz to enter. 'He's in the front room with his feet up. He'll love you for bringing him those. Go on through.'

She saw her husband's eyes light up at the sight of his ex-colleague, and didn't think it was just because he was pleased to see her, or the beers; she didn't expect the small talk to last long.

About five minutes later, Betty tried to suppress a smirk when Evan idly inquired, 'So what's this about you bringing in that lad again on the Rhosddraig case?'

Sitting at the dining table, with Evan slouched in an armchair, and Liz trying to look relaxed on the settee opposite him, Betty didn't have to move her head to watch as the conversation bounced between the two like a tennis ball during a long rally – all she had to do was slide her eyes from one to the other, and drink her beer. It fascinated her, both as a wife, and psychologist.

'I can't tell you anything, you know that, Evan,' opened Liz.

'So you're not bringing Aled Beynon back in?'

'You know his name?' Liz sounded surprised.

'I do. And several other pertinent facts.' *Fifteen-love to Evan*, thought Betty.

'How's that then? Got a source in the division?'

'Better than that.'

'Really? In the village?'

'At its heart.' *Thirty-love.*

'We did have him in, just for questioning under caution, but let him go.'

'Insufficient evidence, or the wrong bloke?'

'Could be either, or neither.' *Thirty-fifteen*

'Come on, Liz, we both know it's usually one or the other at that stage. Why'd you bring him in in the first place if you had nothing on him? I can't believe that would be smiled upon, not bearing budgets in mind, and the overtime that accrues when there's a rush because you're on the clock.' *Forty-fifteen.*

Liz sighed – or, as Betty saw it – she took her eye off the ball.

'It's been difficult,' said Liz sounding deflated. 'He looks like a kid, and yet . . .'

'So you've got circumstantial stuff; hints of opportunity and motive, but you can't tie him to the scene. Right?'

'Yes, sort of.' *Game to Evan Glover.*

'There's a dome of confidentiality over this room, if that helps, Liz,' said Betty, knowing she had to take Evan's side, or he wouldn't sleep soundly for possibly weeks.

Liz put down her beer. Her facial contortions told Betty she'd made a decision. 'We're picking him up again, and charging him in the morning. No real rush, as we're keeping an eye on him and we don't think there's a chance he'll do anything stupid.'

'Have mercy on me, Liz,' said Evan springing from his seat. 'This bloody case has been tormenting me. Just tell me everything, then maybe I can find some peace. Please. Betty's right – not a word, from either of us. To anyone. I promise. Ever. I just have to know.'

Liz crumpled like a newspaper emptied of its chips. 'Alright then. Couldn't find any connection between the dead dealer Hughes and Rhosddraig at all. We couldn't even uncover much activity in terms of drug movement within the village. Most of the residents are well past it, though you never can tell. But then we found out that Aled Beynon's mother died of an overdose back in 2010; she'd lost her job a few months earlier when they knocked down an old pub she used to work at close to what's now the Dylan Thomas Museum in the Marina Quarter – bad reputation for all sorts of illicit goings-on.'

'The Cat and Whistle?' asked Evan, sitting again.

Liz nodded. 'Know it?'

'Too well.'

'As you'll know by now, from the media coverage since we released his name, Dean Hughes was a nasty little dealer from Townhill; nothing big, mainly Spice it seems, but he's been at it since he was a kid and he was never going to give up, just get worse. When we finally got all the permissions we needed, we were also able to access his juvenile record. It turns out Dean had been in the frame for supplying the drugs which killed Aled Beynon's mother – a particularly fatal batch of Spice that was in circulation for a few weeks, and delivered four bodies to West Glam General and the ministrations of the lovely Dr Souza. Do you recall any of this?'

Betty watched with admiration as her husband brought his insights to bear.

Evan sat forward in his chair. 'Of course. Not my case – nothing to do with me, in fact. Bloody awful, it was. Spice was still quite new at the time; well, newish. It had only been doing the rounds hereabouts since 2007 or so, and the grasping sickos who made it kept changing the chemicals and additives they sprayed onto the plant materials in the baggies, trying to stay on the "right side of the law". Used a potion they made by brewing up magic mushrooms for a while I remember – probably because they could pick them for free across half of South Wales, but they varied their concoctions over time. Because of that, the medics could never be certain what a person had taken, so they didn't know how to treat overdoses. Whatever was in that specific batch was deadly, I remember. Two of the victims were suspected to have got their drugs from a young lad, whose name I don't think I ever knew. But Vice didn't have enough to get him on it.'

Betty smiled as her husband's hand scratched through his hair for a moment.

He continued, 'So, do you think Aled found out that this Dean might have "killed his mother", so to speak, and did the same to him?'

Liz replied, 'That's where we were with it when we brought him in the first time, for questioning; enough to have a certain level of suspicion, but nothing concrete. We thought we'd be able to get something out of him in the interviews, but he didn't say anything. At all.'

Betty noticed Evan's expression shift as he asked, 'What do you mean?'

Liz picked up her can, as if she was about to drink, but didn't. 'Exactly what I said. Began with one "No comment", which isn't unusual, but even when his solicitor turned up he said nothing helpful then, either. Not even any more responses of "No comment" which, as you know, is the last resort of the smug, when their legal representative tells them to keep their gob shut.'

'What did his solicitor say to you about him?' Evan sat further forward. 'Anything?'

Liz shook her head. 'Not a lot. I got the impression he hadn't told her a thing. Aled nodded when asked if he understood something, or shook his head when asked if he'd like to say something. That was it. See? Like I said – I've never seen anything like it. They always say *something.*'

Evan nodded. 'Even if it's just "piss off".'

'Exactly.'

Betty wondered where this was going.

'So why are you getting him back in now?' asked Evan, almost sliding off the front of the cushion on his chair.

'Thanks to good old-fashioned detective work, and a bit of good luck as well, we're now in possession of two key facts we didn't have before. To start with, we've got an eyewitness.' Liz took a swig of beer.

'You're kidding,' exclaimed Evan. 'Who? Where've they been until now? It's been months. Too frightened to speak? Living under a rock?'

Liz smiled wryly. 'The last is possibly closest to the truth. It turns out an elderly resident in the area – a certain John Watkins – saw Aled Beynon riding his bicycle away from a fire up at the old RAF listening station late on the night of November 5th. The reason he didn't come forward was because his wife had a heart attack that night, and various complications – including her death, him having a minor attack himself, then his migration to Australia to live with his son – meant he wasn't aware of what was going on in Rhosddraig. Unfortunately, it seems the son he's living with now is one of those people who don't own a TV, so it wasn't until the poor old bloke was propped up in a hospital bed in Sydney – having had another heart attack himself – that he saw some coverage of his village on the Aussie news, where they were doing a bit of a look at places to visit when you're in the UK. They mentioned the grisly death in passing, he put two and two together, and phoned the tip-line we've had going for months. The locals over there have interviewed him; it looks solid.'

Evan was rapt. 'And?'

Betty noticed a hint of a smile at the corner of Liz's lips as she replied, 'He knew Aled well, and gave a full description of the boy's coat and bicycle. That, plus the connection between the dead dealer and Aled's mother, is compelling.'

Betty watched her husband's face and hands as he analyzed this new information. Both were in motion.

'An eyewitness is excellent,' he said, rubbing the ends of his fingers together almost as though he could feel Aled Beynon's shirt collar between them. 'What's the other factor? The witness in Australia has to be the piece of good luck – what about the diligence of the detectives on the case? You?'

Liz smiled broadly. Betty always thought she looked so much younger than her real age when she did that. 'As it happens, yes, it was me who found out something critical. We got a forensic report quite early on about the possible accelerant used; apparently there were traces found in cracks in the concrete surrounding the main burn site. We knew it was a type of flammable oil, but that was it. I discovered that St David's in Rhosddraig uses a type of altar candle that holds lamp oil in a little reservoir, like they had at the church my Scout troop would attend in Bristol. I spoke to the vicar at St David's, who told me they'd had to order more supplies of oil in November due to theirs having run low surprisingly quickly. By his reckoning they'd "lost" three bottles of the stuff.'

Betty noticed her husband's eyes darting back and forth. 'Access?' he snapped.

'Aled Beynon is an altar boy at St David's; in and out of the vestry where the oil is stored pretty much at will. All in all, another solid piece of connective tissue, and a possibly significant one, in that it suggests premeditation. Of course, we'd essentially stopped working the case until we got an ID on the victim, because we literally had nowhere to go with it, but we've moved pretty quickly since then, and we've put a lot of hours into it. It's one of those cases where tenacity has paid off.'

'To be fair to him, although he's a bit pedantic, Ted Jenkins was always good at that. You too,' said Evan. 'Not that you're pedantic, I meant you give good attention to detail.'

Betty was relieved to see him settle back into his chair as he asked, 'And do you have any idea why this Hughes character was in the village on the night in question – which I'm assuming is now confirmed as the 5th to 6th November?'

'It is, and we think we do. They had an event at The Dragon's Head pub that night. Guy Fawkes Night. Door to door has established quite a few of those who attended were not villagers; Helen Jones at the pub confirmed that she and her mother had hoped the festivities would appeal to an outside crowd, and it seems that happened. Our working assumption is that Hughes came to the village for the party, was recognized by the Beynon boy, and violence ensued.'

Betty loved seeing her husband's mind working. 'But how did the victim get to Rhosddraig? Probably not the type to catch a bus, so he'd have driven there, or he'd have been a passenger in a car. I'm assuming there haven't been any vehicles left in the area – you'd have mentioned that. So what about someone from within his circle giving any information about him having gone there with them, but not leaving? Any insights at all?' Betty noted how his voice had shifted gear; it had taken on an edge of despair.

Liz chuckled. 'You're kidding, right? They'd rather set their hair on fire than talk to us lot.' She paused, then added, 'Sorry, that's probably an insensitive metaphor, given the nature of Dean Hughes's demise. He was a human being, after all, and deserves our respect.'

Evan nodded, and started to suck the end of his thumb. 'So you're hoping the Beynon lad will confess this time? To both the killing, and the destruction of the body?'

Liz nodded. 'DCI Jenkins thinks this new evidence might shift him. Revenge is a good motive, he had the means, the opportunity, and we have an eyewitness seeing him flee the site of the fire. DCI Jenkins reckons we could move without a confession, but I wish the boy would say something. *Anything.* Even something in his defense. It's incredibly frustrating.'

Betty decided it would be alright for her to jump in. 'Why do you think he didn't say anything when you pulled him in first time around?'

Liz replied grimly, 'Maybe because he knew he was as guilty as sin, and that anything he said might come back to bite him in the backside? I think he's chosen to ignore the advice of his solicitor about telling us something that might prove useful in his defense. He's a bright boy, by all accounts; his schoolteachers speak highly of him, as does – frankly – anyone you talk to. I think he reckoned keeping schtum was his best bet. And, to be fair, until we got these two new pieces of the puzzle, it worked well for him. We let him go, and he's even returned to school; got a week's compassionate leave – to study for his A levels – then he was back in the classroom. We're going down to Rhosddraig first thing. Which is why I'm off now. And leaving you with a sense of closure, and an absolute understanding that I was never here tonight, and this conversation never took place.'

'Understood,' said Betty, taking her cue.

'Of course. And thanks, Stanley,' said Evan.

'I think you can call me Liz now, Evan, don't you?'

By the time Betty had waved Liz off in her car, locked up, and tidied the kitchen a bit, she wasn't surprised to find she had to shake Evan awake in the chair to get him to go to bed.

Snuggling beside him in the darkness as he snored, happy he could relax so completely, Betty wondered how Aled Beynon being charged with murder would affect the inhabitants of Rhosddraig. A crime in the midst of a community always had repercussions, and now it seemed the culprit was being plucked from within a tight-knit group. She couldn't imagine life would carry on as normal there, but wondered how any changes would manifest themselves. She was particularly concerned that Helen Jones was likely to be facing yet another stressor – her daughter's school friend being locked up on murder charges, rather than just taken in for questioning.

But there was something else bothering Betty Glover; she prided herself on being pretty good at reading people, and she'd noticed that Liz Stanley had talked a good case against Aled Beynon, but she'd almost seemed to be trying to convince herself, not them.

From what Betty knew of Liz, that wasn't at all like her. Not usually.

2nd March

Sadie

I love it here on the hillside first thing, especially when it's still dark, and the tide's going out. It's as though the sea's giving the land back to us, just for a little while. When I woke up this morning I knew it would be the perfect time to walk up to the old place. My place. I left a note for Mam so she doesn't panic when she sees I'm not in bed.

I haven't done this for what seems like ages. As the sun comes up it makes the sea look magical – oily and mercurial. This is my time of day. Me and the hares. They're busy at this time of year – Mad March Hares. No one ever comes here for the sunrise except me. Not even Aled. Not even he knows I do this.

It's fantastic to have something that's just mine. Everyone should have a secret place they can go to, or remember whenever they need to find a bit of peace and beauty inside themselves.

You're not really a whole person unless you have a secret.

And a secret place.

The sort of place that, even if other people can see it, they don't feel the same way about it that you do. Don't relate to it the way you do. Don't know it like you do. But they'd have to find their own place, this is mine.

Mrs Hare showed it to me, a long time ago. This is my shelter, my haven, my connection to everything that really matters to me. Now, more than ever. And she gave it to me. She's shown me, and taught me, so much.

I love seeing the light change. It's like everything is possible, and it will all be good. At least, it used to feel that way. But what Romeo says is true, 'More light and light – more dark and dark our woes'; maybe the sunshine will only make my sadness seem even worse.

Aled's not the same since he came back. Something's changed in him. He's . . . hardened. I could see it in his eyes when he walked into the church straight out of the police car, and it's still there now. We've hardly talked at all since they let him out. Mr Wingfield has driven Stew and Aled to school every day, so I haven't seen him on the bus, and when we're in class, or in the sixth form rooms, he's off on his own with Stew all the time. They whisper together.

He's avoiding me. I know it. He knows I know it. It's the most dreadful feeling. I've been abandoned by him. It's like when Dad went away. No one said anything, he just wasn't there anymore. I felt empty then, like I feel empty now.

I'm worried that the bond between me and Aled is slipping away, like the sea is slipping away from the land. I can't let that happen. I have to find a way for us to be together.

I suppose I've done something for us; people aren't saying as many nasty things about him behind his back anymore. My #wrongboy10 and @wrongboy10 things are working really well. No one knows it's all because of me – they don't even suspect it – and it's becoming a real buzz around the school. People are writing their own Tweets using the hashtag, and Retweeting from the @wrongboy10 account all the time now. It's really good.

I wish Aled and I could be as free as the hares that run around on the hills and moors here. They travel where they please, streaking past the human eye so they're just a blur. Magical. In every sense. Holy, even. St Melangell knew that, and her ancient church is just beneath me, lost to the sand and the sea. That's another reason this place is so special. Even the air smells sweeter, because of her spirit infusing it with love.

If I brush this moss along my cheek, it's almost as though Aled is here with me, touching my skin with his fingertips. Gentle, like he is. That's what no one understands about Aled – he's such a kind, thoughtful person, he wouldn't harm a fly. Well, not unless the fly was being a nuisance. No one really means they wouldn't hurt a fly, do they? It's just a figure of speech.

I wish I hadn't thought of that; figures of speech, metaphors, similes, hyperbole, and alliteration. I'll be thinking about my homework now, until I've done it. Anyway, the sun's up, the wind has changed, and it isn't magic here anymore – I'm getting a bit cold.

I suppose I'd better walk back down and have some breakfast, while I'm stared at across the table by Nan with that horrible monkey-mouth of hers. All those lines she's got are made out of hate. That poison she's been spewing about Aled and his Grannie Gwen? I'm the antidote – my Tweets will beat her village gossip any day now. Just you wait, Nan. I'll win. You'll see.

For Aled.

Helen

Sitting on the edge of the wonky chair in the kitchen, Helen reread the note her daughter had left. She was thankful Sadie was so thoughtful – she'd have been panic-stricken otherwise.

I don't like it when she goes out before dawn, but she's done it for years and never been the worse for it. I mustn't molly-coddle her; she's a bit like a sheep when she's on uneven ground, and she knows the cliff paths like the back of her hand, thank goodness. Helen was grateful that at least it was a lovely clear morning, with no hint of the dragon's breath.

It's almost spring. About time, too, after this past winter. The thought made her anxious; her mother had already started making noises about giving the pub a good cleaning. Helen knew her mum was right, acknowledging that the sunshine showed up a lot of issues that wouldn't have been noticed through the darker months, but she hated the process; it seemed to take forever. Despite her misgivings she wondered if she should talk to her mother about it that morning – taking the initiative she was always accused of lacking.

But first, breakfast. I'll get some eggs out of the fridge to warm up a bit so I can scramble them for Sadie if she fancies them when she gets back.

'Mam, Mam – come quick!' the sound of Sadie's shrill voice at the foot of the stairs made Helen's soul sink. She immediately envisaged her baby girl in mortal danger, or of Bob having somehow appeared on the scene.

'What is it?' she called, rushing down as fast as she could. Sadie stood inside the open door; she seemed to be all in one piece – there was no blood, no torn clothing. 'Are you alright?'

Sadie bleated, 'There's something happening up at Green Cottage, Mam. There are police cars there. I think it's Aled; I think they've come to take him away again.'

Helen's heart stopped thumping; Sadie was safe, just fine.

'Do you want me to come up there with you, to find out what's going on?' Helen suspected the entire population of the village would be out on their doorsteps, necks craned for the best view.

'Yes. But come quick.'

Helen grabbed a jacket, and pulled it onto one arm as she shoved her feet into her wellies – the easiest footwear to get into in a rush. She finished dressing herself as she and her daughter cantered through the village, along the middle of the road. They weren't alone; all three of the Wingfields were doing the same thing, and Helen could see Reverend Thomas running – as best he could, given his portly figure and advancing years – from the boxy 1930's vicarage the church had built when the previous version had been condemned.

As she'd suspected, the villagers had skipped the stage of merely observing through pulled-back net curtains, and most were already hovering at their front doors, standing on slippered tiptoes, shouting comments to each other across the road, from house to house. Helen wondered where her mother was; it wasn't like Nan Jones to miss out on such an epic occurrence.

As they reached the whitewashed cottage where Gwen and Aled Beynon lived, Helen could see Sadie had been right in her suspicion; Aled was wearing baggy trousers, a hoodie, and handcuffs. She was pretty certain that meant they were actually arresting him, not just taking him in for questions this time.

The vicar was comforting a sobbing Gwen, and Aled was crying, looking lost and confused, searching the crowd for a friendly face – maybe a savior.

'Aled!' called Sadie. It was the most viscerally plaintive sound Helen had ever heard come out of her daughter – even considering her infant screams – and it made her wonder about how Sadie truly felt about the boy.

Would she be this distressed if she didn't like him as more than a friend?

Helen was distracted by the arrival of her mother, panting and pink in the face, who snapped, 'Why didn't you tell me what was going on?'

'Because I didn't know until I got here,' was out of Helen's mouth before she could stop herself.

Her cheekiness drew the expected vinegar look from her mother, plus the equally predictable, 'Don't you talk back to me like that, young lady.'

After Aled had been driven away, through a huddle which parted to allow the police car to leave the village, the vicar raised his hands, trying to get all the chatter to stop. Eventually, silence reigned. 'I'm going to be staying here with Mrs Beynon for the moment, but I'm sure the entire community will pull together to support her through this very distressing time.' Helen noticed he caught her mother's glare. 'Maybe Mrs Bevan would be so good as to act as the main point of contact for people who want to come to spend a little time with Mrs Beynon. Would you do that for Gwen, Mair?'

Helen watched her mother's face pucker as Mair agreed to do as the vicar had asked. She wondered if her mother wanted to shout the word 'Judas' at her old friend, or whether she hoped the look of utter disgust and hatred on her face would convey the same message. Mair's blush suggested it had.

The vicar continued, 'I'm sure you all what to know what's happened, and what we've been told is this – Aled has been arrested on suspicion of the murder of Dean Hughes. He's being taken into custody, in Swansea, and will be receiving appropriate legal representation. Detective Chief Inspector Jenkins, as we all know from our interactions with the police in recent months, is heading up the investigation, which he now believes is concluded with this arrest. However, I am sure we all share Mrs Beynon's hope – no, *belief* – that Aled has been incorrectly arrested, and that the whole matter will be resolved by the truth coming to light.'

With the exclamations among the neighbors reduced to a subdued whispering, people began to return to their homes; the vicar put his arm around Gwen and accompanied her into her cottage. As soon as the door shut behind the pair, Helen was horrified to see her mother spit at the doorstep, then turn to leave. Torn between comforting her child and chiding her mother, Helen stayed with Sadie, and hugged her to her bosom, where her daughter sobbed for several minutes.

'This is the worst day of my life, Mam,' she spluttered, her voice thick with tears. 'I know he didn't do it. We have to save him. Will you help me? Please?'

Helen wondered if Sadie had a bit of a crush on the boy.

Sadie was shaking with emotion. 'Mam, please, you've got to help. For some reason Nan hates him and his gran, so it's us against her. Please don't side with her this time – not like you always do. Please Mam. Pick me this time?'

What did Sadie mean, pick *her* this time? Helen couldn't recall a single instance when she'd ever chosen her mother over her daughter. She wouldn't do such a thing. Sadie was asking her to choose; it was an easy decision to make.

8th March

Nan

Nan shouted up the stairs, 'Come on Sadie, it's Saturday so you've got no school to get up for, but we need your help. You can't have a lie in today. Up. Now. We're making sandwiches for the TV people. Out of that bed. You're needed.'

Nan hoped her granddaughter would shake a leg and shift herself; Helen was doing a fair job in the pub kitchen, but more hands would make faster work of it.

If only Nan could get specially discounted sandwiches and coffee from the pub into the hands of all those people out there in their cars and vans, she reckoned she stood a better chance of them choosing to patronize her premises when it came to lunches, and whatever else they might need, rather than the bloody *Cwtch*. It was too good an opportunity to miss.

Since Rhosddraig had first hit the local headlines, Nan had noticed a slight upturn in 'hikers' dropping into the pub, and asking seemingly innocent questions about the Beynon family. Until this morning it had only been the local TV who'd been there, now the others had turned up. And the newspapers, too. Nan reckoned she might make a pretty penny out of them – and maybe not just by selling food; she'd heard that sometimes people were paid for interviews.

For now, they all seemed to be wandering around the small collection of stone cottages, or out along the closest part of the coastal path leading toward the Dragon's Head. Getting themselves acquainted with the area, and battling the ever-present wind. Wrapping themselves in scarves, they seemed to like what they saw, as Nan had suspected they would; one thing you could say about Rhosddraig – it didn't disappoint when it came to picturesque village life, and stunning views.

She'd made a special effort when getting dressed, wearing her new-ish navy slacks, with a rose turtle-necked jumper, and had gone so far as to put on a bit of lipstick – something she usually reserved for church. She didn't think there was anything wrong with trying to make a good impression.

'Where did we put those big baskets we had full of dried grasses beside the fireplace last autumn?' she called to Helen in the kitchen.

'I think they're out in the shed, Mum. The one that doesn't let the rain in. Why?'

'I thought the sandwiches would look good in them; you know, throw in one of those old checked tablecloths as a liner, and make them look all countrified. Presentation is very important in the licensed trade. I'm glad you've given the place a good going over these past few days; it needed it, and it'll pay off with all those people coming here from London. I bet they'll be interested in some nice pies and so forth for their lunches. Have we got any spare menus? Run some copies off on the printer; we can hand them out to everyone out there, so they know what's on offer. Just plain, not color.'

Helen shouted her reply, 'I'm up to my armpits in sandwiches, Mum. Maybe Sadie could help with those other things?'

Nan tutted. 'She's still in bed. Dawdling. You go and get her up. She's not taking any notice of me.'

With that, Nan stepped out of the side door and lit a cigarette.

Bloody ingrate; Sadie was young, she should be helping her mother and her gran. She'd had a right old cob on since they'd carted that Aled away; not talking to anyone, sulking, and coming home late from school every day, all week. Helen was covering for her, saying Sadie was choosing to stay on after classes to do some extra studying, but Nan didn't believe it for a minute. Getting up to all sorts, that girl was. Her mother, too. Helen had even gone out to pick her up in the car a couple of times. That was new.

Nan had seen the way Sadie had been upset by Aled being taken away by the police, and she knew about the card he'd sent her, of course. It was just as well they'd locked him up; it meant he couldn't get anywhere near her Sadie. Best thing for him. Let him rot. Although she'd never seen it, she was sure he had a temper on him. Born and raised on the Dragon's Back? Almost bound to. That was one local legend she knew to be true – the way a person whose first breath was taken on the Dragon's Back could well turn out to have an angry soul. Especially the men.

It was just gone eight when three generations of Jones women set out with baskets of sandwiches, menus, and pots of coffee. Nan was delighted by how happy all the reporters were to have something good to eat and drink. Gallons of coffee and almost all the sandwiches were consumed; her special low prices paid off. Nan even went so far as to offer a ten percent discount on all food bought in the pub by anyone with press credentials – once she found out what they were, and saw what they looked like.

There was no way she was going to let that English lot at the so-called *cwtch* take business away from her.

Helen and Sadie did most of the selling, so Nan was able to talk to the reporters as she took their money, and she learned a great deal. Unfortunately, not all of it was good; it sounded as though many of them had a great deal of sympathy for Aled, seeing this as a story offering the opportunity to bash the police.

Nan didn't like it. She decided to seed some other ideas about the boy.

Helen told her not to say anything, but Nan knew best; she was rather pleased with herself when she managed to let it slip that Aled had lost his mother to a drug overdose. She knew she didn't have to say much, so she just gave them his mother's name, and knew they would find out the whole sordid story; much better to let them think they'd joined the dots for themselves.

When they returned to the pub, one of the reporters followed Nan to ask if he could come to have a private chat with her.

'How much?' she replied, which seemed to surprise him. But she'd decided to take her chance, and reckoned he was a good one to take it with; he was a doughy-looking specimen, white-faced, with pimples on his chin. Looked like he'd never seen the sun.

'I'm just wanting some background information,' he whined. 'It's not the sort of thing we'd usually pay for. We know he used to work for you, at your pub. You could tell me your impressions of him. If you could help me out, I might manage to get my editor to use a photo of you, standing outside the pub – you know, with the name on display.'

Nan gave it some thought. 'Better than nothing,' she said. 'Come to the side door in half an hour.'

She planned to sound him out about what sort of stories were paid for, because she knew quite a lot about the Beynon family, and she might be prepared to share that knowledge, if it helped pay the bills.

As it was, the so-called interview didn't work out as she'd hoped; he'd only been with her in the upstairs kitchen for five minutes, when Helen joined them. She walked in, sat down, and made it obvious she wasn't leaving. Nan felt her daughter's eyes boring into her, so she kept the whole thing pretty straightforward – said Aled had been generally helpful, if given detailed and frequent instructions. Then she posed outside the pub in her church coat for a photo or two.

'Why did you plonk yourself down with me like that? I was doing an interview. It was private.' She allowed her disgust to show when she spoke to Helen as she hung up her coat.

'Mum, these people are our neighbors. They'll be our neighbors long after all those reporters have gone. Don't go saying things you'll regret. You know how you can get, especially about Gwen Beynon.'

'I don't "get" any particular way about that woman. Nor her family. Though I'd have good reason to, if I so chose. It was a cheap way to get the name of the pub into a big newspaper. You might not like to think it, but there'll be a lot of folks who'll want to come to Rhosddraig just because one of our own burned someone to death up there on the hill. Can't help themselves – it's human nature to be curious.'

'Mum, it's not curiosity, its ghoulishness. We don't want that sort of person coming here.'

Nan lit a cigarette. 'You know your problem? You have no idea that we need people coming into my pub to spend money, which you can then go frittering away on whatever you please. This pub has supported you your whole life, and it's supported your daughter. We can't be picky about who we sell our beer and pies to. All money is good money.' That was telling her. 'And don't you go thinking that just because I've managed to get that foreign girl from Lower Middleford, Agata, to agree to do a few shifts behind the bar that you can go gallivanting off all over the place whenever you like. I'll need you here, not running around after Sadie all the time. She's perfectly capable of catching the late bus home after school.'

Nan didn't like the way Helen sighed when she replied, 'Yes, Mum, I understand,' and left the room.

But she'd said her piece; that was important.

11th March

Sadie

It's been a fantastic weekend, and an even better start to the week. Oh my God, this #wrongboy10 and @wrongboy10 thing has really taken off. I mentioned it to a couple of the younger reporters who were in the village at the weekend, and they put it into their stories.

It's gone berserk.

By Sunday afternoon, #wrongboy10 was trending, and not just in Wales. Wandralee Wonder has started Retweeting all the #wrongboy10 and @wrongboy10 Tweets. *Wandralee Wonder!* She's got nearly two million followers. It's made the whole thing so much more powerful. I just wish I could do more of it from home, but Mam and I agree it's best if I only do it from the library in Killay, and she also agreed I could get the bus to Sketty and do some from the library there. If I spread it around, no one will ever know it's me.

Mam even came and picked me up from Sketty a couple of times last week because I'd missed the late bus home. It's our secret, Nan mustn't get wind of it, and I know it'll make a difference to Aled.

I had a couple of study periods this morning, so I went into Killay and did some new Tweets about that horrible Dean Hughes. I've no idea who he really was, and I don't understand how they've come up with his name, but he sounds like a right waste of space, from what I've read about him online.

Someone like that won't be missed.

Not like Aled is missed.

People have to understand that, don't they?

That not everyone is worth the same.

I mean, the Hughes bloke was a real blight on our society. I don't think it's enough that people believe Aled's innocent; when the police try to prove he did it – which they will, by lying – then everyone has to know he was really just getting rid of someone who was doing harm to lots of kids. By dealing filthy drugs.

That Hughes was a leech, feeding on weakness. He deserved to die – that's what they've got to believe too. That's my goal. It's what I can do for Aled.

Just a few minutes after I wrote those Tweets, they had hundreds of thousands of Likes and Retweets. It's getting so fast, now. It's got to be making a difference, I know it.

Nan can gossip all she wants about Aled around the village, but I'm making real people, out there in the real world, change their minds about him. Hundreds of thousands of them. All over the world. Maybe millions. The @wrongboy10 account has over 214,000 followers now. Aled would be amazed.

On Friday afternoon I uploaded a photo of Aled I took at the Remembrance Day service, wearing his surplice and ruffle; it got over a million likes by this morning. Over a million! I never imagined this would happen.

It's fantastic.

15th March

Evan

'You don't look too happy this morning, Mr Glover,' said Betty pouring a cuppa from the pot. 'I know it's chucking it down out there, but you're usually my little ray of sunshine. What's up?'

'I'm fine, Mrs Glover,' replied Evan, forcing a smile.

'Out with it.'

'Have you seen this?' Evan held up his tablet, showing his wife the headlines he'd been digesting.

He'd been slow to accept that using online newspapers would make a good alternative to his previous at-work access to pretty much everything in print, but now he couldn't imagine any other way of accessing information. He could read all the papers and magazines he wanted, watch video clips as he chose, and even follow stories in online publications from around the globe he'd never considered reading.

It was like a whole new world opening up to him – both literally and figuratively. He'd become something of a news-addict since he'd retired. He could barely recall a time when all he'd read was the day-old stuff that came out in print, on paper. Now everything was up-to-the-minute fresh; he'd even set up Breaking News Alerts on his phone.

Betty pushed her reading glasses onto her nose and took the tablet from him. He watched her eyes dart back and forth as she took it all in. He poured out the half a mug of tea remaining in the pot, then moved to boil the kettle to refill it. As he looked out onto their little patch of garden with its bedraggled winter pansies and the daffs all but gone over – the same as every other garden along their street of semis – he was just a little glad he wasn't out there in the weather, chasing down a suspect, or a lead.

How did I ever fit in work? he wondered. The time was flying by; he was busy with projects around the house – and the garden, when the weather allowed. He'd learned the joy of downloading episodes of *Desert Island Discs* from the BBC website and listening to them as he pottered; he'd heard the life stories of some truly amazing people over the past months – the type with great accomplishments behind them but whose names had rarely, if ever, been mentioned by the mainstream press.

He was also becoming fairly adept at using social media, as well as having discovered the pure delight of having time to read. He was pretty sure none of this would sound even remotely exciting to anyone else, but he was luxuriating in the ability to browse bookshelves – either his own, or those at the library – pick up a book on whatever topic took his fancy, then sit and actually read it. The passion with which he gobbled up all sorts of titles was a thrill to him, though he still most enjoyed reading about local history.

'It's quite something when we've come to this, don't you think?' asked Betty, dragging him back to reality.

He nodded. 'That columnist is basically arguing that we, as a society, should have a world-view where those who act against the interest of said society should be treated differently to those who act in support of said society. Don't they understand that's why we have rules – laws? That's what the police and the courts are there for. They're talking about it all as though it's some brand-new idea.' He allowed his annoyance to show. 'I bet the person who wrote that's about twenty-bloody-five. You can't even tell if it's male or female, because apparently the first name "Morgan" is now in use for both.'

Betty placed the tablet on the table. 'First of all, I have to say I cannot see what possible difference the gender of the author makes to the quality, or otherwise, of the piece.'

Evan knew he'd touched a nerve and was sorry he'd done so. He hadn't meant to.

'Secondly,' his wife continued quietly, 'I don't think that's quite what they're proposing, Evan. It seems to me they're baying for the blood of drug dealers, and are saying this boy who's been apparently arrested for murdering that dealer in Rhosddraig should be let off – even if he did do it – because it was a just act.'

Evan stared at the kettle. 'Well, yes, there's that too. Which is also ridiculous.'

Betty joined her husband at the counter and peered through the rivulets of rain pouring down the kitchen window. 'That's all looking a bit sorry for itself out there, isn't it? When it stops, I dare say we'll have a fair bit of tidying up to do. That nice bit of weather we had fooled us all into thinking winter was over.'

Evan turned and held his wife. 'Am I becoming a news bore?'

'I wouldn't say that exactly.'

'But I'm close to it, I know. It's just that I feel so . . . so helpless. When I was on the job, I knew I was making a difference; I was helping to apprehend those who deserved it, and to give some sense of justice to the victims of crime. But now? Now it's as though I don't have any input into society anymore. It's like I'm on the "thanks, you're of no use to us any longer" pile. And it's annoying the hell out of me.'

The kettle boiled, and Betty topped up the pot. They took their seats at the kitchen table. 'So, what are you planning to do about that?' she asked.

Evan knew from experience she was using her professional wiles upon him. 'I don't know. Do you have any suggestions?' he countered.

Betty bit into a piece of toast, the angle of her head telling him she was thinking as she crunched. Eventually the psychologist he'd married said, 'I know you're still coming to terms with not being a detective, and I absolutely understand you can't help but be curious about why people do what they do. It's the part of your nature, your persona and psyche, which took you into your career in the first place. There are deeply engrained patterns of activity observable in most human beings which are the product of the genes we're born with, and the experiences we've had. You're experiencing the totally natural phenomenon of not being able to stop wanting to know what happened, and why, despite the fact your job is no longer a part of your life.'

Evan took in what Betty had said as he poured them both a fresh cup. 'So, to distill your mini-lecture there, you're saying this is a process I'm going through, born of the nature/nurture effect?' He wanted her to remember he had taken all those psychology courses.

Betty smiled. 'Exactly.' She crunched her toast loudly.

Evan almost burned his mouth with his tea. 'So do you think if I allow all of this totally natural desire to know "why" and "how" to be focused on this one case – the case in Rhosddraig – that I'll be satisfied when it's all done and dusted, then? When this angelic Aled Beynon is locked up for having killed the devilish little scumbag the media have now, somehow, discovered possibly supplied the drugs which caused Aled's mother's death, that *then* I'll find my own sense of closure, and be able to think and act like a normal human being again?'

Betty grinned. 'I wouldn't go as far as saying "normal", *cariad*. Maybe that would be too much to expect. But the closure part of it might be true.'

Evan scraped low-fat spread onto his toast, then gave it the thinnest possible coating of lime marmalade. Before he crunched into it he said,

'But the neutrality of the jury pool is being tainted by all this mainstream media coverage; with the frenzy of trending this, and sharing that, on social media making it even worse. Honestly, I can't remember any other case where the victim was so clearly portrayed as a sinner, and the accused as a saint. It's all black and white, if you believe the coverage.'

He allowed himself a moment to chew, then added, 'Life's not like that. Everyone's a swirl of grey, with the choices they make giving them definition. Some of our choices are good, some bad. This Aled Beynon can't be as pure as they say, and I'm sure this Dean Hughes was loved by someone, for some reason. Two young men, each being given a character make-over by the media simply to suit *their* purpose.'

'Sales,' said Betty.

'Eyeballs,' countered Evan. 'That's what they're after these days; not sales from newsstands, but eyeballs on screens – eyeballs they can sell to advertisers.'

Betty shrugged.

Evan pressed on, 'There's something I've noticed about this case in particular; it's about youth. Millennials lap up all this stuff; the generation that would rather look in a mirror or take a selfie than really learn anything about another person. It's all about the packaging. It's playing right to the media's most desirable audience, this story. And good police work be damned.'

Evan was glad Betty was apparently concentrating on enjoying her toast and didn't respond, because he felt like stewing for a while. He suspected she could tell as much by looking at him. They ate in silence, then he pushed himself from the table and decided he'd better make a proper start to the day.

By the time he'd showered and dressed, and Betty had done the same, he was feeling a bit more positive about their discussion. He knew his wife was off to give a few hours' input at the Citizens' Advice Bureau in Clydach later that day, so decided he'd just run a couple of thoughts past her before she left. The fact she'd pulled out the ironing board in the kitchen gave him the chance he needed to corner her.

Enjoying the nostalgic smell of ironing mixed with the remnants of toast, Evan allowed himself the chance to organize his thoughts before he spoke. 'I'm thinking of inviting Liz over. For a coffee, or something. Tonight, if she can. What do you think?'

Betty didn't take her eyes off the collar she was steaming into submission. 'Will what I think really make any difference to what you'll do?'

Evan didn't think her tone was harsh, just realistic. 'Possibly,' he replied, honestly.

'Liz is a grown up. She can decide whether to take you up on your invitation, or not. I can't imagine she won't guess why you're doing it.'

'True.'

'So that's that, then,' she said with finality, popping the crisp blouse onto a hanger, and unplugging the iron. 'See what she says, eh?'

Evan was pleased. 'You're right. I'll ask, and leave it up to her. I'll phone her after you leave; there's no hurry. Now, are you taking a snack with you? I'll do something about dinner while you're out if you like, or will you be coming back via any chip shops? It could be our Friday night treat.'

Betty was examining her blouse, holding it up to the surprising shaft of sunlight streaming through the window. 'I'll bring something home; there's a good Indian place in Clydach. How about a curry for a change?'

'Do they do chips?'

'They're running an Indian takeaway in Wales, what do you think? So, chicken korma and chips for you, is it? Onion bhaji too? Or is that a silly question?'

Evan licked his lips. 'Have I told you recently how much I love you?'

21st March

Sadie

Oh God, I miss him. I can't see him, or smell him, or hear his voice.

It's terrible. Like falling, tumbling, in a void.

If I concentrate really hard I can imagine his hands touching my body under my duvet, feel his breath in my ear.

You're a terrible God – you're Nan's God, not mine, and you've taken him away from me, for all this time. We're supposed to be together. You know that.

Nan says you're all-seeing, and all-knowing. If that's true, then you know what he means to me. Why would you do this to me? To him?

Why are you torturing us like this? Is it because I know you don't really have the power others think you have? Because I know the truth about you.

Is this just you making my life a misery with the little ability you have?

I wonder why I even try to get to sleep these days. Mam's on and on at me to work harder for my A levels, but how can I when there's this huge empty space in my life?

I can picture my darling Aled, locked up with all those horrible criminals in Swansea prison. That's where they sent him after the hearing at the Magistrate's Court. Mam wouldn't let me go to that. I wish she had. At least then I'd have seen him.

Who's going to look after Aled in prison? Everybody knows what terrible places they are, even if you're innocent and you haven't had a trial yet. What if he's being picked on, or bullied?

He's too good for that place. Too young for it, too. But that's where they put him. I think they should have sent him to a place especially for young people, but they said he was old enough to go there. I hate the police, and the magistrates, and the solicitors.

The whole lot of them are against him. I can't allow myself to think about any of the dreadful things that might be happening to him in there. It's too upsetting.

I'm doing everything I can for him. I keep Tweeting about him, and I know it's working, but nothing seems to be helping to actually get him out. If nothing can happen until his trial, why don't they just have that now? Fast.

This waiting and waiting is unforgiveable. I've been Tweeting about that too, and I can see the message is getting through because there've even been things on the news on the telly, using Aled's case to make the public aware of how long people are held before their trials – in so-called remand sections in prisons – when they haven't been proved guilty of anything. It's a national disgrace – everyone agrees.

There's even a website where they're counting the days he's been incarcerated. It's nothing to do with me – it's some organization that speaks up on behalf of young people being remanded before trial. It's fantastic; so many people are helping Aled.

They announced on the BBC last night that he's got a new QC. On the BBC for goodness sake . . . and the *proper* BBC, not just BBC Wales. I'm not really sure what having a new QC means exactly, other than the man from Swansea he had before is getting pushed to one side, and this woman's coming down from London to represent him for free; she thinks the case is a 'terrible indictment of our judicial system'. Apparently she's got a reputation for taking cases like Aled's, where a person has been locked up for no good reason. We'll see; I just want them to get him out, however they do it.

Some people in the newspapers are saying that if anyone can get Aled's case into court faster, she's the one to do it; but others are saying she's pissed off so many people over the years that his case might be slower to be dealt with.

I just don't know.

What I do know is that I didn't set out to change the world with my @wrongboy10 Tweets, I just wanted to get people to see Aled for who he really is. If everything gets slowed down for him, just to make some sort of an example of his case, that would be terrible.

I can't live without him. I'm dying inside. And as for my exams? Well, stuff them. He'll be held back a year when they let him out – which I know they will – and I can stay on with him. Mam can't possibly expect me to be able to concentrate on exams. Not with all this going on.

She's been pretty good about it so far, but she's getting less supportive, now, about the Tweeting business; she was the one who agreed with me it was a good idea, but she doesn't really get it. I know I haven't told her *everything*, but why would I? It's none of her business, and she wouldn't like it. But she's my mother; she's supposed to be on my side.

30th March

Nan

Nan was glad to have Agata behind the bar with her, because Helen and Sadie were just about keeping up with things in the kitchen. Even Agata's kid sister was working as a waitress; she couldn't serve alcohol because she was under age, but she could sort the food, so that was good. Nan couldn't say the girl's funny Polish name, so called her Gen; the girl's English was good – considering – and she didn't seem to mind what Nan called her, so long as she got paid cash at the end of each shift.

It was good they had all hands on deck, because the unseasonably warm weather and the notoriety of Rhosddraig meant The Dragon's Head was bustling; even on a sunny Saturday in March it was unusual for all the outside tables to be in use. Nan loved it.

Having called Helen from the kitchen to help Agata behind the bar, Nan was enjoying a smoke, hovering at the side door; it was a nice enough day that she owed it to herself to have a breath of fresh air. The winter had been as brutal as ever, and now – finally – it looked as though the end might be in sight. The sheep were dotted about the moorland and hillsides as they should be, and at the base of the cliffs the tide was out, so the sand seemed to go on forever.

Best view in the world, she thought, puffing away. *But we could do without the wind, as per.*

For all that most of the locals were a right pain in the backside, Nan loved Rhosddraig. She'd never so much as considered leaving, and had made it perfectly clear during their courtship that, if Jack Jones wanted her hand in marriage, he'd be expected to live with her and her parents at the pub, and work there too.

He hadn't objected; Nan knew he'd discovered it wasn't easy finding work after the war, when all the real men were coming back to take the jobs, and he was only sixteen. Indeed, he hadn't held down a proper job between the time he'd left school in 1946 and the time he married Myfanwy in 1959; he was the one who'd started calling her Nan, and she'd loved it.

'Mum, I've got to go to the cellar to change a barrel; can you help Agata behind the bar for a few minutes, please?' Helen sounded snippy.

'Can't it wait? I'm just having a quick one.' Nan was immediately annoyed.

'You were giving that up last year, Mum,' sniped Helen. 'And no, it can't wait – we've got the chance to sell beer, and beer we shall sell. I remember some woman telling me that should be my reason for living, once upon a time. I'll let you know if I see her around.'

'Oh, ha bloody ha. You're so sharp you'll cut yourself one of these days, my girl. I'll be there now, in a minute.'

Nan was getting sick and tired of the way Helen sighed all the time; it was quite uncalled for.

Pushing through the gaggles of customers, Nan took the reins behind the bar; she'd pulled so many pints over the years she didn't even need to think as she did it, which meant she was able to spot Gwen Beynon peering through the window, before the woman headed toward the door.

'I can't have that,' Nan shouted, much to the surprise of the hiker whose pint she promptly banged onto the counter, only half-filled. She lifted the bar-flap and let it drop with a thud.

Agata carried on pouring the drink where Nan had left off, and handed the puzzled man his beer with a cheery, 'There you are, sir.'

Nan tried to head Gwen off before she entered the pub, but failed; she wasn't as fast on her feet as she'd once been. Gwen stood there, almost filling the doorframe – in terms of its width, if not its height – and her expression spoke volumes. Decades of being a landlady had taught Nan how to spot a problem, and here was one walking into her pub. Gwen had come to make trouble, that much was clear.

'I don't want you in here,' said Nan bluntly. 'Go away with you now, Gwendolyn Beynon.'

'Or what, Myfanwy Jones? Will you throw me out? Is that it? I don't want to be in your horrible pub any more than you want me in it, but you hardly leave it, so I've come here to tell you what I think of you once and for all. My poor Aled's in prison, for something he didn't do, and you're spreading ugly rumors about him all around the village, and in this pub no doubt, as well as saying things to the newspapers that aren't true.'

Nan noticed the look of distaste with which Gwen surveyed the faces surrounding her.

She hoped the woman would shut up, but Gwen continued, 'To top it all, Myfanwy, you see the whole thing as just a way to fill this place with disgusting people who wouldn't be here at all if it wasn't for the fact that an innocent boy accused of all sorts used to work here. Well, he's my flesh and blood, and I won't have it. You're a disgrace to your family, this village, and the church. I've complained to the vicar about your un-Christian ways, and I've written to the bishop in Brecon. So there.'

Nan was aware that her customers had fallen silent; an air of expectation filled the bar.

'I choose to not say anything against you or your boy at this time, Gwendolyn. Though God knows I could. But I don't want you in my pub. I never have. You know very well why not, and it's got nothing to do with Aled.'

'What do you *mean*, it's got nothing to do with Aled? It's got *everything* to do with Aled. This is all about Aled,' screamed Gwen.

Nan could feel her stress levels rise. Her fingers were tingling. She felt ready to explode. The entire pub was agog. 'It's not about Aled. It's about you, and it always has been. You . . . you whore! Get out of my pub now, or I'll phone the police. Agata – find Helen. Fetch her to me, now.'

'I'm here, Mum,' said Helen, suddenly at her mother's side. 'Come on now, this isn't the time or the place, ladies.'

'Go on, let 'em at each other,' shouted a joker from the far side of the lounge.

'Helen, find that man, throw him out, and bar him for life,' shouted Nan. 'And you get out now, Gwendolyn bloody Beynon, or sure as eggs is eggs, I'll push you out myself. I might be half a dozen years older than you, but I'll show you.'

Nan reached out and picked up the nearest object she could find; she swung the bottle of tomato ketchup above her head like a club.

'See what sort of woman has raised your precious Aled,' shouted Nan when she caught sight of Sadie's head peering out of the kitchen. 'She's a dreadful, scarlet woman.'

'She will be if you smack her on the head with that bottle of sauce, Nan,' replied Sadie. Chuckles rippled through the crowd.

'Come on now, Mum, put that down. And you'd better leave, Gwen,' said Helen, trying to grab the condiment from her mother's hand.

'I've said what I came to say,' said Gwen. 'But you all saw what she's like; she'd raise her hand against a saint would Myfanwy Jones, and I know for a fact she has done on many an occasion. The Lord is watching you, Myfanwy, and he sees into your soul.'

'And he knows how filthy yours is,' snapped Nan.

The chatter began to swell, as people returned to their drinks, with plenty of fresh topics for conversation. Helen steered her mother toward the bottom of the stairs, and encouraged her to go up to her bedroom for a rest.

Nan was having none of it. 'I won't let that woman drive me from my own pub. Not ever. I didn't back then, and I won't now.'

A young woman, dressed entirely in shades of red, ran into the pub screaming, 'There's an old woman who's collapsed. My phone won't work. Someone phone 999. And let's get her off the road and onto a seat in here!'

It took an hour for the paramedics to arrive. Word spread quickly that they suspected a stroke. When they finally took Gwen away, Nan said prayers of thanks that the Good Lord had decided to punish Gwen for the terrible lies she'd shouted at her in the pub that day, and for her terrible deceit and betrayal all those years ago.

It had almost been worth the wait.

31st March

Evan

'Wake up Betty. You've got to see this.'

Betty Glover peeled open her eyes. 'Morning, Evan. What time is it? It's still dark.'

'It's almost seven. Well, almost six really, because we lost that hour last night when the clocks changed. Anyway – you've got to look at this. Where are your glasses?'

'Can't you just read it to me?' Evan could hear irritation in Betty's voice, which he was beginning to realize might be justified.

'Right,' he said abruptly. 'They've found Dean Hughes. In Scotland. Alive. It's all over the *Scottish Sunday Recorder*.'

Betty pushed herself up with her elbows, looking sleepy, and puzzled. 'Isn't he the bloke whose remains were found in Rhosddraig?'

'Exactly. But obviously not.' Evan was almost vibrating with excitement.

Betty sat upright, and rubbed her face. 'What in God's name are you talking about, Evan? Dean Hughes was the man they identified; they were his remains. Rakel told you. It's been in all the papers. It was a DNA match. How can he be in Scotland? Alive.'

'That's the thing; nobody understands it. It says here he left Swansea back in November and has been up in Scotland ever since. Living in a squat, largely stoned out of his mind, it seems. One of the reporters for the paper found him sleeping rough on the streets one night, recognized him from all the publicity, and got him into a rehab clinic at the newspaper's expense. They've been waiting until he'd cleaned up his act a bit to do this exposé.'

'They *waited*? How long?'

'See, I knew you'd get it. Yes, they *waited*. Couple of weeks, it looks like. They could be in hot water because of that; I'm not up on Scottish law, but I'm sure they must have something on the books about perverting the course of justice up there. We do down here. This is crucial evidence in a case where charges have been laid. How can the Crown Prosecution Service go ahead when the supposed victim is hale and hearty, and having his photo taken in a newspaper office in

Glasgow?' Evan suspected he was babbling, but he didn't care. 'This is incredible news.'

Betty pushed off the duvet and swung her feet out of bed. 'It's not going to look very good for those people in London who ID'd the victim, is it? I thought DNA was supposed to be reliable. How did they get it so wrong?'

Evan considered his wife's question. 'You're right, and I don't know. I'll phone Rakel, she might have some insights. I tell you what, I wouldn't like to be Ted Jenkins this morning.'

'Nor Liz,' called Betty as she headed for the bathroom.

'Nor Liz,' agreed Evan quietly.

He was still feeling bad about Liz; he'd invited her to come for coffee, to discuss the case, of course, but she'd declined. It had hurt him – not that he'd admitted as much . . . not even to Betty, though he suspected she knew anyway. She usually did.

He'd had a knot in his stomach every time he thought of how curtly he'd signed off from that last phone call with Liz. She didn't deserve it – he'd known he'd been putting her in a difficult position. He hadn't handled it at all well.

Poor Liz. She was a good sergeant. Betty was right – there'd be a huge amount of work for the whole team to do because of this revelation, and he knew a great deal of it would fall on Liz's shoulders.

'I'm going to put the kettle on,' called Betty at the top of the stairs. 'I'm up now, I might as well keep going. Are you coming down?'

'In a minute, love,' Evan replied. He sat on the bed rereading the facts that were going to be headlines for most of the news outlets for the next few days. He couldn't help but allow himself to think through what the team would be up to that day, how Jenkins would be reacting. Making his displeasure clear to the scientists in London to start with, he suspected, and when he'd done that, the team would gather to discuss two critical questions. If it wasn't Dean Hughes they'd found in Rhosddraig, then who was it? And how did Dean being alive affect their case against Aled Beynon?

Sadie

Church was so weird this morning. No one spoke to Nan, Mam, nor me when we got there, and the vicar's sermon was all about forgiving people.

He seemed to look at Nan a lot when he was talking, and he kept repeating a quote from Matthew 6. 'For if you forgive other people when they sin against you, your heavenly Father will also forgive you. But if you do not forgive others their sins, your Father will not forgive your sins.'

It sounds like Mrs Doasyouwouldbedoneby to me. Or The Lord's Prayer. Stupid.

The vicar said he'd been told by the doctor at the hospital that Aled's grannie might recover, given time; the hospital's keeping in touch with him, and he said he was going to go and visit her this afternoon. I thought she'd be dead by now.

Nan's hardly spoken at all since yesterday. She won't talk about what happened, she just purses her horrible, ugly mouth, and sucks on her cigarettes. I hate her. Everyone knows she did this to Aled's grannie. That's why the vicar gave the sermon he did, so Nan would know she should have been nicer. More Christian. Like she tries to make out she is. She's not.

Of course, everyone was talking about the news about the body, too. It was on the telly, in the papers, and everywhere online. I have to admit, I was always really confused about the Dean Hughes thing. Why did the police think it was him, if it wasn't? No one knows. No one's saying, anyway.

And what does it mean for Aled? I'm a bit worried now, because I've worked so hard with my Tweets to get people to believe Aled would have been right to kill Dean – not that he did, of course – but . . . now what?

I don't usually Tweet on a Sunday, because it's hard to get away to do it, but I've been scrolling through my feed, and a lot of @wrongboy10's followers are as confused as me. I don't know what it means. I don't know what to do. I wish I could ask Aled. Or even Mam – but I can't ask her about this.

What's really worrying me is that there are already lots of memes flying about where #wrongboy10 has been given a new meaning; it's being turned around to point out the police identified the wrong victim, not that Aled is the wrong boy to accuse. That's not good; I want everyone to stay focused on Aled being innocent, or at least having had a good reason to do it if they find him guilty.

That's not too much to hope for, is it? It's quite simple, really, though some of those reporters have been writing long, boring articles about how it's an impossible moral stance. But, there, what would they know?

Maybe if they find out who really died it'll make it easier for Aled to come home; after all, if it isn't the drug dealer who gave his mother the drugs that killed her, then why would Aled want them dead?

Of course . . . he hasn't even got a motive for doing it now. Maybe I could risk just one Tweet from home this afternoon. Or maybe, if I scroll carefully, I'll find someone who's saying what I'm thinking and I could Retweet that. That could start the ball rolling. Maybe Aled will be home before we know it.

But I'll have to be careful; Friar Lawrence says it perfectly in *Romeo and Juliet*, 'Wisely and slow; they stumble that run fast.'

Helen

The lunchtime crowd arrived later than usual, which didn't surprise Helen – it always did when the clocks sprang forward an hour; she'd allowed for it when planning the cooking times for the roasts.

What she hadn't expected was to get back from church so late.

She'd been delayed by a bit of an incident as the congregation had filed out, all greeted by Reverend Thomas at the door. Helen had always liked Llewellyn Thomas; he didn't stand for the politicking which was usual within any small church community, and made his views about inclusiveness and acceptance quite clear.

His sermon that morning had obviously been directed at her mother, whose argument with Gwen the previous day was widely recognized as being the reason for Gwen's collapse. Helen realized the entire sad event could have been avoided if only Gwen hadn't come to the pub, but it seemed churlish to point that out when the woman was lying in a hospital bed, flirting with death.

Nan Jones had been the 'housekeeper' at the church – tending to the heating, cleaning, floral decorations, and heading up the altar guild – for many years, but the hundreds of hours of work she'd put in apparently counted for nothing when her fellow villagers all decided they'd had their fill of Nan's acid tongue. Helen knew her mother should have had all her sympathy, but she admitted to herself she saw the point of view of the 'enough's enough' crowd.

However, even with the sensational news about the discovery of a living Dean Hughes, and having to put up with all the sideways glances at her mother, herself and her daughter, it was something else entirely that had kept Helen talking in the graveyard after the service.

When Mair Bevan approach her, Helen had assumed it was going to be to discuss something to do with the church, so it had been a surprise when Mair had whispered to her, 'You've got to get Nan to go and see Gwen in hospital, before it's too late. Those women need a heart-to-heart before one of them's gone. Neither of them should go to their grave with their feud on their conscience.'

'With *what* feud exactly on their conscience?' Helen had asked, never having had the faintest idea why her mother hated Gwen Beynon so much.

'Just tell your mother what I've said, and she'll know what I mean. They've told the vicar Gwen will recover, but you never know. Tell Nan to go to the hospital – quick, if she's got any sense. You should drive her – she'll need a shoulder to cry on when they've talked about it.'

'About *what*?' pressed Helen, but Mair hadn't been prepared to elaborate.

Helen admitted to herself she'd dawdled back to the pub, but when she got there it was full steam ahead, until the main rush had been dealt with. By four she knew she needed to put her feet up for half an hour. Helen went to her bedroom; she couldn't face her mother, and needed her own space for a little while.

Lying on her bed, staring at the ceiling she'd known since she was a child, and counting the spots of mold growing there, Helen tried to take stock of her life; it was a less than rosy picture. The previous night, during one of her now-frequent tantrums, Sadie had viciously accused her mother of living a tiny, pathetic life.

Helen finally took the time to give some thought to the barb, which she'd rejected out of hand when it had been flung at her. She admitted to herself that, in a way, her daughter was right; Helen's life – necessarily revolved around the pub, the village, and the church, with trips to the wholesaler's in Gorseinon, the market in Swansea, and Alis's shop across the road thrown in to spice things up. She hadn't so much as met anyone for a drink since the previous year, and that coffee she'd had with Betty Glover seemed like a lifetime ago.

Helen almost chuckled at that recollection; it had only been about six weeks since she'd received the card from Bob, which was what had set her off jabbering at the poor woman. She still felt bad about that; she'd basically used Betty's good nature to extract a free therapy session from her. Though, truthfully, she had felt a great deal better after having let off a bit of steam that day.

Helen still wondered if Betty had been right – that going for a few formal sessions would help her, but then she reassured herself nothing else had happened, and she was coping very well; she'd been using techniques she'd learned during her previous brief stint of therapy, and had now more or less stopped jumping every time the phone rang, or when she half-saw someone out of the corner of her eye who looked vaguely like her ex-husband. She was much calmer now.

But Helen wasn't back to 'normal', she knew that. And it seemed as though any little thing could throw her off kilter; like the way Sadie was behaving, or the way her mother was acting. In Sadie's case, Helen knew it was because the girl was working all hours to get ready for her exams.

As for her mother? She had no idea what was up with her. Yes, she was getting older; yes, she suffered a fair amount of pain because of the hard work she'd done for decades in the pub; yes, she'd always had a bee in her bonnet about Gwen Beynon. But the past couple of months had been completely different; or maybe it was just since they'd found that card from Aled to Sadie . . . her mother had gone totally over the top about it.

It had all come to a head with the debacle and near-tragedy the previous day, and now there was this cryptic message for her mother from Mair. What on earth had prompted Nan to call Gwen a whore? Why did Mair think the two women needed to talk? It was a real puzzle.

Helen sat up, not feeling terribly relaxed anymore. She had to talk to her mother; she didn't know what Mair had meant by her comment, but was convinced it was important, so she should pass it on. Having been a private, rather solitary child, and – other than those years with Bob – mainly a solitary adult, Helen wasn't one to wade into things. Her soul told her to keep quiet, keep her head down, and do all she could to allow life to move along at a regular pace, with no confrontations or conflict.

But maybe now was the time to insert herself into her mother's life a little more forcefully. She was so lucky with Sadie; she was such a good girl, really. Maybe it was time to focus on her mum.

Once Aled was released, she knew Sadie would be happier; it was bound to weigh on her – even if they were only good friends. Helen had noticed that Stew Wingfield had also all but hidden himself away in his family home – he was another friend of Aled being affected by the whole thing. The Valentine's card from Aled had been sweet, not passionate – Helen was sure it was just a bit of an infatuation Sadie was feeling; few things were as attractive to a young girl as an unjustly accused boy.

Helen got up off the creaking bed, convinced she knew her daughter well enough to be able to give her attention to her mother for a little while. She straightened her cardigan, smoothed down her jeans, and headed for her mother's room. It was time for her to pass on Mair's message – and weather whatever storm might present itself.

Evan

The tension crackled in Liz Stanley's voice. 'I know it's late, but could I come to see you? Informally.'

Evan hesitated for a full half a second before saying, 'Of course. When?'

'I'll be there in a few minutes. Okay?'

'Okay.' He hung up.

Betty called from the kitchen, 'Who was that, at this hour?'

Evan cleared his throat. 'Liz. She's on her way over. Needs to talk, by the sound of it. You want to join us?'

His wife stuck her head into the sitting room. 'It's up to you. Do you mind?'

Evan stood, and the couple hugged. 'God, I love you, woman. You're as intrigued by all this as I am, aren't you? Please admit it. Even if only to make me feel better.'

As Betty pulled back, he could see the love in her eyes. 'You know I am. And that's the truth. I had no idea how frustrating it would be to know only as much about an investigation as the rest of the world – at least, about an investigation I feel is "ours".'

Evan kissed her on the forehead, just as the front doorbell rang. 'I'll get it. Maybe you could stick the kettle on? I'll put money on Liz fancying a cup of something.'

'Will do. Don't keep her waiting.'

Liz Stanley entered the Glover household like a whirlwind. Evan recognized the exhaustion etched into her brow and carried beneath her eyes; he'd been there a hundred times, dog-tired, but needing to push on to get . . . somewhere.

With tea and biscuits on the table between them, Liz's tablet fired up, and no need for niceties, Evan gave his old sergeant the chance to get right to it. 'Say what you want, don't say what you can't. You lead,' he said.

Liz nodded. 'Thanks. I won't say much that either hasn't already been – or very soon will be – in the press. But I would welcome the chance to talk it all through with someone whose opinion I value, and who understands the way these things can go, and should go. I'm also pleased you're here, Betty, because your input would be valuable too. An insightful outsider. But nothing goes beyond these walls, right?'

Evan and Betty agreed.

'Thanks. I just needed to say the words. Quick update: we got the news about Hughes yesterday, twenty-four hours before they made it public, so he's already been brought down from Scotland for questioning, and the Super's looking into prosecuting the newspaper up there for keeping him under wraps. Of course, the people at the lab in London are falling over themselves to remind us they warned us the DNA they found was badly degraded; our own PR people are becoming apoplectic from having to deal with the social media meltdown. Now you're up to date on the big picture.' She beamed manically at the Glovers.

Evan said, 'Have a custard cream, it'll help.' He winked.

'If only,' said Liz, taking one anyway. 'So it obviously wasn't Dean bloody Hughes on that hillside in Rhosddraig – a village I now know almost as well as I know my own flat, thank you very much. I cannot wait to never have to go back to the damned place again, however sodding beautiful it might be. So whose body do we have in tiny little bits? You – and the entire world – wants to know. So we start with the scientists – because they deserve a second chance, don't they?'

She paused to roll her eyes and sigh away her frustration. 'So they suggest a male Hughes sibling. Only thing is, Dean insists he hasn't got any. All his known associates agree – not a sniff of any brothers. Of course, Jenkins is running around screaming at everyone all the time, and seems to have lost the ability to even string two sensible thoughts together within one sentence. He's getting all sorts of heat from upstairs, and he's making damned sure every drop of crap landing on his head is pushed downhill, pronto. So I'm up to my neck in it.'

'Have another custard cream,' said Evan, 'and have some of that tea while it's hot.'

Liz followed instructions, brushing biscuit crumbs off her tablet. 'It's been a slog. I spoke to Dean's mother. Dear God what a mess. How she's alive, I don't know; only in her forties, looks twenty years older. Rough life, in every sense. Anyway, it's quite clear to me from the minute I raise the topic that she knows who Dean's father is, even though she's never made the information known to Dean himself, nor anyone else for that matter. I had to get Jenkins to leave the interview, because his shrill pronouncements about the importance of her telling us the truth were not getting the woman to give us what we needed.' Liz sighed. 'He's bloody useless dealing with women, did you know that?'

Evan nodded. 'I did. Just not got that empathy gene, has he? Need a situation that calls for planning an inquiry, or delegating tasks, and he's great. Good man-manager, and I mean that literally, because he's never been too hot when it comes to overseeing female officers, or staff members.'

'Aware of that. Now,' said Liz heavily.

'And not the best interview technique in the business,' added Evan sadly. 'Not too bad when it's a male career criminal in one of our interview rooms, but out there – in the real world – face to face with people whose cooperation we need, not too good. It's something everyone seems to know about him, but no one seems to be able to change – or help him to change, in any case.'

'Exactly,' replied Liz, allowing herself a moment to stretch her arms above her head. Rubbing her scalp with her fingertips, she continued, 'I finally got what we needed out of her about half an hour after he'd left. Trouble is, it turns out that Dean's father was injured in a stabbing several years back, then disappeared. So the remains could, in fact, be the father. She also claimed to not know if he'd had any more children, but she knew the name of the person she believed was his girlfriend at the time of his disappearance. Got the team to trace her, while also pulling out all the information we had on him – which turned out to be fairly substantial.'

'Anyone I might know?' asked Evan, trying to be helpful.

'Iolo Rees, from Mayhill. Know him? Drugs, car theft, bit of moving of stolen goods, too many drunk and disorderlies to list.'

Evan could see the bloke's face in his mind's eye, and couldn't help but smile. 'Oh yes, I remember Iolo Rees. Ugly looking bugger, with a many-times broken nose. Tattoos up to his chin. Great breeding stock, I'm sure.'

'Seems so.' Liz looked disgusted. 'Anyway, I went to talk to the last-known girlfriend – who's now installed in an ex-council house with three bedrooms and a view of Swansea Bay most people would kill for, because she's up on Pantycelyn Road, isn't she? Whereas I work my backside off on behalf of people like her, and have a one-bedroom flat with a view of a car park, which I've hardly seen for the past two weeks.'

Evan wanted to reach out and give Liz a hug; had she been a friend, rather than an ex-colleague, he'd have done it. Luckily, it seemed he and Betty were experiencing their weird telepathic connection again, because his wife did exactly what he'd wanted to do. Which meant she was the one shrugged off by Stanley.

'Sorry,' said Liz, looking a little embarrassed, 'Not a big hugger. But I shouldn't rant. I wouldn't want her life, so I shouldn't envy her view.' Evan was glad to see her crack a smile. 'So she's now got three kids, which she claims are all her current boyfriend's, but I don't see how that can be, given the timeframe. The main thing is, the quantity of the skeletal remains found tell us we're looking for an adult male, and this girl was just that – a girl – so not old enough to have given birth to any child that would have had the time to grow to adulthood.'

'So Dean Hughes is telling the truth when he says he has no male siblings?' Betty asked. Evan noticed the way her hand was creeping toward the plate of biscuits.

'As far as we could tell at that stage, yes. But I got a phone call around three this afternoon from a neighbor of the last-known girlfriend; it seems the word got around about our inquiries, and I spent an interesting hour late this afternoon with a woman who lives in a council house in Clase, who admitted she'd had a son with Iolo Rees. She hasn't seen the child since approximately last October – sometime. She couldn't recall exactly when.'

Liz held up her hand to fend off questions.

She continued, 'The son is nineteen, and his mother said had the right to live his own life. She assumed he'd found himself a bedsit somewhere. He didn't need to tell her, he was all grown up. She didn't imagine he was missing, just getting on with his life. She mentioned that several times. She also added she was glad to see the back of him because she was sick of everyone staring at her if ever they were together. He has Down's Syndrome, which it seems she found an embarrassment. She and the kid used to live a couple of streets away from Dean and his mother in Townhill, until a few years before Iolo disappeared. This one knew about Dean and his mother, but told me – and I believe her – that Iolo made it absolutely clear to her that she was never to tell anyone that this kid was his, nor that they'd even had a kid together at all. Iolo Rees decided as soon as the boy was born that he didn't want anyone thinking he could have fathered him.'

Betty sounded annoyed. 'What about Social Services? Didn't anyone there notice the boy had disappeared? Surely they must have been involved with some sort of oversight process, even if he had left school. I know Careers Wales get involved around Year 9 to develop transition plans for children with Special Educational Needs, they must have spotted he wasn't around anymore. The Care Act should have kicked in.'

'The team's looking into that now . . . but we all know about the cracks through which some individuals can slip,' said Liz heavily. 'The mother? Said he did well on his own, had an integrated education, and didn't need much support. Used to get himself from A to B on buses, and was good at fending for himself.' She shook her head. 'She downplayed his challenges, possibly to cover her own shortcomings. Or maybe he really was as able to cope as she said. She also made it clear she didn't like to be seen with him in public. Awful.'

'So whose remains are they? Iolo, or Iolo's other son?' asked Betty.

Liz sighed. 'I've gathered an assortment of items that might yield DNA from this son – his name is, or possibly *was*, James Powell. Seems Iolo Rees had a thing about James Dean, hence his two sons' names. Also got some stuff from Iolo's last known address. Not much. Everything is on its way to the lab as we speak.' She checked her watch. 'Nope, it's been there for some time, already. Needless to say, the specialists there understand how critical it is for us to receive fast and accurate responses from them on this one. So I'm waiting for a call. What they've said they'll do is to get as many of the microscopic bits of DNA they've gathered from the remains – and that they are allowed to use, because they can't use it all, of course – to be able to aim for a more accurate match this time. They have, however, pointed out yet again – and in writing to every officer with the tiniest amount of braid on his or her epaulettes – that the fire damage to the remains still means they only have access to compromised samples for comparison. The talk in our team is that this time it might be a toss-up if the powers that be will even accept their findings.'

Evan poured some over-brewed, cool tea for everyone, and they all sipped in silence for a few moments.

'Okay,' he said, 'the victim's identity aside, and any potential motive issues that arise therefrom, do you still think the Beynon boy did it?'

Liz clasped her hands together, her knuckles whitening; she rocked a little in her chair, then leaned forward and spoke softly. 'You see, Evan, that's the problem, I've never been truly convinced he did it at all. But I'm just a DS. What can I do?'

'You don't think he did it?' said Betty sharply. 'Why not?'

Liz sipped her cold tea, placed her mug in the center of the coaster, then threw Evan a puzzling glance. 'I'm afraid it's all your fault, sir,' she said, a twinkle in her eye.

Evan winked. 'No "sir" here, please.' But he understood. 'You don't think he *could* have done it, do you? You can see he might have had the means, the opportunity – and, now that it's possibly the brother or the father of the dealer he thinks of as having killed his mother, maybe he still had the motivation – but you just don't see *this* suspect committing *this* crime, do you? Your gut's telling you something's wrong, isn't it?'

Liz nodded. She rubbed her pink-veined eyes. 'Yes, *Evan,* and you're the one who told me many times that instinct isn't something an officer ignores – it's a critical weapon in our detecting arsenal. And I've taken that to heart. I have watched Aled Beynon sit silently in our interview rooms for hours on end. He's not detached, in the way someone with a mental incapacity would be, nor in the way someone with a psychopathic or sociopathic bent would be – he's just calm, and choosing to not speak up. I can't square that with the sort of person who could be capable of doing what was done to the victim.'

She paused, but Evan knew she hadn't finished. She was weighing exactly what to say next. 'Jenkins won't listen to me. I'm just a DS, why would he? I could possibly imagine someone of Aled's age acting upon an understandable level of antagonism toward either Dean, or even possibly Dean's brother or father, and maybe even getting themselves fired up with alcohol or drugs to such an extent they might lash out at someone. That, I could go with – but only at a push in Aled's case. But to do what was done to that body? A brutal process that must have taken hours of sustained venom, determination, and effort? No.'

Betty leaned forward, rapt. 'Explain Aled's demeanor to me, if you can, would you, Liz? What's he like when you're talking to him? You say not distant . . . what do you mean?'

Liz nodded. 'He's hearing us, listening even, but there are no telltale signs or signals coming off him when I, or Jenkins, or anyone else, proposes a theory of the crime to him. It's almost as though he's only half in the room with us, but not in an absent way.'

Liz picked up a biscuit and crunched into it with what Evan could tell was frustration at her own inadequacies.

She pressed on. 'I don't know what else to say, it's hard to explain. He's there, but not. He's calm, but his hands . . . you know how suspects can get when they're being questioned, Evan?' He nodded. 'Well the hands are always a dead giveaway; picking at the sides of their nails, peeling off ragged edges, that sort of thing. Well it's like he's almost dancing with his; he sits there silently, but his hands are constantly moving, in an almost balletic way.'

Evan spotted his wife's eyes gleaming as she hissed, 'I wish I could spend just an hour with him. Maybe then I'd understand.'

Evan decided to try to help. 'Has Aled been professionally examined? To establish that he's fit to stand trial?'

A wry chuckle escaped from Liz as she replied, 'Yes, he has. Twice. First at his solicitor's insistence, then his new QC's. His solicitor's doing a fair job for him – considering. You know her – Carol Morgan.'

Evan knew her well; a respected representative of the often irretrievably guilty. 'Legal Aid?' Liz nodded. 'One of the better ones. How's she coping with all this?'

Liz raked her hands through her hair; Evan and Betty exchanged a smile, both suspecting she'd picked up the habit from her old boss. 'She's spitting nails. Livid he won't talk, won't give her anything to work with. She did perk up a bit when Olivia Kitchener swept in from London to take over the case. Carol thinks it's going to be a feather in her cap to work with such a high-profile QC. But I'm not so sure.'

Evan said, 'I'm guessing Aled's team has asked for the charges to be dropped – given Dean Hughes's miraculous "resurrection".'

Liz's smile showed how tired she was. 'All over it. Yesterday. CPS is going for lesser charges associated with preventing a burial and obstructing the coroner – which means he could still go to prison for life. They can prove what was done to the body after death, and will use key pieces of evidence we've gathered to seek to prove it was Aled who did it. Whomever the remains might once have been. They also want us to keep trying to prove murder, but I can't see that happening, with no time or cause of death forthcoming.'

'I bet the legal folks all enjoyed working through the weekend,' said Evan with a raised eyebrow.

'Don't we all,' replied Liz dryly. 'They've brought the trial forward, too. Cardiff Crown Court, Monday 8th April.'

'That's fast,' said Evan.

Liz nodded. 'Yes, we've got to shift. Since we received the news about Dean being alive, Jenkins has been all at sea. He's even worse now, given what we've discovered today. We've currently got two potential alternatives to Dean Hughes, both family relatives, and we're rudderless, as a team.'

Evan felt sorry for her; Liz looked to be close to the end of her tether. 'It's all going to crap. You've seen what the press have done with this, haven't you? Any opportunity to point out how rubbish the police are at anything, and they'll take it. Well, this time we've let ourselves, and the victim, down, so maybe we deserve it. The people baying that Aled is the "wrong boy" are having a field day – though I'll admit some of them seem as confused as the rest of us, since Dean turned up alive.'

'The case is certainly filling the media at the moment,' observed Betty.

'It is,' chorused Liz and Evan, both in the same helpless tone. They all managed a smile.

'So, what's next?' asked Evan, doing his best to not tell Liz what he thought should happen.

Liz smiled. 'That's why I'm here. For some tips from my old boss. So?'

Evan glanced at Betty, who was clearly contemplating the last biscuit on the plate – or else avoiding his gaze.

'If you're sure . . .' Evan gave Liz a chance to back out. She nodded, eagerly. 'Okay – I'd be all over the father and the brother. Treat as missing persons, with utmost urgency to locate. Friends and associates, other jurisdictions, you know the drill. If the lab in London says the remains definitely belong to either one, you don't want egg all over you if he shows up alive in a couple of weeks' time. Like Dean did.'

'We're highly focused on those aspects,' replied Liz. 'Even DCI Jenkins knew that was a good idea.'

'Also, if the thought was that Dean was targeted by Aled because of his drug dealing, seek to unearth any connections between James and Aled, or Iolo and Aled.'

'Agreed, and doing it.'

'And . . .?' Evan knew Liz was keen to add something, so opened a door for her, as he always had done.

'I think we should be spending more time looking into Aled Beynon's entire background. Jenkins called a halt when he found the Dean Hughes connection to the death of Aled's mother, Jackie.'

Evan gave the idea some thought. 'Yes, right. And you might look into the mother herself a bit more, too. If Jenkins is pinning his hopes on Aled Beynon and a link to his mother's overdose, you could do worse than understand what led to that, other than just a bad batch of Spice. Under what specific circumstances did she die? As I told you, I wasn't on that case.'

Liz dropped her head into her hands. 'She was scooped up off Swansea Kingsway and pronounced dead. The case was pursued only as far as Dean Hughes, and charges against him were dropped.'

'Dead end?'

'Dead end, at the moment. But you're right – that whole avenue should be pursued. There are too many unanswered questions at this point.'

'*Why* is always the most important question to ask,' said Evan, frustrated that he wouldn't be the one asking the questions himself, nor the one finding the answers.

1st April

Nan

Nan felt a certain amount of pride in her recent achievements; she'd entertained reporters when they'd needed it, fed them bits of information and gossip as necessary, and had made sure she'd been available whenever they wanted to reach her either on her pub or private phone, or in person.

It was all paying off.

Not that she wanted to be the center of attention or anything like that, she just wanted to boost business while she had the opportunity to do so.

Who'd have imagined that a dead body up on the hill would have still proved so lucrative after all these months? The influx of curious visitors to The Dragon's Head wasn't as noticeable on a Monday morning as it was at the weekends, but it was still enough to allow profits to be substantially higher than she might have expected for the time of year.

All that being said, she was glad to have a quieter day; she'd been working too hard, that must be why she was so tired, she told herself. She'd taken Helen's advice, for once; having a few lie-downs during the day was helping her keep her overall energy levels up, and she was beginning to like the new pattern of activity and rest she'd begun a couple of days earlier.

Besides, she needed her wits about her when she was in the pub itself; there were too many people making smart aleck remarks about her recent run-in with Gwen Beynon – all of whom needed to be brought down a peg or two – for her to not be feeling up to snuff.

Nan felt restless lying on her bed, so she got up and looked out of the window, toward the beach below.

She lit a cigarette and opened the latch of the small casement, allowing the fresh breeze in, and the smoke out.

The rain had stopped hours earlier, and there was a true touch of spring in the air. As she looked up from the beach, and across to the hillside, the sharp black lines of the Devil's Table and the Concubine's Pillow made her shiver.

What was it about them that she hated so much? Was it all the stories about pagan sacrifices? Doors to the underworld? They were just creepy.

She reckoned she'd spent years of her life, in total, staring at them, the beach, and the sea, through the same small window frame. She'd lived in the pub her entire life, but she'd been many different people during that time: child, young woman, bride, wife, mother, grandmother.

And a victim of men's whims at every stage.

Her father had been a brute, to both her and her mother.

Her husband? Well, Jack's true nature had come as a complete shock to her. Her son-in-law had been a total idiot, and now it seemed this Aled Beynon was making her Sadie's life – and her life, by extension – a complete misery.

Bloody men.

She'd seen the looks passing between Sadie and Aled, but hadn't thought too much of it; they were both so young. But she shouldn't have allowed him under her roof. Not with him coming from the stock he did.

She should have known better.

Though she'd enjoyed having him under her power.

At least she'd done her best to make everyone see sense since the police had hauled him in. Once they found out who it had really been up there, dead, on the hill, she knew it would be easy for her to restart the conversations about how he was bound to have done it.

She stubbed out her cigarette and took one of her special tablets. She hoped just one would get her through until after the Corries left.

As she pushed the plastic container into the drawer she wondered if she was running a bit short. She'd have to talk the doctor into writing her another prescription. If she couldn't collect them herself from the chemist without Helen seeing what she was doing, she'd get them delivered to Mair like she had in the past, and pick them up from there.

She didn't want Helen to know she needed such strong tablets; she was alright with her daughter seeing her down a couple of over-the-counter pills now and again, but Solpadols? Everyone knew they had a lot of codeine in them, and she didn't want Helen to worry.

Sadie

This is a nightmare. Everything's coming apart.

@wrongboy10 is getting trolled now, and by some really horrible people. I've hardly Tweeted; I don't know what to say.

Even my silence is being condemned.

Why did the stupid police get it wrong?

It was all going so well.

Now – who knows?

I promised Aled I'd help him. 'Don't say anything,' I told him. And I know he hasn't, because if he'd talked, he wouldn't still be in prison.

But now I'm wondering if it's my fault he's not out yet; the telly said he might have been refused bail when they dropped the murder charge because it would be seen as special treatment for a high profile case.

I thought I was doing the best I could to help him, by making his case well-known.

But now?

Now I'm not so sure it's a good thing after all.

What if he thinks I've let him down?

He mustn't think that.

He wouldn't like that, and he's not nice to me when he thinks I've done something stupid, or not been as helpful as I could be.

He's no more cross with me than I deserve, of course, and he always apologizes afterwards – which is lovely.

I don't know why Mrs Lee has us all sitting here in the dark watching this boring TV program about Verona; she said it'll let us see what the real setting for *Romeo and Juliet* is like, but it's got a commentator who's trying to make it all so interesting for 'young people' that he's acting like a complete arse. We don't need some hyperactive twat prancing about in tights to allow us to work out there's a balcony on a building.

Shoot me now.

At least I have a study period after this, and I'll have enough time to get to the library and back. I'll try to Tweet some things that will balance all the nastiness swirling around Aled's name.

I know he'll love me all the more for it.

2nd April

Helen

'Of course Agata will be able to cope on her own in the pub, Mum.' Helen forced her voice to sound patient. 'She's perfectly capable, and this was the only time available to see the doctor. You were lucky to get in today at all.'

'You used to be able to see a doctor whenever you wanted.' Her mother's voice was jagged. 'You shouldn't have to be phoning them up at eight o'clock in the morning, and having to hang on for ages, just to get an appointment. We will get there on time, won't we? Can't you drive faster?'

Helen understood that her mother needed to see the doctor, and was usually only too happy to drive her to the surgery, but this morning, of all mornings, she'd wanted to be able to talk to Sadie before she went off to school, rather than hanging on the phone on her mother's behalf.

Something was wrong with her daughter, she could tell. She'd heard crying during the night, and that wasn't like Sadie. What had her really worried was that she'd been sent away from a bedroom door her daughter had wedged shut with a chair. Sadie had never done that before.

Torn between her mother and her daughter, Helen didn't seem to be able to be everything either of them needed. She was failing them both.

'Look out!' shouted Nan.

Helen swerved just in time to avoid an oncoming motorcyclist who'd cut a corner on the narrow, winding road. She automatically stretched her arm across her mother's body as they crunched to a halt in a gated gap in the hedge.

'Don't do that; I've got my seatbelt on. And when I said go faster, I didn't mean kill us both,' screamed her mother.

'Sorry, Mum,' was all Helen had the energy to squeak out. She put the car into gear and they continued toward the doctor's surgery in Killay. The lanes opened out, then they rattled over the familiar cattle grid at the edge of Fairwood Common. Finally they were driving past the large semis and even more impressive detached homes of the aspirational area of Killay. At least, that was how Helen had always thought of the place.

'About time,' was all Nan said as she extricated herself from the seatbelt when Helen had parked. 'Bloody ridiculous we have to come all this way, when there used to be a perfectly good doctor in Lower Middleford.'

'Consolidation of resources, Mum,' said Helen as she followed her mother inside.

'My back's too bad for me to stand. You go to the counter and tell them I'm here, I'll get us some seats,' said Nan.

'I'll check you in, but I won't wait with you, Mum. I thought I'd pop to the shops and pick up a few bits and pieces while I'm here – there's that place with the nice delicatessen just across the road. I won't be long. Besides, you never want me in there with you and the doctor, do you? You prefer it to be just the two of you.'

Helen hated the way her mother looked at her; disappointment, disapproval, and disdain, all rolled into one withering glance. 'Oh,' was all her mother said. The single syllable communicated volumes.

Having done her duty, Helen left the small building that housed the offices for three doctors, two nurses and a dispensing chemist; it was only about five years old and already the exterior finishes were peeling and looking terribly sorry for themselves. At least there was parking for a dozen cars, which was helpful, given that the rest of Killay offered very few opportunities.

She crossed the busy road with care and patience, and allowed herself to enjoy her little bit of peace and quiet. She browsed the selection of salamis, cold cuts, and cheeses with a smile on her face; she imagined picnics on the hilltops at Rhosddraig with her happy, thriving daughter, her generous mother, and – *if only* – her wonderful father. In her fantasy she was a size ten, and her skin glowed with youthful vitality. Bob had no place in the scenario in her head.

'Fancy a bit of that honey roasted ham? I'll cut it as thick or thin as you like, fresh.'

Helen looked into the face of the boy wearing a striped apron, a straw boater set at a jaunty angle, and a smile revealing some questionable teeth. He looked to be about twelve, but she told herself he was probably in his twenties. She wondered if this was the future his mother had envisaged for him. Was this the sort of thing Sadie would end up doing for a living – slicing meats to order behind a counter in Killay? Surely not. She was going to get her A level grades, get into university, and make something of herself.

'Not the ham then,' said the boy, reacting to Helen's hesitation. 'Anything else appealing to you? The roast turkey's lovely, or maybe something a bit spicy?' He held a large salami dotted with peppercorns and chili toward her.

Come on Helen, she told herself. 'Two hundreds grams of the spicy salami, please, and do you have any *cacciatore* sausage?'

The boy's grin grew. 'Indeed I do.' He reached across the counter and pointed to pre-packaged small salamis. 'Just pop them in your basket yourself, while I cut this. Thick or thin?'

'Very thin, please,' replied Helen. She had to ration herself with such fat-laden treats.

As she watched him work, he did his best to engage her. 'From around here, are you?'

'Rhosddraig.'

His eyes strayed from the slicer, opening wide. 'Oh, you're in the middle of it all then, aren't you? All that scandal about that gruesome dead body, the choirboy who did it, and all that. It must be very exciting. They still don't know who it was he killed, do they? Weird that other bloke turning up alive after all. Do you know the lad who did it?'

Helen sighed. 'Yes . . . no. We don't know if he *did* do it.'

The expression on the boy's face told Helen he harbored no doubt on the matter. 'Yes. Okay. So, what's he really like then? The telly and the papers would have us believe he's some sort of saint. On a mission to rid South Wales of drug dealers, is he?'

'Nobody's one hundred percent good. Are you?'

The boy blushed. 'Well, no, not all the time. Though my mam would kill anyone who said so.'

'That's what mothers are for,' said Helen, taking her wrapped meat and heading for the till.

That's what mothers are supposed to be for, she thought as she queued behind a woman who seemed to be buying a year's supply of tinned steak and kidney pies.

Trust me to get a mother who wouldn't stand up for me in a strong wind, let alone if I was really in trouble. I have to be a mother who supports her child. I'll make sure I talk to Sadie tonight. Mum can cope with just Agata helping her for an hour or two.

Betty

The clutter piled on the little landing at the top of the stairs was a bit of a pain, but Betty didn't mind it too much – both she and Evan were still lithe enough to circumnavigate it without the risk of doing too much damage. They'd both agreed they wouldn't just dump it all back into the unused bedroom when they had the space, but would give it a good going through, and keep as little as possible, while chucking out as much as they could, and donating the rest to charity.

The second of the two spare rooms was no longer spare; the bed had become a seating area, the sliding wardrobe doors a noticeboard, and the chest of drawers a receptacle for folders full of papers. Evan's laptop and printer were set up on the dressing table, its somewhat rickety stool having been replaced with a dining chair from downstairs. To all intents and purposes the Glovers now had their very own murder case management room.

Betty had erected a collapsible card table she'd inherited from her grandmother, via her mum, in a corner, to allow for the constant supply of tea and coffee to be kept away from any electrical items. As she carefully placed a fresh pot and full jug of milk in the exact center of the table – because it wobbled a bit – she wondered how long the remains in Rhosddraig would upend their lives.

She told herself that what she and her husband were doing was quite normal, considering their backgrounds.

Evan looked up from his screen. 'Did you know that Aled Beynon got some of the highest marks in Wales for his chemistry GCSE? Won a prize for it, no less. Yet he still went on to do English, History, and Film Studies for his A levels.'

Betty had to admit she hadn't known that.

'Makes you wonder, doesn't it,' mused her husband, scratching his head with both hands. 'Sounds to me like he's a bright boy who took options that required less effort on his part. I mean, come on – Film Studies? What sort of an A level is that when it's at home?'

Betty had settled into her new role by now – the level-headed psychologist who listened, baited and parried, and provided helpful insights. 'Maybe he wants to work in the world of film-making at some point? English and History would play into being able to understand and work with screenplays and settings, while the Film Studies would furnish him with the technical vocabulary he'd need, and a basic understanding of the history and business of film. That might be it.'

Evan had a glint in his eye when he replied, 'Or else he picked subjects he thought he could coast through, allowing him more time to work to make money, and surf whenever he wants.'

Betty smiled. 'Or there's that, yes.'

'But why, Betty? Why has he been working ever since he was legally allowed to? His grandmother owns their home outright – must do, it's been in the family for generations. We both know what a difference no mortgage makes.'

Betty sat on the bed and sipped her tea while her husband looked at his with trepidation. 'Blow on it,' she said, 'it'll cool off in a minute. And what if Gwen Beynon can't get by on just a pension, when it's her and him? That can't be easy. Maybe the boy just wanted to help out.'

'Making home deliveries of take-away food on a bicycle is a weird way to help out. Couldn't he have got a proper job in a shop, or something?'

'You do know this isn't 1963, don't you?' retorted Betty.

Evan finally dared a sip of steaming tea. 'I don't know what you mean,' he said, sounding a little hurt.

'The gig economy, you know. People having several jobs, all at the same time. Zero hour contracts have made it much more appealing. After all, if you have no idea how many hours you'll be asked to work and therefore paid for, with a so-called "real" job these days, why not become your own manager and rent yourself out to the highest bidder, with the best hours for you, so you know how much money you'll have coming in? It makes sense to me.'

'It makes sense to you because that's been the shape of your career,' said Evan, wearing his sulky expression. 'I've put in the hours over the years, alright, and many of them paid as overtime – though I certainly haven't been paid for all the hours I've worked.'

'Especially if you count the sleepless ones, when you were worrying about a case so much you just tossed and turned in bed,' added Betty, glad at least that was – theoretically – behind them.

'And of course I understand the gig economy. Mind you, I have to admit an awful lot of the people I've run up against during my career have been of the "no visible source of income" brigade. So I understand the jobs' market, and the "too idle or bent to want to even try to earn an honest living" lot. And as for my working life? Well, that's behind me, now.' Evan sounded glum. 'This is now my "hobby", I suppose. So – why the life he's lived? Where has all the money gone?'

'Wetsuits and surfboards, I'd say,' replied Betty. 'Look at those photos of him on social media – the kit he's wearing would have set him back a bit, I'd say – though I admit I know nothing about how much all that stuff really costs. Maybe he would buy second-hand gear? I don't know. Anyway, I bet a state pension wouldn't cover that sort of outlay. I'm saying he works so he can play.'

'Good psychology,' said Evan with a grin.

'I thank you,' mugged Betty, using her best Arthur Askey impersonation. 'Would it help if I Googled the stuff he's wearing and so forth in these photos? I could get some idea of the money involved.'

'Thanks, love,' replied her husband softly, 'that would be useful input.'

Ten minutes later Betty was feeling quite gleeful. 'In just this couple of dozen photos, taken over the past year, he's wearing – or holding – at least two and a half thousand pounds' worth of surfy stuff. That's without all the clothing he's wearing, and the bicycle he's got. If you look closely, you'll notice he's rarely in the same outfit twice, and all the brands he's wearing are top of the line, despite the fact they look as though he's slept in them.'

Evan looked at Betty's figures and the photos she'd highlighted from Aled's social media accounts; he began working out some numbers on his notepad. 'So if he's getting a fiver an hour, he could get that money together in a year – allowing for ten hours' work a week. Doable.'

Betty sighed, grudgingly accepting his point. 'Yes, just, but I still think I'm onto something; everything he's holding and wearing is the newest design, or the latest pattern. Taking everything into account, it all comes in at not far short of about ten grand in the past year or so. That's a lot of money, Evan.'

'Maybe he worked more hours in the summer holidays last year, and the year before. He could have saved up, I suppose.'

'But he doesn't work more in the summer, does he? He's always out on his beloved boards,' replied Betty, her eyes sparkling. She hoped she'd done something truly useful.

'Maybe you really are onto something. Let's come back to that,' said her husband, downing his tea in two gulps. 'Now, back to the timeline.'

'Right,' said Betty, focusing her attention on the papers stuck to the wardrobe doors. Her husband had marked known points in time on a continuous line, with queries and facts, evidence and witnesses noted above and below the critical points. In the voids he'd attached various colors of sticky notes with key words and questions.

Betty was enjoying seeing her husband work; she wondered if this was a true representation of how he'd been during his career, albeit now on a smaller stage and with just her as both workforce and audience. With one hand stuffed into his back pocket, the other raking through his hair, Evan had a pen poking out of the corner of his mouth which he chewed – giving her cause for concern. She didn't mention it.

Evan's voice resonated within the small space, and Betty noted how weird the whole set-up was, in a room where the wallpaper was covered with yellow roses, originally selected because they were her now-late mother's favorite flowers.

Evan paced, to the extent he could. 'A credible witness saw a fire at the spot where the remains were discovered at some time around midnight, on November 5th. This is now the accepted time of the burning, though we cannot be certain the victim hadn't been possibly dead for some time before that, the body secreted, then burned and left where it was found.'

Betty said, 'But how would you get the body from A to B without being seen? And just *how*? A body is heavy. Could Aled have managed it alone? Or could anyone manage it alone, come to that?'

Evan swung around. 'Hang on.'

Betty nodded, and clamped her lips together.

Evan continued, 'There was an unusually high level of coming and going in the village on the night of the 5th November due to the Guy Fawkes celebrations at The Dragon's Head pub. That might have allowed for some unusual activities to have gone unnoticed – okay?' He winked. 'Remains were discovered on November 7th, but the initial ID wasn't given until January 30th. Aled Beynon is brought in for questioning under caution. Reason – the link with the supposed victim. He's released, due to lack of any concrete evidence. Witness statement comes in March 1st identifying Aled as being seen on his bicycle, fleeing the scene of the fire, and Liz identifies the source of the accelerant, to which he had access; he's charged and held. Cock-up in ID is discovered March 31st. New ID of remains as being those of James Powell, half-brother of Dean Hughes, publicly confirmed today; seems there's no sign of him anywhere, and they finally tracked down Iolo Rees alive – so the remains definitely aren't his. I should imagine Iolo's been questioned about having any other male offspring, and has said he hasn't any, or else they wouldn't have made this ID public. Aled Beynon is still Jenkins's prime suspect, according to the DCI's remarks in the press today.'

'Why?' asked Betty.

'Why what?'

'Why is Aled still the prime suspect? I know Ted said it, but I don't understand why he said it. Or even believes it.'

Evan answered immediately. 'One: the brotherly link to the drug dealer Aled believes killed his mother. Two: the eyewitness. Three: lamp oil from the church.'

Betty decided to give as good as she'd got. 'One: even Dean Hughes didn't know James Powell was his brother, so how on earth would Aled know? Two: Aled could have been out on his bicycle that night for any number of other reasons we don't know about. Three: I bet there are loads of people who could have got their hands on the lamp oil in that vestry. Vestries are like that.'

Evan sucked the end of his thumb, then said, 'If Aled was out and about that night on his bicycle for a perfectly innocent reason, we don't know about it because he's not saying – which, trust me – is incredibly unusual. I accept he *might* have now come up with an alibi, and that information hasn't made it into the media yet, but I'm going with him keeping up the silent act. As for the brother thing . . . yes, I agree with you. It's a problem. Do you have any ideas?'

Betty smiled. 'Well, maybe we should look at this the other way around.'

'Meaning?'

'We're looking at it as though the victim is Dean's half-brother – which he is, of course – but what if the link with Dean is just happenstance? What if James being dead is because he was the intended victim? Because he was who he was, not because he was Dean's brother.'

Evan's eyes narrowed. 'Good point. What do we know about James Powell? There's very little in the media about him yet. Though it's early days, I suppose, his name having only just been released.'

Betty's mind sorted through the issues. 'What life did James live? Where did he go? What did he do? With whom did he mix? The answer might be in there somewhere. We need to know more about the victim.'

Evan plopped down onto the chair at the dressing table. 'You're right on all points, and all your questions are good. Unfortunately, I don't know any of the answers. If only you were an eager team of subordinates, we'd get a lot more done around here. How about we both spend a bit of time finding out all we can about James Powell, online?'

Betty liked that idea. 'Agreed. I'll get my laptop fired up down in the front room, you stay here. I'll be back in half an hour.'

Thirty minutes later Betty rejoined her husband, feeling a little disappointed.

'I'll go first,' she said, 'not that it will take me long. It seems James wasn't overly active online, not in terms of social media, in any case. The photos of him I found show him as a beefy boy, usually smiling, but always a little apart from any group he's with; selfies with other people some way off, in the distance.'

'I saw that too,' said Evan. 'It's hard to tell if he's actually with the people in the background, isn't it?'

Betty nodded and continued, 'He went to school in Townhill, then to Mynyddbach Comprehensive when his mother moved to Clase, and didn't do too well academically – which isn't unusual for those with Down's Syndrome. Though it appears he did have a specific talent at which he excelled; most of his social media posts are of photographs he took. I don't mean the selfies, but "real" photos . . . which I would suggest is unusual, as I know that those with Down's Syndrome usually have less acute eyesight than those without it. I wondered if he possibly found telescopic lenses helped him see what he might have otherwise missed.'

'I saw those photos too,' said Evan. 'He was talented. They're good. Slightly odd subjects, though.'

'Oh, I don't know,' said Betty, 'gritty urban shots, some beauties of nature, many of the people and places he saw every day – all well framed and lit. I enjoyed those more than his photos of the moon. He seemed to be a bit obsessive about that, don't you think? I mean, it looked as though he had shots of every phase of it. And I mean every percentage phase of visibility. All in very high resolution – maybe to accommodate his eyesight issues? He was rather detail-orientated, wasn't he?'

Evan smiled. 'See, I preferred those photos of the moon rather than the ones he took of rubbish piled in the gutters near drains, or of the detritus poking out of skips on the side of the road. The photos of the moon were true studies. Wonderful. He must have had some exceptionally good lenses to capture them. And you're right, there weren't many missing from his "collection" from one percent to one hundred. Maybe he had a local spot where he went every day of the month to take a picture. Mynyddbach Common's good and high, and dark, for that sort of thing. He might not have had to go too far from home to be able to do it.'

'I don't think you could do that, though, could you? I mean every shot showed a perfectly formed moon, without a single cloud in the frame. Imagine how long it would take to achieve that, around here. We don't have many days a month without some cloud cover at night. Maybe it was the work of many months, or even years.'

'You're right. I hadn't thought of that. A true passion on his part. But he was good. Poor dab.'

'Yes, a promising life, snuffed out. Gone. All that talent.' Silence. 'Anyway, did I do well? Up to standard?' Betty felt anxious. She wanted to contribute all she could – this was now a shared enterprise.

'I wish I'd had a team full of yous,' said Evan, grasping her hand.

'Your turn.'

'I discovered James Powell was a good runner, apparently; involved with a Swansea group that's part of Disability Sports Wales. Won a gold medal for the 1500 meters in his age group when he was eighteen. Photos in the *Evening Post*. Hints at possible Olympic aspirations. Nothing since then. They mentioned his school in that article too, so it seems he stayed on there until he was at least that age. And there was a bit about a part time job he had at a garden center out past Fforestfach – how he caught the bus under his own steam to work there, and so forth. But no mention of him anywhere after he'd have left school.'

Evan paused and asked, 'It's not something I've ever had to research for myself, at work; do you know what happens to people who need an extra bit of help when they're no longer in school? Especially if they're "blessed" with the sort of mother James seems to have had.'

'It's where the safety net of Social Services is supposed to come into its own,' replied Betty, knowing from experience this often didn't prove as effective as the lawmakers, and even the social workers themselves, hoped.

The couple shared a moment of silence. Betty knew they were both thinking of the tragedy of a challenging, but promising, life having been cut short.

Betty sighed. 'Not much, but it's a start. I think we're about to see a fair bit of press coverage about James in the coming days; stories about a boy who actually did exceptionally well, considering his family background and developmental challenges. They'll have loads of people digging into what we've just begun to unearth; I expect to read lots of interviews with those who knew him, and those who'll speak well of his abilities. A sympathetic victim. Deservedly so.'

Evan poured another cup of tea. 'I agree. I wonder how that will play with those who've painted Aled Beynon as the most angelic murder suspect since . . . well, there hasn't been anything like this before. He's been portrayed as clean-cut, academically bright, and a regular churchgoer. If we believe everything that's been written about him he lived a blameless, hardworking, grandmother-supporting lifestyle that's been hailed as almost Christ-like by some. Millennials have put him up on a pedestal as some sort of iconic figure.'

Betty mused, 'Maybe they need someone to whom they can aspire?'

'I think it's more about them illustrating how wonderful *they* all are, too,' said Evan grumpily. 'How can they put anyone on a jury who's seen that photo of him in his altar-boy surplice? And who hasn't, the way it's been doing the rounds? Who would convict him of this crime?' He shrugged. 'Mind you, there is one thing youngsters – and the media – like better than setting someone up to be worshipped . . .'

'Showing they have feet of clay, and then kicking them when they're down?' said Betty.

'Exactly. It'll be interesting to see how this plays out in the press.' Her husband sounded glum.

Betty stared at the wallpaper, and realized how dreadfully grubby it looked. 'By way of a distraction – when this is all over, we're going to redecorate this room. It's an embarrassment.'

Evan looked around, as if assessing his surroundings for the first time. 'Oh, come on, it's not that bad. Besides – who sees it? No one's stayed over since your mum, and if anyone had, they couldn't have slept in here – the bed was piled high with years' worth of accumulated junk and clutter.'

'It's the roses – Mum loved them, but she's gone now, and it's time to make a change.' Betty kissed her husband. 'Given the changes we've already been through the past few months, I think we're up to one more.'

3rd April

Sadie

I'm glad Mam said I could stay home from school today. I couldn't have faced everyone.

The papers are full of it again.

The police are sure – now – that the thing on the hill was James Powell, Dean Hughes's half-brother. It's weird they were brothers, yet somehow poetic.

There was loads of stuff online about how James was a talented photographer – as opposed to some snap-happy crank, I suppose – despite the fact he had Down's Syndrome.

We've got a couple of kids in our school who've got that. They're okay; not necessarily nicer or more horrible than anyone else. Always bloody smiling, though. I don't get that. I mean, what have they got to be so sodding happy about?

One of them's quite good at gymnastics, I suppose. I never was any good at that balance beam thing; she puts most other girls to shame, she's so sure of herself when she's on it.

My most urgent problem is that @wrongboy10 is getting hit with lots of negative stuff.

At least I've had an hour or so all on my own to scroll and read, and Retweet a few good ones. But the famous people who were all for Aled to start with, like Wandralee Wonder, have shut up now.

And that's not good.

I have to do something to get them supporting him again.

Nan was crowing about this James Powell thing, and I bet everyone at church will hate Aled again by the time they've finished singing the second hymn.

I don't know what to do. I wish I could talk to Aled. I miss him so much it hurts. Not like it hurt when he held me tight by my arms, but it hurts in my soul. I wonder if souls bruise, like my arms did that time? I'm wearing the bracelet he gave me after that incident; it's got hares dancing around it. It's so pretty, the way it glints in the sunlight coming through the window. I can't wear it when anyone can see it, because even Mam would know it would have cost a lot, but I wear it when I'm alone here, and when I go to my place on the hillside, and know I'm safe.

He was so sorry he'd been so nasty to me. He knew I was right; that's why he gave me this. He's given me lots of pretty things this past school year. It's wonderful, though sometimes our text arguments are a bit upsetting.

Some things I use – like my phone cover, and my backpack – and I tell Mam I swapped them at school, or got them dirt cheap online. She's easy to fool. She hasn't got a clue how much my perfume costs, for example. No idea at all. He only gives me the best of things. Exactly what I want. And I always forgive him for the nasty things he's said. Or done. Eventually. Oh, it'll be wonderful when we're married. It'll be the biggest and best wedding this pathetic village has ever seen.

But first, I have to get him out of prison. Mam's not too keen on helping me anymore. I've arranged to see Dad this afternoon; she has no idea, of course. I'm thinking of asking him if he can help. He understands modern technology much better than Mam does, and he travels a lot. He might set up some new Twitter accounts, then he could post to them as he travels and they'd be totally anonymous.

But I can't let on to him about me and Aled. He saw a couple of boys from school pointing at me and laughing when we were having coffee once, and he got really angry with them.

Thinking about it, that was Guy Fawkes Day. A lot happened on Guy Fawkes Day. I always used to enjoy it, because sometimes we'd go up to Swansea for the big bonfire and fireworks display at St Helen's in the evening – when I was younger. That was fun.

I had no idea it would end up becoming such a significant night for me, all these years later.

Growing up has its challenges, they say – Aled and I are going to be so happy when we can be together again. If I concentrate, I can almost feel his lips on me . . .

Helen

I sometimes think the silences are worse than her snapping at me, thought Helen as she drove her mother to the hospital to visit Gwen Beynon.

She won't say why we're doing this, and I know she's stewing on something.

Forcing a smile, Helen announced, 'Not far now, Mum.'

'Good,' snapped her mother, staring out at the lashing rain.

The drive from Rhosddraig to Morriston Hospital should have taken about an hour, but it was taking considerably longer due to the downpour. When they finally arrived it took Helen fifteen minutes to discover there was nowhere to park that didn't require her mother to get soaked to the skin, so she dropped her at the main entrance, promised to meet her at the stroke unit – wherever that was – and drove around the multistorey car park until she triumphantly found a space.

She all but ran into the shiny new atrium area they'd recently built at the old place. It felt almost like a fancy hotel reception area; the comforting aroma of coffee was a lovely surprise. Helen hated the smell of hospitals.

By the time she found the corridor leading to the stroke unit, her mother was walking toward her, her expression particularly grim. 'Let's go,' she barked at Helen.

Helen felt her frustration bubble up. 'Is that it? You can't have been with her for very long.'

'Long enough to say what I wanted to. And long enough to listen to her twaddle. She might be ill, but she's still a lying whore.'

'Mum!' Helen glanced around nervously, afraid someone might have overheard. 'Look, I need the loo before we start the drive back, so why don't you wait on one of those seats over there while I do that. Then we can drive all the way home again.'

'Don't be long.'

Helen sucked in a deep breath as she headed to find the loos. They were signposted in the direction from which her mother had just returned. Suitably refreshed, Helen wiped the last moisture from her hands with a paper towel, then dared to nip along to where she hoped she'd find Gwen Beynon; she'd never understood or shared her mother's animosity toward the woman, and wondered if it might be her last chance to see her before . . .

Gwen was in a little cubicle at the end of a surprisingly jolly-looking ward. Propped up on pillows, her head was bandaged, like something you'd see in a *Carry On Doctor* film. Her face was slack, though the glint in her eyes told Helen she'd been recognized. Gwen let out little grunting noises, and motioned with her fingers that Helen should sit. Machines beeped, and wires and tubes seemed to be attached to her all over the place.

Trying to be as cheerful as possible, Helen said, 'I can't stop long – Mum's waiting for me. I just wanted to say . . . hello.'

Realizing she really meant she wanted to say goodbye, and that she hadn't brought a gift with her, Helen felt immediately and utterly inadequate.

Gwen beckoned her to come close. All the poor woman could manage was a garbled whisper. Her speech was badly slurred. 'Myfanwy wrong. Your dad. Never. Cross my heart.' She sucked in a deep breath. 'New Year. 99. Flu. Bad. Doctor. Mair. Not Jack.' Gwen flopped back into her pillows, her breathing ragged, her cheeks unnaturally pink. One of the machines to which she was connected began to beep loudly. Helen looked around, panicked. Should she call someone?

She didn't need to. A couple of nurses wearing scrubs came jogging toward her.

'Are you a relative?' one of them asked.

Helen shook her head. 'Just a neighbor.'

'Then if you could go, that would help, ta. Mrs Beynon has just had some woman screaming at her, disturbing everybody; she shouldn't really have another visitor so soon. She needs her rest.'

Helen left, in no doubt it had been her mother who'd been screaming at Gwen. As for what Gwen had said to her, she didn't know what to make of it. 99? Flu? Mair? Not Jack? What on earth was she on about?

Spotting her mother waiting for her, Helen noticed how small she looked; sitting on an oversized, boxy seat, surrounded by the sick and the elderly, Nan Jones looked like a woman who'd seen a ghost. Pallid, lined, her eyes suddenly sunken. Helen hadn't thought her mother looked anything but her normal self when they'd got into the car that morning. Now? She felt quite concerned.

'Are you feeling alright, Mum?' she asked gently.

Her mother looked up at her. She'd been crying. 'I wouldn't mind a coffee, if we have time,' she replied quietly.

Helen was completely taken aback; her mother hadn't even cried at her father's funeral. 'Of course we've got time for a coffee, Mum. Shall we go and find some seats in there, or shall I bring one out here for you?'

Her mother looked around, seeming dazed. 'It looks quite nice in that coffee shop. Maybe they'll have a bit of cake,' she said, still in an unfamiliarly soft tone.

'Let's do that then,' said Helen, wondering when – if ever – she'd bring up Gwen's cryptic comments in conversation with her mother.

Nan

I can't believe she's lying there on what's likely to be her deathbed, still not owning up to it, thought Nan as she bit into a piece of so-called lemon cake. She forced a smile for her daughter's sake; it shut her up. *Almost twenty years she's kept it up, but I know the truth of it.*

'Are you feeling a bit better now, Mum?' asked Helen, sipping a bucket of foam.

'I wasn't feeling bad,' snapped Nan, then thought it best to change her tune. 'But thanks for asking.'

She noticed that Helen looked surprised, but decided to not comment. She poked at her cake with disgust; the coffee'd cost an arm and a leg, and the cake had been wrapped in plastic. What was the world coming to?

She needed to sort it all out in her mind. Although Gwen could hardly speak, Nan could tell she'd been angry when she blurted out words. Just words. They didn't make any sense.

'Mum, I just popped in to see Gwen – you know, in case it was my last chance to . . . you know.'

Nan felt hot. 'You had no right.'

A young mother with a pushchair and a toddler bumped Nan's arm; her coffee sloshed. 'There's a pound's worth I just lost on the table there,' she said, mopping it up with a serviette. Helen helped, then took the dripping paper to a bin.

Retaking her seat, her daughter said, 'Gwen said some things to me that don't make any sense.'

Helen was being a pain.

'She rarely did,' replied Nan. 'Not going to change now, is she?'

'She said something about 99, flu, Mair, the doctor, and not Jack. Does she mean Dad? Do you know what any of that means? Mum?'

Nan had no intention of answering.

'Mum? Why were you screaming at her in there? She's not at all well.'

Nan put down the pathetic paper cup. 'None of your business, so keep your nose out.'

'Did something happen in 1999? With Dad? Or Mair? Please talk to me, Mum.'

Nan stared at her daughter. 'Always asking questions, you were, from the time you were little. Questions, questions. "Why?" you'd say. On and on; why are there mountains, why is the sky blue, why are there black sheep? Remember that book you had one Christmas, *Tell Me Why*?' Helen nodded. 'We gave you that to shut you up; whenever you asked "why?" after that, we could tell you to look in the book.'

Nan wasn't sure what the expression on Helen's face meant when she said, 'Oh, Mum.'

'You've turned out alright. Well, since you got rid of that Bob you've been alright, anyway.'

Helen stopped drinking her coffee. The look on her face was changing, she was getting red. 'You couldn't be bothered to give me the time of day, even when I was little, could you, Mum? Dad was the only person in my life who ever took any real notice of me, possibly the only one who ever loved me. The way you've always treated me – and the way you treat me now – makes me wonder why on earth you ever had me.'

'You were an accident, as I've told you on many an occasion. We didn't think we could have kids, then there I was, thirty, and pregnant. My back's never been the same since I carried you.'

'And don't forget your legs, Mum. They've never been the same since then either, have they? Your varicose veins? All my fault. And your piles. You don't usually fail to mention your piles.'

Nan decided that particular comment didn't deserve a response. 'Your father was not at all the sort of man you seem to think he was. He had weaknesses, and I had to deal with them all. You never saw them. I did. You know I don't like to talk about him, so let it drop. Now.'

Nan found Helen's drumming fingers and bouncing knee annoying.

'Dad was a wonderful man, so don't you say anything bad about him, Mum. I was lucky to have him in my life as long as I did, but I wish he were still alive.'

Her daughter was having one of her uppity days.

'Unlike me, I suppose,' sniped Nan. 'Wishing I was the one with all those things poking out of me in that bed instead of Gwen, aren't you? I know you are. Well, I'll be gone soon enough, I dare say. Then you'll see.'

'See *what* exactly, Mum? See how hard it is to keep going every day? See how running a pub is absolutely exhausting? How tough it is raising a daughter alone because the man you married turned out to be the worst nightmare you could have imagined? How being pulled in every direction and never, ever being able to do anything right is so utterly soul destroying? Is that what I'll *see* when you've gone? Well, don't worry, I know all that already.'

Nan decided it was time to stop her daughter from drawing attention to them. She stood. 'I'm leaving now.'

'Not without me driving you, you're not,' said her ungrateful child, also standing.

Nan forced the matter by hobbling toward the exit. She knew Helen would follow her, and she did. Tail between her legs. Looking sorry because she'd spoken out of turn. Just like her father.

Nan decided to keep quiet on the trip home. She wanted to think. But it seemed Helen wasn't going to allow her to enjoy the entire drive in peace.

Once they'd passed Sketty Cross, Helen started. 'See these big houses, set back here, along the Gower Road – did you know my entire horizon of ambition when I was Sadie's age was to live in one of those, with a husband and some children – loving, and being loved. Did you know that?'

Nan had to admit she didn't.

'Dad did, Mum, because he listened to me. He let me talk to him, and he listened. You never listened.'

'Covetousness is against the Commandments, and is unbecoming in a child of mine.' Nan reckoned that about covered it.

'You talk such rubbish, Mum.'

'That light's red,' said Nan, bracing herself.

They screeched to a halt just past the stop line.

'No arm across me to protect me this time?' Nan sneered at her daughter.

'I'm trying to be a quick learner, Mum,' replied Helen.

'Spiteful girl.'

'What was Gwen talking about, Mum? Tell me, or I'll pull over on the side of this road and you can catch two buses to get home from here.'

Nan seethed. She was being held hostage by her own child. To hell with it – he'd been her father, she should know. Nan spoke with all the hatred she felt. 'He had an affair. With Gwen Beynon. End of 1999. I saw them with my own eyes. She's never admitted it, nor did he. But I knew. I chose not to say anything at the time, because marriage is a sacrament, but I know what I know. There. See? Not such a perfect man after all, your dad.'

Nan was delighted that Helen didn't speak for the next five minutes. When she did, Nan was surprised by what she said. 'Dad was nearly seventy by then – what on earth would he be doing having an affair with anyone? Let alone Gwen Beynon. She's not that much younger than you.'

'She's six years younger than me. And your father was the sort of man who had a keen interest in matters of the flesh. An interest I didn't share. Not after you were born, anyway. It wasn't just my back and my legs you messed up, my girl. The stitches I had to have after you came out were nobody's business. That was that, for me.'

Nan watched as Helen puffed out both her cheeks, but kept her eyes on the road. 'A bit too much information there, thanks, Mum. But, even so, I can't believe it. Not of Dad. And not of Gwen. What did you see? How do you "know"?'

In for a penny, thought Nan. 'I knew something was up. A wife can tell. Besides, when you run a pub it's not difficult to notice a person's gone for hours – there's always work needs doing, and him not being there was something I would always find out about. For a while I didn't know where he was off to. Then I saw them together, coming down the hillside path. Pleading with her about something, he was. Holding both her hands in his. I kept more of an eye on him after that. Saw him with his trousers off in the front bedroom up at her cottage once. New Year's Eve 1999. I'll never forget it. Big night in the pub, and we'd brought in extra people to help out. He'd been gone for at least an hour, so I went out to look for him, but there was no sign of him. Then there he was, pulling up his trousers; I saw him through a gap in the bedroom curtains. The light was on up there. He didn't see me. I went back to the pub. Never said a word.'

A long silence followed. Nan noticed Helen was crying. 'Pull over. You can't drive like that, you can't see where you're going.'

They pulled into a layby in Lower Middleford, close to the chip shop and the social club. Helen wasn't sobbing; she was crying silently. Nan had never seen her do that before. She didn't know what it meant, but was grateful for it – she couldn't abide the sound of sobbing.

Eventually her daughter managed to squeeze out, 'I can't believe it.'

'Well, you should. It wasn't the first time he'd done it, either,' said Nan.

Helen's face was blotchy, her eyes wild when she turned to look at her mother. 'What?'

Nan nodded twice. 'There was one he had on the go for a long time, back in the seventies. You were little – you hadn't started school – and he would be gone for hours on end. Back eventually, and never away overnight. But I knew what he was up to. Never knew who it was. Might not have been someone local, even. It was when we had the three-day week, and no electricity for hours at a time. We had to close the pub early some nights, because we couldn't get the stock to sell, and couldn't afford to run generators to keep the lights on, or to make anything else work. Worst time of my life that was, and he was off doing it with someone.'

'Oh Mum.'

Nan could hear sympathy in her child's voice. Sympathy for her. At last.

She just had one more thing to say.

'It was after that the fighting began, but we managed to keep it quiet, so you didn't know what was going on. A bit like you tried to do with Bob. But we were better at keeping it down than you two were.'

Sadie

This swotting every night is totally depressing. It's so hard to concentrate. And what's the point anyway? Aled's going to be in court soon. They're going ahead with it – which is stupid. There's no real information out there about why. It's horrible not knowing. Not being able to see the whole picture. But at least once he's tried for it, he'll get out. So I suppose it's good it's happening now.

Soon he'll be home, and we can go back to how we were. I'll be able to see him whenever I want, and we'll be together forever. He can start giving me nice things again, though I hope we don't have as many rows. I don't like it when that happens. We even manage to keep all that private, too. No one knows. Maybe no one would even believe it.

Dad and I talked about Aled a bit, when we had coffee earlier today. I got the bus into Swansea and we met at the Kardomah Café. I like it there. Mam and Dad took me there when I was little. It was the only place we went that smelled like that – of coffee, and warmth, and safety. That must have been a really long time ago. It didn't smell as much of coffee as I remember it, or maybe more places smell the same nowadays, I don't know. Anyway, it was nice to be there with him.

He's good fun. He made all the waitresses laugh. He said to one of them that he recognized her from some place called The Cat and Whistle. She flipped him with the cloth she was using to wipe the table, and said she wasn't that kind of girl. Girl? She was at least as old as Mam. When I asked Dad what The Cat and Whistle was he said it was an old pub down by the docks – gone now – where all the barmaids were cats and all you had to do was whistle for them. I don't know what he meant, but he seemed to think it was very amusing.

The last few times I've seen him he's been a bit off with me – keeps asking about Mam more than usual. Is she seeing anyone? Does she go out on dates? It's weird he would ask that – I mean, who would want to go out with Mam? She's so old, and she looks as though someone's inflated her like a balloon the past year – she's so fat and flabby it's not funny.

I didn't have a latte or anything to eat with Dad, just a plain black coffee – I've got to watch my figure for Aled. I want him to like the way I look.

Dad's face was more drawn than usual today. He's old too. Maybe it's all the traveling he does – he's always in some hotel or other; he never seems to be at home at all. It must be so boring to have to talk to doctors all the time; I don't like how doctors' surgeries smell, and Dad must smell like that himself at the end of a day going from one place to another, talking about how this new pill does that great new thing, or whatever it is he does. Ha! I suppose you could call him a drug dealer – because he works for a company that makes the sort of drugs that doctors prescribe. I never thought of it that way before.

I told him about what's been going on at school – with the police being all over us about drugs all the time. He said I mustn't worry, that the police aren't interested in people who haven't done anything wrong. He hadn't heard about Aled's Grannie Gwen being ill. He said he might go to see her at the hospital, which was nice of him.

I don't know why Mam made him leave us; there's nothing wrong with him. He'd like to be more of a proper dad to me, but she won't let him. But now that I'm older I'm too clever for her – no one even knows we meet.

We talked about me going to court when Aled is there; Dad said he thinks it's a good idea, because I'll know exactly what's being said. I didn't tell him everything about me and Aled, of course. He ruffled my hair and called me 'his little princess'. Aled calls me a little princess too, sometimes, but not in the same way. Dad told me I have to be very grown up about all this business, and he's right.

I'll be eighteen before long, then I really will be a grown up, so I can at least behave like one now. Which I don't think means revising the Act of Supremacy of 1534, Bloody Mary's repeal of it in 1554, and Elizabeth's new one in 1559.

God, that Henry VIII, what was he like? It was all about him, him, him. And he treated women like things. That's not right. Though . . . maybe they really loved him, like I love Aled.

Mary was no better, in her own way, marrying Phillip of Spain just to try to have an heir. She might have been the first ever Queen regnant of England, but she killed so many people, all in the name of religion.

And Elizabeth? Well, I know she was a great queen, and almost as deadly as her older half-sister, but imagine never marrying, having no one to love you at all. That must be the worst thing in the world, even if you are a queen.

Love, and family, and faith – it's funny how those things are always linked together through history.

8th April

Evan

Looking up at the ornate grey stone façade of Cardiff Crown Court, Evan felt as though he were coming home; he'd spent possibly too many hours inside the building during his years of service. This was the first time for him to enter it as a member of the public; he held Betty's hand as they mounted the steps. You couldn't help but look heavenward as you climbed – the architect had cleverly ensured those arriving would feel awed, and small, as they approached their date with justice.

'We'll finally get to hear all the evidence they've got. The full facts. And see the major players,' said Betty quietly.

Evan nodded; he felt anxious, fizzing with energy. Separated to pass through all the security procedures, he was glad to be able to stay close to Betty as they took their seats in the gallery looking down into the main body of the courtroom.

'How does it feel?' asked Betty, sounding concerned.

'Different,' admitted Evan. 'To be honest with you, it's as though I'm seeing the place for the first time; I never noticed those carved wooden scroll things above the bench before, and I have to admit I don't think I recall the place smelling like this either.'

Betty sniffed the air. 'I know that smell. It's perfume. Expensive.'

Evan looked around, trying to work out who nearby might be the sort of person to wear such a heady scent.

'What's expensive, in your book?' he asked.

Betty smiled. 'Anything over about thirty pounds, but that one's a few hundred quid a bottle. A client I once had used it. It comes with a snake on the box – all that sort of guff.'

Evan was surprised. 'Sounds a bit exotic for any of this lot to be using it.' He couldn't spot anyone who looked as though they could have afforded to spend that much money on all the clothes on their back, let alone on perfume.

'Good Girl Gone Bad.'

'Pardon?'

'It's called Good Girl Gone Bad. I talked about it with my client. She picked it for its name, not its smell.'

'And did she live up to its "promise"?'

Betty wrinkled her nose. 'No names, no pack drill – but yes, she more than did that. Oh look, there's Helen Jones. I expect that's her daughter, Sadie. I wonder why they're here? The links to Aled, I suppose.'

Evan looked across the banked rows of padded benches, and spotted a flaccid woman in her late forties, who looked pallid, strained, and in probably less-than-good health. Beside her sat a girl with glistening long brown hair and a shining complexion, wearing a purple knitted dress.

'I'll just go over to say hello,' said Betty, and she was off before her husband could suggest she didn't.

He watched the reactions to Betty's approach with interest. Helen looked concerned as soon as she recognized his wife; Evan reckoned that was to be expected. The girl was introduced and made polite responses. Betty smiled, bobbed, and looked across at him – obviously explaining who he was. They all exchanged smiles and half-waves.

When Betty returned to her seat she said, 'Helen introduced me to her daughter as an "old friend". They're here because of their connection with Aled Beynon as I thought; both sure he didn't do it. By the way, it's Sadie's perfume you caught a whiff of – they must have passed behind us when they went across to those seats.'

'It must be true what they say about The Dragon's Head pub then,' said Evan just as they were being told to 'All rise'.

'How d'you mean?' whispered Betty.

'People have always said it's got a license to print money, what with its prime location and that view down to the beach. If the granddaughter's wearing three-hundred-quid a pop perfume, how much must the grandmother be raking in there?'

'It might not be the grandmother who bought it for her,' said Betty as Aled Beynon appeared. 'Look at that – almost the first thing he did was look up here, searching our faces. It looks like he stopped as soon as he spotted Sadie.'

Evan looked across at the girl; her mouth was open, her eyes alight, her entire body leaning forward, her hands and fingers in motion. The accused was looking at his feet – she was totally focused on him. It was an interesting dynamic.

Helen

Unconvinced she'd done the right thing by agreeing to accompany her daughter to Aled Beynon's trial, Helen sat on the edge of the bench overlooking the well of the courtroom and wondered how long the thing would take. Days for certain. Possibly weeks. She'd agreed her daughter could come because it was a study week at school, and Sadie had promised she'd keep up with her work in the evenings. But that would be it; she wouldn't be able to come next week, if it took that long.

The world of real trials and courtrooms was a closed book to Helen, though she liked to watch a lot of crime and mystery programs on TV; it seemed to be one of the few things all three generations of Jones women had in common.

This? This wasn't at all what she'd expected. On TV everything went smoothly. Below her, people in gowns and wigs were bobbing up and down, talking to the judge in what seemed to be some sort of coded language. At least, it made no sense to her.

Helen focused on her daughter, who was staring blankly into space and scribbling in a notebook. When Helen asked what she was doing she was delighted to hear her reply, 'Mentally revising the Elizabethan Religious Settlement.'

Thank God Sadie was keeping her head – this was the most important year of her life, and Helen didn't want it ruined by an infatuation with a boy who might have heartlessly, and horribly, killed someone.

Sadie

He looked for me as soon as they brought him in, and he saw me. Now he knows I'm here, watching him. Which is good. It's fantastic to see him again after all this time. It's been agony, not knowing what he's been going through – what he's been suffering. My poor, darling Aled. He's so pale, and they've cut his beautiful hair so short. Such a shame, but it'll grow back. I like it long and curly, all wild and bleached. I think he's lost weight, too; he's wearing his church suit, but it looks like it's hanging on him. I bet the food in that prison is terrible, and Aled likes good food – proper food.

I'll make him all his favorite things when we're together. It'll be good for me, too. No more pub grub for me, oh no. Nor him. And as soon as he's back on the beach, or on his bike, he'll pick up that lovely tan of his, no problem. It must be killing him, knowing he's missing the spring surf. But it won't be long now.

Who knew there'd be this much fussing about at the start of it all? I hope they get on with it soon. Mam said I can come this week, but only this week. It won't take that long, I bet. It can't. There, everyone's getting settled in now.

He's not looking up at me – nor should he. We can't afford to let people spot that we're so closely connected. Not yet. Oh look at him, he's so small down there in that box. He's fidgety. Can't settle. I'm not sure that looks good to the jury – what will they think of him?

What's he up to?

Oh, my God – he's talking to me. He's using his hands and fingers on his thighs to send me messages, like he does sometimes in class. He's making the shapes of letters with his fingers. I've got to write this all down, but I mustn't let Mam spot it. I'll have to concentrate – I've missed some stuff already. I'll just start from here.

U. I. L. U. I. L. U. I. L. U.

He keeps repeating the pattern. He's saying 'I love you'. That's it. I just wish I could signal back to him somehow, but I can't. Oh, there – he just flicked his eyes up to me. I'm sure he saw me smiling down at him. I hope he knows that means I get it. There – the pattern is changing now.

U. I. C. U. I. C. U.

'I see you.'

X X X

Kisses!

This is wonderful. He's so clever. He can talk to me all the time now. All I have to do is not take my eyes off him. He's clasped his hands together now. Maybe that means he has to concentrate on what's being said.

He's looking at that woman in the wig. She's supposed to be good – the best, some say. She's there for him. If I could do what she can do I'd do a better job for him, I'm sure. Because she doesn't love him, or know him, like I do.

It's time for the bloke on the other side to talk now; I'd better listen.

Betty

'So nothing unexpected came out of the opening statements, or the rest of the morning, *cariad*.' Betty was following Evan toward the exit so they could both pop to the loo, then grab something to eat during the lunch break.

'No,' replied Evan, avoiding the crush as best he could, 'but I have to say Geraint Parry-Lloyd for the Crown did well; he put up a convincing argument for Aled having good reason to want the Powell boy to remain unidentified. And he's obviously going to rely heavily upon that witness in Australia; a live link into the courtroom was a nice way to make it as compelling a testimony as possible. Mind you, knowing the Beynon boy hasn't given his defense team anything to work with, they also made a good job of it. Olivia Kitchener, QC, hasn't earned her reputation for nothing.'

'What do you think, Evan?' asked Betty as she was moving toward the Ladies'.

'Oh, far too soon to tell, love. We'll see. You go, I'll meet you out here.'

'Okay – there's bound to be a queue for me. See you when I see you.' Betty pushed the door, and, sure enough, all the cubicles were full, and two women were waiting. A moment later Helen and Sadie Jones joined the queue behind her.

'Hello again,' said Betty brightly. 'How's it going?' She'd meant the question as a general throwaway query, but the look on Sadie's face when she replied told her the teen had inferred a totally different meaning.

'I think it's criminal, the lies they can say about a person in a court, and get away with it. That woman representing Aled should have been much more forceful, she should have told the jury that other bloke was just lying; she should have been more sympathetic. Even she was saying Aled's from a troubled background – he's not. He's just Aled.'

Betty noticed the girl's mother was surprised by her daughter's outburst.

'Come on now, Sadie,' said Helen, 'it's only just getting going. I'm sure she'll elaborate later on.'

Betty decided to not say anything, preferring to see how the conversation played out.

'Oh come off it, Mam. "You only get one chance to make a first impression" – that's what they tell us at school about interviews at university, so it's got to be true here too. That jury? They're already seeing Aled as a misfit, emotionally scarred. It's not fair. He's not. He's as normal as you or me.'

Both women looked at Betty, clearly expecting some response or input. 'My husband says it's very early days, yet,' she offered. 'Maybe Olivia Kitchener is trying to get the jury to see Aled as someone deserving of their understanding.'

'Well she's not doing that, she's making him sound like a right weirdo,' said Sadie sullenly.

Betty noted Helen's anxious expression as she stroked her daughter's hair. 'There, there, now. Don't get upset, love. There's nothing you can do about it. We've done all we can. I know you made a difference with all those Tweets and things—' Helen stopped speaking, and blushed.

Her eyes darted from her daughter to Betty, then she laughed – too loudly, too theatrically, thought Betty. 'You know what these kids are like, with their Tweets and texts and so forth,' she added quickly. 'Sadie said everyone in school got caught up in it, didn't you?'

Sadie was looking at her mother with an expression Betty read to be utter disdain. She found it a little unsettling.

'Yes, we all were,' replied Sadie to her mother, while staring at Betty. 'We often spent all day just texting each other about it.' She flashed an almost manic smile.

A large woman with vivid blue hair vacated a cubicle, and Betty said, 'I'd better not hold up the queue,' nodding at the three women now standing behind them, one holding open the outer door so they could all fit. 'Good luck this afternoon,' she added, not at all sure if she'd said the right thing or not.

Sadie

This is horrific. That Geraint Parry-Lloyd bloke has really got it in for Aled. He said some horrible things about him to begin with, and now he's making other people say horrible things about him too.

They got through all the experts who testified about it being James Powell's remains quite quickly; at least that Olivia woman was good at making them look like idiots for identifying the wrong brother in the first place. Then they got Iolo Rees in to testify he had no more sons. I think Olivia did a great job when she pointed out he might have and wouldn't even know it – given how he'd put it about so much over the years. Then Dean Hughes came along – smug git that he is – to say he had nothing to do with the drugs that killed poor Aled's mother in any case. Olivia couldn't shift him on that, because he just kept repeating that the police had dropped the charges.

One interesting thing I didn't know about came out; that smarmy Chief Inspector Jenkins said several people who'd been at the Guy Fawkes event at our pub had signed statements saying they'd seen James Powell outside our place that night. That was news to me. Olivia pushed Jenkins on it; I don't like that man at all. He's whiny and looks flustered all the time. But I suppose that's good, because it means he wasn't very convincing.

It's all going much faster than I thought it would. It's really scary, in a way. Like it's all rushing past me, and I'm trying to hang on. And I'm trying to keep up with what Aled is saying to me with his code, too. He can't say anything too complicated, of course, but he's been repeating I. L. U. and he's been making little heart-shapes too. Oh, it's so good to just see him again. I can't wait for him to touch me.

I'm not sure what all these people do when they aren't in the courtroom, but I hope it's something important, because we've only been in here for a short time this afternoon, and now they're sending us all away until tomorrow. Why can't they just have a longer day in court? It would make things so much easier for Aled. They're keeping him in Cardiff while the trial's on, not driving him back and forth to Swansea prison. Mam and I have to get home to help Nan at the pub tonight – so I suppose it's good that it's finished so early, in that respect.

I don't even know why all this is happening in Cardiff in any case. I suppose Swansea's not good enough for a trial the whole world is interested in. Typical of bloody Cardiff.

I can't wait to get to bed tonight, then I can imagine Aled's hands all over me.

I hope it's not long until the hands are real.

9th April

Sadie

The drive to Cardiff felt shorter today than yesterday; it's not a journey I've been on many times before, and all the roads seem confusing. Mam and I didn't talk much; she seemed lost in her own little world, and I was in mine. I talked everything through with Mrs Hare last night. She's a good listener, and I know she'll take my messages where they need to go.

Nan was up earlier than usual this morning, so that messed up the bathroom schedule. She wanted to go over to have tea with Mair first thing, she said. Had to talk to her about something, apparently. I'll put money on Mam knowing what that something is – but neither of them has said anything. Oh well, stuff them both. Let them keep their secrets, just as long as I can keep mine.

I don't know how it's going to go here in court today. Aled's got his head down now. I wish I could hold him, and let him sleep in my arms – he'd be able to rest properly then. His signals are different today; he seems a bit twitchy, and he's already looked up at me twice. I hope Mam hasn't noticed. I hope that retired policeman Mam's old counsellor is married to hasn't noticed either; he seems to be paying me quite a lot of attention, which I don't like. Maybe I should tell Mam I think he's a bit of a letch.

That would sort him out.

Aled's saying something with his hands I can't make out. I've been trying to listen to DCI Jenkins giving testimony – Olivia gets a go at him now, which is good. Even though he's whiny, I can tell the jury hasn't taken as much of a dislike to him as I'd hoped they would.

It's Olivia's job to make them go off him – pronto.

I wish Aled would make his signs more slowly. I've seen I. L. U. a few times. But now it's what? He's not making shapes anymore, he's beating a rhythm. I don't understand it. No, wait, we did that back when I was in Girl Guides, it's Morse code. Short, short, short, long, long, long, short, short, short, long, long . . . oh, it's an SOS.

He's asking for help. What's wrong? What's happened?

Hang on – he's got a bruise on his face. That's not right. Who's done that to him? Olivia is saying to the jury that he's been victimized. Oh

God, no! They mustn't hurt him. I can't imagine what sort of people he's mixing with in those cells where they're keeping him. Aled's just a boy – oh good, that's what she's saying.

Maybe the jury will feel even sorrier for him because of it.

Jenkins is being obnoxious now, saying Aled's a young man who had the motive, the means, the opportunity, and he's in no doubt he destroyed James Powell's body. Now he's saying he believes that Aled also killed James.

Go on, Olivia – push back. Hard. That's right, he can't say that. Aled's not on trial for murder.

There, even the judge said that, and she's warning Jenkins. Good.

But why isn't Olivia doing more? She should be telling the jury Aled didn't have the opportunity to even burn the body. But maybe she can't, because Aled hasn't said anything.

But now they all think he could have done it, even though he didn't. He's looking around now . . . oh no, he's actually crying.

My Aled, crying?

I can't imagine him coming to that. He must be lower than low.

Maybe he's on the edge of losing it. Maybe he'll say or do something stupid.

I have to do something.

I have to stop this.

I can't stand it any longer . . .

Evan

'Well now, that's one for the books.' Evan was as shaken as the rest of the people in the courtroom.

'This isn't normal, is it, *cariad*, I can tell,' said Betty.

'It's about as far from normal as you can get. The judge couldn't do anything but call an adjournment. Who knows how long this will take.'

'That look on Helen's face when they took Sadie away. Did you see it, Evan?'

'I did. I can't imagine what's going through her head at the moment.'

He loved the feeling of Betty's hand on his arm.

'What's going through *your* head at the moment – that's what I'm interested in hearing about,' she said.

Evan put his hand into his pocket and pulled out his roll of strong peppermints. He popped one into his mouth and crunched into it. He saw his wife wince, but carried on.

By the time it was decimated, he was ready to speak.

'If Sadie Jones is telling the truth, and she and Aled really were together, having sex – in that very specific manner she announced – down on Rhosddraig Beach from eleven on 5th November until gone two in the morning on the 6th, then it can't have been Aled Beynon that John Watkins saw that night, making off on his bicycle from the scene of the fire. And if – as Sadie claimed – she spilled a few bottles of lamp oil in the church vestry when she volunteered to do the church cleaning on behalf of her grandmother, but was too frightened to tell anyone about it, then he had neither the opportunity nor the means. Add the fact the motive's always been shaky, and you have a Crown case in tatters, I'd say. Might be a pretty straightforward dismissal.'

'No wonder they're all scurrying about down there,' said Betty, peering over the balcony. 'Look, there's Liz. She's staring up at us. Should we go down to her?'

Evan weighed his decision. 'I'm not sure this is the time or the place to be seen with her. Could you text her? Use girl-code.'

'Give me a minute, I'll have to turn on my phone.'

As Evan waited, he ran the case through his mind for the thousandth time. If Aled and Sadie were together during the critical period down on the beach – had they at least seen something?

Might Sadie be able to give a statement that would allow the police to open a fresh line of inquiry?

Jenkins had disappeared.

Evan could imagine the flurry of activity going on behind the scenes; hurried arrangements for meetings in private rooms, organizing legal representation, and so forth. But, however frenzied it might all feel, nothing would happen quickly. Experience told him that much at least. He didn't think it likely there'd be any significant developments that day. Unless . . .

'Liz says it looks like she'll have to cancel our plans to have coffee tomorrow morning. Duty calls.'

'I thought as much. She'll be up to her neck in it. Never mind. I think we should leave, and get back to that "decorating" we've been working on in the spare room.'

'Agreed.'

Helen

Hoping to find somewhere to sit and wait, Helen felt as though she were trying to navigate an unknown landscape hidden by treacherous swirls of dragon's breath. She took the coffee offered by a police constable, and suddenly realized her hands were trembling, almost uncontrollably.

Since Sadie had stood up on that balcony and had screamed that Aled couldn't have burned anyone's body on the night of November 5th because she and he had been involved in some very particular sexual undertakings on the beach at the time, and that she was the one who had made the lamp oil 'disappear' from the church by spilling it, she'd said nothing – other than to tell Helen she'd better organize a solicitor to sit with her when she made her official statement.

Sadie's passion had blazed in the courtroom, but her voice had been chilling when she'd spoken directly to her mother. Helen recognized neither person as her daughter.

Helen sipped the coffee, aware only of its temperature.

She felt dazed. Numb. The reality surrounding her hidden by a fog of confusion.

'It shouldn't be too long now,' said the constable. He had a surprisingly deep voice for such a young, slight man.

Even as she thought this, Helen wondered why that one detail had impacted her.

Given they were in Cardiff Crown Court – which seemed to be awash with legal and policing types of all sorts – Helen couldn't imagine why it would take so long to get an appropriate solicitor to represent her daughter's interests; it had already been a couple of hours, and Sadie had refused to say anything until she had one. Helen wondered if it wasn't a bit late for her daughter to shut up, given the pretty comprehensive nature of her outburst. She also wondered if the news had broken beyond the walls of the court yet.

At that thought, her chest tightened. *Oh my God, what if it's on the news already! What if Mum sees it?*

The crushing panic shattered Helen's troubled train of thought. It hadn't occurred to her to get in touch with her mother. She balanced the coffee on the wide wooden arm of the bench seat, pulled out her phone and speed-dialed the pub – that was where her mother was bound to be at this time of day.

There was no answer, which was odd. She phoned their private number.

Still nothing. Just the answerphone.

In desperation, she phoned Agata's mobile, knowing she was working to cover her own absence.

'Thank God you answered, Agata. I'm trying to reach Mum. Can you put her on, please? It's important.'

Agata was gabbling. Usually Helen could understand everything she said – her Polish accent was negligible, because she'd been raised in Wales – but now she couldn't make sense of anything she was saying.

Helen took a deep breath. 'Slow down, Agata. It's all okay. Just let me talk to Mum.'

Agata spoke more slowly. 'She's in the ambulance, outside. She had just returned from Mrs Bevan's house. She was there a long time. She saw the news on TV here about Sadie and Aled – the reporter said the two of them had been having sex the night Aled was supposed to have burned that body, and they also spoke about Sadie cleaning the church and spilling oil. The reporter said all this, standing outside court in Cardiff. Mrs Jones shouted at the TV, shouting "No, no, no, it can't be true!" She looked at me, her face very angry, then she fell onto the floor. Grey. Not moving. Genowefa called the ambulance; my little sister is good in a crisis. I made people leave the pub. The ambulance arrived . . . but not so fast, and . . . Mrs Jones is in there now. But . . . I don't know how to tell you . . . she is gone. Just like that. In a minute. Before they ever got here. I could tell. Gone. I am so sorry. We did everything . . . they did everything . . . but the Lord took her.'

Despite the fact her head was swimming, Helen leaped to her feet. She felt cold. Hot. Sick. Her ears were roaring. She managed to squeak out, 'Help me' before she felt the heat of spilled coffee on her leg.

10th April

Betty

'Who on earth is ringing before eight in the morning?' Evan sounded groggy as he flapped his hands along the kitchen counter, trying to locate his mobile.

He growled, 'If this is one of those bloody silly people trying to sell me double glazing, I'll make sure I report them.'

Betty looked up from buttering toast. 'Your mobile's plugged in here.' She poked at it with her elbow.

She couldn't help but notice the screen said PRIVATE.

A blocked number.

Her heart sank a little.

Evan answered the call. 'Hello,' he snapped.

He paused, and Betty noticed his eyes widen. 'Yes, sir. Glover speaking, sir.'

As he listened, Betty watched her husband closely.

His face betrayed a shifting range of emotions. He stood taller, his body straightening from the slight stoop he'd recently developed. She noticed that although his brow was furrowed, his eyes sparkled. She didn't think they'd ever looked as blue to her as they did in that instant.

Betty's mouth felt dry.

She slathered twice as much Marmite onto her toast as usual, then sat quietly at the kitchen table, and crunched.

What would he say?

What would he tell her, or ask her?

She believed she knew.

Finally, it was over. 'I understand, sir. First thing tomorrow morning, sir,' said Evan.

He placed the phone on the table, and sat. 'Aled's been released. Jenkins is off the case. They need a fresh pair of eyes.'

Betty dreaded what was coming.

'I was first on the scene. They're calling me in. Re-interviewing me.'

Betty was awash with relief. 'They aren't pulling you back in?'

Evan looked surprised. 'Me? Back in, to work on the case? No. I'm just a witness.'

Betty could have wept. 'I'll go up and get something sorted for you to wear. Most of your work clothes have been relegated to the wardrobe in the spare room. I'll dig something out. You could wear that tie I bought for your leaving do.'

The irony was lost on neither of them.

20th April

Evan

'Put your foot down, the funeral's in half an hour.' Evan knew he should have driven – he was much more familiar than Betty was with the winding roads of the Gower Peninsular, but he'd lost the toss.

'Yes, *sir*,' replied Betty. Evan could tell she was smiling, even without looking at her.

Taking a sharp curve at the ruined Penrice Estate gatehouse, Evan braced himself as Betty added nonchalantly, 'I've never heard of a double funeral before. Have you? It's a bit odd, don't you think?'

'It is,' chuckled Evan. 'Two separate funerals would mean two opportunities for a get-together, which would usually be preferable, I should imagine . . . starting with sandwiches and shared memories, and ending up with beer and singing, no doubt. However, given the people in question, it seems to make sense that they'd do it as a double booking, I suppose.'

'I can't imagine there'll be many coming from beyond the local villages.'

Evan had to put her right on that one. 'I don't know about that. Nan Jones managed to make herself quite a well-known figure – and not just in the press over the past few months. She was a landlady reputed to be so rude, you had to meet her to believe it. I know people who went to The Dragon's Head just to be insulted by her.'

Betty dared a sideways glance on a straight – if perilously narrow – stretch of road. 'I know we haven't been in that pub for quite some years, but I didn't recall her being that bad. But, if it brought in the business, she'd play it up, I suppose.'

'Oh no, she didn't play it up at all; she had no idea she was being offensive, she honestly thought she was a cheery type. Which was what made it so entertaining. My mother said she was always the same way – absolutely tone deaf to every situation.'

'Your mother knew her? Of course, she was from that area. Your dad was from Gorseinon, wasn't he? Given the distances involved, how did your parents even meet up?'

'He had a bike.'

'A bike?'

'My dad did a fair bit of cycling when he was younger – clocked up the miles on his old bike, he did. No car; couldn't afford one back in the 1950s, so his bike got him back and forth between Lower Middleford and Gorseinon. He went there on a daytrip once, met her, and kept going back. It's the best part of twenty miles each way, so he'd spend a good few hours in the saddle to be able to court my mum. They often talked about that. I'd almost forgotten. Then they'd go out and "canoodle amidst the cairns and tombs" – that's what they used to say.' Evan sighed at the recollection. 'They had a good, long marriage.'

Betty focused on the road as she asked, 'I can't recall any cairns or tombs down that way. Where are they?'

'Up on the hillside above Rhossdraig Beach. Two Neolithic burial mounds, dating back about five or six thousand years, depending on which books you read.'

'Where exactly? I can't picture them at all.'

'They're a good way around the hillside – out above the sweep of the beach. The one in the best shape is the entrance to what is now a collapsed long barrow; there's a capstone standing on top of four dolmen stones, like a tabletop on four legs. The Devil's Table – so called because it looks just like a massive table, and – well, it's the sort of thing they must have looked at hundreds of years ago and they couldn't come up with a reason for its existence, other than for it to have been somehow conjured up by the devil himself.'

'I've never noticed it.' Betty sounded annoyed with herself.

'They're not that big if you're looking at them from the side of the bay where the car park is, but they're easy to spot once you know where they are. There's another one not far away from the Devil's Table, called the Concubine's Pillow, where two of the uprights have given way, and the capstone has slipped, so it's like a giant pillow you can lie back against. There's still a sort of triangular covered area, and the stone kerb and steps leading down into the long barrow – the burial chamber itself – are still intact. It wouldn't give much shelter in a storm, but . . .' Evan paused.

Betty smiled. 'I think I just heard a lightbulb switch on above your head, like in a cartoon.'

Evan's mind was racing. 'You might have done. It would provide a great place to keep a body out of sight for a few days. As you recall, in our conversations, you and I have now agreed the assumption that James Powell was killed as well as burned on November 5th to 6th is not necessarily a sound one, because DCI Jenkins admitted in court they showed only James's photo to people who claimed to have seen him at the Guy Fawkes event. I should imagine they're re-interviewing everyone who said they'd seen him there, this time with a six-pack. I can't believe Jenkins didn't do that in the first place. That was a poor decision on his part.'

'A six-pack? I'm assuming that's not the promise of a few cans of beer.'

'A photo array of six similar-looking people, from which the potential witness chooses one face. Of course, the team will have a heck of a time of it now, with all those photos there've been of James in the press, and on TV. But it's worth them trying, I suppose.'

'You're the professional.'

Evan continued to think aloud. 'They've put out public calls for sightings of James up until November 7th, the date the remains were found. Now, I think that's the new chap displaying an abundance of caution, because it sounded to me at the trial as though John Watkins in Australia was pretty sure of his facts – at least about his sighting of the fire being on the night of November 5th, even if he's only sure he *believed* the person he saw was Aled Beynon.'

He paused, then added, 'If James Powell was killed some time before the night of the 5th, his body would need to have been secreted from view until then. The cairns, the stones marking the ancient tombs, offer a possibility, with the Concubine's Pillow being my first pick.'

'Trust you to pick a concubine,' said Betty. Evan wondered if she was trying especially hard to keep the conversation light.

Evan raked his hands through his hair. 'Goodness knows the weather's been through the sites for months now – the sheep too – but they're worth checking. We could pop up there for a bit of a stroll after the funeral.'

He noticed Betty squirm a little in the driver's seat.

'I'm not really wearing the right shoes for going yomping up hills to look at ancient ruins, *cariad*. I came dressed for a funeral. Haven't you noticed? Marks and Sparks, head to toe.'

As they reached the bend just past Lower Middleford which allowed a view of the Dragon's Head and Rhosddraig itself, Evan felt a strange sense of foreboding; usually, the view lit up his soul, but today it seemed as though he were approaching . . . he didn't know what, he just knew it wasn't pleasant.

'It would be quite a break in the case if someone came forward with evidence of a sighting of the victim between the last time his mother can be sure she saw him, on the 30th October – and the discovery of his remains on the 7th November,' he mused.

'It would, but everything we've been able to find out about him suggests he was a shy boy, and known for keeping himself to himself. It was also in the paper that he went off on buses all over the place. So maybe a bus driver spotted him somewhere, I suppose. I dare say they'll be trying that. And I bet your lot are doing their best to get something out of the lads who hang around on the streets in the general area, in case any of them spotted him.'

Evan snorted.

'Want to share?' asked his wife.

'Expecting to get anything out of that load of losers? The same sort of useless idiots who set fire to a car parked right next to the police station in Penlan last month? It was lucky no one was injured, or worse. What on earth do they think something like that accomplishes?'

'Nothing, *cariad*. That's not the point.'

Evan nodded emphatically. 'Correct. It's pointless.'

'They probably see it as a way of making their feelings known,' added Betty quietly. 'Not a particularly positive, or useful method of communication.'

Evan shook his head in disgust. 'Complete waste of space. Now, putting that to one side, if we believe everything Sadie Jones screamed out in the court, we have to discount Aled Beynon as being the figure Watkins saw departing the area. However, we still have his description to work with. Watkins saw someone on a bright turquoise bicycle, wearing a yellow vinyl coat with a hood. Both of which Aled owns.'

Having crunched a peppermint to shards, Evan added, 'I bet those brainiacs in London won't ever be able to come up with a cause or time of death. So all we're left with is what everyone knows. One – on the afternoon of the 31st October there was definitely no mound of stones covering a heap of bones at the RAF place; we know this because the Reverend Llewellyn Thomas was up there that day, around two-ish he said in court, and everyone agrees he'd have noticed it. Two – the remains were found on the morning of 7th November by Hywel Evans and his dog.'

'That pile of stones on top of the remains? That sounds like a cairn itself,' said Betty. 'But they're built as a mark of respect, aren't they, not to hide things.'

'That's a thought . . . a *cairn*.'

'Has another lightbulb popped?' Betty was mugging surprise.

'Yes. Maybe. Tell you what, let's park in the main car park, not the one at the church, and let's walk and talk. You made good time at the end there – well done.'

'Thanks,' said Betty in a strange tone. 'Will you pat me on the head in a minute?'

'Sorry.'

Evan delighted in the sun's warmth on his face when he stepped out of the car. 'Weird weather this year,' he observed. 'This tie straight, is it?'

Betty fiddled with his collar a bit. 'Can't even dress yourself. Never told me that before I married you, did you? What else have you been keeping from me?'

They set off toward the church, arm in arm.

'Nothing worth knowing,' said Evan. 'Mind you, sometimes people don't mean to keep something a secret, but it's really hard to tell even a significant other absolutely everything about your life – because there are bits you forget yourself until something reminds you. Like the Devil's Table, for example; I remember coming to visit my grandmother in Lower Middleford for a week one summer, and walking up onto the moor with some local girl. Can't even remember her name now. Anyway, we kissed; a very innocent kiss. I must have been about twelve, I suppose. I hadn't given it a thought – during my adult years – until today. I haven't meant to keep that from you, I just hadn't recalled it, until now. I promise I've not been trying to keep you in the dark about my earliest experiments with the opposite sex.'

Betty chuckled, and play-thumped her husband. 'Okay, I believe you. Now – what about cairns?'

Evan kissed Betty's cheek. 'Yes – cairns – the symbol of an honorable burial for a person of significance. A memorial of their life. I don't know why I didn't think of it before. My initial assumption – and that of Jenkins's investigation – was that the stones and so forth piled on top of the skeletal remains were put there as some sort of forensic counter-measure, right?' Betty nodded. 'Well, what if they weren't? What if they were put there to specifically mark a resting place, as a signal of respect, or loss? Like they were originally meant, as you said.'

Betty sounded puzzled, 'You're thinking the mother?'

'James Powell's mother? No. Not her. All those interviews she's given? However hard she might try to sound as though she adored him, she clearly didn't respect her son in life, so there's no way she'd go to all that bother in death. But what about someone to whom he really did mean something? Maybe there's a yet-to-be revealed relationship with an unknown person. You see, we can't even be certain the culprit was from this area, can we? I mean, anyone could have done it. We have to question every previous assumption.'

'But why James Powell, and why here? And why a cairn?' Betty sounded sullen.

'Good for you for asking the question it's the duty of every professional detective to keep asking – *why*? But we'll have to pick this up later,' said Evan. 'Time for a double funeral. Eyes peeled, and off we go. Let's see what we'll see.'

'I hope Helen's coping okay,' said Betty solemnly. 'She's having a really difficult time of it at the moment, I should think.'

Sadie

I'm so glad all the reporters have stopped coming to the pub, and phoning all the time.

Mam was right to make a fuss about them not being able to see me. I don't want my photo everywhere, without my say-so; I had to save Aled – I did, and that should be an end to it.

It's just as well that baby was found dead in a ditch in Newcastle – they all ran off to write about that instead.

And now I can really celebrate, because it's finally here – the first time the whole village will see me and Aled out in public together. It's so exciting. He'll look lovely in his suit, I know. I texted him to suggest he got it dry-cleaned after wearing it in court, and I bet it'll come up looking nice. And a black tie will set off his white shirt a treat. He's so handsome, he'll look heavenly, even though he's dressed for a funeral.

We'll be walking in together, of course. Both our grandmothers, laying side by side in their coffins, and we're each going to place a little bunch of flowers on top of one coffin. We agreed.

It's not quite how I'd expected to walk up the aisle with him, but it'll do for a start. We've hardly had a chance to see each other at all, let alone be together just the two of us, since they released him. Of course he went straight from the jail in Cardiff to his grannie's bedside in hospital. He slept there for a whole week, holding her hand, even though she wasn't really conscious. Then she died. They didn't have to do anything much to her body afterwards, because they knew why it had happened.

Not like Nan. They kept her body for ages after she died; I expect they cut her up into tiny pieces. Serves her right. I think it's hilarious that Nan and Grannie Gwen are having a joint funeral; it was cheaper to open and close both graves the same day, so Mam and Aled agreed to do it this way.

His Grannie Gwen said she wanted him to wear bright colors for her funeral, but he agreed with me a black tie was best, because his suit is dark grey, not actually black. Nan would have wanted everyone in deepest black, Mam said, so I've got a new frock, because Mam said I had to wear one. I already own lots of black, but she said none of it was suitable. I have no idea where I'll ever wear a black dress again, but at least it's chiffon and long, so maybe I could make it look a bit more dressy with some jewelry if I need a grown-up, formal outfit at some point – though why I would, I cannot imagine.

It's a lovely day for it; a perfect blue sky, with cotton wool clouds. My favorite. Nan would have come up with some reason or other to hate it – but I think it's lovely. The sun's shining, the birds are singing, the wind is blowing, and the sheep are dotted about on the emerald grass, as they should be. Rhosddraig is truly beautiful on days like today.

Oh good, there's Aled now, waiting for me at the end of the path into the church. Mam left the pub ages ago; I wanted to be about five minutes late, so they'd have to wait for me and Aled, and they could all watch us walk up to the coffins looking suitably unhappy, but at least as a couple. I thought it would give our entrance to the world as we truly are a bit more gravitas. It's an important day for us – the first day of the rest of our lives. The start of us becoming what we were meant to be – a force to be reckoned with.

The Head at school told Aled he could either do his A levels when they hold the re-sits – or put them off for twelve months. He agreed to wait a year. Once I heard, I asked if I could do that too. It's for the best. Though having been away from school for a few weeks now, I didn't enjoy the feeling of being back there. In just over a month, when I'm eighteen, I'll be able to work behind the bar with Mam, which will be great . . . I think. Agata's still doing most of the shifts at the moment; I'm not sure I really like her, but Mam says she doesn't know where she'd be without her – or me, of course.

We spent a lot of time making Welsh cakes and *bara brith* yesterday, for the get-together at the pub after the funeral; Agata said she and her sister would make the sandwiches fresh, before we're due back there.

Mam's still having to take it easy; the doctor said she got a mild concussion when she fainted onto the marble floor in Cardiff Crown

Court. I'm sure she'll be fine; rugby players are always okay after they have a concussion, and she doesn't go running around like them all the time.

Any moment now, I'll finally be at Aled's side. I'll kiss him on the cheek, just lightly, but he'll know how much the kiss means. He'll open the door for me like the gentleman he is, and it'll be our time. I can hear Hywel Evans playing 'How Great Thou Art'. That must have been one of Grannie Gwen's requests, because Nan hated it; thought it was modern rubbish.

I wonder if she's spinning in her coffin?

Helen

Keep it together, Helen.

Standing in the front pew, with Gwen's woven straw coffin on one side of the altar, and her mother's sleekly varnished wooden one the other, Helen Jones felt utterly alone, and completely empty.

Hywel had been playing repeats of various suitably solemn hymns, followed by more up-tempo theatrical pieces, for ages, then the vicar gave him a nod; he played an introductory verse to 'How Great Thou Art', and the congregation began to sing. The little church was full – unusual for the Saturday of Holy Week.

Helen glanced toward the door. *Where the heck is Sadie? She knew what time the service was supposed to begin.*

Finally, the door opened, and Helen was relieved to see her daughter and Aled enter.

They both had pink, puffy eyes, and a slightly unhealthy glow about them; they walked solemnly along the short aisle, and each placed a little posy of flowers on top of the casket containing their grandmother.

It was an incredibly touching moment, and noses were blown in a chorus – but Helen felt queasy, and not just because she knew she had to speak in front of so many people in a few minutes' time.

Sadie joined her mother to the left of the aisle, where all the seats were filled with people dressed completely in black. Aled sat in the front pew to the right of the aisle next to the little pulpit; the seats behind him were filled with people wearing the most vivid colors imaginable. Helen thought the church looked as though it was set up for some weird sort of ritual, and noticed the Reverend Thomas was looking a little uncomfortable. Did he, like Helen, see this as a symbol of the villagers quite literally 'taking sides'? Even the Corries had split up.

When the time came for Helen to speak, she chose to stand between the two coffins, rather than mount the couple of steps to read at the lectern in the pulpit; she didn't want to feel as though she were preaching. She'd hardly slept the night before, worrying about what she'd say. She'd thought about it a great deal and had written reams of notes, which she'd read aloud to a bored-looking Sadie on several occasions. But now her hands trembled, and she knew she ran the risk of her voice not holding out, which annoyed her – this was an important speech, the last time she'd have the chance to tell people what she thought of her mother.

Not that she had any intention of sharing any honest feelings with them, of course; that wouldn't be proper. No, she'd carefully constructed a speech mentioning all the right sorts of things about Nan. She shook as she unfolded her notes, then looked up at the sea of faces, and it all just seemed to flow out of her. She mentioned her mother's childhood in Rhosddraig during the war years, and spoke of the fifties when she'd helped with growing fruits, vegetables, pigs, and sheep because of rationing; she elaborated on the fanciful tales her father had whispered to her about his courtship of Nan – and even told people about him inventing that name for the woman some of them had known until then only as Myfanwy; she talked about how Nan had relished motherhood, being at the heart of the community, and even grandmotherhood.

Then she stopped. *Enough lies,* she thought.

Still just about able to make out the features of the people filling the church through her tears, with Sadie and Aled in front of her, she folded her notes and added, 'This has been a time of great division in our little community. We're not numerous, we true People of the Dragon, so we should all stand together. Because of what . . . happened in court . . . everyone here knows that Nan's granddaughter Sadie, and Gwen's grandson Aled, have . . . formed a bond. I say today is the day we all start afresh, and take heart from this young couple who came here to share their grief. If that's what it takes for us all to forgive each other's unkind thoughts, and maybe even harsh words, then let's help them move on, and begin to share some happiness.'

Both Sadie and Aled looked at Helen with wide eyes. A farmer sitting at the back of the church – not a regular attendee – managed four vigorous claps before realizing no one was about to join him, though there was a significant rearranging of backsides on wooden pews, and many satisfied glances exchanged. Helen nodded her own head, just twice, as she retook her seat.

She dabbed her eyes as Sadie clutched her hand, and they both watched Aled mount the steps to the pulpit. He, like Helen, pulled out a folded piece of paper, then spoke in a bell-like voice, telling the congregation that his grandmother had asked him to read a part of the sermon written by a priest at St Paul's Cathedral upon the occasion of King Edward VII's body lying in state in 1910. He explained it was often referred to as a poem, though it was not written as such, and was known as 'Death Is Nothing At All'.

Helen, like the entire congregation, was transfixed as he read aloud. Aled appeared to have a halo around his short, curly hair; Helen knew it was just the effect of the sunlight streaming through the window beside him, but it gave an ethereal air to his entire person. His eyes were moist, and he almost glowed with an unusual-for-him pallor; it all made for an intoxicating picture.

By the time he had finished, everyone in the church was crying, and Helen was as convinced as her daughter had always been that this boy could never have killed anyone, nor have burned human flesh.

'Amazing Grace' was sung for Gwen, and 'The Day Thou Gavest, Lord, Has Ended' was sung for Nan. Helen, Sadie, and Aled joined the Revered Llewellyn Thomas in the porch to shake everyone's hand as they exited, before they all moved to the Beynon family graveside, for the interment of Gwendolyn Jane Beynon, then to the Jones family plot, for the interment of Myfanwy Valerie Jones.

Not one person left before it was all over, and Helen reminded the crowd that everyone was welcome at the pub where the food would be free, and the bar would be too, for a couple of hours. She'd thought that fair; her mother would never have forgiven her if she'd had an open bar all day.

It was only when they'd all got back to the pub, and most people had a drink and something to nibble in their hands, that Helen finally found a moment to be able to thank Mair Bevan for the friendship she'd shown her mother over the decades; she brought Mair a selection of sandwiches and a glass of Mackeson to a table where she'd made sure the nonagenarian had a comfy seat.

'I know Mum was so grateful to you, for everything you did with her, and for her,' said Helen, taking the chance to sit down, just for five minutes.

Mair's voice was so cracked and breathy, Helen needed to get close to be able to hear her over the general hubbub. 'Nan was many things,

Helen; grateful wasn't one of them. She took what she wanted, and did as she pleased. All her life. Don't forget, I was thirteen when she was born; I never had any misconceptions about your mother's capacity for anything.'

Helen didn't know quite what to say. She'd never been sure why Nan and Mair were such 'friends', despite her mother never showing any gentility or kindness toward the older woman. She tried her best to not look uncomfortable. 'I'm so pleased you were able to be here today. You're looking quite like your old self again,' she ventured. 'I'm glad you got over the pleurisy alright. It's a nasty thing. Have you had problems with your lungs before?'

Mair cackled. 'My own fault. Smoking for more than sixty years will do that to you. Still, who'd have thought I'd have seen off Dilys Watkins, and now both Nan and Gwen? All of them so much younger than me, yet here I am, and they're all gone.'

Helen wondered if Mair sounded just a little too pleased with herself. She decided to let it pass. 'Hearts and strokes, all of them. It's terrible,' she said, shaking her head sadly.

'Dilys and your mother had heart attacks, yes, but they were getting on and heart disease is the biggest killer by far each year in Wales – more than a quarter of all deaths are related to it. It's heart, circulation, or cancer that usually gets the old ones.'

Helen was surprised, and suspected her face portrayed as much, because Mair added, 'I've had many years to learn all about pretty much everything that can kill a person – I've made it my business to find out. It's why I gave up smoking when I was eighty; I reckoned if I'd made it that far I should at least give my old body a bit of a helping hand. That, and the fact it got so expensive, and I couldn't smoke here in the pub any longer because of the ban.' She leaned even closer and hissed, 'I'd kill for one right this minute, to be honest with you, but I can just imagine what my doctor would say. I was lucky they didn't want to keep me in hospital after they'd done all their tests.' She cackled again, and Helen managed to squeeze out a smile.

Helen was thinking it was time to take her leave and mingle a bit, but Mair put her hand on her arm and stopped her. 'But you've got one thing wrong, Gwen didn't have stroke, she had a bleed.'

'But she was in the stroke unit, in hospital, and Mum said she'd had a stroke.'

Mair put down her glass of stout, which was already half empty. 'They need to do things to you much the same for a stroke as a bleed, see, so that's why she was there. High blood pressure for years, a mini-stroke two years ago, and on warfarin ever since. The sister at the hospital told me her INR was 9.6 when they got her in there.'

The letters and numbers meant nothing to Helen. 'I don't understand.'

Mair looked slightly shocked. 'Oh, what it is to be young – well, under fifty, anyway. There are so many things you don't need to know about at your age. The INR is the International Normalized Ratio and refers to blood clotting. Because Gwen had suffered a little stroke the doctor put her on warfarin to keep her blood a bit thinner – a reading between 2 and 3 is the usual thing. It is for me, anyway. I had my mini-stroke about five years ago. If she had an INR of 9.6 when they got her into hospital she must have taken a double dose of warfarin at least . . . or maybe she'd knocked back half a bottle of vodka, or something, I don't know. But that's what happened. She had a bleed, not a stroke. They're difficult to come back from, even with the surgery they did.'

Helen was surprised Mair knew so much about it all, but didn't have time for a longer discussion. She turned her mind to the rest of the people she needed to talk to. 'Can I come over to your cottage soon for a bit of a chat, Mair? I really should circulate a bit. I know Mum came to see you the morning she died; maybe we could catch up about that?'

Mair finished her drink. 'Of course. But could I bother you for another Mackeson before you go?'

Helen writhed her way to the bar through the throng, and poured Mair's drink herself. Her Mum had enjoyed a Mackeson, too. Helen thought it tasted like cough medicine, and said as much when she placed it on the table in front of Mair. 'I don't know how you stomach it,' she quipped.

'It's something of a landlady's favorite; it doesn't matter if it's warm or cold, it's got a body that lasts, and one glass can get you through the whole night, if you need it to,' said Mair. 'I dare say it's why Nan and I both learned to enjoy it.'

Helen was puzzled. 'I didn't know you were ever a pub landlady, Mair. Where was that? When?'

Mair smiled across the head of her beer. 'That was my other life. I ran a place called The Cat and Whistle, down by the docks. Knocked it down now, they have. And good riddance. It was nearly the ruin of me, that place.'

Helen was about to ask what she meant, exactly, when Hywel Evans touched her on the shoulder and mentioned they were running short of Welsh cakes. Helen apologized to Mair that she had to abandon her, then apologized to Hywel for her lack of attentiveness, and promised to tend to it right away.

Before she turned toward the bar she happened to glance out through the window.

Her stomach clenched; there was Bob, her bastard of an ex-husband standing with his arm around Sadie's waist, who was hanging around his neck, kissing his cheek. And he was shaking hands with Aled.

Helen's heart thumped in her chest. She felt dizzy. What did it mean? The man who'd made her life a complete misery was now standing just a few yards away, and seemed to be bonding with her daughter – the daughter she'd tried so hard to protect from him.

Hywel whispered in her ear, 'The sandwiches are getting a bit thin on the ground too – if you know what I mean.'

Helen plastered a smile on her face, did her best to stop her hands trembling, and headed toward the refuge of the kitchen.

Evan

Having visited the pub after the funeral to express their condolences to Helen more fully than they'd been able to when they'd shaken her hand at the church door, the Glovers had decided it was too full for them to stay; Betty had popped to the loo, and they'd left. Standing beside the car Evan asked, 'Do you think you can manage to get up there with those on your feet after all?' He pointed to the hillside.

'Is there a path?'

'Most of the way . . . well, some of the way.'

Betty wriggled her toes. 'These shoes are old enough that I don't mind them getting a bit messy. I'll manage.' Evan suspected she didn't want to miss out on anything.

The couple set out, Betty following her husband's lead; the path was really only wide enough for one.

Over his shoulder Evan asked, 'What were you gabbing to the vicar about after the interment, by the way?'

'Remember he said in court he'd been up at the place where they found the remains on October 31st and said there was nothing there then?'

'Yes.'

'Well, I was asking him why he went there at all. They didn't ask in court.'

'And?'

'He said he'd been past the RAF ruin on his way to the sites we're about to visit, to bless them and protect them with holy water before Halloween. So what's all that about, then?'

'Tell you when we get there – not so easy to climb and shout over the wind,' was just about all Evan could manage. He'd have to consider at least thinking about getting some regular exercise soon.

Finally reaching the Concubine's Pillow, Evan announced – somewhat breathlessly, 'It won't compromise the area if we approach the site.'

'After all that, I'm glad to hear it,' replied Betty with a cheeky grin.

Evan reached out for her, and they both stood for a moment, hand in hand, taking in their surroundings.

'If nothing else, *cariad*, it was worth the climb for the view alone,' said Betty close to her husband's ear.

Although not quite at the top of the hilly moors – which offered the highest points of the entire Gower Peninsular – they were almost there. The semi-collapsed Concubine's Pillow, and it's still-erect mate, the Devil's Table, which was about a hundred yards away, stood on what was almost a shelf – a wide, flattened plateau just beneath the steeper climb to the top. Both allowed a view across the beach below to the Dragon's Back headland, and the Dragon's Head itself far out in the sea. It was a magnificent sight which had never failed to stir Evan's soul. He looked at his wife, knowing she would love it too; her expression told him he was right.

Beneath his feet, the springy and much-chewed grass was dotted with sheep droppings and some native wildflowers. There were a few annoying signs of humanity, in the shape of the odd plastic water bottle and some snack bar wrappers, caught within tufts of spikey grass and rock outcroppings.

Betty remained quite still, apparently soaking it all in, while Evan got on with a bit of rooting about. The Concubine's Pillow offered no more than a semi-shelter from the elements, but he wanted a good look beneath the angled rock.

He shouted, 'There's been a fire in here; the structural stones are significantly charred. Might have been yesterday, or five years ago. Maybe one, or many over time. There's also a plastic sandwich wrapper. Maybe dropped here, or possibly the wind drove it into the opening.' Evan pulled out his phone. 'I'm going to take some photos,' he explained. 'Have a wander, if you like, but please take care – the grass can be slippery, and we're neither of us particularly well-shod for this expedition – you even less so than me. It's a nasty drop.'

'Yes, sir,' replied Betty, saluting. He watched as she walked about twenty yards along the shelf, then returned his attention to the task at hand. He snapped furiously.

Once he felt satisfied, he stood upright and took in the miles of beach stretching below him; Evan felt soothed as he was buffeted by the ozone-laden winds. The tide was out, though he could spot dozens of tiny figures along the distant sea's edge, and in the ocean itself; surfers, enjoying their time in the waves, without a thought of mangled remains, double funerals, or anything other than the way nature sometimes blessed them with her bounty.

Evan wondered if he'd have enjoyed surfing. At fifty-eight, he knew he was unlikely to ever find out, and admitted to himself it had a certain appeal, but didn't seem to be quite his thing; he didn't really fancy the idea of having to be zipped into the suit.

He looked over to where Betty was taking photos of the Devil's Table with her phone; the flat stone on top of the four dolmen was level with her shoulders. He'd never been keen on the Devil's Table – he'd heard such dreadfully frightening stories about it from his grandmother when he'd been a lad. He had words with his adult self as he strode off to join his wife.

'It's impressive,' she said when he arrived. 'I cannot imagine how ancient hands built this five or six thousand years ago, but it must have created awe in all who saw it.'

'So much so that it is – of course – surrounded by many legends.'

'Do tell – I know you love that stuff,' encouraged Betty.

'Well, the story goes that the dragon out there in the ocean had been captured by the devil and secured in place with chains, doomed to watch over all those who lived on its back, because their souls belonged to Old Nick himself. The devil would come up from hell through the opening beneath the table, and his concubine would do the same at hers, then they would sit here to watch his dragon breathe fire over the sea at the end of the day, creating the sunset. When he was happy that his "pet" was doing a good job, he and his consort would descend again to his realm through the gaping holes in the hillside.'

'Interesting. So many psychologically significant motifs in that story. Human beings are truly fascinating creatures,' noted Betty. Evan loved the way his wife's mind worked. 'So, are the residents of Rhosddraig all supposed to be blessed, or cursed, because they live where they do?'

Evan chuckled. 'Well, bearing in mind my gran came from Lower Middleford, the next village along, and that the residents of neighboring villages often have a healthy disrespect for each other, you won't be surprised to hear that – in her mind at least – they were cursed. Those who live in Rhosddraig believe they are blessed, of course.'

'Of course. Interesting. Listen, *cariad*, while you and I were snapping away, I began to give some serious thought to what we were discussing earlier about cairns. The idea of someone building a memorial atop sacred remains was niggling at my brain. Was James's a natural death maybe being marked by someone? Was he being revered in some way? So, maybe not a murder at all . . . maybe a tragic accident, with the victim being memorialized? What if someone had found the corpse of James Powell, and they had chosen to set his body in a place of prominence? But why the burning, twice, and the smashing? That's the problem with my ideas, the threads don't mesh, psychologically speaking; the treatment of the remains before they were covered with stones suggests anything but respect, wouldn't you agree?'

Evan gave her words the consideration they deserved, staring out at the waves crashing against the 'throat' of the Dragon's Head. 'Maybe the cairn idea was just a step too far on our part, and the police really are seeking a brutal murderer who did what they did to hide evidence of their crime.'

Evan was delighted when Betty countered with, 'Then why place the remains where they'd be found? Surely it would have been better to hide them away somewhere – just a pile of charred, broken bones, buried under what is, after all, an abundance of moorland. Or even just scattered about the entire area. They might never have been found.'

Evan grappled with the paradox for a few minutes, trying to balance the ideas of reverence and respect, with the maliciousness and mania of the cremation and mangling of the remains. Then there were the missing teeth.

Finally he said, 'On balance, I don't believe anyone would do what was done to that corpse if they'd merely happened upon it. So – an accident or a murder at some point, then the burning, removal of teeth, smashing, then burning again, followed by the covering with stones.'

'Stop it, Evan – you're making another assumption . . . the teeth could have been removed at any point along the way there, you're placing too much trust in what Rakel told you was her assumption of when they were removed.'

'You're right,' said Evan. 'I'll think on that. But, for now, why don't we just enjoy what's here, then we'll pore over our photos tonight, and we'll open a nice bottle of wine while we do it. How about that?'

'I love you, Mr Glover.'

21st April

Betty

After something less than four hours' sleep, Evan had got out of bed and had gone into their 'murder room'. Betty had heard him make his way downstairs a couple of hours later. She was worried about him, but was doing her best to offset that concern against having seen him blossom into the 'old Evan' since he'd got stuck into thinking about the Rhosddraig case for himself. She knew he was frustrated, but he was slightly less so because he was doing something about it.

Lingering in the shower, Betty kept asking herself what she'd be saying to a client facing her situation – how she'd try to help them work through it. She was annoyed that she didn't seem to have any useful advice for herself. She made her way downstairs before eight. Evan was snoring on the settee. She was relieved; he needed his sleep.

Betty was filling the kettle when her mobile phone rang. Who on earth could it be, so early on an Easter Sunday? 'Hello?'

She was surprised to hear an anxious female voice. 'Is that you, Betty?'

'Yes. Who's speaking?' The number on Betty's screen meant nothing to her.

'It's Helen Jones. From Rhosddraig.'

Betty was immediately on full alert. 'Hello, Helen. To what do I owe the—'

Betty all but held her breath as words tumbled out of Helen. 'He's back. Bob's back. My ex-husband is back. He turned up after Mum's funeral yesterday, and he spent some time with Sadie and Aled. He stayed in one of the rooms they rent out at the social club in Lower Middleford. He's coming here today. I don't know what to do. What should I do? What can I do?'

'Well, I could—' began Betty, but Helen hadn't finished.

'I should have got an injunction against him when I had the chance, but I didn't. I thought it would all stop when we got divorced, and it really had. Sort of. Well, all except the phone calls. And him turning up everywhere I went. That was bad. Really bad. But then he did stop. Really. Absolutely. Until the card came. The Valentine's card. Now he's here. He wants to come into my home. I just buried my mother – how can he do this to me? What am I saying? He knows exactly how vulnerable I am, of course he'll take advantage. I should have done something when he sent me that card, but I didn't. Why didn't I?'

Betty took a deep breath, and expelled the air as quietly as she could. She didn't want Helen to know how challenging she was finding the surprising situation.

'Okay, Helen – he's not there, in your home this minute, is he?'

'No. Sadie said she invited him for lunch. My daughter *invited* him. What can I do?'

Another deep breath.

'So we have a few hours to come up with a suitable course of action, good.' Betty used her calming voice, for her own sake as much as Helen's.

Helen continued. 'What was Sadie thinking? I know I kept everything from her, but she must understand that her father's not good for me. For us. Why would she invite him to our home?'

Betty gathered her professionalism about her, and reacted without any further hesitation; she could tell Helen needed immediate help and support, and was pretty sure the woman had no friends. 'I could be with you, at the pub, in just over an hour, how about that? I'll bring Evan, too, alright?'

Helen's voiced cracked. 'Oh would you? Oh, thank you Betty. You're wonderful. I knew you were a true friend when we had that heart to heart in Swansea Market. It made ever such a difference to me, that chat did. Come to the side door, I'll let you in there. Just knock.'

Betty woke Evan and packed him off to get showered; she dressed, filled thermal mugs with coffee, and grabbed some chocolate biscuits. They were in the car within fifteen minutes, and heading to Rhosddraig once again.

It was a lovely day for the drive, but Betty suspected an emotional storm would have to be weathered upon their arrival. She felt especially nervous because she was only too well aware that, as a therapist, she'd be out of her comfort zone. Helping people work through their problems in a neutrally furnished office was an entirely different kettle of fish than being, possibly literally, on the front line of a psychological and possibly physical battle between an abuser and his victim. She'd never had to face that sort of a situation before, so she was especially glad Evan was by her side.

Sadie

It's going to be wonderful – we'll be a proper family at lunch, and I'll be everybody's princess. Mam made such a fuss about Dad joining us, but she's wrong. It'll all be lovely. And I suppose today's as good a day to do it as any other.

Of course, I disagree that Easter Sunday is so significant, but it's really quite typical of that church lot to get it all wrong – they say Christ rose after three days, but they also say he died on Good Friday and rose on Easter Sunday. Anyone can see that's not right. If anything it would be Easter Monday he rose. *That* should be the special day.

I'm glad to be back here, in my special place, beneath the Devil's Table, looking out at the dragon, seeing the world awash with color and vibrations. It's going to be a unique day.

Another first.

I saw a hare on my way along the path. She shot past me. So fast. Sleek. Beautiful. They're very sensible to sleep aboveground, watching the stars, enjoying the fresh air. I'd do that too, if I could. And they're so fortunate that they can go to the other side whenever they want, it's just that we can't see them do it. They're true messengers; like canaries, they try to tell us when things are getting bad for us. They aren't as numerous as they once were, and we should wonder why that is. And people should be really worried about that myxomatosis that's killing them off over on the east coast of England. That's terrible, that is. It must be a warning. The same thing with the bees. And the sparrows. But no one seems to care.

I care. I care about lots of things no one else cares about. I care about this place. I saw some people up here yesterday afternoon, when everyone was squashed into the pub. I know they didn't see it as I do, alive in so many ways.

Some people in the village really do know what it's like, but they only whisper about it, because they understand its power.

For me? It's the place I've come to since I was young. My other home. Maybe even my proper home. And now, as I look down to the beach, I can see my other place of power. The part of the beach I told them about in court. The part of the beach where everyone from the village – and even visitors – will look, and think of us.

Aled and Sadie. My Romeo, and the beach.

We'll be together forever, now.

Betty

Betty noticed that Helen's eyes were pink and her voice sounded husky when she thanked them for coming. 'Sadie's gone for one of her walks, so we're alone. Come up to our kitchen, we can have a pot of tea. It's much better than the pub. Too many windows there – I keep thinking he's outside, looking in at me.'

Betty had told Evan she would take the lead in their conversation with Helen, knowing he would understand. She spoke as gently as she could, aware this was a delicate moment.

With tea on the table, they sat opposite Helen.

'You can say whatever you want, Helen. Evan and I will listen, and we'll do what we can to help.'

Helen's expression told Betty she understood the gravity of what she was about to do. She began, her voice faltering now and again as she spoke. 'It really started when Sadie was a baby. Up until then we were fine.' She looked guilty and shook her head. 'Well, I thought we were, but I suppose we weren't really. I know that now. However, it was Sadie coming along that seemed to change Bob significantly. Maybe I didn't give him as much attention as I had before, but Sadie was a bit . . . well, needy, I suppose you could say. She'd take every bit of attention I could give her, and still want more. Hardly slept at all. Cried a lot. Drove him to distraction. That's when he starting staying away for extra nights on his trips.'

Betty wanted to build a picture of the man she knew almost nothing about. 'So he traveled – on business?'

Helen nodded. 'Rep for a pharmaceutical company. When we met at uni, he knew that was what he wanted to do. I admired him for his focus, and he got a job right away. We lived in London for a bit, then moved to Slough. Not so bad for coming back here for visits. Just along the M4. But we didn't come often. I was glad to have a bit of a break from here. Young and ambitious back then, I was.'

'What did you study?' asked Betty.

'Archeology.' Betty suspected her surprise, and maybe Evan's delight, had shown when Helen added, 'I know, you'd never think it of me, would you? But I loved it. It made me feel so connected to the lives of those who had gone before. Growing up here got me hooked. I used to look at those cairns and megaliths up on the hillside, and the other Neolithic sites over at Parc le Breos in Parkmill and up on Cefn Bryn, and wonder about the lives of the people who had built them.'

Betty noticed a spark in Helen's eyes she'd never seen before; she told herself to not read too much into it, but it was worth noting. 'You didn't follow your passion into the field after university?' She was as interested in watching Helen answer almost as much as hearing what she had to say.

Helen shook her head. 'You need to stay within the academic world to thrive in it, because there are so few other opportunities. And Bob needed to move to Slough for the job he'd got, so that was that, really.'

Helen stared at her tea as she added, 'I didn't mind giving it up at the time. Bob and I had become very close at uni, and I never really socialized with the people I studied with, so I felt most complete when I was with him. It was only later, after the divorce, that I realized what I'd lost, what I'd left behind. But even now, when I have the time, I still read about archeological investigations and finds; I'm not a complete numbskull when it comes to keeping up with it all. I hope I passed my love for ancient times on to Sadie – it was important to me, though I don't think she became particularly enamored of it. She'll be doing her A level in History next year, when all this tragedy and upheaval is behind us – but that's more about dates and documents than the stuff I enjoyed . . . I *felt* history, I wasn't big on memorizing lists of data.'

Betty asked, 'And you and Bob moved here before you'd had Sadie, because your father died and you came to help out at the pub, is that right?'

Helen agreed. 'And I never left. I meant to, but Mum needed me, and she needed the pub. It was the only life she'd ever known, you see. Bob agreed he'd travel from here, and it all went okay – until Sadie, like I said. In fact, it was still not too bad when she was in her cot. Because she cried such a lot I had the cot in the bedroom with me, and Bob used the room at the end of the hall – the one that's Sadie's room now. Then, when she was old enough to sleep in a bed, she had that room and Bob and I shared my room, our room, again. But it was . . . difficult.'

Betty took one of the Welsh cakes she was offered. She knew she had to push ahead. 'Do you think you can tell me about what happened when it was bad?'

Helen looked past her, and Evan. She blushed.

Betty's heart went out to her. She understood how difficult this was for the woman.

Helen licked her dry lips. 'No, not all of it. I don't want to, and it doesn't really matter. Thinking about the details of it just makes me angry – with myself. First it was the sex – he wanted it, I didn't.'

She leaned in, glanced at Evan and said quietly, 'Sadie's was a difficult birth. She came so fast, I ended up delivering her in the pub. Couldn't even get upstairs. No doctor, until after she was out. Just the women of the village to help me. Always in a hurry, that girl was, even then.'

Betty was taken aback when Helen threw back her head and laughed, then began to cry.

Eventually Helen wiped her eyes and said, 'My mother blamed me for her being cut to ribbons when I was born. Most of her infirmities were my fault, apparently. As I uttered those words just now, I heard her speaking through my mouth. I would never say any of this to Sadie – I don't want her to feel the weight of the guilt my mother used to heap upon me every day. However, as I said, sex wasn't pleasant for me after Sadie was born. But Bob insisted. Forcefully.'

Helen nibbled her lip. 'I know we live in the twenty-first century, but, honestly, the idea that a wife could deny her husband sex didn't come naturally to me. I've never had friends, you see – not the sort I could talk to about all of this, anyway. It wasn't until I started seeing what other people wrote in some chat rooms that I realized I had been raped, over and over again, by my own husband. It never occurred to me I could turn to anyone to help me say no, and have him hear it, and take notice.'

Betty spoke gently. 'That's when we first met, I think. But you weren't able to tell me any of this.'

Helen looked helpless. 'No, I'm sorry, I couldn't. I thought there was something wrong with me, you see? He was always telling me I wasn't normal, and I believed him.'

It was a story Betty had heard too many times, and it still had the power to make her angry.

Tears rolled down Helen's chapped cheeks as she confessed, 'He knew I didn't want Mum to guess what was going on, and that I wouldn't make a noise to disturb Sadie; he took advantage of that. I wasn't as strong – emotionally or physically – back then as I am now, so I would tell him no, he'd beat me, and he'd take me anyway. No publicly visible bruises, of course. Except maybe once or twice.'

'I'm sorry, Helen. No one deserves that,' said Betty gently.

Helen appeared to gather herself. 'I left him once. Took Sadie, of course. He was away for work, and I caught the bus to Cardiff. We stayed at a little B & B in Cathays. Nice people. They thought we were on holiday. I made the mistake of phoning Mum, just to make sure she didn't worry. I did it from Cardiff station. He found us. Mum heard an announcement when I was on the phone, then he just went from place to place with our photos until someone in the library told him where we were. I used to take Sadie to the library there – she always loved books.'

'So you came back.'

Helen sniffed. 'We came back. He threatened to tell people I was a bad mother, to take Sadie away from me. He did well at work, and really had people fooled. Everyone would have believed him, not me. But I was more determined to end it after that, and I hoped he might get tired of all the fighting. It took a while.'

'Your divorce?'

'Believe it or not, he found someone new. Someone he said he could be happy with. He welcomed the divorce. You know, when I found out about his new woman I wondered if I should tell her what he was like – but I had to save myself, and Sadie, you see, so I didn't say anything. I feel bad about that now. I allowed the divorce to be an easy one, no blame, no fault, no mention of everything he'd put me through, just to get it over with. Though I insisted he couldn't have any unsupervised visits with Sadie. He signed all the papers without a fuss. I just hope he didn't do the same to his new woman as he did to me.'

'You had your peace?'

Helen shook her head. Betty noticed she was picking at the sides of her nails. 'There were phone calls – which went on for months. And he would turn up out of the blue, standing outside the pub, staring at me. Then, for no apparent reason, it stopped. Until now. It started with that card. A Valentines card – like we were still a couple. Do you think he did the same to her as he did to me? Do you think she's managed to get rid of him, and that's why he's come back?'

'Do you?'

Helen's eyes blazed. 'Betty, I don't *know*. Please don't treat me like I'm your client, just asking me the same questions I'm asking you. I need advice. I need some practical help. This man will be in my home in a couple of hours, and I have to face him – just feet away from the bedroom where he raped me for years on end. How do you think that makes me feel? How can I deal with it? What can I do to stop it?'

Betty was wounded by the savagery of Helen's tone. Evan squeezed her leg under the table.

'Only me, Mam. Aled's here too,' called Sadie, the door below slamming shut.

'I'm up here with some friends,' called Helen shakily.

'Oh.' Sadie sounded surprised. 'Okay then, Aled will have a coffee in the pub kitchen. I'll be up in a minute.'

Betty had to act fast. 'Have you spoken to Sadie about any of this?'

Helen shook her head. 'I wanted to protect her, not traumatize her.'

'You have to tell her about it, Helen. She needs to understand why her father being in the same room as you is not healthy for you,' pressed Betty.

'I can't,' croaked Helen, just as her daughter entered the kitchen.

'Mam – what's the matter? What can't you do?' She glowered at Betty. 'What have you said to upset Mam? You know she's already very low because of Nan dying. Why are you here anyway? And you? You're one of the policemen who tried to have Aled put in prison forever. You're not welcome here.'

Helen blew her nose. 'Sadie, you have no right to say that. Betty and Evan are my guests. You'll be polite. My roof, my rules.'

Betty was stunned when Sadie hissed angrily, 'Oh listen to you, Mam – just like Nan. That's what she used to say to us all the time, wasn't it? Well, I took it from her then, but I'm not taking it from you now. I'm almost an adult and I'll do as I please.'

Betty watched Helen, wondering how she'd respond; would she crumble, or rally?

Helen reacted as though she'd been slapped in the face; her eyes were wide, her mouth open. She stared at her daughter in shock, and dismay. Her feeling of betrayal was tangible for Betty. The room fell silent.

'You invited your father here for lunch,' said Helen quietly. 'I won't have him under this roof. Not ever again.'

'You've no right to stop me seeing him. He's my blood,' said Sadie indignantly. 'You've tried to stop us being a family all these years. Well, he and I have been getting together for months, I see him quite often in fact, and he's very happy to have finally met Aled. We're all going to have lunch and be nice to each other. So there.'

Betty grabbed for Evan's hand, out of sight, waiting.

'You have no idea what you're asking of me, Sadie.' Helen's voice trembled.

'What, to have lunch with the man you threw out of here all those years ago? The man you've tried to keep me from seeing? My *father*. That can't be so difficult.'

Helen stared into Betty's eyes. In them, Betty saw true despair and shame. Then resolve.

'Betty, Evan – I wonder if you'd mind letting me and Sadie have a few minutes together. Alone. Maybe Aled could make a coffee for you downstairs.'

Betty and Evan stood. Before they left the room Betty felt compelled to say, 'Sadie, your mum's in a fragile state – please be respectful of her.'

As she turned to leave she heard Sadie snort. It wasn't a pleasant sound.

Halfway down the stairs she whispered to Evan, 'You go on. It'll be a good chance for you to get the measure of Aled. I want to hear what I can.'

Evan hissed, 'You can't listen to them, it's private.'

'This isn't a client relationship. I don't like the sound of how Sadie's treating her mother. I think it's important for me to get the full picture.'

Evan puffed out his cheeks with what Betty judged to be an 'on your own head be it' expression on his face.

She squatted down on a stair that didn't seem to creak too much.

Helen

'This is one of the hardest things I've ever had to do in my life, Sadie.' Helen's voice sounded muffled inside her head. She'd cried so much since the previous day even her ears were blocked up. 'I don't know where to begin.'

'You threw Dad out after you had a nervous breakdown. Start there, if you like. Or tell me about how me being a naughty child made you have a nervous breakdown. That would be okay too.'

Helen was astonished at the coldness in Sadie's voice. She stuttered, 'I . . . I never had a nervous breakdown. And certainly not because you were a naughty child. You weren't. You had a fair pair of lungs on you as a baby, but I loved you more than I loved myself. I did everything for you, and because of you I allowed myself to be . . . wait, what makes you think I had a nervous breakdown?'

'Dad told me. He said you abandoned me here one day and took yourself off to Cardiff. He was terrified about what you might do to yourself. He came and found you and saved you.' Sadie spoke with the certainty of youth.

'I did go to Cardiff, but I took you with me. I was going to start a new life there for the both of us, away from your father. I would never have left you, Sadie. You were . . . you *are* my life. You were about three. Don't you remember us visiting the library there? You loved it. We went every day for a week. We used to picnic in the cemetery beside it, listening to the birds. There was a nice librarian there who let you take one of the toys with you at the end of our first day. You kept it. You've probably still got Mrs Hare around the place somewhere – you wouldn't go anywhere without her until you were about six or seven. It's why I hunted for ages to find a hare-shaped mould to make your birthday blancmange. All the other children had rabbit-shaped ones. You were really quite particular about the difference.'

Sadie screwed up her face. Her voice was hesitant. 'Mrs Hare? You're making it up.'

For a moment, Helen wondered if she'd dreamed it all – the library, the stuffed toy. 'Come on, I bet you've still got her somewhere,' she said, moving away from the table, 'let's look now.' She headed toward Sadie's bedroom; her daughter was wrong-footed, and scampered after her.

'You're not going into my room, Mam. It's private.'

'My roof, my rules,' shouted Helen, her mind racing through the details of her time away from Bob, in the capital city. She hadn't imagined it. She hadn't dreamed it. It was all real. She still had the weakness in her left arm.

'No, Mam,' screamed Sadie.

Helen was having none of it. Flinging open the door to her daughter's room she didn't care that it was a complete mess. She pulled open Sadie's wardrobe, expecting to have to hunt about in the mounds of discarded old plimsoles, scarves, and winter tights with holes in them to find the toy, but she didn't.

Sitting on the shelf across the top of the flimsy 1940s utility wardrobe was Mrs Hare. She had half a floppy ear, no eyes or nose, one leg, two arms, and an entirely bald belly. She wore a tiara of diamante stones, several glittering necklaces, and sat on a velvet cushion. Plastered onto the knotty wood around her were several printed icons of St Melangell – identifiable because of the brown hare she was holding – all decorated with glittery stickers.

Helen was stunned. 'Mrs Hare. A librarian named Jane gave her to you.'

'No!' shouted Sadie. 'A giant gave her to me. Her hair was on fire. It was in a church. A huge, dark place. No one spoke. The windows went up and up to the sky. It had a spire. She was the priestess. The Devil's

Concubine. She gave me Mrs Hare and said I was her special girl. I had to take very great care of her. Treat her with honor and respect. Forever. Because I was chosen.'

Helen's mouth was dry. She felt the panic rise in her stomach. Sadie looked and sounded as though she were in a trance.

'I think you've got things muddled up a bit, Sadie love. She was a large woman, I suppose, and she did have long red hair. And Cathays library does look a bit like a church. But the rest? You were only little. You weren't used to strangers at all. We'd never been anywhere – your father wanted us here, at home the whole time, and you weren't allowed down into the pub. He wouldn't even let you play with the children in the village. You and I used to stay up here, and I would read to you from my old archeology textbooks. He wouldn't let you have any children's books. Mum and I would read you whatever was on the shelves already.'

'The hare is sacred, you know,' continued Sadie in her odd voice. 'The hare is able to run from our world to the next, carrying messages about our hopes and wishes with it. Mrs Hare helps me all the time. She makes my dreams come true, because I treat her with respect. She communicates with the concubine down there for me, and with a saint up here. She has a magical life, between two worlds.'

'Sadie, you're not making any sense. Have you . . . are you taking something I don't know about? Something you shouldn't?'

'Oh shut up, Mam. I only put natural things into my body. I'm special. Besides, it's not me talking rubbish, it's you. *You* told me that the old church here, the one that was swallowed up by the sands below us, was called St Melangell's. When they built the new one they changed the name because too many of the locals here revered the hare more than Christ. *You* told me that. It was in your precious books. They should have kept the original name. St Melangell is the patron saint of hares; they're her little lambs. Her feast day is May 27th, my birthday. It can't be a coincidence. I really am hers.'

Helen was grappling with her emotions, and her recollection of ancient lore. 'Maybe this all came from some of the books I used to read to you about Welsh mythologies, but it's all joined up wrong in what you're saying.'

'It's not myth, it's true, Mam.'

Having mentally faced the prospect of having to explain to her daughter how her father had been a horrific abuser, Helen now found herself off balance, needing to work out why her child seemed to be worshipping a stuffed toy, and believing all sorts of muddled, strange tales from millennia past. She sat on the edge of Sadie's bed, at a loss.

Sadie's voice had a harsh edge when she said, 'Maybe you did take me to Cardiff with you, but I know you left me alone too. I remember being here with just Dad. Only him and me. Talking through the night. Why did you leave me? You just said you never would.'

Helen knew there was no going back. 'Your father tracked us down in Cardiff and brought us back here. He was very angry. Even more angry than usual. We were fighting. He broke my arm. I ended up in hospital. There were three nights I was away from you. Only three nights, in your entire life. They had to operate. I had to be there. Don't you remember me having my arm in plaster for months? We've got photos of your birthday that year – it was in plaster then; your father wouldn't let me be in any of the pictures he took, but you can see part of my arm in one of them. Just one.'

Sadie's brow furrowed. 'Was your arm blue?'

Helen nodded. 'There was a wrapping over the plaster.'

'Maybe I remember,' said Sadie quietly. Helen watched her daughter's face intently; Sadie was thinking, that much was clear. 'You're saying Dad hit you?'

Helen's heart lurched. 'Yes. He . . . he was quite brutal. In many ways. You really don't need to know all the details.'

'Is that why Nan called him the devil? When I would ask her about the scary noises in the night. When I would ask her why you were crying in the bathroom?'

Oh God, you heard us. Helen's heart was breaking. 'Maybe. I tried to always be quiet. I did my best, love.'

'I get it now,' said her daughter flatly. 'You should have done a "Hashtag Me Too" on him. A woman shouldn't allow herself to be treated that way. Women are far superior to men.'

Helen couldn't believe her daughter's nonchalance. She felt hot tears roll down her raw cheeks. 'Oh Sadie, love – that sort of thing is for celebrities, and Hollywood types. It's not for women in tiny villages where they have no options, and no power. Where they have a child they love more than life itself – and a husband who's always threatening to tell the police they're mad, or worse, and never let them see their darling baby again. I didn't even have a car back then – we caught three buses to get to Cardiff. How can a victim escape if she's got nowhere to go, no way to get there, and no future, even if she makes it?'

'Dad said you—'

Helen could feel her face getting hot. 'Forget what he said, Sadie. Your father's always massaged the truth to fit his idea of what it should be. When he left us for another woman, it was the best thing that could ever have happened to us. Yes, don't look so shocked – he left us for another woman. I never told you because I didn't want you to think his leaving was your fault. But even then he stalked me for months. He terrorized me with phone calls and unexpected visits. He wouldn't let up. *He* moved on – but he wanted to make damned sure I didn't. Just the sound of the phone made me want to throw up. *His* fault.'

'You're lying.'

Helen couldn't take it any longer. She let it all out. It was time. 'You young people – you bear your souls on social media – you beat your breasts online about injustices, inequalities, and exclusions. It's idealism run amok. It's not reality. Reality is needing to have somewhere to live that isn't a horrible little room with mice in the walls. It's about needing to see your child educated and socialized and raised with love around them, not hate. Escape isn't easy, and for some it's an impossibility. Good for you for shouting about it, but instead of spending hours ranting about things online, why not get up and do something about it? Raise money for safe places, for free therapy, counselling, and self-defense classes. Don't just sit on the sidelines whining that no one else is changing things. Nothing changes on its own – you have to take action. But no one does. Better to bleat and blame, than act and help. Dear God, what's our society going to be like when you lot are in charge? A complete and total mess – with everything debated to death in a virtual world, and not one person rolling up their sleeves and getting things done.'

Helen watched as her daughter leaped to her feet, red in the face, screaming, 'It'll be no worse than the mess you lot have made of it.'

She was caught completely off guard by her daughter's open-handed slap to her face. She toppled, trying to save herself by putting out her arm.

She heard the break before she felt it.

Evan

Sitting in the deserted pub with his wife crouched silently on the stairs – a strange feeling so early on an Easter Sunday morning – Evan wondered what had become of Aled. They'd shared some perfunctory pleasantries over a coffee, then the lad had said he had to slip out to get something from his friend Stew Wingfield. That had been a while ago, so he assumed he wasn't coming back.

Evan had expected to hear some raised voices coming from the upstairs living quarters, but the thud startled him.

That can't be good, he thought.

Reaching the foot of the stairs, he could see Betty was bounding up them two at a time. He followed, likewise.

'Help!' called Sadie. Evan and Betty followed the shout, and found Helen in a heap on the floor at the foot of Sadie's bed.

'Don't try to get up,' said Evan, taking control of the situation he'd sized up in an instant. 'Sadie, get your mother a glass of water, now.'

Evan saw how glazed Sadie's expression was, and knew Betty had spotted it too. 'I'll get it,' she said. 'Sadie can stay with her mum.'

Sadie started to cry. 'I'm sorry, Mam. I didn't mean it. Please forgive me? Here – have this.' Evan was amazed to see her hand her mother a long silk scarf. 'It's pretty. It'll make it all better. Pretty things always make it better.' Sadie sounded like a six-year-old talking to a doll she'd just dropped.

Evan was horrified, and fascinated, in equal measure. This girl – not quite eighteen, and clearly living a protected life – seemed to think an act of violence would be forgiven upon receipt of some sort of gift. He wondered where she had learned such connections. It concerned him; having chatted to Aled for just a few minutes, he'd at least had the chance to notice the boy was slight, but muscular. And evasive about his relationship with Sadie.

Betty arrived with the water. 'Just give your mum some space, okay? Evan and I will help her up. Helen – Helen? Do you think anything is broken?'

Helen was glassy eyed. She nodded. 'My wrist crunched. I think I broke it.'

Evan could see that Helen's left wrist and hand were already starting to swell. 'Right-O, Betty love, can you go and find some peas or something in the freezer, and a towel?'

'On it.' Betty dashed out, and returned minutes later with the requested supplies.

When Helen's wrist was bound and chilled, Evan and Betty each took an arm, and helped her onto the bed.

'I'm phoning for an ambulance,' said Evan.

'It'll be quicker if we drive Helen to the hospital ourselves,' said Betty.

Evan knew she was right. He watched with admiration as his wife comforted the injured woman. 'Do you want to talk about what happened, Helen?'

Helen seemed to be studying the pattern on the tea towel wrapped around her hand. 'I fell. Tripped over something on the floor. My own stupid fault.'

'Yes,' said Sadie airily, 'Mam's a bit clumsy sometimes. Maybe it's the concussion she got at the court coming back again.'

Evan was chilled by the girl's cool demeanor; he was in little doubt about the truth of the situation. 'So that's what you'll both say, is it?' he said. Betty shot him a warning glance, but he felt it was his duty to press Helen to tell the truth. 'Come on now, Helen; how many times over the years you were with your husband did you tell someone you'd slipped, or tripped, or bumped into something? Is that how you want to teach your daughter to react within a relationship? And you, Sadie – isn't it healthier to own up to the truth of what you've just done, and face the consequences?'

He was completely taken aback when Sadie stamped her foot and screamed, 'Consequences? What do you know about consequences? I'm the only one around here who has any idea what that means. I've had to live through the consequences of my mother throwing my father out, my grandmother being a bitch, and you lot taking my Aled away from me. I've had to bear all those consequences. Well, Nan's dead, Dad's coming for lunch, and I've finally got Aled. So there. He's mine now. Forever. I'm all he'll ever need, and he's all I'll ever need. We are complete. You? Rubbish, that's what you are. I have forces on my side you can't possibly understand, and I've had to use all my powers to achieve what I have despite the consequences of other people's actions. Love and blood and faith, that's what it's all about.'

She pushed past Betty. 'Say what you want, Mam, I'm out of here. I'm going down to be with Aled.'

'He left. Said something about Stew Wingfield,' said Evan.

Sadie had an unfathomable look on her face as she said, 'He won't have gone far away from me.' She clattered down the stairs.

'You telling her about her dad didn't go too well then,' said Betty.

Helen shook her head. 'Not really. And there was a lot of other stuff too. My daughter's a bit mixed up about a few things. She's confused. Angry. She hit me.'

'I know,' said Betty. 'I stayed on the stairs. I listened.'

'Could you phone our helper Agata, please, Evan?' asked Helen feebly. 'Someone's got to open up if Aled's not here; Sadie can't serve because she's not eighteen yet. Agata will do it. Her number's on the noticeboard in the kitchen. Ask if her sister can come to serve the food. It's Easter, we'll be busy. We'll have to offer just sandwiches or—'

Betty said, 'Stop. I'll phone Agata. Let us handle it.'

Helen started to sob. 'Thank you. I'm so useless.'

Betty hugged her. 'No you're not. It's just all a bit much for you at the moment.'

Helen's voice was thick, her eyes pleading. 'I've always tried my best. For Sadie. For Mum. For the pub. But it's never enough. I've let everyone down. Mum's gone, and Sadie? I don't know who she is anymore.'

'She's a teenager,' said Evan.

Betty nodded. 'A breed all their own. I tell you what, I'll phone Agata, then I'll drive you to the hospital. Evan can wait here until Agata arrives; keep an eye on things. Alright?'

Helen sniffed her acceptance.

Sadie

Mam's so weak. And so stupid. I'm neither.

By the sound of it she always has been. I wonder if what she was saying is true? Did Dad really beat her? Did she try to run from him – with me? I do remember her blue arm – that was *broken*? Maybe Dad made up Mam's nervous breakdown, to make a point. Sounds like she wasn't far off one in any case.

I'll go and see if Aled's gone back to his house. It's his now, not his Grannie Gwen's. He can sell it and we'll have loads of money. Fantastic. Stew's been staying over with him this past few nights, for company. Once I'm eighteen, I can go and stay with Aled.

The two of us alone. That would be brilliant.

Everything's a possibility now his grannie's gone. And Nan too. Good riddance to them both. Old women should know when it's time to go – they have no use, no power. They should just step aside and let us have our time.

Stew's parents are weird. When I knocked just now to ask them if Aled was there, and they told me that he wasn't, and that Stew was over at Aled's, they sounded . . . cold. Hard. I mean, I know they're English, but they've been here long enough to have warmed up a bit.

His mum seems nice when she's in the *Cwtch,* but everybody's public face is different to their private one. Has to be.

They sat on Gwen's side of the church for the funeral. Of course. Maybe they blame Nan for Gwen's death. I know a lot do. Maybe they think I'm like Nan. Just goes to show how wrong people can be. I'm nothing like Nan. Nothing like Mam, either. I'm truly unique.

I'll get rid of Stew if he's there, so Aled and I can be alone for a while. It's been ages since we had time for just the two of us. Months. I can't stand it any longer. The funerals are over now – and Mam, for all her faults, said those lovely things about how everyone should be supportive of us as a couple – which came a surprise, I must say. Good for her. It all helps.

There goes Mam now, in the car with her 'friend' Betty. 'Friend' my eye. Betty's her crutch. I'll wave and smile. I should. Serves her right for being against Dad coming for lunch. I'd better phone him, I suppose; no point him coming now. More time for me and Aled to be alone.

I'll rearrange the lunch for tomorrow. That's soon enough, and Dad doesn't have to leave until Tuesday morning, after the Bank Holiday, which is good.

Evan

Finding himself now completely alone in a pub before it opened, Evan wondered what Rakel's husband Gareth would make of his situation; heavenly, he imagined.

Knowing Helen and Betty might be gone for the better part of the day, and with the word from Agata being that she wouldn't be able to make it to the pub until half eleven at the earliest, Evan had helpfully written a note which he'd stuck to the outside of the pub's door announcing the revised opening time.

He helped himself to an orange juice, and sat at a table beside the wall of windows which looked toward the beach and, looming over it, the hillside where he and Betty had walked the day before.

He pulled out his phone and scrolled through the photos he'd taken, thinking about what the signs of life trapped within the angle of the Concubine's Pillow might mean. Realizing he had the time to do it, he phoned Liz Stanley, to offer to send her the photos, if she liked the sound of his idea about the possible role of cairns in the case.

She shouted her name when she answered his call. Her voice echoed a little.

'Hello Liz, Evan here,' he replied. 'Happy Easter. How are you?'

'I'm okay, thanks. You? Happy Easter to you and Betty, too.'

'Thanks. Look, I know you're busy, but wanted to share a thought with you. Is that okay, given the current oversight situation?'

'Go for it. My new-new boss is open to anything. He'll be asking the office cleaners for their thoughts next. Please tell me you've had a bright idea.'

Evan outlined his thinking about cairns and the secreting of a body. He offered to email the photos he'd taken. Liz thanked him. 'I'm on my way to Rhosddraig right now, as it happens,' she added.

'I'll see you in the pub then. I'm holding the fort.' He explained the situation.

'That doesn't sound good. Not you being alone in charge of a pub, but the Jones family dynamic. And if Helen's not there I might just turn around; I need to talk to Sadie, and I can't do that without her mother or an approved adult being there.'

Evan couldn't help himself. 'Why do you need to talk to Sadie?'

Silence.

'Liz?'

'I'm thinking. About what I can and can't say.'

Evan waited.

'I'll be there in about half an hour. Can't talk now.'

Liz was gone. Evan hoped it meant she was going to give him some information face to face that she didn't want to divulge over the phone. He felt the old excitement rise in his belly, then thought it might be the orange juice. He took the empty glass back to the bar. A hesitant knock at the door drew his attention. He opened it, ready to point at the note, but when he saw the hollow eyes and pallor of Mair Bevan he helped her inside, and made her take a seat while he brought her a glass of water. She drank it, gulping it down.

'Better?' he asked. The woman looked dreadful.

'I'd have preferred a glass of Mackeson, but beggars can't be choosers,' she replied, a wicked glint in her rheumy eyes.

Evan wasn't too sure that she was in any fit state to drink beer for breakfast – or at any other time, for that matter. 'Maybe I could find some somewhere,' he suggested.

'I'm just kidding. I know I shouldn't. Not with the tablets I'm on. I had two glasses yesterday, and regretted it all night. Didn't sleep at all well. But here I am. I came to see Helen before church.' She looked at her watch. 'With everything that's been going on, and me being ill, the vicar's got some of the younger one's on the altar guild now, so I don't need to get there until the service starts.'

Evan explained everything that was going on, without mentioning Sadie's involvement in her mother's fall.

Mair sucked her dentures. 'This family. Always the same. Trouble.'

Evan was curious. 'How do you mean?'

Mair narrowed her hooded eyes. 'I know you. You used to come here when you were a youngster. Shirley Pritchard's boy, aren't you? Married some bloke from Gorseinon, didn't she?'

Evan nodded. 'She did. David Glover. I'm Evan. You knew my mother?'

'I did. In passing. Your gran, too. Vi. Still alive, is she? Your mother, not your gran.'

'Left us a few years ago. Too young.'

Mair sighed. 'One of the problems you face if you live as long as I have is that there's almost no one left alive to remember with. Even the ones I recall being born, like your mam, and Myfanwy here, have gone. Being old is bloody hard work. Lonely, too.'

'Better than the alternative,' said Evan as brightly as possible.

Mair's expression suggested she didn't agree. 'Pain all the time, a constant parade of doctors and specialists, and the people you know dropping around you like flies? Oh yes, barrel of laughs it is. Policeman, aren't you?'

'Retired.'

'You're not old enough to retire.'

'I'm old enough to want to.'

Mair looked toward the bar. 'Nan wouldn't have begrudged me one little bottle of orange juice. Don't bother with a glass. Find a cold one in the fridge for me, would you? Good lad.'

Evan smiled at being called a lad, and returned with a chilled, opened mixer-bottle of orange juice. Mair picked it up with two rope-veined, claw-like hands and drank deeply. Evan found the sight unsettling.

'Have you lived here all your life?' asked Evan, by way of conversation.

'Worked in Swansea through the war, and after. But yes, born in the house I live in now,' she replied. Having wiped her thin, purplish lips with the tips of her wizened fingers, Mair added, 'So Helen won't be back for hours. Pity. I was going to tell her what Nan and I had been talking about the day Nan died. It'll keep, I suppose.'

Evan couldn't resist. 'I could pass it on when she gets back, if you want to get to church.'

Mair rolled the bottle between her hands. She stared at Evan, but her raisin eyes gave nothing away. She made chewing motions. Spittle gathered at the corners of her lips. Evan studied his nails.

'Can't hurt,' she said, 'it's a later start at church today, for Easter, so I've got a bit of time yet, and they'll be forever up at A & E. I go to bed early these days.' She took another swig from the bottle. 'I won't beat about the bush. Nan and her husband Jack had problems. Years back. Before Helen was born. Jack was a man who had certain . . . tastes. Did you ever come across a place called the Cat and Whistle in your time?'

Evan was surprised. 'I was a policeman in Swansea, how would I not have come across it? It was the pub for which the term "den of iniquity" was invented.' He wondered where Mair was going.

'Used to be the landlady there, I did.'

Evan was gobsmacked. 'When?'

Mair's lips stretched into a smile. 'Barmaid there from 1942. I was still a teenager – not that we were called that, back then. Used to hide in the cellars with the barrels during the Swansea Blitz. Like the Windmill Theatre in London, we never closed. I took the reins in 1960. Retired when I was seventy.'

Evan let the idea percolate. He was looking at a woman with a reputation for running a knocking shop above a pub, who'd been questioned in more cases of prostitution, theft, violence, drug-trafficking and even murder, than he could recall.

'You're *Mary* Bevan?'

Mair nodded.

Evan pictured the notorious woman he was speaking about; he'd never met her face-to-face, but he'd seen a large photograph above the bar in The Cat and Whistle, which had shown her as curvaceous, flame-haired, and fearless. Had that woman become this shrivelled thing in front of him?

'My father insisted Mary went on my birth certificate, but my mother always called me Mair. I married Dewi Bevan in 1953. Used the English version of my name at work; it allowed me to keep the lives of Mair Bevan of Rhosddraig, and Mary Bevan of The Cat, totally separate. Never did time, or nothing, so that was good. Lived upstairs when I worked there early on, then I got a car. Very fancy. I was able to spend the odd night every week here, with my mother. Came back here when I retired.'

Evan was at sea. 'And what's that got to do with Jack and Nan Jones?'

'Before Helen was born, Jack would visit The Cat sometimes. Nan used to hit him about, see? Strapping woman she was back then, not like you'd have seen her recently. Jack must have found he liked it, or maybe he always did. Either way, my girls did a better job of it than Nan, and he was prepared to pay for the superior service. Then Helen came along, and he stayed home. Eventually he started visiting one of my girls who lived here, in the village. Jackie Beynon started at The Cat as a barmaid when she was about twenty. Kids growing up in Rhosddraig? Nothing here for them at all. And Jackie was never the quiet, studious type. Took her a while to get into the drugs though. I know for a fact she was clean when she started there; we overlapped by a couple of years, and all my girls were clean.'

Evan shook his head. How often had he heard that?

'And don't look at me like I'm dirt on your shoe,' croaked Mair. 'Enough of your lot used to skulk up the back stairs so they wouldn't be seen by the drinkers below when they wanted a bit of a treat on the house. It's why I never did time. Backs being scratched all over the place, there were. They trusted me. Especially when AIDS came along. Terrible thing, that.'

Evan was starting to feel angry. He'd never been able to consider working vice – he'd have wanted to shake everyone and tell them to wake up to what they were doing to themselves and those they loved. No, not his cup of tea. And too many people like this woman – ready to enable all sorts, then excuse it to anyone who challenged them.

'So what did Nan Jones want to talk about?' he asked bluntly. Why not revert to his old interviewing techniques? He was certain Mair/Mary would cope.

'Nan hated Gwen Beynon. Everyone knew it, but no one knew why. I certainly didn't. But when I guessed Gwen Beynon was dying in hospital, I told Nan to go to talk to her; have it out with her, once and for all. See, I've lived with the consequences of not having spoken my mind to too many people who've died. Of not having asked them questions I should have done. And when they're gone? Well, it's too late then. It eats away at you. So, Nan did as I suggested, and confronted Gwen. Then she came to see me because Gwen told her to. She got everything off her chest when she came to see me. It turned out Nan believed that Gwen and Jack had been having an affair. Told me she'd seen them together on New Year's Eve 1999, with her own eyes. Now there's a date when everyone knows exactly where they were. I expect you do, don't you?'

She paused, and Evan nodded. He wasn't going to give this woman the satisfaction of engaging in an actual conversation with her.

She continued, 'Me? I was at home, nursing Gwen who had the flu something awful. With me for five days, she was. I missed an epic night at The Cat. So there was no way Nan could have seen Jack with Gwen that night. On what turned out to be her deathbed, Gwen sent Nan to me, knowing I'd been nursing her that night. Knowing I could tell Nan her suspicions were rubbish.'

'So Nan was wrong?'

Mair nodded. 'Stupid woman. I told her so, too. All those years she's been such a cow to Gwen? Very unfair. And all because she thought she knew best, and knew everything. Always did. I thought Nan deserved to hear a few home truths about her own family, so I told her all about her Jack's little habit, and how he'd really enjoyed how she'd treated him. You should have seen her face. Purple, she went.'

Mair paused and drank from her bottle. 'I didn't tell her with any relish, mind you, but because she was talking rubbish. Nan went off in a in a terrible state after telling me to my face I was a liar. She was going on and on about her being sure Jack had his trousers off when she saw him through a gap in Gwen's bedroom curtains, then she went all white, and started swearing her head off about how she'd always known Aled Beynon was the wrong boy for Sadie, and how she was glad he was locked up and on trial. Barmy, that one. Always was.'

Evan waited. Nothing. 'And that was it?' He'd expected more.

She nodded.

Evan thought about what she'd said. 'Could Nan have seen her husband Jack with Gwen's daughter Jackie that night?'

Mair studied her bottle. 'No. Jackie would have been down at The Cat. That night of all nights? Bound to be a cracker there that night. She wouldn't have missed it.'

'If you say so.'

Mair nodded. 'I do. Maybe it's best you tell Helen, rather than me having to do it. I don't want another Jones woman going off on me. Or maybe don't tell her everything about her dad. Just tell her about the other stuff – you know, the bits her mam asked about.'

Evan didn't think it would be the right time to tell an already reeling Helen Jones that her mother had beaten the father she'd worshipped, who had himself enjoyed a predilection for masochistic sex at the hands of prostitutes overseen by a retired madam who lived up the road.

He puffed out his cheeks. His gran had been right when she'd said people in villages hung net curtains in their windows with good reason; there really was no way to guess what went on behind them.

'I'll do my best to convey the essence of what you've just told me about your conversation with her mother to Helen,' said Evan. 'I'll see how she's faring when she gets back from the hospital. As you can imagine, she's still a little raw after her mother's death.'

Mair put down her empty bottle. 'Not much love lost there. Nan and her? Oil and water. Nan dominated Jack, Helen was dominated by Bob. Not a nice man, Bob Thistlewaite. Polar opposite of Helen's father; liked to play-act the tough man just a little too much with the girls, did Bob. In the end, they had to tell him he wasn't welcome at The Cat anymore.'

Evan's years of experience were the only reason he didn't gasp. 'Helen's ex-husband, Bob, was also one of your customers?'

Mair shook her head. 'I'd left by the time he showed up. But I kept in touch with my replacement, of course. Professional courtesy – and curiosity.' Evan noticed a truly unpleasant gleam in Mair's eyes. 'Bob found The Cat long before he and Helen ever moved here, when he was visiting Swansea on business. It's funny how things happen, isn't it? I saw a bruise on Helen's arm one day; she tried to hide it, of course, which made me notice it even more, and the others that followed. I mentioned it to Nan, but she told me it was none of my business. I heard from my successor at The Cat there was a nasty piece of work about; I didn't put two and two together at first, then it turned out it was Bob Thistlewaite. Returned to The Cat after he and Helen got divorced. He finally got slung out around 2009, not long before they closed the old place down altogether. Best thing for it.'

'Why wasn't he shown the door long before that, if he was known to be violent?' asked Evan. It wasn't the norm for those who ran brothels to allow their source of income to be endangered, he knew that much.

Mair nodded. 'Yes, well, when you've got a punter who has easy access to all sorts of pharmaceutical samples, it means he has some leverage, see.'

Evan's train of thought was interrupted by knocking at the door. He was torn. 'Back in a minute,' he said.

An anxious-looking young woman wearing every color of the rainbow, and a few extra, stepped through the door as he opened it.

'I'm Agata,' she announced. 'You're Evan, correct?' Evan nodded. 'Thanks, I'll take it from here. My sister will be here soon to help prepare the food. She was at a friend's house, revising. She'll come on her bike, along the coastal path, and get here as soon as possible.'

'Is that safe?' Evan couldn't help himself.

Agata grinned. 'It's forbidden to cycle it, but for the kids around here, that path is like a motorway. They all get bikes that can cope with its rugged surfaces. She'll be fine.'

As Evan stepped aside to allow Agata to get on with her work, he spotted Liz Stanley striding across the road from the car park. He could imagine she was working on an opening quip.

'So is this how you're spending your retirement, sir? Doorman at a pub? You'd think they'd shell out for a nice uniform, with braid on the epaulettes. Get paid in beer, do you?'

'Oi, less of the lip, you,' said Evan, truly pleased to see Liz. 'Come on in. I just have something I want to ask a very interesting woman I've been chatting with. Follow me.'

When they entered the lounge, other than Agata singing to herself behind the bar, it was empty. 'Where did Mair go?' asked Evan.

'I haven't seen Mrs Bevan,' replied Agata. 'Surely she would be in church at this time? The bells were ringing as I arrived.'

Liz rolled her eyes. 'The incredible disappearing woman? Or is it something more serious – should I be phoning Betty?'

Evan was annoyed. He'd wanted to ask Mair some more questions, but it was clear they'd have to wait. He turned his attention to Liz. 'Maybe Agata will put a pot of coffee on for us. I have to wait for Betty to come back with Helen, so I could be here some time. Good to see you, by the way,' he added.

Liz cracked a smile. 'You too, Evan.'

'So? What couldn't you tell me on the phone?' he asked eagerly.

Liz nodded toward a table in a corner. 'I'll show you.' Sitting, she woke up her tablet. 'I was originally on my way here to go through Sadie's statement with her again – just a bit of fact checking, which my new boss wants us to do with everyone. But I got a call on the way, and pulled over to take it. Things have changed. You know James Powell was a keen photographer?' Evan nodded. 'He belonged to a photographic club in Treboeth, and they had a group cloud-storage area he used. It seems all his photos were automatically uploaded as he took them. They gave us access. The team found these.'

She handed the tablet to Evan. He scrolled.

'Good grief,' he said. 'I see what you mean about things having changed. You'll need to do more than just check Sadie's statement.

And, yes, at least her mother needs to be with her, possibly a solicitor too. Were you planning on taking her in?'

'I think we might need to do that.' Liz's tone was grim. Having seen the photos, Evan could understand why.

Betty

The drive to the A&E department at West Glam General had been as fast as the speed cameras allowed. Helen and Betty had hardly spoken. Helen seemed to be in a daze, blurting out half-sentences now and again; Betty wondered about the concussion Sadie had mentioned. She decided she'd speak up about it at the hospital.

Fortunately it was still early when they reached the registration area – or holding pen as Betty thought of it after half an hour. Surrounded by the walking wounded, she could imagine how the scene might have been twelve hours earlier, when the effect of alcohol upon the part of the brain responsible for decision-making had taken its toll on many.

As it was, they only had to wait an hour for Helen's name to be called. X-rays, more waiting, consultation, more waiting, then setting, strapping, and plastering all followed. They left the car park almost exactly four hours after they'd entered it. Betty was impressed.

'I might be able to help in the pub when we get back,' said Helen as they headed toward Rhosddraig.

'You'll do no such thing,' said Betty. 'You're going to listen to the doctor and take it easy. The tablets he gave you will make you sleepy, too. You need a good rest. Your body needs it, and your psyche needs it. Trust me, I'm a therapist.' She was trying her best to lighten the mood.

'What if Bob turns up? I won't be strong enough to cope.'

'He won't.' Betty tried to sound convincing.

'You don't know him. He might.' Betty noticed Helen was staring at the road ahead as though she might spot her tormentor at any moment. She looked more than strained; she looked close to collapse.

Betty's mind raced. What if Bob did turn up? 'We'll help in the pub, if Agata can show us what to do, then we'll stay the night. You must have somewhere we can sleep. How about that?'

'There's Mum's room, I suppose. There are clean sheets on the bed. I did that before the funeral. I don't know why.'

For some reason the idea of sleeping in the recently-deceased Nan Jones's bed didn't immediately appeal to Betty. She told herself it would be just like sleeping in a hotel bed. It wasn't as though Nan had died in it, after all. 'Perfect,' she said.

This wasn't the day Betty had envisaged when she'd woken up. 'I'm just going to stop at that garage, to see if I can find a few bits and pieces Evan and I might need if we're not going home until tomorrow.'

By the time the pair walked into The Dragon's Head pub, there was a good crowd enjoying a sunny afternoon, Agata and Evan were serving at the bar, and Agata's sister, Genowefa, was ferrying plates of sandwiches from the kitchen.

She saw the look of relief on her husband's face as she arrived. 'You go on up, Helen,' she said. 'You'll be alright on the stairs, won't you?' Helen nodded.

Rushing to the bar she said to Evan, 'I'm going upstairs to settle Helen, then I'll be down. We're staying the night. In Nan's old room. Don't pull that face. We'll be fine. I bought an emergency toothbrush; we'll share it. We'll have to manage with the clothes we're wearing. Back in a few minutes.'

She found Helen sitting at the kitchen table. 'No, not here. I'll make you a cup of tea if you want, but you should get into bed. Will you need a hand to get undressed?'

Helen's eyes focused briefly. 'I don't think I'll be able to get my bra off. Would you . . .?'

'I'll put the kettle on, and I'll be with you in a minute. You go and get started. And don't worry, I've seen it all before.'

Helen looked a bit wobbly when she stood, thought Betty. 'I don't know what I would have done without you,' she said, then left the room.

With a pot of tea brewing, Betty knocked on Helen's bedroom door. 'Ready for me?'

Helen called her in. 'I can't get my socks or my bra off. But I got my nightie over my head.'

Eventually tucked in, Betty handed her a fresh mug of tea and the tablets the doctor had prescribed. Her charge duly medicated, she said, 'I'll be downstairs. If you need anything, or anyone, just phone the pub. Your mobile's beside you, and it's fully charged. Evan and I will be sleeping in your mum's bedroom. I'll check in on you later, but I won't wake you. Promise. Now sleep.' Betty suspected she would; Helen was completely wiped out.

As she left the bedroom, Helen called, 'Is Sadie alright? I haven't seen her. Where is she?'

'I'm sure she's fine. Don't worry. I'll check where she is. If I'm uncertain about anything, I'll talk to you. Go to sleep.' Betty closed the door.

'Here I am, what can I do?' she asked Agata when she entered the bar.

Agata looked Betty up and down. 'I don't know, what *can* you do?'

Betty felt somewhat deflated. 'I can open bottles, pour drinks, possibly use the till, if you show me how to, and maybe even manage to pull a pint – after proper instruction.'

Agata nodded. 'Come around. I will show you, then I'll see how you do. I hope you're good because your husband is slow, and I need a break. It's not too busy. We will manage.'

And manage they did. It was gone eight before Betty really knew what was happening. Her feet were sore, she never wanted to see another half of Guinness – which turned out to be an almost impossible drink to pour properly – and she was fit to drop. Agata took pity on her inexperienced helpers and sent them for a break together.

'Do we have any idea where Sadie is?' she asked her husband as they sat beside each other at one of the empty wooden tables out in the pub's beer garden. Below them the wet sands of the beach, and the sea itself, glowed red and purple beneath the breathtaking sunset.

'Haven't seen hide nor hair of her since she took off to look for Aled this morning,' replied Evan. 'Possibly she's thinking leaving well alone is best? Spending time with her boyfriend?'

'I reckon,' replied Betty. 'Anyway, I'm not worried about her. She'll keep away from here, if she's got any sense, until she's cooled off, good and proper.' She tried to sigh away her stress. 'My God this view is wonderful. I see what those legends mean about the dragon's fire on the horizon. What a sunset. Imagine seeing this every day of your life. How inspiring.'

The couple allowed themselves a few moments of companionable silence to drink in the beauty around them.

'Remember those sunsets we saw in the Caribbean, when the sun just dropped out of the sky?' said Evan. 'This is better. Slower, so you can savor it.'

'It's not as toasty here,' noted Betty, 'but you're right, this is wonderful. Though I have to admit I don't like the idea of Sadie being out on her own after dark.'

'I have a sneaking suspicion she won't be alone,' said Evan gently. 'Aled's got his gran's house all to himself now. Don't you think a teenage couple would make the most of such an opportunity?'

Betty reached across the table and squeezed her husband's hand. 'I dare say they might want to, but I'm not sure Helen would be in agreement. It's not our decision to make, you know. It's between her and Sadie.'

'The girl's almost eighteen, and it's not as though it's illegal. I should imagine many thousands of other teens are getting up to all sorts behind their parents' backs. After all, Sadie was quite open about what she and Aled had been doing on the beach when she spoke in court . . . sorry, shouted in court.'

'Didn't you think that was odd? To share so many intimate details, like that?'

'How d'you mean?'

Betty chose her words carefully. 'I understand she was determined to give him an alibi, and I also understand that he'd been gentlemanly enough to not speak out about their liaison. However, all she needed to do at that time was give the bare minimum of information. The details were quite unnecessary.'

'You're right, but it turns out this is a family with an interesting relationship with sex.'

Betty was surprised. 'Meaning?'

Evan regaled her with a recounting of the conversation he'd had with Mair Bevan.

Betty was nonplussed. 'You just never know, do you?' And here's me, with my training, saying that.'

Evan leaned in. 'And there's more. I've had a busy day, you know. Liz was here earlier, and showed me some pretty interesting photos.'

'Liz was here? Why didn't you mention this earlier?'

'When? We've been up to our ears in bar work since you got back. This is me telling you, now. She initially intended to check Sadie's statement, but couldn't because . . . well, Sadie wasn't here for a start, but nor was Helen. She's going to come back tomorrow at nine, and she'll have an approved adult ready, just in case Helen still isn't up to being with her daughter when Sadie's being asked some new questions. Probably at HQ.'

'New questions? About what?'

'Sadie said she'd never seen James Powell before his demise, yet they've found photos taken by James on Halloween that suggest that's not true. A few show a couple of people – grainy, in the distance. I think James was using one of his powerful lenses, but the light wasn't good. However, it's clear that one of the figures is Aled Beynon. His hair was still long and almost white back then, before they chopped it all off for the trial. He's with a female. Sadie. They appear to be struggling with each other. He's holding her, possibly shaking her. They're fighting.'

'But all that means is that James Powell had seen Sadie, not necessarily that Sadie had seen James Powell. If James Powell was a long way off, would Sadie have even known she was being photographed, let alone by him?'

'Possibly not, but there are a couple more pictures which show Sadie, semi-naked, running toward the lens looking very angry.'

'Semi-naked?'

'Topless, hair flying about, wearing lots of necklaces, and so forth. The Concubine's Pillow is visible in the background.'

'Good grief. That's . . . quite something,' said Betty quietly.

'They're the last photos James Powell ever took.'

Betty was immediately concerned. 'We should find Sadie.'

'Want to take a stroll toward Green Cottage with me?'

'Good idea. I'll tell Agata she'll have to battle on alone for a little while longer.' As she stood, Betty told her feet they weren't sore, but they didn't listen.

Helen

Helen could do nothing but feel; the power of thought, of processing her feelings, had deserted her. Her wrist, arm, and shoulder ached; her head thumped; her stomach cramped. She hoisted herself up to a sitting position, but it took a mammoth effort. The simple act of pushing the duvet off her body required major contortions.

Finally she sat on the edge of the creaking bed, her feet dangling uselessly. She wasn't at all sure she could walk. She contemplated phoning down to the bar to ask someone to bring her something to drink, but she didn't want to be a bother. She slipped her phone into the pocket of her nightie, almost smiling as she recalled mentioning to her mother how she thought it was utterly pointless for a nightie to have a pocket.

Staggering from one piece of furniture to the next, she made it out to the hall, where she slid along the wall, stumbling. Finally reaching the kitchen, she took an upturned mug from the draining board, sat it in the sink beneath the tap, and filled it with water. She didn't spill too much taking it to the table, where she flopped into a chair and gulped down every mouthful.

I'll be worse than useless in the pub like this, she thought to herself. *And there's no one I can turn to for help.*

She lay her plastered arm on the table, and examined her swollen fingers. She managed to move them all just a little; it didn't even hurt too much. Cradling her forehead with her good hand, she closed her eyes and let her tears fall freely, hearing each one land on the bare wooden surface with a gentle plop. She was past sobbing. She was surprised she could even cry.

She jumped violently when her phone rang. She fished about in the folds of her nightie for it, hoping she'd get to it before it stopped ringing. She did.

'Hello?' *Who on earth could it be?*

'Hello Helen. Sorry we couldn't get together for lunch today after all. But I'm looking forward to seeing you tomorrow instead. It'll be just like old times, the three of us together.'

That voice.

Helen hit the disconnect button and lay the phone on the table in front of her. It rang again within ten seconds. She didn't answer. She tried to control her breathing.

It stopped ringing.

A little ding told her she had a voice message.

Then another ding told her she had a text.

Then another, then another . . .

She realized her entire body was shaking, and she was – unbelievably – sobbing.

Sadie

I know he's got a lot on his plate – after all, Aled felt quite differently about his Grannie Gwen than I felt about Nan and he'll probably miss her a lot, to start with – but he could at least have set *some* time aside to be just with me.

I told him I thought it was unfair, but he said he'd made arrangements to go surfing with Stew, his first time since he got out of prison – then to eat with Stew and his family; he thought he'd have a free afternoon and evening, and lots to think about having spent lunchtime with me, Mam, and Dad. And he'd have been right, of course, if only everything had gone to plan.

But I'm good at dealing with the unexpected – good at turning a problem into an opportunity. I know that, and so does he. So I brought myself back here, to my special, secret place, and no one's any the wiser. I feel so completely connected to my spiritual self here, it's wonderful. And the sunset tonight was spectacular. Good one, dragon.

There's just a little bit less than a full moon tonight; waning gibbous, but she'll have grown to be nearly full again by May 27th; my birthday, and St Melangell's Day. It could be better, because a truly full moon is always more powerful, but it'll do, I suppose.

It was a full moon on November 5th – I'll never forget that. Such a special night. A night of absolute transformation. Of metamorphosis. So much extra power to call upon for me, and for Aled. The moon shone so I didn't miss anything. She's wonderful. It was worth waiting after Halloween until she was full again for that final transformative act; I'm not sure he felt the same way, but it was important to me. I made that crystal clear to him, several times, though he kept begging me to let it be otherwise.

Mum's in a state. I've thought about what she said; maybe there's some truth in it. But if it *is* all true, and if she really doesn't want to be in the same room with Dad, how will I make our family perfect? She'll just be jealous of me and Aled all the time, and the Dad thing will always be between us. How can I fix that? How can I fix Mam?

I would ask Aled about it, but it would be difficult for him to understand, because he hasn't had a mother for a long time. Mothers are a heavy burden; even though she said she was sad Nan died, I've seen Mam change since then. She's started doing things a bit differently in the pub, and she's even cut back on eating bad things, and is getting out and about a bit more, walking around the village, when she can. So I think she's really a bit glad Nan's gone. Deep down.

Now there's this. With Dad. What'll I do?

Why isn't Aled answering my texts? Surely he's got a few minutes, even if he is having a jolly old time with the Wingfields. I bet Maggie is stuffing him with all her organic, grain-fed thingymebobs.

I suppose it's late enough for me to go home now. I expect Mam will be fine about me having that little outburst earlier on today. She always forgives me, though why she didn't want my nice scarf, I don't know. Aled gave it to me after we'd had a row in school one day. It's very attractive.

Oh no, there are those two old farts, Betty and Evan Glover, shouting for me now. What are they up to, coming toward my path, calling my name like that? I'm not a dog, or a little kid.

Oh well, I suppose I'd better go back to the pub.

Helen

Helen dragged herself from a fitful sleep.

'How are you feeling?' Betty was hovering just inside the bedroom door.

Helen managed a groggy, 'Not too bad, thanks. Is Sadie alright? Maybe she could pop her head in before she goes to bed? I'd like to apologize to her for being so nasty earlier on today.' The fight had been preying on her mind.

Betty was holding a cup of tea. 'Time enough for that. I thought a cuppa with your tablets would be a good idea. Don't worry about Sadie. She's been out for a bit of a walk and she's on her way back now. Evan's gone to meet her as she comes down the path. It's dark, and he doesn't want her to hurt herself.'

Helen forced her mouth to form words. 'She's good on the paths. No problem. Maybe see her later.' She swallowed her tablets with a drop of tea. It was hot; it felt good. Although her stomach felt cavernously empty, she knew she couldn't face food.

Betty perched on the foot of the bed and said, 'Mair came over to see you this morning, before church. While we were at the hospital. She and Evan had a bit of a chat.'

Helen gathered her thoughts, as best she could. 'Oh yes, I wanted to talk to Mair about Mum, and Gwen.' She felt if only she could sit up she'd be able to focus better, but she seemed to be caught up in her sheets.

'Here, let me,' said Betty, unwinding the sheet and duvet.

Helen was grateful for her help. 'Thank you. Can Mair come to see me now?'

Betty shook her head. 'It's a bit late for someone over ninety to be out and about, I'd have thought. But she did tell Evan what your mum and she talked about. I could tell you, if you like.'

Helen desperately wanted to know how her mother's last morning had been filled. 'Please.'

'Well, it might not help much, because what she said doesn't seem to make much sense, to me. What Mair said was your mum believed your dad had been having an affair with Gwen, and told Mair that she'd seen them together on the night of New Year's Eve 1999.'

Helen felt a peculiar sinking sensation as she recalled her mother's words to her in the car that day. 'Yes, Dad and Gwen . . . Mum said that to me too. I think it's all rubbish, but I don't know why Gwen wanted me to see Mair.'

Betty replied, 'Mair said your dad couldn't possibly have been with Gwen that night because Gwen was with her at the time. Gwen had a rather bad case of the flu and was staying with Mair, you see. So there, maybe that will help you sleep a bit better. It seems your mum got hold of the wrong end of the stick; she told Mair she saw your dad dressing himself in the bedroom window of Gwen's cottage. However, Gwen wasn't there at the time. So you have nothing to worry yourself about.'

Helen's sluggish brain juggled the information. Of course her mother had got it all wrong – she often got things wrong. She'd always been blind to the detail, the nuances surrounding her. But how could she have got it *so* wrong? Had she imagined Jack Jones, in a bedroom window, getting dressed? Helen struggled with it all. She felt drained.

'Now come on, time to snuggle down and let those tablets do their work,' said Betty, standing, and pulling the bedclothes up around Helen's chest. She was a bit over-fussy, but Helen couldn't complain. She was especially thankful that the Glovers were going to stay overnight.

'Okay,' replied Helen. As she tried to find a comfy spot on her pillow she realized that tomorrow would soon arrive, and with it the prospect of seeing Bob. She hoped the tablets would be strong enough to allow her a dreamless sleep.

22nd April

Betty

'Evan, wake up. I think there's someone moving around downstairs.' Betty checked the time on her phone. 'Evan, it's not quite half past four. Do you think there's an intruder?' Her mind leaped to Bob, and Helen's safety. She shoved her husband in the ribs. 'Wake up, Evan.'

Sitting upright, Evan looked puzzled.

'You look like you've been shot. Out of a cannon,' said Betty quietly.

He scratched his head. 'I feel like I have been. Dear God, this bed's a mass of lumps. What's the mattress filled with? Horsehair? What's wrong, anyway?'

'Listen,' hissed Betty. They did. 'There, did you hear that scraping sound?'

'I can hear many sounds that are utterly unfamiliar to me, love. We're in a strange bed, in a strange place; everything's either too quiet, or a weird noise.'

'I'm having a terrible night, Evan. Awful dreams when I can catch a nap, but mainly just lying here listening, thinking. I can't stop thinking.'

Evan sat more upright. 'Come on, love, you need your rest. Look, we've taken on this task of looking after Helen for tonight, but this can't go on. It's got to be resolved within her family.'

Betty sighed. She knew he was right. That was why her mind was racing. 'That scraping noise isn't downstairs, it's outside,' she said quietly. She felt more than a little annoyed with herself.

'Probably. But tell me, what's the plan for the morning? Are we staying? Going?'

Betty tried to plump up the ancient pillow she'd been wrestling with for hours. 'Don't you think we should stay at least until Liz gets here? I know we can't be involved in the interview, but we can be here for the fall out.'

Evan sighed his acceptance. 'Cool as the proverbial cucumber Sadie was when she got back here tonight, wasn't she? Amazing. As if nothing had happened. Seemed to be surprised her mother was in plaster. And so dismissive of us two running around the village trying to track her down, when she'd been swanning around God only knows where.'

Betty smiled. 'I know we've sometimes wondered if we've been unfortunate to not have kids – well after a few hours with that one I can tell you it was most definitely a blessing. I'd be locked up for murder or madness by now if I'd had to put up with that for years.'

'The word "madness"? From you? That's not a word you professionals use, is it?' mugged Evan.

'Turn of phrase, *cariad*.'

Evan whispered, 'Maybe she took a chance before going to bed to apologize to her mother, in private. You know, saving face in front of outsiders. We're not family, and we're also not People of the Dragon.'

'And you can stop all that malarkey, too. Dragon's this, and Devil's that? This is the twenty-first century, Evan. Move on.'

He grunted. 'What about Bob possibly coming here for lunch? Is that something we should stay for, do you think? Even if Sadie's taken in for questioning, maybe Helen won't be up to going with her, and he might still show up.' Evan sounded a little testy.

'Unless there's a way to stop him coming, then, yes, it might not be a bad idea. It's so frustrating that your lot can't do anything until a stalker crosses a line. It must be a living hell for the victims.'

Evan sounded tired. 'I love you, and I respect what you're saying, but we've been through all this before. However, I will talk to Liz about it in the morning. Since the last time all that stuff happened to Helen things have changed; there are new charges that can be brought. The victim still has to play an active role in gathering evidence and presenting it to the police but, yes, there are now actions that can be taken that couldn't even be considered back then. And before you say anything – no, there still isn't enough done about it, and yes, there are thousands of victims we still can't help, and no, I don't think the money will ever be there for the police to be as effective as they could be, and no, I don't think that there's adequate protection for victims when a culprit is released. I get it, love, I do. But . . .'

'I know all about the changes, Evan, and I'd like to say "too little, too late" for many women, but I understand that something is better than nothing, and that at least now the law has some teeth.'

Betty knew her husband understood, and was as frustrated as she was.

She added, 'Removing a stalker from society can allow them to get the professional help they need to be able to come to terms with the fact that what they are doing is abnormal, as well as giving the victim a chance to get their life back.'

'I know. But it's still all about resources, isn't it?' said Evan heavily. 'However, on this occasion, we can be the resource, the support system. I understand why Helen doesn't want to be in the same room as Bob; he treated her in a truly criminal manner, so we should take our chance to stand up for her. We'll stay.'

'I love you, *cariad.*'

'Good. Now let's try to get some sleep.'

Betty snuggled down, as best she could, beneath the skimpy eiderdown – the like of which she hadn't seen since she was a child, staying with her grandmother.

She was delighted Evan had suggested talking to Liz about the situation between Helen and Bob the next morning.

However, as she tried to ignore the strange sounds which seemed to echo through the house, she realized how terribly isolated the village was, and she even began to understand why the old beliefs, and ways, might linger in a place like Rhosddraig – where the thick stone walls of the picturesque cottages had the potential to trap people inside them, rather than keeping unwanted visitors out.

Evan

Creeping as quietly as possible across ancient floorboards which creaked with irritating and deafening regularity, Evan made it into and out of the bathroom in record time. The sun was up, and it looked as though it would be a lovely morning. He hated the feeling of putting on the clothes he'd worn all the previous day, but had no choice.

He looked down at his wife, fast asleep, and snoring. She looked pale. He touched her cheek. 'Sorry, love, but it's time to get up.'

Betty groaned. 'I've only just got off. But alright. I can't stick this bed for another five minutes in any case.'

Evan watched her do her own version of the tiptoeing he'd just performed, and tidied up the bed as best he could. They met again in the kitchen.

'The kettle's on, and the pot's ready to go. I haven't poked about trying to find something to eat; I don't want to disturb Helen or Sadie.'

Betty nodded. 'We should let them both sleep in. Especially Helen. I have a feeling she'll emerge when she's up to it. How about a cuppa, then a walk? It's lovely out, and we're unlikely to ever be here so early in the morning again.'

'Right you are.' Evan was delighted. He even drank his tea while it was still really too hot for him, just so they could get going.

Sadie appeared as they were about to head off. 'I'll take Mam a cup of tea,' she offered. 'Is there some in the pot?' She was dressed, but still sounded half asleep.

Evan tethered his irritation with the girl, and managed, 'Good idea. And don't forget DS Stanley will be here by nine to see you.'

The girl grunted and threw him a dismissive look. He fizzed with anger. Couldn't help himself – Sadie Jones was quite the girl.

A few minutes later, with his wife beside him, he felt immensely uplifted by the freshness of the air. 'Wouldn't it be something to be able to walk by the sea every day?' he mused, delighting in the sight of the lacy necklace of surf on the beach below them.

'It's a bit far for us to run down to the bays on a daily basis,' replied Betty, 'but maybe we could make an effort to do it a bit more often? My hours are flexible, after all.'

'A couple of blokes from work have sold up and moved into those flats for the over 55s down on the seafront near the Brangwyn Hall. The photos look nice.' He wondered how Betty would react.

She did no more than glance sideways at him as she said, 'Well, we're both old enough for that, now. But they're quite small, aren't they, those flats?'

'Why do we need all the space we've got? I know we bought the house imagining we might one day fill at least one of the other bedrooms with offspring, but we don't need two spare rooms, do we? And how often do we use the middle room downstairs? We live in the kitchen and the front room. We probably don't need a lot of the stuff we've accumulated. We could have a good old clear out, and even buy some new furniture, if we moved.' He left it at that.

Betty pulled on his hand, and stood still. 'You're serious about this, aren't you? You've put some thought into it.'

Evan looked into the face of the only woman he'd ever loved – in a romantic way. 'I am, and I have. It occurred to me when we cleared out the room we've been using for our little "enterprise". Everything that's now sitting on that landing could go, and we wouldn't miss it. We didn't even know most of it was there. We could spend a bit on doing up the house, make it look tidy enough to sell, and cash out. "Downsize". It's all the rage, you know. Get a smaller place, on the seafront. We could walk, enjoy strolls like this every day, if we wanted.'

'I don't like the marina area – too boaty for me,' said Betty starting to walk again, slowly. Evan could tell by the angle of her head she was giving the matter real consideration. 'And I'd prefer to be a bit further away from the city center than down near St Helen's, to be honest. But not this far out. This is way too isolated for me. Mumbles maybe? Up on the hill, not right down on the front. Too much traffic. But that would cost a fortune, and who knows if our place would sell.'

'A three bedroom semi like ours? On a street with a really good school not too far away? In a heartbeat, for a king's ransom,' mugged Evan. 'Or not. But it's something to consider, isn't it? I'm not really one for fancy cruises, love. Nice to do it once, but no need to make a habit of it. Your Auntie Barbara's money would do us a lot more good if it gave us a chance to get out and about on a daily basis, not just going off on an exotic jaunt once in a blue moon.'

'Food for thought,' said Betty enigmatically. 'Maybe a fresh start is just what we need. We've got what I hope is a long future ahead of us yet, Evan. But for now, how about we start back toward the pub? I've never been this far out along the back of the dragon, before. It's a surprisingly long way out to the head, isn't it? It must take some doing to get out there, and back in, before the tide turns and traps you on the island.'

'You're right. And many have fallen foul of that very issue; there's a sign at the best crossing place, telling people the times of the tides, but some choose to ignore it, either ending up spending twelve hours out there, or – worse still – injuring themselves, or even losing their lives, trying to make a dash through the surf when the tide's on the turn. I know you say it's all rubbish, but these sayings about not messing with the dragon all have a seed of truth in them. That's why they become sayings.'

As they headed back toward the pub and the village, Evan spotted some sort of activity over on the hillside further around the arc of the bay, near the Devil's Table. 'Look, some other people are out and about early, like us.'

His wife squinted toward where he was pointing. 'Is that Sadie? Maybe with Aled? That orange color is just like the get-up she had on in the kitchen earlier on.'

Evan squinted into the morning sun. 'Might be, I suppose. Though what she's doing gallivanting over there when she knows Liz is on her way to see her, I don't know. She's quite special, that girl. Insouciance personified.'

Betty thumped him playfully. 'Hark at you. Been eating a dictionary for breakfast?'

'Listening to Radio 4 too much, I expect.'

Agata had promised to arrive early to make sure all the preparations for the lunches for Easter Monday were made, and Evan could smell she'd been busy as soon as he and Betty entered the pub. The aroma of roasting chickens made him feel immediately, and achingly, hungry. He pulled Betty toward the kitchen. 'Come on,' he said.

'Good morning, Agata. Thanks for getting here so early. Any chance of something to eat? We don't want to clatter about upstairs and wake Helen.'

A few moments later he was happily chomping into a sandwich made with thickly cut, home-roasted ham. He whispered to Betty, 'Sandwiches for breakfast? It's like camping.' She smiled.

Agata announced, 'Sadie said she would take her love to her holy place. Does that mean something to you?' she sounded puzzled.

Evan replied, 'We think we spotted her over by the Devil's Table just now, with Aled. Surely she can't mean that?' A nerve jangled deep inside him.

Betty asked, 'What time is Liz due?'

'I said nine, but I'm already here,' said Liz, popping her head through the open back door. 'Any more of those going, by any chance? I'm starving. Didn't have anything at home remotely suitable for breakfast.'

Taking their sandwiches and mugs of tea, the threesome moved to a table in the sunniest part of the pub, allowing Agata full run of the kitchen, which she needed; she'd decided to only offer chicken for the lunch service, and it seemed to Evan she'd elected to roast an entire flock of the blessed things.

Evan explained to Liz about Sadie having gone AWOL.

She wasn't impressed, he could tell.

'How about the mother?' Liz asked sharply. 'Do you think she'll be up to supervising? I've got a stand-in acceptable adult on speed dial; I told her I'd come and scout things out before I dragged her away from her family on a Bank Holiday.'

Evan and Betty exchanged a worried look, and explained the detailed background of the situation that had blown up between Helen and Bob. Liz took notes as they spoke – as Evan had known she would – and nodded, or looked horrified, at the appropriate points in the sad tale.

'When do you think Helen might put in an appearance? I need to know if she'll be able to accompany Sadie to HQ,' she asked when they'd finished.

Betty checked her watch. 'Sadie took tea in to her before half seven, so I'll go and see if she thinks she's up to it. Alright?'

Liz didn't object, so Betty headed off.

Taking his chance to have a quick one-to-one, Evan asked, 'So, any progress to report on your case?'

Liz wiped crumbs from her blouse. 'To be honest, Sadie Jones is our main focus, at the moment,' she said. 'We need to know why she lied about her movements on the night of the 31st October, when she said she was at home all evening but clearly wasn't, and why she said she'd never met James Powell, when those photos suggest otherwise. We also need to be sure she hasn't lied about anything else.'

'Like what she was doing on the night of November 5th, for example?' asked Evan.

'Exactly. It's the double-alibi angle, isn't it? I'm really annoyed she's not here, though I suppose, to be fair to her, I did say nine o'clock. Bloody teenagers.'

Helen

Helen's first thoughts when there was a knock at her door were, *I don't want to get up and face today. Can't I just hide here until it's tomorrow?*

'Come in,' she said, with as much strength as she could muster.

'Hello Helen, I was just checking to see how you're doing. Wondered if I could maybe help you to the bathroom, or something.'

Betty sounded positive, upbeat – Helen had forgotten how that felt.

No, leave me alone! was what she screamed inside her head.

'Thanks, that would be great,' was what she said aloud.

Betty was good to her – she gave her just the amount of help she needed, but left her to her own devices once she was sure she was safe. Helen made a bit of an effort to clean herself up – but she felt sweaty and limp even when she'd dressed, with Betty's assistance, in clean clothes.

'Where's Sadie? And what about lunches in the pub? I can smell chicken – is Agata here?' She knew she was letting people down.

'Don't worry, everything's under control,' said Betty.

But, groggy as she was, Helen sensed something wasn't right. 'Where's Sadie?'

'She's gone for a walk, that's all. With Aled, I believe. Now, how about we get you downstairs, then you can see that Agata's got everything sorted, so you can stop worrying.'

Helen knew that was a good idea, and was able to make her way down to the pub quite easily. She was a bit wobbly, but that was to be expected. Pleased with Agata's preparations, she finally noticed Evan and Liz Stanley having a chat at one of the tables outside, in the beer garden. 'Why's DI Stanley here?' She couldn't imagine.

Betty smiled warmly. 'Well, she needs to talk to Sadie. Some sort of mix-up about her statements. Do you think you'd be up to attending that interview with your daughter? The police need a parent or a person recognized as an acceptable adult to be with a minor. Now don't worry, if you're not feeling up to it, Liz has someone she can call on to sit in.'

Helen was confused. 'Oh course I'll do it. She's my daughter. But what's wrong with her statements? I . . . I don't understand.'

Betty helped Helen into a chair and said, 'Hang on, back in a mo,' and disappeared.

Helen hated the fogginess she was experiencing. Sadie's statements were a problem? What did that mean, exactly? Nothing good.

As she sat and waited, she watched Betty, Liz, and Evan, all conferring beyond the picture window. A dumb show. Odd.

Her mind wandered to her mother seeing her father through a bedroom window at night, dressing. But Gwen had been at Mair's house. She wasn't at home. So why would he have been dressing in someone else's empty house in the middle of the night?

1999 would have been before Aled was born, so it would have been only Gwen living at Green Cottage at the time . . . no, Jackie, Gwen's daughter lived at home then, didn't she? Well, sometimes. When she wasn't off with her questionable friends in Swansea.

Helen's sluggish thoughts sharpened.

Her father and *Jackie* Beynon? Jackie had been three years below Helen in school, so surely he wouldn't . . . no. *Not Dad.* Helen tried her hardest to focus.

If her father had been with Jackie on New Year's Eve 1999 . . . and Aled had been born in September 2000 . . .

The horror of it hit her.

'Oh my God, no!' she cried aloud.

Agata's worried face appeared behind the bar, 'Helen?' She dashed out of the back door. Soon Liz, Betty, and Evan were hovering over Helen, as she felt the pub swirl around her.

Betty's face seemed blurry. 'Helen – what's the matter, love? Can you tell me?'

Helen fought to form thoughts, and turn them into words. 'New Year's Eve 1999, you said Gwen was staying with Mair, right?'

Evan answered. 'That's what Mair told me. She said your mum couldn't have seen your dad at Gwen's house, in a state of undress, because Gwen was with her.'

'But there was Jackie Beynon, too. What about *Jackie*? Aled's eighteen. Born September 2000. Right age. Is he my brother? I think he's my half-brother.' She felt the heat of tears on her cheeks.

Evan spoke calmly, 'Now don't worry about that, Helen. I'll admit I had the same thought, but I mentioned Jackie Beynon to Mair, who said she'd probably not have been in the village at all that night. Jackie would have been at a big party in Swansea. Mair seemed pretty sure about it.'

Helen felt her heart pound, her toes tingle. 'She wasn't. I know that for a fact.' She waved her good arm toward the bar. Everyone looked around. 'There's a photo up on the wall by the optics taken that night – around one in the morning. The first photo taken in this pub in the twenty-first century. Jackie Beynon is in it. And Mum. And Dad.'

Helen felt as though she were sinking into the chair.

As if through the swirl of the dragon's breath, Helen saw the people around her stare at each other, the looks on their faces telling her even they realized the importance of what she was saying.

Liz's voice sounded harsh. 'You mean you think Aled might be Sadie's . . . half-uncle? Step-uncle? Is that even a word?'

Evan replied, 'I don't know if it's a word – but if Jack Jones was Aled's father, then Aled is Helen's half-brother, making him related to Sadie in a way that . . .'

Helen couldn't hold it in any longer, but she couldn't form words. She had to let out all her anger, frustration, and horror.

She opened her mouth as wide as she could, and wailed. She didn't know she was going to do it until the sound was coming out of her body. She just closed her eyes and let it all roll out of her.

As the noise reverberated inside her head she saw colors, felt vibrations and then . . . nothing. Everything stopped. She realized she had stopped screaming. She felt completely drained.

Betty was asking how she felt. All she could do was retch – dry, and raw. And sob. She wanted to say so much, but she felt so tired that all that came out was, 'Sadie. Aled. My Mum. News on TV. Worked it out about Jackie. Heart attack. My baby girl. With Aled. Wrong.'

Somewhere Helen heard disembodied voices. One asked, 'What tablets is she on? She seems to be really out of it to me.' Another replied, 'They gave her Co-codamol at the hospital, just a few, enough for three days. I gave her some last night, and this morning. Oh God . . . let me check.' Another voice said, 'Let's get her outside, into the fresh air – Agata, can you bring some cold water, please.' Finally, 'Look, these were beside her bed. It's a bottle of Solpadol, with Myfanwy Jones's name on them. Do you think she took these?'

Helen felt herself being shaken. It felt bouncy – but not too bad. She tried to focus her eyes on the face in front of her. 'Did you take extra tablets, Helen? Helen? Have you done something to yourself?'

A voice said, 'I've called an ambulance. They said to keep her moving if we can. Keep her conscious.'

'I'll do it,' said someone.

Then . . . nothing.

Betty

'Evan, I'll never forgive myself. We were here. We should have seen this coming. When I went up and found the tablets, I also saw Helen's mobile phone beside her bed; over a hundred text messages. Forty missed calls. It must be Bob again. It must have been too much for her.'

Betty was close to tears. She felt the guilt as a physical force, her body vibrating, tingling. 'I wish she'd said something. The bastard didn't need to try to get into the pub itself overnight, he was already inside her head, and on her phone.'

'This isn't your fault, love. She could have turned her phone off,' said Evan.

Betty was shocked. 'You know what she's like. She probably thought he'd start phoning the pub instead, then she'd be involving other people – including her daughter. The lengths to which a victimized person will go to to hide the fact they are under attack can be extraordinary. Sometimes they don't want anyone to know because they feel guilt, other times they try to absorb all the effects of the harassment themselves, because they see it as their fault.'

Evan shook his head. 'Sorry, love, I didn't mean that. What I meant was she knew we were here for her – she didn't need her phone to be switched on in case of an emergency last night. She should have told us if he was harassing her; we knew about what she'd been through. Surely she could have let us help her?'

Betty hated feeling so useless. 'I don't know. Maybe. But these things are never as straightforward as they might seem to an outsider; there's such a complex set of potential responses . . .'

Betty's flow was stopped by the abrupt arrival – through the pub's kitchen – of Aled Beynon, accompanied by a couple she half-remembered from the funeral.

'She's got Stew, you've got to help him,' wailed Aled. Betty was horrified to see blood dripping from a wound on the boy's head, and noticed he was dragging his left leg, which was also bloodied.

'Is that policewoman around?' shouted the man. 'I saw her park her car and come in here. Where is she? Sadie's taken my son off somewhere . . .'

Evan replied. 'DS Stanley is outside attending to an emergency situation. I'm a retired police officer, Evan Glover. Who are you, and what exactly is happening? Betty? Come and tend to Aled, please love.'

Betty did as her husband asked, steering the dazed youth to the chair recently vacated by Helen, where he flopped. 'I'll get a towel and some water,' she said, but Agata raced in from the kitchen with just what was needed. As Betty mopped Aled's forehead she could see he had a deep gash in his hairline. It would need stiches, she reckoned. There was a lot of blood. He was worryingly pale.

She concentrated on staunching the flow by applying pressure to the wound – so couldn't see the unknown man behind her as he barked, 'Stephen Wingfield. Wife Maggie. Rhosddraig Cwtch. Sadie Jones has abducted our boy. He was staying with Aled last night. She went to Green Cottage this morning and viciously attacked Aled, as you can plainly see, then made off with our son Stewart. We don't know where she's taken him, or why. But Aled says she threatened the pair of them with a gun. A gun!'

'We saw Sadie out on the hillside earlier on. We thought she was with you, Aled,' said Betty.

Maggie Wingfield wailed, 'The hillside? Thank God. Please get that real policewoman to help. Whatever the emergency is outside, we need her more. Our son . . . she's got a gun.' Betty could hear the terror in the poor woman's voice.

Agata responded to a pounding on the front door of the pub, and another woman in her forties Betty had never seen before burst into the lounge. 'I don't know what's going on, but I've just seen some funny business going on at . . . oh my God – what's happened to him?'

'Sadie attacked him,' replied Stephen.

'And she's taken Stew,' added Maggie.

'And you are?' asked Evan calmly.

The woman was agog. 'Um . . . Alis Roberts. From the shop. Why? Who are you?'

'Detective Inspector Evan Glover, retired. You were about to say there's something amiss somewhere? Where?'

'Up at the Devil's Table – I think there was some sort of fight going on, and now someone's dancing around on top of it. It's dangerous, that is. I saw DS Stanley come in here a while back. I thought I'd tell her. She should do something about it.'

Betty turned, momentarily, from tending to Aled's wound to gauge how her husband would react; he was surrounded by anxious people, but looking perfectly calm.

I expect this is how he's always been in times of crisis, and I've never known it, thought Betty.

'How's Aled doing, Betty?' he asked.

Betty weighed her response. 'I think he'll need stitches in his head and it looks like his leg's been slashed by some sort of blade. The ambulance that's on its way here for Helen will be put to good use.'

'Agata, take over from Betty putting pressure on that wound, please. Betty you come with me. The rest of you stay here. I'll be back in two minutes. Don't leave. Anyone,' barked Evan forcefully.

Taking control comes to you naturally, thought Betty.

She and Evan joined Liz, who was more or less dragging Helen around the grassy picnic area; her husband communicated the news succinctly.

Liz nodded. 'Betty, as you can see I've kept Helen mobile. I've advised central control about the medications we believe Helen might have ingested, and the paramedics should have treatments with them for an opioid overdose, but the Solpadol also contains acetaminophen, which can lead to liver and kidney failure. We can only hope we've caught her in time. Her condition might worsen before they arrive. Do you know how to administer CPR?'

Betty replied rapidly. 'No, I'm sorry. Can you show me how to do it?'

Liz replied, 'At a pinch. But check in the pub if anyone's trained in it. Quick.'

Betty did as she was asked, and returned with Maggie Wingfield in tow who told Liz, through her tears and panic, 'I've got a first aid certificate, for the restaurant. It's up to date. Did my refresher day about a year ago. We covered CPR. Can I help with Helen? And will you please, please help my son? He's in terrible danger.'

Liz said, 'You keep Helen upright and moving, while I attend to your son's needs. I suggest you collect your thoughts, and take a few moments to think clearly about your training, in case you need to use it. You could do worse than refresh your memory by checking current CPR practices online, while I sort out the situation with your son.' She then repeated everything she'd said to Betty about the pills Helen appeared to have taken.

Betty followed her husband and Liz back into the lounge bar, where Liz was immediately assailed with loud requests for her to take action.

'Quiet! I need information before I do anything. Who knows about Sadie being armed with a gun?' Liz's voice rang out strong and clear.

Aled timidly raised his hand.

'Tell her what you told us,' shouted Stephen. 'She threatened to kill him—'

'Please, Mr Wingfield, let Aled speak,' said Liz forcefully.

Aled's voice was weak, hesitant. 'Sadie's got a gun. A real one. It looks like a gun they have in old westerns. It's her great-grandfather's. From the war. From her attic. She . . . I know she's carried it in her backpack sometimes. I don't even know if it works. But . . . it might. She hit me on the head with it. There's this ring thing on the end of it. It really hurt. She was shoving it in Stew's back, then she hit me again. She must have . . . made him go with her.'

Liz nodded. 'Give me a minute.' She whispered something to Evan that Betty couldn't hear, and stepped outside the pub's front door, her phone at her ear.

All eyes turned to Evan. 'DS Stanley is making arrangements for an armed response unit to be dispatched to this location. She has to go through her superiors to do this; it's standard operating procedure. The nearest unit is stationed in Bridgend, but they could be mobile when the call reaches them, so we cannot be sure how long it will take for them to arrive.'

'Dear God – I'm not waiting until some blokes with guns get here from Bridgend, man,' interrupted Stephen Wingfield, loudly. 'I'll go over there myself. Better she shoots me than my son.' He moved toward the door, and Betty saw Evan move faster than she thought he could.

'Please don't, Stephen,' he said. 'It's not wise. We'll need backup before we confront a young woman with a weapon which might still be able to perform its deadly function.'

Betty – and everyone else – turned as Liz reentered the lounge. 'It's being done, they'll call out armed response. And they're sending additional officers. We're asked to sit tight. Observe, if we can.'

Betty could see that Stephen Wingfield was about to blow his top, so nudged her husband, who said, 'I know this is difficult for you to understand, Stephen, but we have to think about the personal safety of—'

Stephen pushed past Evan, who almost fell to the ground. 'You're all insane. I'm not staying here. He's my son. What are you going to do? Arrest me? I'm off.'

Liz was wrong-footed, and Stephen had made it to the road before she could get past Alis and Agata. Evan followed, with Betty screaming after him, 'Evan, no!'

But he'd gone.

Evan

Evan followed Liz as she ran to the car park, jogging to keep up with her. 'You haven't got a spare tactical kit in there for me by any chance, have you?' he asked.

Liz was pulling equipment from the boot. 'No, and you won't need one because you're going to stay here and hold the fort.' Her eyes were no more than slits. 'You're no longer on the job, Evan, and you have no police powers. You're a civilian. I cannot risk involving you, as well as Wingfield. You're needed here.' She slammed the boot shut, and turned.

Evan sighed. 'One, I have experience; two, you don't know how to get to where you need to get; three, I can distract as well as engage. Let me at least get you to the site? Then I'll back off, and you can take over. You need to go in this direction, not the way you're going'

She didn't reply, but he believed Liz would follow as he headed off, and she did. Evan knew he had to pace himself, so jogged, rather than setting out at an unsustainable speed. He pulled his phone from his pocket and speed-dialed Betty.

'Tell Maggie Wingfield to phone her husband and get him to wait for us. Tell him to catch his breath, because he might need it. Just get him to stop. We're on our way now.' He hung up after he'd allowed Betty to beg him to be careful for a full ten seconds.

Betty

The pub was unnaturally quiet. 'Can I cut into your trousers so we can clean up that gash on your leg?' Betty asked Aled.

He looked puzzled. 'I could just take them off. I'm wearing shorts underneath – Stew and I were going to the beach.'

He did, and Betty wiped the drying blood from his leg. The long gash wasn't as deep as she'd feared. She couldn't help but notice the bruises peeping out above and below his shorts. 'Surfing must give you a lot of bumps,' she said.

The boy's eyes filled with tears. He started to shake.

Aled spoke softly. 'Not surfing. Sadie. She . . . she hits me. Not just today. Lots.'

Betty pulled a chair close, and sat between him and the gossiping Alis and Agata, so they had less chance of being overheard. She'd read so much about him, and she'd been there when he'd spoken at his grandmother's funeral, but she'd never talked to the boy before. Betty wondered what sort of person Aled Beynon truly was.

'What do you mean?' she asked in no more than a whisper. She felt her shoulders tense. Was Sadie being abused by this lad in the same way her mother had been by her father? The bruises on the boy's torso suggested Sadie had chosen to fight back at least once.

The boy's chin quivered. 'I don't know how to explain it. Only Stew knows . . . I haven't told anyone else. I . . . I can't.'

Betty decided to dive in; she believed that if an abuser could be caught early enough, they might be able to learn to follow an entirely different path – she had to try her best.

'Look, Aled, I'm not just married to an ex-policeman, I'm also a psychologist and trained therapist. I've heard most things, and although you're not my client, I can be discreet. I'm used to helping people. So why don't you tell me all about it? I thought you and Sadie were happy together, but even happy young couples can have problems.'

She recalled the photos the poor dead boy, James Powell, had taken that Evan had described to her.

'You see, Aled, sometimes a young man doesn't understand how to manage his impulses, and has to learn how to act and react in heated situations. If you've been fighting, and you've ended up being violent toward Sadie, and she's had to fight back, you should consider getting some professional help – learn how to manage your anger.'

Aled's eyes opened wide. 'But I don't hit Sadie, ever. And we're not a couple. At all. We never have been. I do everything I can to avoid her.'

Betty was confused. 'Pardon?'

'I'm not Sadie's boyfriend. I've never felt anything for her. Never led her on either, honestly I haven't. I've never so much as gone out with her, or kissed her, or anything – I mean, why would I want to?'

He broke eye contact with Betty, and stared at the gash on his leg, tears rolling down his face. 'Sadie makes my life a complete misery. She's always phoning me and texting me. All the time. Day and night. She won't leave me alone. I try to ignore her, but she knows that I . . .'

He squeezed his eyes shut. 'She's got something on me that could get me into trouble.'

'Trouble with the police?' Betty knew she had to tread carefully.

Aled looked lost. He was nibbling his dry lips, and seemed to be trying to make a decision. Eventually, he nodded, and wiped away his tears. He looked at her with what Betty judged to be a flash of guarded defiance. 'Yes, with the police, and – if it came out – with some other people too. It would be even worse if they found out about it.'

Betty wished her husband were there to lead the questioning. 'I see,' she said, not really understanding at all. 'That must be frightening. A difficult situation.' She decided to take a chance. 'You probably made one silly decision, and you didn't realize how big a mistake it would end up being.'

Aled sat up a little straighter. 'That's exactly right,' he said, a glint of what Betty believed was hope in his eyes. 'All I did was get a job. Just a job. I love surfing, see? It's what I do to be my true self. But surfing costs a lot; Stew's been great, lending me all his new and used stuff, but Grannie couldn't afford to buy the things that had to specifically fit me, so I got a job, delivering food, on my bike.'

Betty nodded her encouragement.

'I'd take my bike to school with me, on the bus, then work up in Sketty, in the evenings. Delivering pizzas, burgers, fish and chips, that sort of thing. It was too late when I found out I wasn't always delivering *just* food. By then they had me. I had to carry on because . . . because the blokes who ran the business, they could prove I'd broken the law, if they wanted to. The only way I could think of to get out of it all was to tell them I'd got a job down here, in the village, so I wouldn't be doing bike stuff anymore. For anyone.'

Betty handed him a paper serviette to wipe his eyes.

He looked mournful. 'I hate drugs; drugs killed my mum, see? Why would I ever want anything to do with them? I know people think everyone who surfs is always stoned, but you've got to have your wits about you when you're out in the ocean. I won't touch drugs. Nor will Stew. We hardly even drink. We're the same that way, too. I couldn't believe what I'd got caught up in. I never meant to. Working here at the pub was my only way to escape. The blokes who ran the delivery business believed that I wasn't going to work at all in their area any longer, which was good, but then it meant I was stuck here, in the pub with Sadie, all the time.'

'And that meant what, exactly?' urged Betty.

Aled blew his nose. 'It wasn't too bad to start with, I suppose. When I began here, back in August, she seemed a bit keen, you know, just a bit of attention, and I could cope with that alright. Then, in September, she saw me hand over a package to a really nasty, older bloke who came to our school on a big motorbike to get it from me. He was from another gang who work up in the Swansea Valley area. Big noise, apparently.'

He looked terrified. 'I wasn't dealing, honest. I just had to pass it onto him . . . for the people who ran the delivery service. They *made* me do that one last thing. But . . . Sadie took a photo of me doing it, and she threatened me with it. All the time – blackmailing me. And if I ever ignore her, or disagree with her in any way, she holds it over me – tells me she'll show the photo to the police, which would get me into a real mess. And if the photograph became public, the police would also get the bloke who's in it with me . . . and that would be even more dangerous. She even tells me I have to buy things for her to make up for being . . . disobedient. I've spent a load of money on all this stuff she insists I give her. She's *really* specific. And it has to be *exactly* the right thing, or I'm for it. I don't know what to do. She never stops. I have nightmares about it.'

Betty took a deep breath. She hadn't been expecting such revelations. 'But you and she were down on the beach together the night you were accused of setting fire to that body on the hillside. So you're at least having a sexual relationship.' It had to be said.

Aled blushed. It had been a long time since Betty had seen a teenager do that. 'No. We weren't. We aren't. I told you. There's nothing like that going on between us at all. When she shouted it all out in court the way she did, I had to decide if I was going to go along with what she said, or not. I had to get out of there, somehow, so I took my chance. Backed up what she said about us. It was . . . unbelievably bad, being in prison. And now she's got that to hold over me too. I mean, I know it got me out of jail, but she's ten times worse now. The day of my gran's funeral? It was awful. I loved Grannie so much. She was everything to me. As if it wasn't bad enough that Grannie was dead, Sadie kept going on and on at me as we walked into the church about how it was the start of a new life for us – then her mother said something about how the whole village should see us as a couple, and some sort of symbol or other, and . . . it's terrible. No one understands at all. Only Stew.'

Betty's mind was racing. 'But if you weren't with Sadie the night she said you two were together, why didn't you ever tell the police where you really were?'

It was only once the words were out her mouth that Betty realized what she was asking. She wondered if she'd gone too far.

Aled shook his head. 'I couldn't.'

His eyes darted about. 'It's Stew, see? Stew hadn't come out to his parents, then. I couldn't say anything because he and I were together that night. Grannie always said she knew I was gay before I did. I never thought about girls, or boys, until a few years ago, and I knew then. Stew's parents thought we were just – you know – good mates.'

Betty nodded as encouragingly as possible. 'That night? November 5th?'

'We went for a walk – just a walk – but we were alone, down on the beach, where Sadie said she and I were. When she shouted all that rubbish out in court I thought she'd seen us there, and that she was going to blackmail me about that too. But I had to agree with what she'd said, because I couldn't cope with being locked up any longer. And I thought I could get out of there without having to drag Stew into it by just repeating everything she'd said. But I couldn't tell the police where I really was. Because of Stew.'

'And do Stew's parents know about his sexual orientation now?'

Aled shuddered with a deep sigh. 'He was terrified to tell them, but we both knew it had to be done. Stew and I talked and talked about it. He finally told them last night. About him, and about us, not about how Sadie's been with me – no one else knows about that. In fact, Stew's mum and dad even said how good it was of Sadie to lie for me. They have no idea what she's put me through.'

He looked directly at Betty, his eyes pleading. 'I've put my A levels on hold, and I'm not even sure if uni is right for me anymore. Losing Grannie's been really hard for me – and being in prison? I don't even know how to explain that. Stew's been great. I don't know what I'd have done without him. He was in court every minute for me. Sitting as close as he could get, just feet away from me. We think we love each other, see? We know we're young, and this is the first time either of us has . . . been in a relationship. We talked to Stew's mum and dad about this last night; we both know this might not last, but we are happy, now.'

Betty said, 'That's good. He must mean a great deal to you.'

Aled nodded. 'I promised him I wouldn't talk. That I wouldn't say we were together that night. He thought his parents would chuck him out, see? Thought his whole life would be over if I told about us. He really loves his mum and dad. Everyone wants a family, don't they? But he's got this uncle who's gay – his father's brother – and he's been cut off from the whole family for years so we thought . . . well, he thought. You know?'

Betty nodded her encouragement. 'How did it go when he broke the news?'

Aled almost smiled. 'It was weird. They were . . . surprising. They were fine with it. Said all they wanted was for him to be safe and happy. Apparently everyone turned their back on Stew's uncle because he acted like a complete idiot at a family wedding; nothing to do with him being gay. Stephen and Maggie are good with it. Like Grannie was. Who knew? Stew didn't. I didn't. But we're going to be okay. So I kept my mouth shut for him, see? And, no, I didn't set fire to that bloke on the hill. I was with Stew the entire night. First on the beach, and then at home. Grannie knew, but I made her swear on the Bible to not tell, too, and she didn't. She did that for me, even though it was very hard for her.'

Betty sat up, feeling the strain of crouching forward, hunched over for so long. 'Do you still think Sadie gave you that alibi because she wanted an additional insurance for your compliance with her demands?'

Aled nodded. 'Yeah, I reckon. She's nuts, you know.'

Betty's annoyance at the use of the word must have shown.

He added, 'No I mean it, seriously nuts. Everyone at school says so, ask anyone. She hasn't got a single friend, never has. But since this school year started? Now she freaks everyone out with all her mumbo-jumbo about how life and love are "mutable", and how there's some saint or other who's better than God himself. Oh, I don't know, I swear she makes it up as she goes along. She's merciless. Everywhere I go – she's there. She sent me thirty texts before seven o'clock this morning. I jump when I get a text now. I can't escape her. I met her father after the funeral. He was really nice – not like her at all. I wondered if I should say something to him about her. I don't think her mother would believe it, see? Well, that's my problem, really. I don't think anyone will believe me. Do you?'

Betty was honest. 'I believe you.'

Aled managed a smile. 'Thanks.'

'So what happened this morning?' Betty used her coaxing voice.

Aled shifted on his chair. 'After last night's heart to heart, we all had dinner at Stew's house, then he came over to the cottage.' Aled paused. 'It's funny to think the cottage really is mine now; it'll always be Grannie's in my heart. It feels so empty without her being there. Anyway, Stew and I were going to go down to catch some waves this morning, when Sadie rang the bell. We didn't answer. Then there she was peering through the back door – where she had no right to be – and she saw Stew and me messing about in the kitchen. I mean we weren't doing anything . . . you know . . . just kissing. Anyway, she went ballistic. She smashed the glass in the door, fought her way – through Stew – into the house, then she starts waving her bloody gun about and this long thing, like a big rusty sword. It was terrifying. I honestly thought she was going to shoot me, but she whacked me really hard with it, and down I went. I don't know how I cut my leg. No idea.'

'I think she might have sliced you with that blade you saw. We'll tell the medics when they get here that it was rusty.' Betty worried about the cut more than she had done.

'I was woozy, you know? I don't know how long I was like that. Then I sort of came to, and she was going on and on about how I'd let her down. She kept saying I was telling her in the court room that I loved her – that I'd asked her for help, and she'd given it to me. I had no idea what she was talking about . . . there was no way I would have talked to her. No way I *could* have done. I just sat there in front of the judge, looking ahead of me, numb. Thinking about the surf, like I did when they were asking me questions in the police station. I just allowed myself to be in the waves, in my head. Riding. I do it in class, sometimes, too. If I concentrate I can feel the waves in my hands, feel the water rushing between my fingers and across my palms, it's wonderful. It's like stroking an animal, sort of . . . at least, that's how it feels to me. Like the sea is alive. Anyway, I eventually tried to get up off the kitchen floor, when she finally stopped gibbering, but she smacked me with her gun again. I'm sure I saw her pushing Stew out of the front door with the gun in his back – like they do on TV. I was shaking such a lot. Then they were gone. I managed to stagger over to the Cwtch to get hold of the Wingfields, and they brought me here. I'm not surprised she's taken Stew to the Devil's Table – she's obsessed with that place, too.'

Betty reached forward and held his hand as his tears started again. 'Come on now. It'll be alright.'

Aled looked panicked. 'But what if it's not? What if she really hurts him? She was screaming that no one should get between her and me, because we're a family now – which is crazy. If she thinks I'm her "family" then why does she hit me every time I'm alone with her? Trust me, that's as infrequently as possible. If I have to give her a "gift", as she calls them – my penance for having not replied to her texts fast enough, or not having talked to her in school, or whatever – she makes me meet her out by the Devil's Table, always as the moon is rising for some ridiculous reason, and then I have to apologize, and she whacks me with her fists, as though I'm some sort of punch bag. Like I said, she's nuts. If I try to back away she threatens me with showing that bloody photograph to the police. So I have to stand there and take it. I can't hit a girl. It's not right. I will admit I grabbed her once – just once – to try to push her off me, but she even took photos of the bruises on her arms and threatened to show them to the police too. So what can I do?'

Betty smiled. 'You've done it, Aled. You've told someone. It can't have been easy for you, I know you don't have a mother, and now your grandmother's gone too, but there's me.' Betty tried to get another smile out of him, but reckoned it was too much to hope for.

'I couldn't have let Grannie know what Sadie was like. No way. Nan Jones was horrible enough to her, without Grannie having a reason to hate Nan back. I couldn't risk Grannie wanting me to give up my job here – I needed the money, and this is the only job in the village I can do . . . otherwise I'd be thinking about having to go back on the bikes. I had no way out of it – I couldn't escape Sadie at all. Here. School. Everywhere except at home. That was the only place I could get away from her. In person, anyway. Grannie was my protector as far as me and Stew went, that was enough for her to do for me, having raised me and everything. I didn't want her to know about how Sadie's been with me. It's so . . . embarrassing.'

Betty had to ask. 'So does Sadie know about you and Stew being a couple?'

Aled didn't hesitate. 'No, see, that's the weird thing . . . I thought when she blurted all that stuff out in court she'd seen us together on Guy Fawkes Night. But she didn't mention it after I got out, and now I don't think she's worked that bit out at all. Seeing how she was this morning, I reckon just knowing he kissed me is too much for her. I'm so frightened for Stew. Is that policewoman any good? And your husband – is he up to it? If Stew's dad gets hold of Sadie, he might hurt her, even if she has got a gun. Maybe especially if she's got a gun pointed at Stew; Stephen Wingfield is ex-army – a paratrooper. They're all bonkers; you've got to be to go jumping out of planes all the time.'

Betty hoped an ex-paratrooper, a retired DI, and a young DS would be able to defuse the situation she could only imagine was developing at the Devil's Table. The information about the gun terrified her, even more than when it had first been mentioned. A teenage girl, sounding as though she had some serious psychological issues, in possession of a gun and a grudge? It worried her a great deal.

The weight she'd felt descend on her shoulders every time Evan had walked out of the front door to go to work was back again, and this time it felt much more difficult to bear.

'There, there,' she said to Aled, patting his hand, 'I'm sure it'll be alright.' She could feel his entire body trembling. He sobbed freely. Betty suspected the cathartic effect of sharing his story with her was beginning to take effect; she'd seen it often, though usually in the more controlled confines of her office.

Betty knew she had to get word to her husband about the true nature of the relationship between Sadie and Aled, and about how Sadie probably thought of Stew relative to her perceived power over Aled. She'd dealt with enough victims of abuse to know Aled was telling the truth, and it gave the whole situation a very different dynamic.

Betty didn't want Evan making a wrong move, or saying something that might touch a nerve with Sadie, who was clearly not as stable as she'd believed her to be.

Evan

'Thanks for waiting, Stephen, you did the right thing.' Evan shook the anxious man's hand as the threesome finally met up with each other at the ruined RAF listening station, where the path they needed to take toward the Neolithic monuments diverged from the main one.

Liz said, 'As you know, armed response and backup are on their way, so, please, leave it to us, Stephen. We've been trained for this. Stay here – we'll handle the situation. '

'*Utrinque paratus* – Ready For Anything. Paras. Fifteen years in. Lead scout of my section. I can still live up to our motto,' replied Stephen Wingfield.

Evan processed the information. He knew Liz was the only one of the trio with any legal standing to act in any confrontation. He watched her face contort as she weighed options – a habit she'd always had.

Liz had made her decision, he could tell. 'Great to know I have two men with me who are trained in a wide variety of skills, many of which might come in handy. Evan knows where we're headed, as do you, probably, Stephen. I'll allow either one of you to take the lead for now – but I am in command of this, understand? If I say step back, you do it. Right?' Evan and Stephen exchanged a glance, and each nodded. 'Both got a phone?' asked Liz. More nodding. 'Right, get them out and let's all exchange numbers. Set them to vibrate, and place them somewhere on your person where you have easy access.'

Stephen led off. Evan didn't believe for one minute that the man intended to take orders from Liz if he saw his son in mortal danger and – of the three of them – Stephen was likely to be the only one with any practical experience of being shot at; Evan had never come under fire in all his years of service, and knew he'd have heard if Liz had done. Knives, blunt instruments and even cars had all been used against him while on duty. But a firearm? This would be a first for him.

He was impressed by the way Stephen moved; he'd obviously kept himself in shape, and Evan wondered if he might be one of the locals who enjoyed hang-gliding – he seemed the type. Or maybe, like his son, he was a surf fanatic. Either way, he nimbly led them along a slightly more circuitous route than Evan would have chosen, but it had the advantage of bringing them to a spot just above, and adjacent to, the Devil's Table.

As they walked, then stooped and shuffled, Evan answered a call from Betty, whose concise recounting of what had clearly been an emotional heart-to-heart with Aled Beynon surprised him. He briefly passed these new and revealing insights to Liz, and checked facts with Stephen, who was horrified to hear about how Sadie had been treating Aled. The ex-soldier's resolve seemed to strengthen even more.

Liz observed, 'Alright, Sadie's less stable than we thought. We'll need to be extra careful; if she sees Stew as a threat to her imagined relationship with Aled, she might be more likely to take action against him, or us.'

'I never liked her. She was always just off-kilter,' said Stephen, swearing quietly. 'If she does anything to harm my boy, I'll—'

'Enough,' said Liz. 'You will not break the law while you're under my command. Got it?'

Evan could tell she was aiming to tap into the ex-para's training to take orders from a superior officer. He wondered if it would be effective.

They finally got close enough to their target area to have to stop even whispering, and made their way on their bellies for the last few minutes, creeping forward like three caterpillars possessed of varying levels of flexibility.

Finally peering over the edge of the escarpment, the sight that met Evan's eyes was remarkable, somewhat confusing, and potentially lethal. Stew Wingfield was limp, lying on his stomach on the flat, tabletop stone. Sadie stood astride him, her long dark hair streaming in the wind, her vivid orange top and trousers billowing. In one hand she held what Evan thought was a somewhat dilapidated stuffed rabbit and what looked to be a rusty old bayonet, in the other she had a gun – a revolver, as far as he could tell. She was ululating, swaying her hips, and waving the rabbit and blade above her head.

Liz used her binoculars to survey the scene and hissed, 'Can't tell if the revolver's loaded, of course; it's certainly old. Bayonet in her other hand likely to not be sharp. We're too far away to rush her without endangering Stew.'

'She's completely lost the plot,' whispered Stephen. 'She could do anything to my boy, at any minute. We have to act.' Evan noticed the muscles in his face twitch as he spoke. It gave him great cause for concern.

'I think it's best we all follow the orders I was given, and wait,' said Liz. 'She seems to be more concerned with some sort of ceremonial whatever-it-is than harming Stew. He doesn't seem to be in immediate danger.'

Evan wished he were in charge, but he wasn't, so he had to 'make a suggestion'. 'Given we don't know her game plan, nor how long this incantation stuff might go on, we could split up, and make a three-pronged approach – left flank and right flank, with one of us remaining here, in the central location. The person in this spot would be the first to engage Sadie, if that's what's needed. Their subsequent descent to the Devil's Table would also be the most precipitous.'

'I'll do it,' said Stephen. 'I'm trained to drop and roll – least likely to get hurt doing it. Also, I want my son to hear his dad's voice . . . to see me, if he can, and know I'm here for him.'

'I say we wait,' said Liz, forcefully.

But Evan knew it was too late for that, when Stephen rose to his feet and called his son's name.

Betty

Maggie Wingfield shouted, 'I need help out here – Helen's on the verge of collapsing.'

Betty helped Agata and Alis to drag Helen into the pub.

'I think she's past being walked about,' said Maggie. 'She's conscious, but only just. I think we should lay her down on the floor in the recovery position. Can you all give me a hand?'

Once Helen was correctly positioned on the floor, she seemed to come to her senses for a moment. Looking up at the battered and bloodied Aled she rallied, and began to crawl. Betty was amazed at her strength, given her state.

'Keep away from Sadie. You're my brother. It's wrong. Disgusting. Leave her alone.' Helen's speech was slurred, as though she were heavily intoxicated.

Betty had to stop Aled from getting up out of the chair to run away.

'Keep her off me,' he shouted. 'They're all nuts, the Jones women. Nan all but killed my grannie, Sadie's made my life a complete misery, and now this one's gone bonkers too. What the hell is she on about? I'm not her brother. She's crazy.'

'My dad. An affair with your mother. You – they had you,' said Helen, reaching for Aled's leg.

Aled curled into a ball in the chair.

'Shut up!' he screamed. 'I know exactly who my father is, thank you very friggin' much; he's from Newport. Lives in Spain now. Got a wife and four little kids. Just because my mum didn't tell anyone else in this village who he was, it doesn't mean I don't know. It's none of anyone else's business. You're allowed to keep secrets in a family, aren't you? Everyone does.'

Betty judged that Helen had used up the last remnants of her energy, and she collapsed, sprawling across the floor. Betty shouted, 'Maggie, we might need CPR any minute. I think she's going into respiratory failure – blue lips.'

Maggie was shaking, and all but in tears. 'Oh my God, I hope I can do this. It's different when it's a dummy, in training. And what about Stew? Is there any news about him? Oh my God, Stew!'

Betty held both Maggie's shoulders, and looked her squarely in the face. 'You can do it, and it will be just fine, Maggie. And Stew will be fine too. Stephen, Evan, and Liz are on their way to where Sadie and Stew are now. They're three highly capable people. Now, let's get Helen into the correct position for CPR . . . there – listen. I can hear an ambulance in the distance. Come on – you can do it, Maggie. Let's try to make sure the paramedics have a living patient to help when they get here.'

Evan

As Stephen towered above them, shouting down to his son, Liz swore under her breath. 'You go right,' she whispered, 'I'll go left.' Evan nodded. They belly-wriggled away.

The moist, springy grass smelled sweet; Evan tried to ignore the sheep droppings. He scrambled to his feet as soon as he dared, and looped around behind such mounds in the hillside as existed, aiming to approach Sadie's position from beyond the Devil's Table. He knew Liz would be coming from the direction of the Concubine's Pillow, and would be able to use the wide curve of the hill to remain hidden until she was almost at the scene.

In the distance he heard an ambulance siren, a faint sound of hope. Then it stopped. They must have been told to come in silent; lights only. He flattened himself against the steep incline of the slope behind the plateau upon which the massive monuments stood.

He could tell he was getting close because he could hear voices, but he couldn't make out what was being said. When he finally had a clear view, he could see Liz mirroring his actions. Sadie was still on top of the Devil's Table, but now she was facing Stephen's clifftop position, rather than the sea, and she was pointing the gun at his son's head. Stew was still face down on the slab – and he wasn't moving. Evan could see that his back and sides were bloodied. What had Sadie been doing with that bayonet?

For what he hoped would be the only time in his life, Evan cursed his lack of familiarity with facing firearms. He was grateful he'd not had to do it before, and delighted it was a rarity for a non-specialized officer to have to do it at all. But he wondered how he would react. He was about to find out how brave he really was.

He broke cover; Liz did likewise. Sadie reeled wildly, waving the gun around, aware she was surrounded. 'Don't come any closer,' she screamed above the gusting wind, 'or I'll shoot him. He'll be a worthy sacrifice.'

'Touch my boy once more, and I'll kill you.' Stephen's reply was guttural, menacing. Evan believed him.

'Quiet now, Stephen. Come on, Sadie, love,' called Liz. 'This can all end now. Listen – your mum needs you, Sadie. She's not very well. There's an ambulance on its way for her. Why don't you come back to the pub with us to see how she's doing? You'll want to go to the hospital with her, won't you?'

Good approach, thought Evan.

But it didn't work.

Sadie laughed dramatically, and play-acted shock. She mocked, 'Oh my mummy's not well? Taken a few nasty tablets has she? There's no point me going in an ambulance with her, because if she's not dead yet, she will be soon. Nan had some wicked pills hidden away – her secret stash – and I gave Mam some in her tea this morning. She shouldn't have said she didn't want Dad around, should she? We could have been a family again – but oh no, she didn't want that, did she? Well I fixed her – she can go and join Nan, with the worms, for all I care.'

Evan's line of vision allowed him to see ant-like figures moving around the sweep of the bay, toward them; the armed response unit. He had to get Sadie to look at him, and away from them. He had to be the one to engage her now.

Evan sucked in air, and called out, 'Did you hurt your grandmother as well as your mother?' He moved toward Sadie, his hands raised, unable to let Liz and Stephen know why he was doing what he was doing. He hoped they both worked it out.

Sadie laughed again, this time hugging the stuffed rabbit, and the bayonet, to her breast. 'Nan? No. I didn't need to. Went down all on her own, she did.'

Evan was at least a little relieved. 'And what about Aled's Grannie Gwen – did you maybe have something to do with her becoming ill?'

Sadie stopped twirling the gun. 'Oh aren't you a clever mister retired policeman. You guessed. Yes, it didn't take much. I went over to her and gave her a mug of hot chocolate and her tablets, like Aled used to do every night. But a few extra, you know? Loved the fuss I made of her, she did. Missing him, you see – because you lot had taken him. Which wasn't nice at all. I went and made her tea the next morning and gave her more pills. Do you know they use warfarin to poison rats? It's horrible stuff. I wasn't sure when it would kill her, but I knew it would. And it did, in the end. It was just good luck that everyone blamed Nan.

She always thought she was the queen of the village. But that's me –
I'm the special one, not her. She's in a box now. And I'm here.'

Evan could see Sadie was about to turn in Liz's direction, and he
couldn't have that.

He shouted, 'But why, Sadie? Why did you do that? Aled loved his
grannie. Wouldn't she have been a part of your family?'

Sadie rocked on the balls of her bare feet. 'No, she wouldn't. She and
Nan didn't get on, and Nan was my blood. I didn't know Nan would die,
see? So Grannie Gwen had to go. Besides, Aled and I will need the
money.'

Each time Sadie spoke, Evan slithered his feet along the grass just a
little, so she wouldn't notice he was moving ever closer. Liz mirrored
his actions, Stephen held his position.

Evan pressed. 'What money?'

'The money for the cottage, of course. God, you old people don't live
in the real world at all, do you? Green Cottage is worth at least a
quarter of a million, just for the outer shell and its location. People will
be lining up for it. Do it up, keep the look of it right for the
conservation lot, and sell it on or rent it out. Worth a fortune. And all of
it for Aled and me. Of course, when Nan died the pub became Mam's,
and when she goes – if she hasn't already – it'll be mine. So we can live
there, and have Aled's money too. See? Perfect.'

'You don't want to leave Rhosddraig? You want to stay here?' Evan
had to keep her talking.

'Leave my secret places? No, of course not. This is where I come to
be myself – my true self. My time will come, very soon, then I can
reveal myself, but not until I'm eighteen. Not long now. On May 27th the
world will celebrate the Feast of St Melangell, and I will finally take my
place here, at the left hand of my master, and will become her current
embodiment; it is my day of final transformation. See here –' she held
the stuffed toy above her head – 'hares are the lambs of St Melangell.
They travel between worlds as they wish, they are my messengers.'

Evan knew he was getting caught up in a lot of mumbo-jumbo that
Betty would be much better suited to deal with. He wondered if he
should follow Sadie down what might be a literal rabbit hole. Was that
the best way to find out what he needed to know?

'I saw some photographs of you here one night – on Halloween, in
fact. Was that a special night for St Melangell too?'

Sadie started to talk to Stew, poking his limp body with her foot.
'He's really thick, isn't he? Everyone knows Halloween belongs to the
devil himself – it's his night, when all those he has taken come back to

visit the world above. I was up here, communing with my master, when I saw flashes. Someone was taking my photo. A boy with a camera? On such a magical night? I didn't want him seeing my secrets; we fought over the camera, but he was large, and clumsy. He fell into the chamber beneath the Concubine's Pillow – I think the devil himself grabbed his ankles, and in he went. Poor thing – he cried like a baby. Said his leg hurt. There was blood, and it was all bent. He couldn't leave, so I pushed him further down, right inside, and kept him there.'

'You kept James Powell prisoner in the chamber beneath the Concubine's Pillow?' Evan wanted to be sure he got all the facts.

'Well, not really as a prisoner. He couldn't walk, so of course he had to stay there. I fed him, gave him water. Right there and then I gave him a little bit of my holy food, and that's when I knew he'd been sent to me that night. He saw the truth, like I do. He saw the colors, and the way the earth and the air move.'

'So you kept James Powell hidden up here, all the time from Halloween until November 5th? Why, Sadie? And why did you kill him then?' Evan could see the tactical team fanning out from the path in the distance.

'I didn't kill him. Why would I do that? The devil was the one who took his life-breath. I came back one morning, and he was dead. Hadn't even eaten the sandwich I'd brought him the night before. I stayed with him for a bit, and ate it for him.'

Evan was working his way mentally through the timeline on the wardrobe door of his spare bedroom. 'So why did you burn his body on November 5th? It was you who did that, wasn't it?' He felt he was getting closer to the truth at last.

'Oh yes, that was me. I had to really, because it was meant. See, to start with, I couldn't move him when he died, of course, because he was a real lump. So I set fire to him where he was, inside the mouth of the door to the other place, beneath the Concubine's Pillow. It took hours for him to burn, but that was okay – there weren't big flames, so no one saw anything. I left him to it. Came back the next morning, and he'd transformed, as I knew he would. But I didn't want him telling tales in the other world, so I had to take his teeth out, of course. Did you know it's really hard to get teeth out of a skull? I thought they'd just fall out, but it seems they don't; I had to go and get a big hammer from the pub's cellar and smash his skull to bits. Once the skull was smashed, I just kept going. It didn't take long. In fact, once I got into the swing of it, it was fun. It's amazing how brittle bones can be. Some of the big bits were tougher, but even they gave way when I really put some effort into it.'

Evan hid his creeping disgust at Sadie's unfeeling words. He was now within about six feet of the Devil's Table. 'So why the big fire on November 5th? And why place his remains in a pile where they could be found, covered with stones?'

Sadie bent down on her haunches, poking Stew's back with the barrel of the gun. Evan was horrified to see that the boy still didn't react. He couldn't see his face. He wished he knew if his eyes were open or not; that would tell him a lot . . . maybe too much.

'You're so thick. It's true what they say about policemen. It was a full moon on the 5th, of course. Don't you know how special a full moon is? How powerful it can be? Well, take it from me, it is. Very. I didn't know the boy's name, didn't really care, though I did think it was weird that he ended up being related to the bloke who killed Aled's mother – so it definitely must have been *meant* – but I knew he'd been sent to me even before I learned that. You see, I'd been planning to sacrifice a sheep to my master, but I couldn't find one, then along he came and . . . well, there you are. He was sent to be a sacrifice. He gave his life so I could become stronger, more fit for my master; so I felt it fair to mark his passing with a memorial – his own cairn. I couldn't believe it when everyone got so excited about it. That came as a surprise.'

Evan was truly puzzled. 'You didn't think people would be interested in a pile of bones buried under stones? You must have suspected the police would want to know whose body it was.'

Sadie stood again, and began to sway. 'No, not really, because it wasn't a body you see. The boy had transformed. No one ever talked about "a body" did they? Everyone talked about "remains". That was all they were – bits of leftover stuff from when he'd been a person; he doesn't need them in the other place – ask Mrs Hare, she'll tell you . . . no one there has need of a body, they're just raw emotion.'

Sadie whispered something into the ear of her stuffed toy, and laughed, nodding her head.

Evan's gut was all over the place; he knew this girl had killed, he knew she had weapons at her disposal which meant she could do so again, and he didn't doubt she might. But surely she was mentally ill? Some sort of psychosis? He wished he could ask Betty a few questions. Sadie was spouting a lot of mixed-up, made-up twaddle. He couldn't imagine where she'd dredged it from. But he was in no doubt that, to her, it all seemed real, and meaningful.

So dangerous.

What would a teenager with such a warped set of beliefs do when confronted by masked men brandishing firearms and loudhailers?

He couldn't be sure – but what he did know was that he might find out in a few minutes; the response team had stopped moving. He reckoned they must be getting into their final positions. But to do what? That was what worried him.

Surely both Stew and Sadie could be saved.

'So who was it Mr Watkins saw on Aled's bike on 5th November? Was it you?' he shouted.

'Yes. I needed to get over to Lower Middleford while the second transformation was taking place, so I took Aled's bike and raincoat. He always leaves them around the back of Green Cottage, and my old bike had a puncture, so I took his.'

'And why did you need to get to Lower Middleford, Sadie?'

'To chuck the boy's camera away, of course. And all the bits of his clothes that didn't burn properly. You really aren't very observant for a policeman, are you? Rhosddraig doesn't have any large bins or anything, and if you throw something down to the beach it's going to be found, sooner or later. Besides, St Melangell wouldn't want me to litter. So I rode over to the social club in Lower Middleford where they have those big wheelie-bins that are collected every week. I just shoved the camera and stuff down to the bottom of one of those, and that was that.'

Evan noticed the girl was beginning to sway more, now that she was standing again, and her eyes seemed less focused.

'Sadie!' He called her attention back to him; he didn't want her to notice what was going on around her. He dared to allow her to see he was moving toward her, hoping she'd train the gun on him, not Stew.

It worked. Evan should have been pleased, but his mouth dried up.

'Stop moving,' she shouted forcefully. 'I won't let you take him. He's too special to Aled. I saw them kiss. Stew must have forced himself on Aled, because I know Aled loves me. I must be the only person Aled needs. Once I'm transformed I will be complete. I will be his everything, and he will be mine. Like Romeo and Juliet. Then we will eat the holy food together, and be as one with the earth and all that is beneath it. He will become my master, and I his concubine. I have been shown how to allow others to transform, you see. Because I was chosen, even before my birth.'

'What's the holy food, Sadie? Is it a secret?'

Sadie smiled coquettishly, then giggled. 'No, it's like my secret place – everyone sees it, but no one knows what it is. I do. I know where to forage for it, and how to use it. Others don't.'

The penny dropped for Evan. 'But I do, Sadie, because I have also been chosen.'

Sadie laughed, mocking him. 'You're lying. You're too stupid to have been chosen. Besides, you're old. Go on then, tell me, where does the holy food come from? Tell me.'

'It's all around here, sometimes in the grass, and much more often under the trees in the woodlands; but not now, of course. I bet you found it first in September and October, didn't you? When the days were damp, and you were out early in the morning. The holy food was given to you; it grew up from beneath the soil, not out in the open, but in hidden places, that only you knew about. You ate it, and then you were able to see what others can't. The colors in the air, the vibrations of all living things. Am I right?'

Sadie stopped swaying. She looked intrigued. Puzzled. Evan was pleased – that was exactly what he'd hoped for. But the gun was still trained on him. That wasn't good.

'Okay then, mister retired policeman, if you know so much about it, how does it taste, and feel, in your mouth?' she asked petulantly.

Evan smiled. 'Not so good – but it's holy, so it's not supposed to taste good. It's a bit slimy if it's freshly picked, but if you let it dry out, it's not too bad. A bit chewy. Earthy. Do you eat it all the time?'

Sadie swayed, and shook her head. 'Only on special occasions. Full moons. Halloween. And I've got some for my birthday, of course. Then it will be given to me again when the days shorten, and the master has more control than in the summertime. You're right that it's not nice, but nor is the holy food in church . . . that starts dry, and ends up slimy, but everyone eats that. It's all flesh – the holy food in church that Nan was always so righteous about, and my master's holy food. I gave some to Stew when I brought him here. Look at him, he went all floppy. I don't know why. Probably because he's not special. Just ordinary. I had some too – just a little. Today has been difficult for me. I needed to see the colors. Love, and family, and faith . . . it's all so tiring.'

Evan was very close now. 'Come down, Sadie. Let me share my holy food with you. I love the colors too. We can talk about them. No one else will understand, but we will. Throw the gun away, and the knife. You don't need them. This is all so exhausting.'

Evan was hoping the psychedelic properties of the magic mushrooms Sadie had ingested would be carrying her toward a sleepy phase, not a manic one; she seemed to be more relaxed than she had been when they'd arrived.

She smiled down at him – a beaming, innocent smile – and the gun and knife clattered onto the stone slab. She clutched her stuffed toy as black-clad figures clambered onto the ancient stones, shouting orders she either didn't hear, or which she chose to ignore. Stephen Wingfield came barreling down the slope to gather his son into his strong arms, laying him on the grass, where he held him, and wept.

As Stephen pushed his son's long hair from his bloodied face, shaking him gently, Evan saw the boy open his eyes a little. He croaked, 'You're all silver and gold. Your hair's a river, Dad. And those wings! I bet you could fly now, if you tried.' Stephen gathered Stew into his arms, sobbing.

Liz reached Evan and hugged him. 'I hope I'm allowed to do that,' she said. 'Thank you, Evan. You were brilliant. Well done.'

'I had to keep her attention away from that lot coming toward us. I didn't mean to take over. The job would have fallen to whichever one of us was this side of the monument. It just happened to be me.' He knew Liz would have been able to achieve the same outcome.

'Good call on the magic mushrooms, Evan. And a very convincing explanation of how they taste and feel in the mouth.' Liz winked.

'People tell you a lot of useful things in interviews,' replied Evan, grinning. 'I'll let you take it from here,' he added – glad to be able to do so. 'I want to get back to my wife.'

Betty

Once the paramedics had taken responsibility for Helen and Aled, Betty had managed to find an old pair of binoculars which she'd trained on the scene unfolding across the sweep of the bay at the Devil's Table. She'd watched the advance of the armed response unit, and could see Evan was engaging Sadie, getting closer and closer to her. With her heart pounding, she wished with every fiber of her body she could hear what was being said. Her inner being begged her husband to not do anything dangerous – though it was clear to her the entire situation could become horribly tragic at any moment.

She understood Maggie Wingfield's desire to run along the path to help, but stayed close to the petrified woman, sharing the binoculars with her, so she at least had a chance to see how her son and husband were faring.

Finally, the end came, and the only unknown was exactly how badly Stew had been injured; the blood on his body was obvious, even at a distance. Once they saw Sadie being subdued by the figures in black, the two women ran from the pub, heading toward the monuments. As they cantered along, Maggie's phone rang; she stopped to answer it, and Betty stopped to listen.

Betty's heart lifted when she saw Maggie's expression change from anxiety to relief. 'He's alive,' she said tearfully. 'Cut, and bruised, and drugged – but alive. They're going to carry him back here, and there's another ambulance on the way. I need to see him.' She took off again.

Betty managed a few more steps before her own phone rang. She let Maggie keep going, but wanted to hear Evan's voice. '*Cariad*, you okay?'

'Fine. Love you.'

'Love you too. I'm coming.'

'Meet you halfway.'

When the pair finally met on the path, Betty burst into tears and blurted, 'I am so proud of you, my darling. You did a wonderful thing. You've saved both Stew *and* Sadie.'

Evan hugged his wife close, which she enjoyed very much.

She added, 'Sadie's going to need a lot of help. I hope she gets it.'

'I'll make my statement, as will everyone else, and we'll let the experts decide that one, shall we?' replied her husband, cuddling her tight.

'Best to always do that,' said Liz Stanley as she caught up with the couple. 'And on that note – and just so you all know I'm a really amazing detective – I've just received a text from colleagues in Slough. Bob Thistlewaite is wanted for failure to appear in court there – beat up the new wife, and ran off, apparently. I dare say that's why the renewed interest in these parts. I've asked local to pick him up at the social club in Lower Middleford where he's staying. So that should help Helen Jones for now, at least. And I promise I'll keep an eye on her case over the next few weeks and months. What news about her from the paramedics, Betty?'

'They can't be sure, yet. She should recover from the effects of the opioid poisoning alright, but they won't know what damage might have been done to her liver and kidneys by the acetaminophen in the Solpadols until they run some more tests. Since they have no idea how many she swallowed, they'll have to wait to find out how she's going to be, long term. They're cautiously optimistic, and hope she only ingested a few. She didn't tell us what she'd done. We'll have to keep our fingers crossed. I'd like to check on her at the hospital when we're finally able to get away. It could be a difficult future for her – and not just because of what she'll have to cope with relating to her daughter's actions.'

Evan kissed Betty's head. 'Sadie would know how many tablets Helen took, because she's the one who gave them to her; Helen didn't try to commit suicide, her daughter tried to kill her.' Evan sounded as grim as he looked. 'Putting the bottle of pills beside her mother's bed, so we would think she'd taken them herself, is chilling. And Sadie admitted poisoning Gwen Beynon with warfarin. That was certainly premeditated.'

Betty was shocked by the news, and realized she still had a lot to learn. She happily let Liz get along, so she could get all the facts from Evan. The FIT people were on their way, so Betty knew Liz had a long day ahead of her, and suspected she and her husband did too.

Eventually, she and Evan were able to enjoy a fortifying pot of tea, while Agata took up a position at the pub's front door where she was telling what appeared to be the entire population of the village that the pub would be closed, until further notice.

Once Evan had told her everything that had transpired at the Devil's Table, Betty asked, 'What do you think will happen to Sadie now?'

'I don't know, exactly, love,' was her husband's gentle answer. 'But I hope, and trust, our justice system allows her to get whatever help she needs, and whatever else it is she deserves.'

'I know what you deserve,' said Betty, 'a medal. You were ridiculously brave, *cariad*.'

'After today, a quiet retirement is all I'm hoping for,' said Evan.

'Got any sense of closure yet?'

Her husband sighed heavily. 'Closure? For this case? I'm not sure I ever will, love. I know Sadie's got an illness – some sort of mental imbalance, probably exacerbated by her use of magic mushrooms over the past months – but I'm still grappling with her horrifically nonsensical reasons for doing everything she did. I have to admit I know in my heart I'm feeling more certain than before that I'm past all this. Yes, there's the frustration of being on the outside of a case, of watching it unfold in the media without being able to be useful. But maybe that's the lesser of two evils. Maybe I can find peace pottering about the house and garden, and with my history books, after all. And I have you. I should focus on allowing us to become all that we can. Together.'

Betty was relieved, in so many ways. 'Let's play our part here then, and we'll pop in to check on Helen at the hospital on the way home. And how about, over the next few weeks, we see what sort of flats might be available for sale down in Mumbles? Or maybe even Caswell Bay? A complete change might help us both settle to our new future, whatever it might hold.' said Betty.

Evan kissed her. 'Tidy.'

Acknowledgements

This book has gnawed away at me for the better part of two years. Finally, here it is. During that time I've been encouraged to keep going by my husband, without whose continual patience and support I wouldn't have managed to get it written. My mother and sister have also cheered me along every step of the way, and my beloved Poppy's been at my feet, or allowing me an excuse for a long walk when I/she needed it.

I've received valuable input from two members of my extended family in Wales – one of whom works in law enforcement, the other within the legal system. They will remain anonymous, but know who they are. Readers should know that any inaccuracies in either the legal or policing elements of this book are not because I was given poor advice, but because I 'might' have chosen to ignore parts of it – the fault, therefore is wholly mine; this is, after all, a work of fiction.

Sue at the Bay Bistro in Rhossili was a great help – thanks, Sue; Emma Mugford knows the Gower Peninsular intimately, and that shows in all her work – thanks for letting me use your photograph for the cover, Emma. I changed the name of Rhossili to protect the innocent – the people there are lovely, and it's a wonderful place; maybe you'll be inspired to search it out online, or even visit.

Early readers gave me critical feedback. To the following, thank you for ploughing through my raw output: LM, SS, KA, SW, NP, KL. My editor Anna Harrisson and my proofer Sue Vincent have made my work better – thank you both.

To the fellow authors who blurbed the book, the bloggers and reviewers who wrote about the book, the booksellers and librarians who helped you find the book – thank you so much; your efforts helped me get the word out about my work, and helped readers find it. I really appreciate it.

And to you, who have chosen to read this book, thank you for doing so.

This book raises some challenging topics. Online search engines can be useful when trying to locate up-to-date local laws and resources, and can often allow those in need to reach out – anonymously, if needs be. There's no shame in asking for help.

21113295R00178

Made in the USA
San Bernardino, CA
08 January 2019